The Legacy

Angela Woodward

Angela Woodward was born in Bradford on Avon. An early interest in horses was interrupted when as a teenager she spent three years in Singapore where her interest changed to swimming going on to achieve international honours.

On returning to England and completing her education, she qualified and pursued a career in Medical Laboratory Sciences, working in hospital pathology departments.

By combining her interest of horses with the sciences, she has produced a thoroughly fascinating debut novel in 'The Legacy'.

The Legacy

Angela Woodward

Cowan Publishing Limited

First published in 2001 by Cowan Publishing Limited
A Cowan Publishing Paperback

10 9 8 7 6 5 4 3 2 1

A CIP catalogue record for this book is available
from the British Library

ISBN 1 903892 007

Typeset by Palimpsest Book Production Limited,
Polmont, Stirlingshire
Printed and bound in Great Britain by
Omnia Books Limited, Glasgow

Cowan Publishing Limited
83 Princes Street
Edinburgh
EH2 2ER
0131 247 6778
01877 339290

To my mother, Rosemarie Brown, to whom this book will be a complete surprise.

1

Julian Anderson-Brown glanced again in his rear view mirror and concluded that the black Ford car was definitely following him. He turned off onto a country lane. The black car followed. He accelerated as much as he dared in the dark conditions – his headlights barely distinguishing the lane from the muddy grass verge. Damm, the car behind had accelerated too.

His eyes reverted to the road and too late he saw the sharp bend in front of him. He flung the steering wheel to the right, but in doing so lost control. The car hit the grass verge and seemed to take off, somersaulting once before coming to rest with a sickening crunch back on it's wheels on the other verge.

The air bag had seemed to explode from the steering column, hitting his face with an unbelievable force, and during the tumbling he had felt an unbearable pain down his right side.

He lifted his head off the air bag. His nose throbbed painfully and something wet and warm dribbled from it down over his lips and mouth. It tasted metallic. He wiped his mouth with his left hand and realised it was blood.

The stabbing pain in his chest seemed to get worse and made him catch his breath.

He looked out of the crazed windscreen and noticed that the car that had been following him had now stopped about 20 yards in front. Someone was getting out.

A dark foreboding inside warned him that the man wasn't coming to give assistance. In desperation he looked round and saw the lights of a farmhouse across the fields – he could get help there.

With a superhuman effort he managed to open the door and literally fell out of the car. Hoping beyond hope that the man had not seen him, he crawled round the back of the car.

He managed to pick out a gap in the hedge and decided to go for it. He crawled over the verge, his breath coming in short, painful gasps, when he suddenly found himself tumbling down into a ditch, landing with a noisy splash in the foot or so of icy water that lay in the bottom.

The coldness of the water revived him, and he lay completely still, holding his breath, hoping the man had not heard him.

In the stillness of the night the ominous sound of footsteps came from behind the car. He tried to pull himself out of the ditch towards the gap in the hedge, but with his right arm and leg apparently broken and virtually useless, he could only claw at the bank with his left hand.

Suddenly he saw a man standing over him, and held out his hand for help. He heard the man laugh. Instead of help, a foot came down on his head, pushing it under the water.

Anderson-Brown struggled desperately to free himself, but his left arm flailed in vain. He tried to hold his breath, but to no avail, and as his efforts diminished with the inevitability of death, he suddenly thought of his dream that he would not be able to achieve.

As the moment before darkness finally descended and his twitching had almost ceased, his last thoughts were of his niece Emily. It would be up to her now. Yes – she would see his dreams turn into reality and he would get his revenge on Nathan Grant. She had to, or all this would have been in vain.

'What on earth have you been up to, Emmy?'

Emily paused, as she was about to take a bite out of her piece of toast.

'What do you mean, Greg?'

She looked up as Greg sauntered into the kitchen holding the post, paying particular attention to one of the envelopes.

'Well, it's not every day that my sweet little girlfriend gets a letter from a firm of solicitors, so spit it out, Emmy, what have you been doing?'

He handed her the letter and sat down opposite her, staring at her with curiosity and expectation, waiting for the letter to be opened.

Emily put down her toast and examined the envelope. Yes, it was definitely addressed to her – Miss E. Lloyd – and had the name of Pierce Adams, Solicitors, next to the postmark.

A cold shiver ran down Emily's spine – she had absolutely no idea why she should receive such a letter, so the icy feeling could not have been due to a guilty conscience. It was probably the fact that her only previous dealings with solicitors had been following the tragic death of her parents just over three years ago, causing her to associate them with the most traumatic time for her life.

'Open it then, the suspense is killing me.'

Emily looked at Greg. He was devouring his breakfast without a care in the world. Nothing seemed to bother him. He had certainly received a few solicitors' letters in the past, all chasing bad debts that he had collected – a result of his inability to kerb his free-spending habits.

Emily felt mildly irritated. Whatever was in the letter was her own business, and his cavalier attitude had annoyed her to such an extent that she was determined not to open it in front of him.

'I can't think what it's about, I'll open it after breakfast,' Emily replied, and with that resumed eating her now cold toast.

She then noticed the other few letters that Greg had put on the sideboard.

'So, what else was in the post?'

'Oh, not much.'

The overly casual way with which Greg said that made Emily get up and fetch the other two letters. She opened them, and seeing the contents sat down in exasperation.

'Greg, you promised to pay these two last week, now they're threatening to cut off the phone and electricity!'

'Sorry, Emmy, I was a bit short of cash last week – you know how it is, and pay-day is still a couple of weeks away. You couldn't pay them for me this time, love, please? I'll pay you back – promise.'

Emily glanced up to see Greg giving her one of his doleful looks, which irritated her since he knew she couldn't resist it. She was desperately in love with her tall, dark, brown eyed, ruggedly handsome Greg, and would do anything to please him – and he knew it.

She always felt so insecure in their relationship as they were total opposites. She was the envy of all her friends, to be living with the charming, extrovert 'Gorgeous Greg' – as they called him.

Emily knew she was not exactly a beauty, and was shy and reserved in comparison to Greg. She was medium height, had shoulder length wavy auburn hair, hazel eyes and a trim figure, yet lived with the daily insecurity that Greg could easily find another far prettier girlfriend.

He certainly had the opportunity, as most evenings were spent out at night clubs with his friends when money seemed no object; then when it came to paying his share of the bills – there was always good old Emily to bale him out.

When he first moved in with Emily, he had cheerfully agreed to pay his share of the bills, but now he always seemed to manage to avoid his responsibilities. Emily couldn't help but resent this, after all, it was her house – a small two bedroomed terraced house in a less than fashionable area of town. She had bought the house with the money left to her by her parents, so it was only fair to share the costs, but one look into Greg's deep brown eyes and her initial resentment would dissolve and she would forgive him every time.

Emily finished her toast and stared at the letter next to her plate. Curiosity eventually got the better of her and she opened it, trying not to appear too anxious.

'So, what does it say then?' asked Greg in between mouthfuls of coffee.

'Give me a chance to read it.'

Emily read the letter before sighing with relief at the contents.

'They want me to make an appointment to see them about Uncle Julian's will.'

'Uncle Julian? Wasn't that the old boy whose funeral you went to a week or so ago? The one they found in the ditch after that awful accident? Hey – was he loaded?'

Greg was trying not to sound too excited, but his mind was obviously racing. A dead relative meant a will – a will meant inheritance – inheritance meant money – and the solicitor's letter meant that Emily must be due something.

'Hardly,' replied Emily with indignation at Greg's apparently enthusiastic attitude to the death of her only surviving relative.

'He was always rather eccentric. I remember when Mummy and Daddy died, he sort of offered to look after me – I think it was more out of a sense of obligation than anything. At the time, that was the last thing I wanted, to live with a mad scientist in his hovel of a flat. Besides, I've no doubt I would have ended up looking after him rather than the other way round.'

Emily sighed as she thought back in time.

'When I was young, he occasionally used to turn up at our house – usually when he needed help – apart from that we never saw much of him. Daddy used to refer to him as the black sheep of the family, since he always had these way out controversial opinions. I suppose he was one of those people who was brilliant but a quite odd at the same time.'

'Well, he must have had something for these solicitors

to contact you,' Greg persisted, although Emily noted that his tone was a little less enthusiastic than before.

'It's probably a load of old books and clothes.'

'You never know, it's usually the ones who spend the least on themselves that have a bundle of cash stashed away somewhere. Just think – my girlfriend could be an heiress.'

Emily laughed. 'I doubt it. I'll give these people a ring as soon as I get into work, although I can't possibly see what Uncle Julian might have owned that could possibly be of value to anyone.'

'That's my girl. See if you could find out anything today, I would hate to be in suspense all over the weekend.'

Greg got up and put his jacket on.

'Ring me if you have any news. We could certainly do with a new car if there were any money. Anyway, I must dash or I'll be late.'

"You mean you could," thought Emily, feeling a little annoyed at his attitude.

Without so much as a peck on the cheek, Greg left, humming to himself, leaving Emily to clear up alone.

Emily felt a little depressed at the thought of Greg planning all the things he could buy with a little extra cash – all, no doubt, things that he wanted.

Part of her wished there would be nothing, so at least they wouldn't fall out over it.

Emily sighed. Greg would be unbearable until she had some news. Well, there was only one way to find out.

That afternoon, Emily was sitting in the reception of Pierce Adams, Solicitors. She recalled the rather odd conversation she had with Mr. Pierce when she phoned earlier.

He had suggested that she come early in the afternoon, since, to put it in his own words, "there were urgent matters to be cleared up regarding Mr. Anderson-Brown's will." Not only that, but he indicated that it would be rather complicated and would take some time to go over, so an early afternoon appointment was agreed.

Emily was intrigued as to what Uncle Julian could possibly have in his will that was either complicated or would take all afternoon to go over. Still, he was eccentric in his life, so Emily could only conclude that he was just as eccentric in death.

She looked round the spartan reception area. It was depressing, dingy and in serious need of decorating and some new furniture. On the table next to Emily was an untidy pile of outdated magazines, which appeared to have been well thumbed through over the years.

The receptionist appeared close to – if not past – retirement age, with grey permed hair, a little overweight and wearing a tweed skirt with twin set jumper and cardigan. "Only the string of pearls was missing," Emily thought wryly. She seemed to be typing, answering the phone and delivering files to various offices with a dexterity that only decades of practice could bring.

The phone buzzed and was immediately answered.

The receptionist looked up.

'Mr. Pierce will see you now, Miss Lloyd.' She motioned the direction with one hand. 'Down the corridor, second on the right.'

'Thank you,' replied Emily as she stood up.

The corridor was even dingier that the reception room,

with high ceilings, which seemed to provide a haven for numerous spiders – judging by the amount of cobwebs Emily could make out above her.

She reached the second door, hesitated for a moment, then knocked.

'Come in,' a muffled voice answered from within the office.

Emily opened the door tentatively.

'Ah, Miss Lloyd, please come in and sit down.'

Mr. Pierce stood up and held out his large, chubby hand, reaching out to shake Emily's.

Emily sat down in the large leather chair opposite him, and wondered how long ago it was that Uncle Julian had sat here too.

Mr. Pierce fetched a file from the pile on the filing cabinet behind him before sitting down. He opened it, quickly reading the first page.

Emily watched him; his half glasses perched on the end of a bulbous nose. He was overweight, with sparse grey hair, and a double chin, which seemed to fold over his collar. His suit was old and crumpled, and his shirt looked as though he had been wearing it all week. The tie and top button were undone, to ease the restriction his double chin obviously caused.

She quickly glanced away, hoping he had not noticed her staring at him. She looked around the office. Two walls were taken up with battered filing cabinets, some of the drawers of which wouldn't shut properly, judging by the way they jutted out at strange angles to the rest of the cabinets.

Another wall was taken up entirely with shelves upon which were row upon row of leather bound legal books, most of which looked as though they hadn't been touched for years.

Mr. Pierce's desk was a huge dark wood desk with a worn brown leather top that sported scratches, scuffs and coffee cup marks accumulated from years of hard work and abuse.

The office carpet was worn and faded, the original colour of which Emily couldn't possibly guess.

Mr. Pierce cleared his throat and looked over his half glasses at Emily.

'Miss Lloyd, as you know from the letter you received, your uncle, Julian Anderson-Brown, has left a will, which I would like to go through with you today.' He looked rather uncomfortable as he shifted slightly in his chair. 'How well did you know your uncle?'

'Not very well at all.'

'I gather you are his only surviving relative.'

'As far as I know, yes. He certainly never married.'

'And I believe your parents died a few years ago.'

'Yes, just over three years ago.'

Mr. Pierce sensed that he had touched on a rather delicate subject, and looked away, embarrassed.

'I'm sorry to ask you all these questions, but your uncle did leave rather a bizarre will, and I'm trying to understand his thinking behind it.'

Emily looked up at him. It was obvious that he was feeling uncomfortable asking these questions, and she couldn't imagine where they were leading.

'My uncle never did anything that seemed to amount to normal behaviour,' she said, smiling at the thought of all the rumours and wild stories that had circulated in the family about Uncle Julian. 'He always seemed to me to be a little eccentric, and took great pleasure in rubbing authority up the wrong way, judging by the number of universities he worked for.'

'As I recall, he was a scientist,' Mr. Pierce said as he heaved himself out of his chair and wandered over to the window, staring out at the passing traffic. 'Tell me, do you like animals?'

'Er, well, yes.'

Emily stared at his back as he continued to look out of the window, thinking that this conversation was definitely getting a bit weird.

'Horses?'

'I suppose so, although I've never been riding, but yes, any animal.'

'Good. Would you like a cup of tea or coffee?'

Emily couldn't help thinking that this man was as batty as her Uncle Julian.

'Tea, please.'

Mr. Pierce sat down at his desk and pressed a button on the intercom.

'Two teas please, Violet.'

He started reading the paperwork in front of him again, and an uncomfortable silence descended on the room.

The silence was relieved when the receptionist entered with the teas, leaving them on his desk and departing again with barely a word.

Emily noted that Mr. Pierce had become rather red in the face, and that a few beads of perspiration had appeared on his brow.

He looked up and pushed one of the teas towards Emily and sighed.

'Well, no doubt you have been wondering what is in

the will, and I apologise for the odd questions earlier, but I think you will appreciate why I was asking once I tell you the contents.'

He picked up his cup and took a sip before turning over the page.

'I'll give you a summary of the will as simply as I can, then we can go over it in depth later. Firstly, his personal possessions he has left to his housekeeper – a Mrs. Monroe. His books and papers he has left to be shared amongst three of those he considered his most brightest pupils, the names I have here if you want to know.'

'No, that's OK,' replied Emily, relieved at the thought that she wouldn't receive a mass of scientific books, which she had no interest in or use for.

Mr. Pierce coughed and shifted uncomfortably again.

'Last, but not least, we come to what he has left you. Firstly, he has left you a horse, specifically a race horse – which is in foal.'

Emily almost dropped her tea with shock, spilling some of it in the saucer. To avoid any further accidents, she put it down on the desk.

'A race horse?' she said in astonishment.

'Yes – a race horse. Not only that, but I gather the foal is imminent, so I suppose you could say two race horses.'

Emily sat there for a while, trying to absorb the news.

'I never knew he even had a horse.'

'Yes, your uncle did indicate that you would be rather surprised.'

'But I don't know anything about horses – race horses or otherwise!'

'You love animals,' replied Mr. Piece weakly, 'so that's a start.'

'I know, but I can't possibly keep it. Firstly I don't know how, and secondly I couldn't afford it – I barely get by on my salary as it is.'

'Now, wait a minute, you haven't heard the rest of the will,' Mr. Pierce said hurriedly, in an attempt to pacify Emily, who was by now quite flustered. He had rehearsed how this conversation would go a thousand times in his mind since he knew of his client's death, and each time it seemed more ridiculous than the last. 'Secondly, he has left a sum of £50,000, which is to be spent solely with the intent of entering the foal in the 2003 Derby. Mr. Anderson-Brown nominated myself as a trustee of the fund, so all expenses you would have to submit to myself for approval and payment.'

Emily, by this time, was beginning to think that she was in some surreal nightmare.

'I have no idea at all about racing, the Derby or horses – even if there are funds to cover the costs,' she protested.

'That's what owners pay trainers for,' he replied, trying to make this as easy as possible.

'I'm sorry, I couldn't possibly do this,' Emily said, weakly.

'I'm afraid, in that case, that brings us to the third and last part of the will, which I have to say I found most unsavory and told Mr. Anderson-Brown as much at the time. Should you decide not to accept the first two items of your inheritance, then the mare and foal are to be destroyed and the money is to go to the Institute of Genetic Research.'

Mr. Pierce looked up at Emily to see an expression of shock and horror on her face.

'You couldn't possibly do that – that's outrageous!'

'I'm afraid that if it came to it, I would have no other choice.' Mr. Pierce was clearly embarrassed by the whole episode, and looked at Emily, concerned at what she must be feeling.

When Mr. Anderson-Brown had first come to him to draw up the will, he had objected most strongly to it's contents, but Mr. Anderson-Brown insisted that these were his wishes, and that if he didn't want the business, then he would go elsewhere.

He had hoped in vain that his niece would be an outdoor horsey type and would relish the challenge, but Anderson-Brown soon dispelled that notion. The only ray of hope was that Anderson-Brown had said that Emily had been brought up to do what was right, and that he had every confidence in her.

He could see that Emily was thinking hard by the way her hazel eyes were flicking from side to side without actually focusing on anything.

He could only imagine what turmoil she must be going through as he waited anxiously for a response.

Eventually Emily sat up in the chair and looked directly at him.

'So, basically, I haven't got a choice. I can't possibly allow them to be destroyed. I thought my uncle was a bit eccentric, but he must have been totally mad as well. So, what do I do next?'

Mr. Pierce could see that Emily's eyes were beginning to fill with tears. A paternal feeling overcame him as he patted her hand.

'I've made a copy of the will. Take it home and study it over the weekend. Don't rush into a decision just yet.' He passed her a copy of the will and an extra piece of paper. 'That's the address of the livery where the mare is. It's about ten miles from here. Why don't you go out there over the weekend and see what you're letting yourself in for? I believe the mare is called Andaman Sea. Your uncle was so excited about her, and as for the foal she's carrying, he kept saying what a champion it was going to be.'

Emily looked at the address on the paper and sighed.

'How on earth am I going to explain the situation to them?'

'Don't worry, I've taken the liberty of writing this letter explaining the situation and the prospective change of ownership. It's not as daunting as you might think; when it comes to racing, I'm sure most owners haven't a clue. After all, the trainer trains it, the jockey rides it and the owner gets to pay the bills and have the fun.' Mr. Pierce passed the letter to Emily and hoped that he had sounded convincing enough to allay some of Emily's fears. 'Oh, and you'll probably find that there will be some outstanding bills from the stables, so if you could let me have them I can settle any outstanding accounts.'

'Yes, of course.'

Emily thought for a moment.

'Isn't the Derby quite a big race where all the wealthy people enter their horses?'

'Well, I suppose it is.' Mr. Pierce hesitated, trying not to concern Emily even more than she was already. 'But it's not so much about who you are as the horse's ability, from what I gather.'

15

'How could Uncle Julian be so sure that the foal will have that ability?'

'I can't see how he did, but I know he kept saying how it was bred for the Derby.'

Emily folded up all the paperwork she had been given and put it in her handbag.

'Anyway, the alternative is too awful to consider,' she said, getting to her feet. 'I will go over to the stables this weekend and see what I'm letting myself in for, and will ring you on Monday.'

'That's my girl.' Mr. Pierce stood up and shook hands with Emily.

'I'll look forward to your call on Monday. Just think what a whole new interest in your life it will be.'

'You could say that again,' Emily muttered under her breath as she left the office.

Once outside, the cold January air brought her back to reality. Emily walked slowly back to her car, and once inside closed her eyes for a moment.

What on earth was she going to tell Greg?

Emily sat at the kitchen table with Uncle Julian's will spread out in front of her. Beside her was half a mug of tea, which had been forgotten about and had long since gone cold as Emily struggled to understand what on earth had possessed her uncle to make out such a will.

She had no idea he was interested in horses, let alone owned one and had embarked on breeding from it.

She remembered, years ago, from the odd comment her mother had made, that he was an avid gambler, but gambling was one thing and owning a horse was another.

As for the condition that the foal, once eligible, was to run in the Derby – why – Uncle Julian must have lost his senses.

Emily rested her head in her hands. How on earth was she going to explain this to Greg? The thought of trying to explain £50,000 tied up for spending solely on a horse was bound to upset him.

Emily heard the key in the front door and realised that Greg had arrived home. She took a deep breath, waiting for Greg to appear, which he did in record time.

'So, am I speaking to an heiress then?' he said, giving her a quick peck on the cheek before sitting down opposite. 'Why didn't you ring me at work? I've been in suspense all afternoon. I rang your office after lunch, and they said you had taken the afternoon off to see the solicitor. You could have rung me, Emmy.'

'I've only just got home,' replied Emily, defensively.

'Took that long, eh? Well, it must have been important and more than those old books you suspected.'

'It's rather complicated.'

Emily thought of how the solicitor had stumbled though the will, and realised that he had weeks to think what he was going to say – she had only an hour to work out what to say to Greg. The best way, she concluded, was to read it word for word.

Greg sat in silence until he heard the words £50,000.

'Oh, boy,' he exclaimed, as his eyes gleamed with anticipation. 'Just think what we could spend that on.'

'Before you get carried away, listen to the rest of it.'

Emily read out the conditions attached to the money.

'You can't be serious!' he gasped incredulously. 'There must be some way round it, like sell them or something.'

Emily tried patiently to explain the conditions of the will again, and after ten minutes of argument from Greg, his initial excitement had turned to fury.

'There must be something we can get out of it. I know, what about a Land Rover – we could say it was for towing a horse box for that bloody animal!'

'No,' said Emily firmly, 'I would have to abide by the terms of the will, after all it's my inheritance and therefore my responsibility, not yours.'

'Stuff your inheritance, I'm going out!'

Greg stormed out of the kitchen, grabbed his jacket and left, slamming the front door behind him.

Tears welled up in Emily's eyes. It had gone worse than she had planned, and what was even more upsetting was that she had witnessed a side of Greg she had never seen before – greedy, selfish, abusive and downright unreasonable.

She had hoped she could discuss it rationally with him and plan what she could do. Perhaps when he got used to the idea he would come round.

All she knew was that at this moment in time she needed support, but if she had to, she was determined to do it alone.

She wiped her eyes and resolved to go to the stables first thing in the morning – with or without Greg.

Emily barely slept that night.

Two things kept her awake – the first of which was the will. The second was Greg not coming home that night.

In a way, Emily was relieved, as she didn't want to deal with Greg if he returned in the same mood as when he left. She hoped that he had spent the night as his friend's house, which he sometimes did if he was out very late or had too much to drink.

She dressed quickly in jeans and a thick jumper, hoping it would be the appropriate attire for visiting the stables.

Following breakfast, she made a quick call to the stables and arranged to see the owner – a rather well spoken lady called Mrs. Forsyth – there at 11a.m., with reference to Andaman Sea.

Mrs. Forsyth had heard that Anderson-Brown had died, and was obviously anxious to know what was happening with the mare.

Emily had made a list of all the questions she had thought of asking, but then screwed up the piece of paper in frustration. The list had seemed ridiculous – all the sort of questions that any novice would have been able to answer.

Mentally, she narrowed it down to the bare essentials, and at 10.30 – with still no sign of Greg appearing – set off for the village where the stables were.

Following the directions that Mrs. Forsyth had given her, and despite getting lost twice, Emily eventually turned into the drive with a few minutes to spare.

She couldn't help but be impressed as she drove down the long, tree lined driveway, where clumps of snowdrops were beginning to flower beneath the evenly spaced poplar trees. At the end of the drive, the lane split into two, with a drive to the large and impressive Cotswold stone house off to the left, and what Emily concluded were the stables to the right.

She parked her car next to a battered and mud splattered Range Rover, feeling as nervous as when she went for her first job interview.

Angela Woodward

Pulling her thick jacket round her, she got out of the car and looked round her.

The yard had a large barn on the right hand side – behind which Emily could just make out the edge of a steaming muckheap. An L shaped row of stables was to the left and in front of her. In the centre was a large courtyard, which, due to the rainy January weather, was wet, muddy and littered with pieces of straw. Wheelbarrows stood outside two of the boxes, and from some of the stables, horses of various sizes and colours looked out, some munching on apparently nothing at all whilst others eyed the outside world like any nosey neighbour peering through the lounge window.

Wishing she had put a pair of wellingtons in the car, Emily picked her way through the less muddy areas of the yard, until she spotted a head bobbing up and down in one of the boxes. She went over and peered into the stable, where a girl in her early teens was grooming a dark grey horse that seemed to be paying more attention to the bucket in the corner than the girl.

'Excuse me, I'm looking for Mrs. Forsyth.'

The girl looked up and walked over to the stable door, pushing the rear of the horse out of the way with her shoulder.

'See that door over there at the end of the stables, she'll be in the office there.'

'Thank you,' replied Emily, as she watched the girl give the horse an affectionate slap on its rear before continuing grooming.

By the time Emily had reached the office door, she couldn't help but wonder if she could claim for a new pair of shoes off the inheritance, since hers were now

20

soaking wet and covered in mud, straw and God knows what else.

She knocked on the door, and on hearing a muffled 'come in,' entered.

'Mrs. Forsyth?' Emily asked tentatively, 'I'm Miss Lloyd. I phoned earlier this morning about a horse called Andaman Sea.'

'Yes. Please come in and sit down. I was so sorry to hear about Mr. Anderson-Brown.' Mrs. Forsyth motioned to a battered old sofa that took up most of one wall of the office. 'Can I make you a coffee – I'm dying for one.'

'Yes, thank you.'

As Mrs. Forsyth busied herself making the coffee, Emily looked around. She estimated that Mrs. Forsyth was in her late thirties, a tall woman who had long fair hair tied back in a ponytail. Under the bulky jumper and shirt, she was probably quite slim – it was hard to tell. Her face was tanned and weather beaten, with a healthy rosy glow from the obvious outdoor life.

The office itself was warm and cosy, heated by an old two bar electric fire, in front of which was a big blanket-lined dog basket. In it lay a black Labrador, who lazily surveyed Emily with one eye, and deciding she was no threat to his warm space, sighed and closed his eye again, resuming his sleep.

Next to the fire was a big old bookcase, every shelf groaning under the weight of piles of paperwork and books – all on horses.

An old desk stood in the corner, covered in yet more paperwork, magazines and empty coffee mugs.

Mrs. Forsyth handed Emily a coffee and sat down.

Emily quickly explained the circumstances of her visit

but only up to the point of her inheriting Andaman Sea.

She took out the letter from the solicitors and handed it to Mrs. Forsyth, who opened it and quickly read its contents.

'I had heard that your uncle had died, and I have to admit I was getting a little concerned as to what to do about Andaman Sea.'

'Yes, I can well imagine. I only found out about her yesterday, and I have to admit it came as a bit of a shock since I never knew he was interested in horses, let alone owned one.

Mrs. Forsyth nodded sympathetically. Having noticed the state of Emily's shoes, it was obvious to her that Emily had never been in a yard before.

'Firstly, you would no doubt like to see Andaman Sea.'

'Yes please.'

With Emily following, Mrs. Forsyth went out to the second box from the office and opened the stable door, went in, and with a few encouraging noises reappeared leading the mare.

Emily was transfixed. The mare looked magnificent, standing as high as Emily's shoulder, with a dark bay coat and mane and tail that shone like burnt copper, and a small white mark between the eyes.

She had recently been groomed – no doubt for Emily's benefit.

The mare pricked her ears and nuzzled Mrs. Forsyth's jacket pocket. Mrs. Forsyth reached in and pulled out a couple of mints.

'Here, give her these – all horses love them,' she said,

handing them to Emily. 'Hold out your hand flat, that way she won't take a chunk out of you by accident.'

Emily held the mints out, and Andaman Sea nuzzled her hand, tickling palm as she deftly picked up the mints. The mare nuzzled her hand again looking for more, letting out a snort of warm air on not finding any.

'That's enough, you are fat enough as it is,' said Mrs. Forsyth, slapping the mare's neck with affection.

Emily had been so busy staring into the big deep brown eyes of Andaman Sea, that she hadn't noticed the bulging girth. The thought crossed her mind that the mare looked as though she was about to burst.

'How much longer has she got to go?' Emily asked, thinking that there was no way Andaman Sea could possibly expand any further.

'Oh, about three weeks,' said Mrs. Forsyth as she rubbed the mare's back. 'We have a couple of foaling boxes which are a bit bigger, so we'll soon put her in one of those to give her a bit more room.' Andaman Sea let out another snort and started pawing the ground.

'Oh, I know, old girl, it won't be much longer.'

Mrs. Forsyth rubbed the mare's ears before slipping her another mint.

A few spots of rain started to fall, so Mrs. Forsyth led the mare back into her box and they retreated back to the warmth of the office.

'She's a reasonable mare, and the sire is one of the best money can buy, so the foal should be quite useful.'

'I do hope so,' replied Emily, not daring to tell Mrs. Forsyth about her uncle's plans for the foal. Emily, hoping to expand her knowledge a bit continued, 'So you think the foal is fairly well bred then?'

'Well, from the sire's point of view, you couldn't get much better. He was a multiple classic winner and must have cost your uncle a fortune in stud fees. Andaman Sea, however, didn't exactly set the racing world alight – did reasonably well in a couple of smaller races. She does have a couple of big names in her pedigree. Still, for all the theories of breeding, you can cross two of the greatest and end up with something totally useless, and on the other hand, sometimes, from nowhere comes a real star. That's the magic of breeding – until it comes to the crunch, you'll never know.'

Emily sighed; it all sounded like a lottery to her. She then remembered what Mr. Pierce had said about the livery bills.

'The solicitor said that there were a few outstanding bills which need paying.'

'Yes – that's a bit of an understatement I'm afraid. Your uncle was never very prompt with settling his account, so I'm afraid there's quite a sum outstanding. I've enclosed copies of the outstanding invoices together with the latest ones to bring us up to date.'

She handed Emily a bulging envelope.

'I'll forward it to the solicitors on Monday,' promised Emily. 'Well, I think I have taken up more than enough of your time.'

'No, that's fine, I'm just relieved that Andaman Sea's future is on the way to be sorted out. It has been a bit of a worry over the last few weeks, having an ownerless horse in the yard – so to speak. I presume you want her to stay here for the time being?'

'Yes please, if that's possible.'

'Nothing's too much trouble as long as the bills are

paid.' Mrs. Forsyth stood up. 'Do come and see her any time you want, or you could always ring. If you could leave me your address and phone number, so I can contact you. She may be due in a few weeks, but anything can happen.'

Emily wrote the details down on the pad Mrs. Forsyth offered. She had no idea how much it was costing to keep the mare here – that she could find out from the invoices once she got home – but for the time being, Andaman Sea seemed to be in good hands, and besides, she didn't have any other alternative. At least there were funds to meet the bills, so she wasn't unduly worried.

Emily thanked Mrs. Forsyth again, and watched as she disappeared across the courtyard into one of the boxes. Emily couldn't resist going to see Andaman Sea again.

The mare moved from the back of the box and put her head over the door, nuzzling Emily's pockets.

'I'm sorry, I haven't got any mints,' Emily laughed, 'but I promise I'll bring you some the next time I come.'

She patted Andaman Sea's neck, and wished she could give her a big hug, but was uncertain how the mare would react.

For the whole drive back, Emily couldn't take her mind off the mare.

How could Uncle Julian have put that awful condition in the will about having her destroyed if she didn't agree to the conditions. How could anyone be so cold hearted to such a beautiful animal.

The more she thought about it the angrier she became. She wished she could give him a piece of her mind and get it off her chest, but that was now impossible.

Her anger turned to a steely determination to protect

Andaman Sea and her foal, starting with ringing Mr. Pierce first thing Monday to agree to take over their ownership.

By the time Emily reached home, she had calmed down slightly in her anger towards her uncle, and was relieved to have come to the decision to keep the mare.

As she opened the front door, she could hear the TV in the lounge, and felt a twinge of guilt at having forgotten all about Greg – until she remembered that he hadn't come home last night.

She walked into the lounge to find Greg slouched on the sofa, feet up on the coffee table, beer bottle in one hand, watching the football on the television. An empty pizza carton lay open, in which lay an empty beer bottle.

'What happened to you last night?' she said, biting her lip and trying not to sound too accusing.

'I could ask the same about you this morning,' came the reply from Greg, without him even turning round to look at her. He took a swig from the bottle and continued to watch the football.

'I went to see the horse,' Emily said defensively.

'Expert now, are we?' came the sarcastic reply, 'or have you decided to send it to the knacker's yard?'

It was all Emily could do to contain her anger.

'No, I'm going to keep it, and if that's going to be your attitude, I see no point in discussing it any further. From now on it's my business and mine alone.'

'My Emily – racehorse owner,' sneered Greg. 'Boy, are my mates going to have a laugh about that. Chuck us another beer, Emily, and I'll drink to that.'

'Get it yourself.'

Emily stormed out of the lounge and threw her handbag on the kitchen table.

Greg followed her in, and without a word or glance, helped himself to another beer from the fridge before returning to the lounge.

It was then that Emily realised how hungry she was – not surprising since it was almost three o'clock. Judging by the empty pizza carton in the lounge, Greg had already eaten – not that she was in any mood to cook him anything.

Quickly she made herself some cheese on toast and a cup of tea before settling down at the kitchen table.

She fetched the envelope from Mrs. Forsyth, and opened it, unfolding the four invoices it contained.

A quick calculation revealed almost £1500 outstanding for a period of three months. Only three months, she thought with astonishment.

Weekly livery fees were £90, which was almost half her take home pay and more than she would ever dream of spending on herself. She had no idea that it would be that much. If Greg knew, he would be even more furious than he was at the moment, so she dared not tell him.

Emily comforted herself with the thought that at least there were funds to cover it, and she wouldn't have to spend any of her own money – not that there was anything spare to spend.

Monday morning soon dawned. For Emily it had been an awful weekend.

Greg had been so cold towards her. The only time he had spoken, it would be some sarcastic comment about her, Andaman Sea or her uncle.

Emily felt relieved to be back at work and away from his hostility.

She had phoned Mr. Pierce and agreed to the conditions of the will, and put the invoices in the post to him, keeping copies, which she tucked neatly into a folder. Mr. Pierce, in turn, would forward documents to transfer ownership to her.

Emily didn't want to say anything to any of her work colleagues for fear of finding the same amount of incredulity and ridicule she had received from Greg. No – she would give herself a week or two to allow herself to get used to the idea and feel more confident with her plans before revealing them to anyone else.

All the while, she couldn't help but wonder how on earth Uncle Julian had come to possess a racehorse, let alone one in foal. Add to that the bizarre clause about the Derby and Emily decided he must really have lost his mind.

Much as she loved Andaman Sea from the minute she laid eyes on her, she found herself cursing her uncle for leaving her in such a ridiculous predicament. One thing was for certain, Emily's life had now changed direction in a way she could never imagine, and she felt very uneasy about the lack of control she had on it now.

From beyond the grave, Uncle Julian had apparently mapped out a course that Emily would have to follow, like it or not.

Emily shook her head and kept coming back to the same question – Why?

What she didn't know was that the answer lay in a chance meeting between her uncle and a multimillionaire some two years previously.

2

Two years before Emily Lloyd found out about her strange inheritance, Nathan Grant was at Epsom racecourse, moistening the end of his cigar before lighting it, inhaling deeply, savouring the feeling of smug satisfaction that this year, the Derby, the greatest horse race in the flat racing calendar, was going to be his. He blew out a long slow stream of cigar smoke, which coiled lazily skywards before vanishing in the warm Epson air. He had the best horse and the champion jockey on board. The going was also perfect for his entry, Northern Lights, the hottest favourite for years, and nothing it would seem could stop them.

Yes, this year it was going to be his turn. Nathan closed his eyes for a moment and envisaged himself leading Northern Lights into the winner's enclosure, followed by collecting the winner's trophy. He had even thought about the short speech he would be called upon to give. Today, after years of trying, it was going to be his turn. He could feel the win – almost taste the victory.

He opened his eyes and gazed out over the Derby crowd. The atmosphere and anticipation of the record crowd was infectious. With barely room to move, the ladies, dressed in their finest summer dresses interspersed by their less colourfully dressed partners, gave the effect of multi coloured sardines, covering what seemed to be every available square inch of space, jostling together in what appeared to be futile attempts to get from a to b. He smiled as he watched the crowds, grateful that he could enjoy the day from the civilised surroundings of his private box.

It was a long time since he had been to a race meeting like this and had to watch with the general public. The mere thought of it made him shudder. Now, as head of Grant Global Communications and a multi millionaire, he had a box at all the important race meetings and could watch the racing as he had become accustomed to – in style.

He glanced down at his Rolex watch – almost half an hour to go before the start of the race. It was time to make his way down to the paddock. He turned and walked across the room, acknowledging his guests as he passed them, not wishing to engage in any lengthy conversations that might delay him from what he almost arrogantly regarded as his destiny.

Walking towards his wife, he wryly noticed that she had a glass of champagne in one hand and yet another canapé in the other. His heart sank slightly at the sight of her. With all the canapés he noticed she had eaten, it was no wonder she was overweight. He sighed to himself. He despised Lydia. He had put up with her for nearly twenty years now. She was short, plain, fat, and no matter how much money she spent on her hair, designer clothes, face lifts and God knows what else, to him she never looked any better.

He looked at her a little closer, trying to see what had

possessed him to marry her in the first place. Lydia was short – a little over five foot – and definitely not petite with it. Her excessive appetite for food had resulted in her being a good couple of stone overweight, which even the most expensive haute couture found impossible to disguise.

Her hair was dyed fair to hide the grey, and was cut and permed in a totally unsuitable style for her age and shape in a vain attempt to make her look younger.

As usual, she was wearing too much make-up, but then again there was a lot to cover up.

Nathan chuckled to himself – perhaps it was better for her to use too much make-up – after all, he had the dubious honour of knowing what she looked like underneath it all.

He glanced down at her legs – yes – predictable as ever – the ankles were beginning to swell. Hardly surprising with the weight they had to carry whilst wearing those ridiculous strappy high heeled shoes she liked to wear to make her look taller than she was.

Nathan looked away, not wishing to depress himself too much on such an exciting day, and sighed. From his point of view it had been a marriage of convenience from the start.

Lydia's father owned a company that Nathan was desperate to acquire. It was the link that was missing in his global communications empire. Lydia – being an only child – was adored by her father, and when all offers to buy the company failed, Nathan courted Lydia and married her. The only problem was that Lydia's father bequeathed the controlling interest in the company to

Lydia on his death, and so Nathan had been saddled with her ever since.

Lydia had long since realised that Nathan had married her for business reasons – a realisation that came as quite a shock. She knew that she was no beauty, but was totally taken in by Nathan when he started showing an interest in her.

Naively she thought he had married her for love – after all, he was tall, handsome, very successful, and at that time – one of the most eligible bachelors in the country. It didn't take her long to realise that he was a serial womaniser, and following the birth of their second child, the marriage became one of convenience for both of them.

Nathan – through Lydia – had the vital link in his business empire, and being 'married' kept his succession of girlfriends in their place, whilst Lydia had the status and spending power that she could previously only have dreamt of.

'Come on, Lydia, it's time to go down to the parade ring,' Nathan said impatiently as Lydia popped yet another canapé in her mouth.

Quickly she downed what was left in her champagne glass.

'It wouldn't do to be late, would it?' replied Lydia with some degree of sarcasm.

It was one of Nathan's many habits, which irritated her. He always had to get down to the parade ring early in order to gain maximum exposure from the media – most of which he owned anyway. A few well-chosen words here or there were guaranteed to be headlines the next day. She also knew that in having the favourite in the race, he would want to lord it over the other owners.

He could be so unbearably conceited sometimes, it was almost embarrassing.

'For God's sake, Lydia, will you hurry up!'

'Coming, dear.'

Lydia hurriedly finished adjusting her hat in the mirror and duly followed her husband, who was obviously in no mood to wait.

It wasn't long before Nathan was striding confidently into the parade ring. Lydia, meanwhile, was having trouble keeping up in the high heels, which, despite the dry conditions, seemed to sink into the turf – probably due more to her weight than the state of the ground.

There were already a few owners in the parade ring, and a couple of horses being walked round.

Nathan walked over to one of the owners he knew quite well.

'Good morning, Tom,' he said, shaking hands with the somewhat portly fellow owner.

''Morning, Nathan, you lucky dog. The rest of us don't stand a chance against Northern Lights with this going. We've all been praying for rain to soften the going and give our entries a chance. Still, a place will do me fine today.'

Nathan beamed.

'We'll see.'

Lydia, meanwhile, was busy chatting to Tom's wife, exchanging the latest gossip.

Nathan knew most of the owners. It seemed to be the same old faces every year, just different horses, since only the rich could afford racing at this level.

The owners seemed to be subdivided into three categories – the super wealthy Arabs who seemed to dominate the

Classic races, and in particular, the Derby, for which over the last five years they had seemed to have a rota system amongst themselves for winning.

Then came the very wealthy, of which Nathan was one. They would win the odd Classic and maybe be placed in the Derby.

Lastly came the enthusiasts who would have a once-in-a-lifetime opportunity with a Derby entrant, but who had no realistic hope of winning. For them, taking part was sufficient.

Nathan was on polite nodding terms with the first category, knew all of the second group, and despised the third.

This year, however, it was going to be different. Having been placed in the Derby for the last two years and having been beaten by the Arab connections on both occasions, Nathan, in a moment of madness and sheer frustration, outbid them at the yearling sales and had bought Northern Lights for a record sum. Despite the considerable dent in his fortune he had felt very pleased with himself, and felt even more smug now. Northern Lights was, after all, unbeaten, and had won the 2000 guineas in considerable style.

Winning the Derby was Nathan's lifelong ambition, and would give him the status and recognition in the racing world that up to now he thought he had been deprived of, and in his opinion, certainly deserved.

Once the Derby was under his belt, Northern Lights would be retired to Nathan's stud, where he would hopefully sire more Classic winners – and with any luck – perhaps another Derby winner. His initial outlay in buying the horse would then look like small change.

The Legacy

The sight of Northern Lights entering the parade ring brought Nathan's mind quickly back into focus. The horse looked magnificent, his dark bay coat gleaming in the sunshine, the contours of his muscles rippling as he moved.

Ears pricked, the horse looked round, taking in the scene with the experienced air of a seasoned campaigner, despite his relative youth. Slightly on his toes, he seemed to float round the parade ring, oozing power and charisma with every step and looking every inch a champion.

Nathan glowed with pride. Northern Lights had never looked better. Lydia glanced at Nathan as he watched the horse stride by. She couldn't help but feel a twinge of envy and sadness as she saw the look of adoration in Nathan's eyes. If only he could have shown something close to that look for her, but no. Maybe he had at some time, but it would have been too long ago to remember. As soon as someone or something proved to be a disappointment to him, they were discarded, rather like a small child who grows tired of his toys.

Northern Lights was certainly Nathan's toy of the moment, and Lydia hoped beyond all hope that he would win. Nathan would be unbearably conceited, but at least when he was happy, everyone else was happy – not to mention relieved. If Northern Lights got beaten, Lydia had promised herself two weeks at their villa on St. James's Beach, Barbados, to get away from the foul mood that would inevitably follow. In fact, to cover the possibility, she had even booked her flight on Concorde – just in case.

Nathan in a bad mood – from her previous experiences – was not something she wished to endure.

Meanwhile, in the weighing room complex, James Ryan, Northern Lights' young jockey, was changing into Nathan Grant's silks. Despite having ridden in countless races and won quite a few Classics, the Derby was the one prize that he had always dreamt of winning, ever since he could remember.

He was surprised to find himself feeling very nervous, since the atmosphere of this big race was totally different from any other, and of course, the expectations were so much greater.

He had hardly slept the previous night, going over and over again in his mind how to ride the race.

Surely he would never have such a wonderful opportunity to ride the winner.

He would swap everything to ride the winner of the Derby – the champion jockey title and all the other Classic races. Somehow, when you win the Derby, be it horse, owner, trainer or jockey, you become part of racing history and everything else pales into insignificance.

Usually the weighing room would be full of chatting and joking jockeys, but today there was almost a reverent silence.

James glanced quickly in the mirror. He knew that in the morning the winning jockey's picture would feature in articles all round the world, and according to the bookies and the racing fraternity, it would be him. The thought made him feel even more nervous.

He ran his fingers through his straight, sandy coloured hair, and after completing the pre-race formalities, took a deep breath before striding out into the paddock, trying to cut himself off from the excitement and expectations of the crowd and focus on the race ahead.

By the time he reached the parade ring, Stuart Lawson, Northern Lights' trainer, was already there, engrossed in deep conversation with Nathan Grant.

'How did Northern Lights travel?' Nathan Grant was asking Stuart.

'No problem,' came the reply from the large framed, portly, cigar-smoking Stuart. 'He's certainly on top form today. Never been better.'

All three of them anxiously watched Northern Lights walking round, each silently praying that there was no avenue in his preparation that had been overlooked, which, given Stuart's reputation for being one of the top trainers in the country, seemed highly unlikely.

For the umpteenth time, Stuart went over the race plan with James, who, despite knowing the tactics off by heart, listened almost reverently to the trainer, nodding in all the right places.

The parade ring was beginning to fill with the connections – owners, trainers, jockeys and anyone else who had an excuse to be there – legitimate or otherwise – all huddled in their respective groups, all discussing last minute scenarios and trying to cover all the possibilities of how the race might evolve.

The horses, meanwhile, continued to parade round – some getting very hot and agitated, whilst others lobbed round as though this was an every day occurrence and was all very tedious.

The bell sounded. It was time to mount up. The jockeys, having been given their final instructions yet again, mounted up, and the horses were led out onto the course for the parade.

Nathan could barely contain his excitement, and even

Lydia had to admit to herself that she was feeling tense and nervous.

'Well, it's all up to Ryan and Northern Lights now,' Nathan said to Stuart as they made their way back though the crowds to the comfort of his box, stopping to chat with other owners on the way.

The horses by now were well on their way to the start. Through his binoculars, Nathan could pick out Northern Lights by Nathan's distinctive colours that James was wearing – gold with a red circle on chest and back, red sleeves and red cap.

The grace with which his horse was cantering to the start made Nathan swell with pride. He studied the other horses – the cream of racing – but there were none as handsome as his own.

Lydia, meanwhile, was chatting to one of their friends, and out of the corner of her eye watched Nathan's personal assistant take him a glass of champagne and start chatting to him with a degree of familiarity, which she had, long since learnt to recognise.

Nathan seemed to have a quick succession of personal assistants – all young, tall and stunning looking. Whatever their role in assisting was, Lydia was sure it would be of an extremely personal nature.

They never seemed to last long in their 'job' and were quickly replaced by another just as stunning looking.

This current assistant was tall – almost six foot, with luxurious long blonde hair, a flawless complexion and a figure that Lydia could only dream of. Grudgingly, Lydia had to admit that she was certainly very beautiful, and exceeded Nathan's usual standard. Her simply cut red dress hugged her figure in all the right places,

The Legacy

accentuating her bronzed tan. They certainly made a handsome couple, but Lydia was comforted by the fact that Nathan could not afford to divorce her – or be too indiscreet with his relationships.

She sighed, having long ago accepted Nathan's affairs, and in a way relieved that he never bothered her now in that department of their marriage.

The horses were now being loaded into their starting stalls – some easily, others having to be persuaded by the capable stall handlers. Northern Lights went into his stall with the minimum of fuss and waited, ears pricked and eyes fixed on the course ahead, which looked as smooth as green baize, disguising the arduous course ahead.

Stuart Lawson joined Nathan on the balcony.

'It's all up to them now,' he commented yet again in resignation.

Stuart knew how much this race meant to Nathan, not to mention to himself and the prestige of the yard. Nathan had put enormous pressure on him to bring Northern Lights this far. The horse had not let him down, and he was confident that he would do the business again today.

He also had great confidence in James as a jockey, and the James Ryan/Northern Lights combination had been a dream ticket for him this season.

Amongst the other runners, he couldn't see Northern Lights getting beaten, but in racing, there was no such thing as a certainty. The only thing that Stuart was certain about was that only a win would do for Nathan – being placed again this time was not an option.

He winced as he remembered last year when Nathan's horse came a close second. Nathan was furious, and spent the rest of the season complaining about the dominance of the Arab connections in the racing world. They had so much money, they could buy the best and breed the best, and the average owner barely got a sniff of the major prizes. Not that Nathan could ever be classed an average owner, but even he found it difficult to come by Classic winners.

Despite his global empire and enormous wealth, Nathan always felt in the second division, and beating the Arabs had become an obsession with him.

The last horse was being loaded into the stalls, and a silence descended over the course as all eyes turned to the start.

Some people in Nathan's box joined them on the balcony whilst others, like Lydia, stayed inside to watch the race on the TV screen.

Nathan was oblivious to all his guests; he was so focussed on Northern Lights in stall eight.

There was a split second when it seemed that time stood still. One of these great horses would run it's way into the record books, and the others would just be extras in the greatest race of the year.

Nathan held his breath.

The stalls opened, the horses sprang out and the crowd roared.

Within a few strides, Northern Lights was tucked in behind the leaders, just where Stuart had told James he wanted him.

Up the hill they galloped, some being held back as they tried to run too freely, others getting the odd reminder with the whip to focus their mind on this being the Derby and not just another training gallop.

Northern Lights had settled four off the lead and was travelling smoothly, avoiding the bumping going on behind as others jostled for places.

As they rounded Tattenham Corner, he was still well placed and travelling sweetly, now up into third place.

With three furlongs to go, James gave Northern Lights a slap on his neck, and the horse responded by storming into the lead, appearing to leave the others rather one paced.

Everything was going to plan. Nathan's excitement mounted. The second and third favourites were dropping back, and by now, Northern Lights had a three-length advantage. Only two horses gave chase, Sandstorm and The Silver Fox.

Two furlongs to go and Northern Lights still held a two-length lead, and only had to maintain his stride and rhythm to win the race, as the chasing two seemed to be making little headway.

Suddenly, in the final furlong, the unthinkable happened. Northern Lights began to falter, losing his rhythm and starting to hang to the left.

Sandstorm, who was giving chase, swallowed up the tiring Northern Lights and, to the roars of the crowd, passed him in the last stride to snatch racing's most coveted prize.

The tumultuous cheering of the crowd seemed to wash over Nathan as his horse crossed the line, beaten into second place by the unfancied second string horse of yet another Arab.

Nathan stood in silence, totally lost for words, his eyes fixed on the finishing post, unable to comprehend what had just happened.

Stuart, beside him, was equally shocked, his mind racing on to what Nathan's reaction would be. He knew what Nathan was like, and realised that the rest of the day was going to be very unpleasant, not to mention the next few weeks.

There would be no way he could explain that with the Derby being over a unique distance, no one ever knew if a horse would get the trip until the event. He had been convinced that Northern Lights would have no problem; obviously he was wrong.

Nathan would be looking for answers, and in an act of self preservation for the prestigious job that he held as Nathan's trainer, he decided to make James the scapegoat.

'That bloody jockey! He should have pushed him harder over the last furlong and held his line. Couldn't even steer him in a straight line. How could he have let Sandstorm through? Call himself a champion jockey!'

Stuart hoped he had sown the seeds of doubt about James in Nathan's mind. Knowing Nathan, someone was going to be out of a job by the end of the day, and he didn't want it to be himself, even though in his heart he knew that there was nothing James could have done. Northern Lights just didn't get the trip, but having spent so much money to buy the horse, Nathan would be unable to accept that the horse wasn't up to it.

Nathan's guests all started to congratulate him on his second place. Only Stuart and Lydia knew that second place wasn't good enough for Nathan.

Nathan, with barely a word, started making his way down to the course. Stuart quickly followed in silence.

Lydia caught sight of the thunderous look on Nathan's

face as he left the room. She downed the remaining champagne in her glass in one go and made a mental note to confirm her flight on Concorde first thing in the morning. A couple of weeks at their villa would be paradise in comparison to having to suffer the sort of foul mood that Nathan was going to be in. By the time she returned he would hopefully be in a more civilised mood.

Nathan, beside himself with rage, arrived on the course as Northern Lights was being led in. It was only because of the massive crowd and James's popularity amongst the public and the fact that the world's press were there that stopped him from hauling the jockey off and punching him. Perhaps in the back of his mind he knew that James wasn't to blame, but Nathan being Nathan had to find someone on whom to vent his anger, and that unfortunate candidate on this occasion was James.

As James saw Nathan striding towards him, he sensed that he was far from happy.

Stuart, who had been trying to keep up with Nathan, had a very worried look on his face.

James felt he had a clear conscience, he had run the race as he had been instructed, done all the right things, but when he asked Northern Lights for that one last effort, there was no response.

'I'm sorry, sir, Northern Lights did everything that was asked, but he just didn't get the trip and faded in the last furlong,' James tried to explain to Nathan as he unsaddled Northern Lights, who was blowing heavily and was wet with sweat – every blood vessel pulsating and bulging beneath his saturated darkened coat.

'What do you mean "he didn't get the trip"? He's bred

to get the trip, trained to get the trip, and you say he couldn't!' Nathan fumed, his face contorted with rage.

'In the last furlong, he changed his legs and the camber took him away from his line. I changed my whip over, but Sandstorm flew by and when I asked for more there was nothing there.'

'In the Derby, you don't ask for more, you're paid to demand more, and in no uncertain terms. This is the Derby, not a bloody tea dance!' ranted Nathan, barely able to string a coherent sentence together, so great was his rage.

Stuart was standing behind Nathan, staring at the ground, embarrassed by the public spectacle that was happening in front of him. He felt desperately sorry for James, who he knew had done well to hang onto second place, but there would be no pacifying Nathan.

James looked almost pleadingly at Stuart for some sort of support, but Stuart tried to avoid looking at him and shrugged his shoulders. It was a case of every man for himself and Stuart was not about to throw away his position to support a mere jockey – owners were far more important. There were, after all, plenty more good jockeys but very few owners who owned the calibre of horses that Nathan Grant did.

James realised that nothing he could say at this moment would defuse the situation, and being too well mannered to get involved in a public slanging match with his boss, reasoned that perhaps, when Nathan had seen the replay and calmed down, he would see the truth.

He also realised that Stuart was not going to enrage Nathan by disagreeing with him.

There was no other course of action but to unsaddle

the exhausted Northern Lights and hope that everyone would calm down by the next day.

With nothing left to say, James nodded towards the owner and trainer and miserably departed the scene to weigh in.

The sight of the Arab connections in the winners' enclosure was more than Nathan could bear and he stormed off, ignoring all calls for interviews, and headed for the sanctuary of his private box, leaving Stuart to deal with the slowly recovering horse.

When he arrived back in his box, Nathan was appalled to find his friends still celebrating his second place.

No one ever remembered who came second in the Derby, they only remembered the winner – everyone else was a loser, no matter where they came.

Lydia knew better than to speak to Nathan when he was in a mood such as this, but his 'assistant,' who Lydia had since found out was called Samantha, rushed over to congratulate Nathan, only to be met with a thunderous glare and a very curt reply.

"Yet another one falls by the wayside;" Lydia thought to herself with wry amusement.

Nathan, unable to bear any more patronising, decided to leave. Without any explanation he departed, leaving Lydia to make up some excuse about urgent business, and to continue to entertain the guests for the rest of the day. At least she was good at entertaining, thought Nathan as he stormed out.

Nathan was fortunate in that few people were leaving immediately after the big race and quickly reached his car, startling his chauffeur who was engrossed in the

Racing Post whilst listening to the radio. The chauffeur immediately shut the *Racing Post*, turned off the radio and sat up straight, as close to attention as he could muster.

'Hard luck, sir,' he said, sensing that his boss was in an awful mood.

Nathan didn't reply, just sat back and thought for a moment. He had found the company back at the racecourse so unbearable, that he had left without a thought of where he was going or what he was going to do next.

He closed his eyes for a second, thinking of his dreams and the fortune that had just gone down the drain today. He might as well blow some more money tonight.

'The club, Alex,' said Nathan, as he tried to regain his composure.

As the car pulled away, Nathan thought over the day. It seemed that no matter what he did or how much he spent, his dream still eluded him.

To be beaten by the second string horse of an Arab owner added insult to injury. It wasn't fair. There seemed no way he could win. He had spent a record amount buying Northern Lights, and what had he got for it – defeat.

Time to take control again. He picked up his mobile phone and dialled.

'Stuart, Grant here. I don't want James Ryan riding for me again. I don't care if he's got two rides booked for me on Monday, sack him now. I'm sure there's someone in the yard that can take his place. Failing that, you ride the horses if you bloody well have to.'

He switched off the phone and looked out of the window.

Alex glanced in the rear view mirror and winced to himself. From what he could gather from the racing commentary, James had done nothing wrong. Still, Alex had worked for Nathan long enough to know that he didn't tolerate losers, whether it was their fault or not.

He watched Nathan make another call, this time to the head of Grant News International.

'Andy, Grant here. I want you to include in your Derby coverage in all our papers tomorrow that James Ryan is no longer my retained jockey. Why? Let's just say he didn't ride the finish as one would expect a champion jockey to do – Lydia could have done better! Yes, you can include it in all our sports reports on our TV channels too. While you are at it, you can cancel his contract for writing the daily racing column with immediate effect.'

Poor bastard, thought Alex. James Ryan had been stitched up good and proper by Grant. By the time Grant had finished with him he would be unemployable, he thought sadly. Still, Grant hadn't become the multimillionaire he was without being totally ruthless. Nathan's success was achieved by a combination of astute business brains and by using people when he needed them and dropping them immediately they were no longer of any use. He had no conscience what so ever.

He heard the tell-tale signs of yet another number being dialled.

'Simon, Grant here. Terminate Samantha's employment with immediate effect. Give her the usual payoff and cancel her company clearance, I don't want her in the office again. Oh, and change the locks on my Mayfair apartment within the hour. You can also make arrangements for any of her personal effects that are there to be delivered round to her flat. You heard what I said – within the hour!'

Boy, was he having a busy day, thought Alex. He smiled at the thought of that pompous Simon Winter having to arrange all that whilst still in Nathan's box at Epsom.

He certainly had to hand it to his boss, who, in a mood like this, was a master of revenge.

Outstanding business completed, Nathan sighed and sat back as Alex drove to the centre of London.

Within a short time Nathan had arrived at his club, having discarded his top hat and tails for an expensive jacket he kept spare in the car.

Once inside, he felt relieved and almost comforted by the familiar surroundings, which seemed to insulate him and cut him off from the current unpleasant realities of the Derby.

It was like being in another world – another existence – calm, quiet and dignified.

His confidence soon returned as he strode towards the blackjack table, arriving with a sizeable pile of chips, which, to the average man, would represent their annual wage.

He sat down, nodded to the dealer in acknowledgement, and without a word started playing, gambling on each hand the sort of money, which raised eyebrows amongst the other gamblers, but for Nathan, who was renowned for gambling large sums, was just average.

Someone came up to Nathan and slapped him on the back.

'Well done Grant, second in the Derby. What an achievement!'

Nathan acknowledged with a mere grunt, and continued to concentrate on the cards.

The man sitting next to him looked up.

'Second – hard luck. Second sucks!'

Nathan looked up at him, surprised. This man had been the only person today who seemed to know how he felt, and had summed it up so simply in those two words – 'second sucks.'

He looked at the man, a studious pale looking chap, thin and wiry with greying, unkempt hair. Nathan was surprised he had been allowed in wearing such a fraying tweed jacket.

As they played on, with each hand his neighbour thought long and hard before tossing each £50 chip over from the ever decreasing pile in front of him, losing every time.

There was an aura of desperation about him, which cheered Nathan slightly – at least someone in the world seemed to be having a worse day than him.

Nathan continued to play, his concentration reverting to the cards. Some hands he won, others he lost – he was about even.

His neighbour, however, was becoming increasingly pale as the small pile of chips in front of him dwindled ominously. Beads of perspiration appeared when he was down to his last two, and he started to finger his fraying collar nervously, almost as though it was tightening around his neck.

When down to his last chip, he studied the cards more intently – almost desperately – before picking up the last chip with a trembling hand.

Whoever he was, he certainly wasn't a seasoned gambler, thought Nathan. Firstly, you should never show emotion, and secondly you should always be able to afford to lose.

Nathan looked at his hand of cards – a good one – and tossed over a couple of the larger chips he had.

The dealer turned her cards over – 19. Nathan had 20, and his winnings were returned. His neighbour threw his cards over and slumped back in his seat – his eyes closed- with a look of utter despair on his face.

He really does look as though he has had a worse day than me, thought Nathan, almost feeling sorry for him. Somehow he almost knew how he felt, even though he didn't know the reason for it. Despair felt the same, whatever the cause.

'Here, have these on me,' Nathan said, in an uncharacteristic gesture of compassion which surprised even himself, as he tossed over a couple of £100 chips.

A couple of hundred pounds would hardly make a dent in the pile in front of him, but to his neighbour it seemed like a lifeline. His eyes lit up and some colour returned to his cheeks, as he sat up and tried not to sound as overwhelmed as he felt.

'Thank you, that's very generous of you,' he stammered.

The dealer dealt another round of cards. Nathan's neighbour studied them intently before hesitantly betting a £100 chip. It was double what he was used to gambling, but he would have felt too embarrassed to change them for a lesser denomination.

To his delight he won, and a few hands later he had a tidy pile of chips stacked neatly in front of him. His luck had certainly changed, as had his mood, which had gone from one of total dejection to almost euphoria.

The urge to continue his winning streak was tempered by the value of chips in front of him, and he decided to stop. He turned to Nathan.

'Please let me buy you a drink – I certainly owe you one.'

'Yes, thanks,' replied Nathan, having grown a little tired of blackjack and feeling in need of a break.

He didn't usually associate with strangers, but this chap didn't seem to know who he was, and didn't seem to be the sort of person to care either, which Nathan found a refreshing change.

They retired to the lounge area, where the stranger ordered two double brandies. He reached out and shook Nathan's hand.

'I'm Julian Anderson Brown, by the way.'

'Nathan Grant,' replied Nathan as they sat down.

'Second in the Derby then,' said Julian, trying to start up a conversation and break the almost embarrassing silence between them. 'You must be pig sick.'

'That's an understatement,' sighed Nathan 'I spent a record amount of money to buy that horse with the Derby in mind, and he got stuffed on the line'.

'So near and yet so far,' sighed Julian as he downed his brandy in record speed.

Nathan ordered another round, this time a single for

himself and a double for Julian, who seemed to drink with the same recklessness as he gambled.

'The horse just didn't seem to get the trip, although the jockey should have kept him balanced – he only had a few strides to go,' Nathan said angrily. 'I really thought this year I'd win it. I had the horse, the jockey and perfect going. It seems that no matter what you spend and how much you prepare, there is always the unanswered question until the actual event – will he make the distance.'

Nathan stared into his brandy glass, imagining what might have been – what should have been. He felt that familiar veil of depression beginning to descend on him with this line of conversation, and decided to change it before he reverted back to the black mood that he had arrived in.

'What line are you in?' he asked, trying to sound interested, but what he was really interested in was getting back to the tables again.

'Oh, I'm a geneticist at McFarlane University, – or at least I was. I found out yesterday that my research grant had been withdrawn and my post terminated, so I've got a couple of weeks to round up my research, find a new job and find some new accommodation since I had a house supplied by the university.'

'Why did they withdraw your grant?' Nathan asked, not particularly interested, but pleased that the topic of conversation had changed completely.

'Well,' began Julian, taking a large sip of brandy, 'the grant was for research into genetically modified crops – all very tedious. Everyone's doing that sort of thing these days, and I could do it almost blindfolded. What

I'm really interested in is genetically enhancing animals. In fact, I had genetically modified some hamsters on the side, and that's really what upset my sponsors. Apparently it's all right to tamper with crops, but as soon as you do something to animals it's a whole new ball game and is deemed unacceptable.'

'What on earth had you done to these hamsters to get yourself dismissed?' asked Nathan, becoming fascinated by Julian's story.

'I found out that there is a gene which controls the efficiency of the oxygen uptake in the blood stream. If you think about it, why are the Ethiopians and certain Kenyan tribes so successful in middle and long distance running – it's because it's in their genes. Find the gene and you can add it to other species that are lacking it, and their performance will be enhanced accordingly.'

'I think I get the picture,' replied Nathan, trying to comprehend the very complicated subject that Julian was trying to explain. 'So how were you found out?'

'The Dean of the Faculty came round and happened to go into the room where I kept my experimental hamsters. They were exercising on their treadmills like there was no tomorrow. With having added this gene, they just kept going and going. One of my assistants, feeling rather pleased with the results of my work started to explain it to the Dean. Needless to say, he was furious and I was effectively dismissed the next day.'

'How on earth can they possibly dismiss you for doing something as incredible and exciting as that!' exclaimed Nathan.

'I don't know. Perhaps I was playing a little too

close to God for their comfort,' sighed Julian, not in a conceited way, but honestly believing in himself and the experimentation he had carried out. 'Also, I guess the Dean didn't want his department trashed by the Animal Liberation Front. That, together with the sponsors wanting to be seen as environmentally friendly and as uncontroversial as possible. In the end, though, plant or animal – what's the difference?'

He then chuckled.

'The way those hamsters were performing, you could probably have powered the electrics for a whole house. And as for your horse breeding – why leave anything to chance? I could engineer you something guaranteed to have the staying power and for a hell of a lot cheaper than you could buy one.'

At this point, Nathan wasn't sure if he was talking to a genius or a drunken madman. Part of what he said seemed incredible, but the more he thought about it, the more obvious it sounded.

Nathan, being the head of a global media empire, knew a little about most things, but genetic engineering had never been a subject that had fired his imagination. In fact, it usually raised quite a few controversial issues in his papers.

What Anderson-Brown claimed to have achieved seemed quite incredible.

Perhaps it was the brandy talking, or perhaps Anderson-Brown had actually stumbled upon something to revolutionise breeding. Instinct told Nathan that this was a story worth pursuing.

Nathan, realising that he would get no more coherent information from Anderson-Brown, made his apologies and left, leaving the scientist slumped in his seat, rather worse for wear after all those brandies.

A few moments later, oblivious to the late hour, he phoned Simon from the back of his car.

'Simon, Grant here. You've done everything I asked today? Good. No problems? Good. Now I want you to do a complete dossier on a Julian Anderson-Brown, geneticist at the McFarlane University, and have it on my desk for 9a.m. Monday morning. Yes – the full works – personal, financial, career, everything. Yes – you heard – by 9a.m. Monday. You can also do the same for the Dean of his department at the same university – no – I don't know his name. See you Monday.'

Nathan put the phone down and closed his eyes.

He could now see a glimmer of hope on the horizon, and Anderson-Brown could be the one to help him achieve it.

For the first time in quite a few hours, Nathan smiled. The past was forgotten – only the future was important.

If what Anderson-Brown had claimed he could do was correct, then the future would be very interesting indeed. He could only hope that it wasn't the brandy or a deluded scientist that had raised his hopes.

Alex, as he drove his boss home, noticed in his rear view mirror that Nathan was in a totally different mood now. He seemed to have that same smug expression on his face that he had in the morning as he drove him to the races.

Alex couldn't help but wonder what had happened to cause the change in mood. No matter how much money Grant had won, that wouldn't explain the odd, almost excited mood he was in. He couldn't put his finger on it, but one thing was for certain, his boss was up to something, and Alex wished he knew what it was.

3

The morning after the Derby Lydia was down for breakfast considerably earlier than usual for a Sunday. She had arrangements to make and packing to do before flying off to Barbados the following morning.

She poured herself an orange juice and sat down to mull over the events of the previous day after Nathan left so abruptly and in such a foul temper. Following his departure the rest of day had degenerated into farce.

Everyone was left feeling rather uncomfortable, not sure whether it was correct to stay and indulge in the hospitality of their absent host or not. Lydia had tried to act as if nothing was wrong, but the atmosphere had changed from heightened expectation before the race to one of embarrassed confusion and tension afterwards.

Stuart Lawson, the trainer, had received a phone call, obviously from Nathan, which whilst leaving him apparently relieved, had an unsettling effect on him.

Simon Winter, Nathan's right hand man, received the next phone call, which had him in a real flap. He disappeared out onto the balcony to make numerous phone calls, shutting the door behind him for privacy. Lydia then noticed him take Samantha onto the balcony, again shutting the door behind them.

Samantha had been thoroughly confused by the abrupt departure of Nathan, leaving her in the company of Lydia without Nathan's moral support. The conversation that followed between Samantha and Simon resulted in Samantha rushing out of the room in a flood of tears.

The few remaining guests by this time were so embarrassed that they made their apologies to Lydia, thanking her for a wonderful, entertaining day, and departed early.

Lydia thought the day had been anything but wonderful, but it had certainly made up for it in entertainment value.

She quickly looked through the Sunday newspapers – all Nathan's own publications.

Glancing at the racing pages, she saw that each of them carried articles on James Ryan's 'poor' ride and his subsequent dismissal as Nathan's retained jockey. She also noted that the daily column James wrote was missing.

Lydia couldn't help feeling sorry for him. Another life ruined by the great Nathan Grant.

She turned her mind towards her trip to Barbados, her escape from the inevitable misery of yet another one of Nathan's foul moods.

Barbados was her haven at times like these. She seemed to spend more and more time there. Life there seemed so simple and uncomplicated.

Nathan, on the other hand, only spent a couple of weeks a year there, mid winter, when all the flat racing set descended on the island, and maybe another odd week if he knew the 'right people' were going to be there. Nathan always had to have a reason for going somewhere or doing something. Apart from that he spent little time away from his business empire, afraid that he might miss a golden opportunity or the prospect of a battle with a rival.

Lydia closed her eyes and thought of the sun and sand she would be enjoying tomorrow. Those walks down St. James's Beach, relaxing by the pool, the excellent Creole cuisine, rum punches, fiery sunsets, and most of all a few thousand miles between her and Nathan. What bliss.

Lydia was just visualising sipping a rum punch when Nathan strode in.

She was extremely surprised to see him. Not having heard him come in the previous night, she had assumed that he had spent the night at his club. Then again, after taking two of her sleeping tablets she wouldn't have been capable of hearing anything.

'Good morning, dear,' said Nathan, in such a polite and civilised tone that Lydia almost choked on her orange juice. She had expected him to still be in a snarling rage after Northern Lights' defeat.

'Good morning, Nathan,' she blurted out.

Nathan helped himself to a coffee and a couple of croissants from the breakfast table and then sat down to read the papers.

'Rotten day yesterday, wasn't it?' he said without looking up.

Lydia agreed, not knowing what to make of the mood he was in. She couldn't even remember the last time they had spoken over breakfast.

'I hope you don't mind, but I thought I would go off to the villa tomorrow,' she ventured, taking advantage of the reasonable mood he seemed to be in.

'What a wonderful idea, the break will do you good

59

after all the trouble you've gone to hosting the Newmarket parties, not to mention the one yesterday,' Nathan replied, still engrossed in the papers.

Lydia could not understand why Nathan was behaving in such an understanding and civilised manner – it was so uncharacteristic of him.

He did seem rather preoccupied with something, upon which his whole attention seemed to be fixed.

Despite this, Lydia was relieved that he approved of her trip. She always hated arguing with him before she went away, so it was nice to have his approval, which she appreciated more than she realised.

She wondered what he was thinking. He was certainly up to something, and to cause such a radical change of mood it had to be something big.

Maybe he wanted her out of the way for a while, hence welcoming her trip abroad. He usually preferred to be alone in the house when he had a lot of thinking to do.

Lydia knew better than to ask, so she carried on with breakfast, whilst her thoughts returned to that rum punch by the pool.

Stuart Lawson was also sitting at the breakfast table at his training yard. He was feeling very unsettled.

The day before he had the unpleasant task of sacking one of the best riders in the business, whose ride, through no fault of his own, just happened to get beaten by a better horse on the day.

From the moment Stuart had got the call from Nathan to dismiss James, he felt a combination of relief and regret. Relief in that his own position seemed secure, and regret in that one of the greatest jockeys he'd had the privilege to work with had been so emphatically discarded by his boss.

Stuart was also put in the difficult position of firing James.

Nathan knew that Stuart always gave James a lift when he was due to ride in big races, so there would be ample opportunity on the way home to break the news.

As James was also a good friend, Stuart had known that there was no easy way to do it, so he just came right out and told him. James was understandably devastated. As a retained jockey his livelihood had been in Nathan Grant's hands, and it had been taken away – just like that.

James had pleaded with Stuart to contact Nathan to ask him to reconsider, which Stuart agreed to do just to put James's mind at rest for the rest of the trip, but when he saw the reports in the papers the next morning he knew there would be no point.

To cap it all, Stuart now had to find a jockey for all Nathan Grant's horses entered in the forthcoming races – starting Monday.

He sighed. It was going to be a long day, and a miserable one at that.

Northern Lights lad had reported that the horse seemed lethargic first thing, and hadn't eaten up from the night before. Stuart could only hope that it was the effects of the hard race the previous day and nothing more serious.

Northern Lights had been led out that morning and had seemed very subdued. It was amazing the difference between a winner and a loser. Somehow, the horse had sensed the depressing atmosphere around him and had reacted accordingly. Northern Lights, following his previous wins had always been on his toes and full of himself the next day, almost as euphoric as the stable staff. Yesterday, after the high expectations not fulfilled, a sombre atmosphere hung over the yard and over Northern Lights himself.

A few miles down the road James Ryan was having an even more depressing breakfast.

He had hoped that in the dawn of a new day things wouldn't seem as bad as they had the previous one; after all, it could hardly have got any worse.

One look at the headlines of the racing pages told him otherwise.

All the blame had been heaped at James's door, with opinions ranging from incompetence to him having taken a pull.

James was outraged. Any chance of him riding for Grant again was purely academic.

From the reports in the papers he could not believe that they were reporting on the same race, but that was journalistic licence – Nathan Grant style.

His wife, Jackie, was distraught. Their baby was only a month old, and the family income, together with the glamour that came with being associated with Nathan Grant, had disappeared – just like that.

James had tried to reassure her that it was only the one owner he had lost and that there were plenty more, but secretly he was more worried than he let on.

He knew that when he took on Nathan Grant's retainer there were other high profile owners who had been hoping to sign him up, but James put all his eggs in one basket and went exclusively to Grant – a decision that was now haunting him. By going to Nathan Grant he had upset the other owners who had been hoping to procure services of the up and coming maestro of the racing world.

James could only hope that he hadn't burnt too many boats as he was now going to have to approach these owners for rides. The only problem was that they too now had retained jockeys and by contacting these owners James would be upsetting a lot of his colleagues.

Still, it had to be done – after all- he had to keep his wife in the luxury to which she had come to expect and take for granted.

James sighed to himself. It was a long time since he'd had to ring owners in order to pick up rides.

Perhaps – he hoped – when they realised that he was available, the owners would contact him, but with not a single ride booked ahead of him, he couldn't afford to wait and was already drawing up in his mind a list of owners. One thing that worried him was that so far, the phone had been ominously quiet, apart from the inevitable journalists. Unable to stomach any breakfast he picked up the phone and started dialling.

Monday morning could not arrive soon enough for Nathan. He had spent Sunday in his study, reading articles on genetic engineering, cloning, and anything else connected with the subject. Most of it was way beyond his comprehension. One thing was for certain – it was astonishing what could be done. How it was done, he couldn't understand, but that was irrelevant. What mattered to Nathan was the results. How they were obtained was unimportant.

Nathan wished Lydia a good trip, but she hardly

seemed to notice, she was so engrossed in organising her wardrobe for her holiday.

He was relieved that she would be away for a couple of weeks since he had a considerable amount of planning to do. Having Lydia twittering away in the background like a nagging headache would have been an unwelcome distraction.

As he drove his boss to work earlier than usual that Monday, Alex noticed that Nathan was in a buoyant mood. From his experience as Nathan's chauffeur, he had come to realise that his boss was an extremely complex character, and you never knew what to expect next. Certainly Nathan had gone through all moods possible over the last forty eight hours, and Alex was grateful that the one he was in currently was one of his better ones.

Alex pulled up outside Grant Global Communications head office – an imposing building that towered over the others in the area, dominating the skyline.

He got out and opened the door for Nathan, who grunted what Alex took to be a thank you, and watched his boss stride inside. He noticed how uncharacteristically keen his boss had seemed to be to get to work. Nathan was usually enthusiastic, but today he seemed almost excited.

Alex wished he knew what was in Nathan's mind. He had, in the past, been able to pick up a few bits of gossip, and had invested accordingly, building up a tidy nest egg for retirement. Being Nathan Grant's chauffeur certainly had its advantages, and by keeping his ear close to the ground, the financial gains he had made had certainly outweighed the disadvantages of being at Nathan's beck and call twenty four hours a day, seven days a week.

If it weren't for the confidentiality clause in his contract, he could have written quite a novel by now, since his boss led a very colourful life. Perhaps he still could – but just alter the names.

He pushed the thought to the back of his mind immediately. Nathan Grant was the one person in the world he would not dare to cross. He had seen the results of indiscretion by other employees and business colleagues, and had vowed that it would never happen to him.

Nathan strode through the luxurious foyer of his empire, acknowledging the greetings of his employees who were surprised to see him in this early.

He took the lift straight to the top floor where his office was situated.

From the lift, he continued down the wide corridor, upon the walls of which hung original oil paintings by various masters.

At the end of the corridor, he reached his secretary's desk. Janice, his personal secretary for the past ten years, was already working away. She was always in early, and always stayed late.

Nathan Grant expected one hundred and ten per cent from his staff – nothing less would do. Since Janice joined the company as an office junior fifteen years ago when Grant Global Communications was in its infancy, she had always given far more than anyone else.

She was fiercely loyal, discreet, honest and frighteningly efficient, and rapidly rose to become Nathan's personal secretary.

Janice also had the advantage of being quite plain in appearance, and, always being immaculately and demurely dressed, certainly wasn't going to distract Nathan like some of the new young girls – with their short tight skirts and long blonde hair.

Nathan once described Janice as being sexless, which to most people seemed to be a very unkind remark, but Nathan meant it as a compliment. Janice had certainly earned her position by sheer hard work and unquestioning loyally, and as such had Nathan's respect and confidence.

Nathan also knew that Janice had a fearsome reputation amongst his staff. To get to see Nathan, you had to get past Janice, who weeded out the time wasters and opportunists with a ruthless efficiency that Nathan found amusing.

Janice looked up as she heard Nathan approach. She too was surprised at how cheerful he seemed. After what she had read in the papers, she had been expecting the worst, and had been bracing herself for a tougher day than usual.

'Good morning, sir. Can I get you a coffee?'

'Good morning, Janice. Coffee would be great. Make it strong and black – it's going to be a long day. Could you also organise a couple of bacon rolls, Lydia's still into croissants every morning, and I can't survive on them.'

'Of course.'

'Oh, and when Simon arrives, show him straight in.'

'Yes, sir.'

Nathan went into his office, closing the door behind him. Janice rang down to the senior staff restaurant and ordered the bacon rolls to be sent up immediately – complete with brown sauce – just as Nathan liked them.

For all his wealth and affluence, it amused Janice

that Nathan still had a weakness for bacon butties with brown sauce.

With lightning efficiency the bacon rolls arrived, looking a little out of place on bone china, with silver plated cutlery and a white linen napkin folded neatly.

She quickly poured the filtered coffee, put it on the tray, knocked on Nathan's door, and went in.

Despite the number of years that Janice had been Nathan's secretary, she still found his office intimidating.

A huge mahogany desk dominated the room, with two large leather chairs in front of it and an even bigger one behind. Despite Nathan's large frame, he seemed almost dwarfed by this massive chair in which he was seated.

To one side of the office was a lounge area with two matching leather sofas. Two armchairs were separated by a huge coffee table with the finest Italian marble top. Two bookcases lined an entire wall from floor to ceiling and in the centre of the wall were two carved mahogany doors which housed Nathan's cigar collection, a fridge and a fully stocked bar containing anything that Nathan could possibly want.

Janice saw to it personally that his favourite cigars never ran out, and all the necessary refreshments were there.

Janice would not dream of allowing anyone into Nathan's office unless they had an appointment or were the cleaning staff. She also made sure that she was always present when the cleaning staff were there, having ensured that all the waste paper had been shredded first. These days you couldn't trust anyone.

Nathan was busy reading his mail, so Janice put the tray down on the desk and made a discreet departure without disturbing him. She didn't get a thank you, but then again she never expected one – it was all part of her job.

Janice had just settled down to her work when a flustered Simon Winter came rushing down the corridor, briefcase in hand.

'Good morning, Simon, Nathan's expecting you,' said Janice, a little amused at the flustered state of Simon, who was usually so calm and in control.

'God, he's not in already, is he?' exclaimed Simon, anxiously looking at his watch, and relieved to see that there were still a few minutes to go before 9am.

'He's been in for over half an hour,' replied Janice, not asking what had got Simon in such a state.

That was another thing that Nathan liked about Janice – she wasn't nosey, she didn't pry and didn't get distracted from her job. She was, however, far more astute than most people gave her credit for, and knew just about everything that was going on in the building – past, present or future. She would pick up comments and bits of information that would come her way, and file them away in her mind, thinking no more about them. If there was anything Nathan wanted to know about anyone or anything in the company, he just had to ask Janice.

Janice buzzed through.

'Simon has arrived, sir.'

'About time too,' came the reply over the intercom. 'Oh, and come in and clear this tray away.'

Simon knocked politely on the door before going in, followed by Janice who removed the tray and was asked to bring some more coffee.

Janice duly returned with the coffees and then left the two to their meeting.

'So, what have you got on them?' asked Nathan, barely able to suppress his enthusiasm for getting his hands on the two folders which Simon was just getting out of his briefcase.

'A very interesting couple of characters,' Simon replied, handing the files over. 'It took a lot of favours to get all that information in such a short space of time, and on a Sunday as well, but I'm sure you'll find it interesting reading.'

'Thank you, Simon, I'll start working my way through them.' As an afterthought he added, 'Oh, and could you clear out Samantha's personal items from her office and send them round to her flat.'

'I took the liberty of doing that yesterday.'

'Excellent.'

With the meeting effectively over, Simon stood up and left Nathan engrossed in the rather thicker dossier on Dr. Julian Anderson-Brown.

Simon wondered what on earth Nathan wanted with full dossiers on these two. After all, they weren't exactly business rivals, and he couldn't see how their expertise could be of any use to Grant Global Communications.

Perhaps Nathan was on the trail of a scandal – they were certainly both colourful characters, and had been involved in a considerable amount of controversy. But if that were the case, surely Nathan would have handed it to his top investigative reporter.

Simon came to the same conclusion as Lydia and Alex. Nathan was up to something. No doubt he would find out soon enough what it was.

*   *   *

After Simon's departure, Nathan buzzed through to Janice, instructing that he wasn't to be disturbed. He settled back into his chair and started to read the dossier on Julian Anderson-Brown. The more he read, the more convinced he was that Anderson-Brown was his man.

He was forty two, unmarried, unattached and currently holding a position at McFarlane University, being funded by a research grant from a pharmaceutical company – or at least he was until last week. His parents were deceased, and he had one sister – also deceased.

A rebel from an early age, despite excelling in his class, he was expelled from his first grammar school for carrying out experiments on laboratory rabbits which were 'not part of the curriculum.'

Nathan smiled and wondered what on earth he had done.

He had excelled even more at his second school, before going on to a place at Cambridge University, where he soon gained a reputation for brilliance, arrogance and a disrespect for his tutors.

A first class degree was a mere formality, but his reputation for being a rebel preceded him in the research world, where he found it difficult to obtain posts in which he could further his ideas. Since his ideas were fairly radical, any post he did find was usually short lived.

In being continuously thwarted by the research establishment, Julian Anderson-Brown had vented his frustration on gambling. It would appear that he thought he could apply his genius to gambling the same way he applied it to research. The effects were quite different. Analysis of his financial position revealed that he was in serious debt –

some of which was to the sort of people it was ill advised to associate with. In short, having now lost his position at McFarlane University, Julian Anderson-Brown was in serious financial trouble.

It was obvious from his attitude at the gambling tables on Saturday night, that he was in desperate trouble – and knew it. What he had won that night would secure him a little time, but not much.

Nathan smiled to himself. Perfect. He was about to throw a drowning man a lifeline. He would have no option but to grasp it willingly, with both hands.

Nathan put down the file on Anderson-Brown and leant back in his chair with a feeling of satisfaction. Part of the jigsaw had fallen into place – now to see what the other part had to offer.

He buzzed through to Janice for another coffee, which appeared immediately, and settled back to read the dossier which Simon had prepared on Professor William Middleton, Dean of the Department of Biological Sciences, McFarlane University.

Whilst sipping his coffee, Nathan read the first page, which covered general family details. It was the second page that left him speechless. It would appear that the William Middleton, now Dean at McFarlane University, who gained a first degree at Stanford University U.S.A., had died in a skiing accident a year after gaining his degree.

So, if the brilliant William Middleton had died some twenty years ago, then who was the William Middleton at McFarlane University?

Reading the dossier further, it transpired that this William Middleton had gained a second class degree at a secondary university, and on finding out that his namesake was deceased, had adopted his qualifications as his own and had subsequently risen through the ranks at the university to hold the elite position he was currently in.

This gets better and better, thought Nathan. He couldn't believe how well his plan was coming together. In a way he couldn't have organised it better if he had tried – a desperate scientist and a Dean with a big secret – boy, was this his lucky day!

He buzzed through to Janice.

'Janice, contact a Dr. Julian Anderson-Brown at McFarlane University. Tell him I want to see him this afternoon – say 2p.m. If he wants to know what it's about, tell him his gambling benefactor of Saturday night wants to make him a proposition he would find most interesting. After that, contact Professor William Middleton, Dean at the same university. Inform him I would like to set up a substantial research grant for his department. Make it clear I must see him at 3p.m. today.'

It wasn't long before Janice buzzed through to Nathan's office.

'Excuse me, sir. You have an appointment with Dr. Anderson-Brown at 2p.m. and Professor Middleton at 3.'

'Thank you, Janice. Could you organise a steak and salad lunch for me? Yes, I'll have it in my office.'

Janice wondered what on earth Nathan wanted to see these two people about. Generosity was not one of Nathan's characteristics, and what these two could offer the company was beyond her.

She rang down to the staff restaurant and ordered a medium rare steak, French fries and side salad with

French dressing, followed by strawberries and cream. Janice knew from experience what Nathan meant by a steak and salad.

As the order was for Nathan Grant, the meal was rushed up to the top floor in record time.

'I'll take it in,' Janice announced firmly, extinguishing the hopes of the young waitress who thought that she would eventually get to meet the great man in person.

As the disappointed waitress returned to the restaurant, Janice picked up the tray, and knocked on the door. She went in and placed the tray on Nathan's desk, who by now had cleared away the files to make room for his lunch.

'Strawberries and cream too – how thoughtful of you, Janice,' he remarked uncharacteristically.

'I know they are your favourites at this time of the year, sir,' she replied, surprised that he had recognised that their presence was due to her own initiative. Unusually that sort of thing was taken for granted and almost expected of her.

She departed to leave Nathan to have his lunch in peace, returning half an hour later to remove the tray and bring yet another coffee.

'I've a busy afternoon, Janice. Let me know when my appointments arrive. Apart from that, I don't want to be disturbed.'

'Of course, sir.'

At five to two, Janice buzzed Nathan.

'Dr. Anderson-Brown has arrived.'

'Thank you, Janice, I'll see him shortly.'

Nathan thought through his plan and a couple of minutes later asked Janice to show him in.

Janice opened the door and ushered Julian Anderson-Brown in. He looked exactly the same as he did on

Saturday night – same frayed jacket, same shirt and trousers (but this time even more crumpled) and same unkempt hair.

'Please come in, Dr. Anderson-Brown,' said Nathan as he stood up and offered a handshake.

Anderson-Brown walked across the room and tried desperately not to be overawed by the size and splendour of it. Offices like this he had only ever seen in films, and he never believed – until this moment – that they could possibly exist. He felt intimidated by it.

He shook Nathan's hand.

'You must forgive me. I had no idea who you actually were on Saturday night,' he said, apologetically.

'That's all right. Socially it doesn't matter what one's line of work is,' replied Nathan, trying to put him at ease.

'Anyway, please sit down. I would like to talk over a proposition I have for you, which I'm sure you will find both interesting and challenging.'

They both sat down. Anderson-Brown stared at Nathan across the vast expanse of his desk. This sounded interesting. In fact, bearing in mind his impending unemployment, any proposition was worthy of his attention.

'From what you said on Saturday night, you're a research geneticist.'

Anderson-Brown thought for a moment. He had drunk so much brandy that night; he could only remember fragments of the conversation. He wished he hadn't drunk so much – goodness knows what he had said or claimed. He knew that his tendency to exaggerate increased on a par with the volume of alcohol he consumed.

'I also gather that your research grant has been withdrawn due to some experiments which didn't meet with the Dean's approval.'

Anderson-Brown blinked hard. "Oh, God, I told him about the hamsters," he thought, wishing the chair he was sitting in would swallow him up.

'From what I've read of your qualifications and employment record, I would guess that your expertise – and should we add – enthusiasm is under used and undervalued.'

Anderson-Brown sat up. This was beginning to sound interesting.

'The proposition I have is that Grant Global Communications take over your research funding. In return, you will continue your research more on the animal side than crops. Your debts at the club will be paid off, together with the outstanding amounts with those two loan sharks you have been dealing with. I would not like to have your scientific mind distracted by such worrying matters.'

Anderson-Brown squirmed and turned bright red. How on earth did he find out about those two?

'Your wages will be paid as usual by the university, But Grant Global Communications will pay you an extra monthly bonus of £1000 nett.'

'That's extremely generous of you,' stammered Anderson-Brown, who had quickly calculated that it would make him better paid than the Dean.

'However,' said Nathan, as he leant forward, placing both his hands on the table and looking Anderson-Brown straight in the eyes, 'your monthly bonus is for work I would like to do for me personally. The work is to remain totally private and confidential – I cannot stress that enough.'

Anderson-Brown tried to avoid the piercing stare of Nathan Grant. What on earth could he possibly want, and why did all the best offers come with a 'however'?

'What is it you would like me to do?' asked Anderson-Brown tentatively.

'Saturday night you told me about your experiments with hamsters.'

Anderson-Brown squirmed. "Oh, no, I did tell him about the hamsters," he thought with dismay.

'You also said that you had increased their stamina by a considerable amount.'

'Yes, that's correct. Of course, it's all still in the experimental stages.'

'You implied that the gene you had altered could be altered in other animals as well.'

'Yes, in theory, although I got sacked before I could try it on any other animals.'

'What I want you to do, and you claimed on Saturday night that you could do it, is to create a genetically modified horse with this gene, with the sole intent of winning the Derby.'

Nathan Grant sat back and waited for the reaction.

Anderson-Brown gasped in astonishment. His initial reaction was that this man was mad.

'Could it be done?' asked Nathan, trying to get a response.

'Well, yes, it's possible,' replied the astonished geneticist.

'This must remain totally confidential. Let's say the

Jockey Club would not be very happy if they got to hear about it.'

'So, you mean it's illegal,' said Anderson-Brown tentatively.

'Only if they find out about it,' said Nathan Grant with a smile. 'So, what do you think of my proposal?'

'Yes, it could be done. It would take a year or so of work, but yes, I would have every confidence in a successful outcome.'

'I forgot to mention, you have only six months before the breeding season starts. I realise that it would involve a lot of extra work, and so I propose a bonus of £50,000, half payable on confirmation that the mare is in foal and the rest on birth of the foal. There will be an additional similar bonus when the horse wins the Derby.'

Anderson-Brown sat back in his chair. No one had ever put such a bizarre and outrageous proposition to him before. It could be done, he thought, but six months would be a very tight schedule. The apparent illegality of it didn't bother him that much, neither did the ethics – after all, he was just going to engineer the foal – what Nathan Grant did with it afterwards was his business.

He thought about the product of his research appearing on the world stage and in such a prestigious event. It certainly appealed to his warped sense of humour.

Then an awful thought struck him.

'The Dean at the University would never agree to me continuing animal experimentation,' said Anderson-Brown, realising that it had all been too good to be true.

'You leave the Dean to me,' replied Nathan. 'He's coming here later this afternoon to discuss the grant. I'm sure I'll talk him round.'

Anderson-Brown looked at Nathan. If anyone could talk him round, it was Nathan Grant.

'Meanwhile, give my proposition some thought. I'm sure our confidential project is just the thing to extend your expertise to its full potential. Let my know your decision in the morning.'

Nathan stood up, indicating that the meeting was at an end. Usually Nathan would want an instant decision on his proposals, but he knew that Anderson-Brown had no other choice, given his desperate financial position. He would also be unable to resist the challenge.

'I'll phone first thing in the morning,' replied Anderson-Brown.

After leaving Nathan Grant's office, Julian's mind went racing over the extraordinary meeting. This could be the chance of a lifetime – but could he pull it off? He was already beginning to think of the ways and means to achieve it.

Professor William Middleton arrived promptly for his three o'clock appointment, and was a little annoyed to be kept waiting. Back at the university, no-one ever kept the Professor waiting.

The phone call from Grant Global Communications had come totally out of the blue to William Middleton, who although downhearted at having lost the grant, was euphoric with the imminent departure of Anderson-Brown, who had been like a thorn in his side since his appointment.

He loathed Anderson-Brown because he was everything William Middleton wasn't. Popular with the students, who regarded Anderson-Brown as almost a cult figure – a radical, a free thinker, and unafraid to clash with authority if his views differed from theirs. He was also unconstrained by red tape and totally uninhibited by thoughts of what other people might think of him.

With this meeting there was a chance that the grant funding would be restored, enhancing the prestige of his department, and ultimately of himself.

Professor Middleton waited with growing impatience in the reception area outside Nathan's office, which, having had time to study it, he regarded as a little ostentatious.

The dragon like receptionist received a call, which indicated that the meeting was imminent, and at last he was shown into the office of Nathan Grant.

Professor Middleton's first thought was that the desk at which Nathan Grant was sitting was bigger than his office, and that the office was about the same size as the total sum of his staffs' offices put together.

To say that he was a little taken aback was an understatement. He had read about people who had offices like these but so far he had never had the good fortune to meet one.

The man who was sitting behind the massive desk seemed to have the stature to match, and had stood up, holding out his hand.

'Professor Middleton, I'm Nathan Grant. Thank you for making this meeting at such short notice.'

Nathan Grant shook his hand with an authority, which made William Middleton wince.

'Please sit down. Can I arrange a tea or coffee?' Nathan asked, lulling William Middleton into a false sense of security, like a snake before it strikes it's prey.

'Tea please, white, one sugar.'

Nathan buzzed through to Janice.

'Could you bring in two teas, one white, one sugar. Thank you.'

Almost immediately Janice appeared with the respective drinks and a selection of biscuits, before disappearing with the same efficiency.

'Let's get down to business then,' said Nathan, as he picked up a biscuit. 'Grant Global Communications would like to take up the funding of the research grant which you lost recently.'

Professor Middleton wondered how on earth Nathan Grant had got to hear about the withdrawal of the grant so quickly, since it had only happened a few days ago. Still, in big business, news travels fast, especially in the media world.

Professor Middleton began to think that this really was his lucky week. Grant funding restored and Anderson-Brown leaving. It had taken over a year to get rid of him, but he always knew that Anderson-Brown would slip up in the end.

'The university would certainly welcome that,' replied the Professor.

'Good. However, I would insist that Dr. Anderson-Brown is reinstated and continues the work. I think his work is outstanding, and I would like to see him make further advances.'

Professor Middleton could not believe that Nathan Grant was insisting that he reinstate that upstart. He would rather forgo the funding than have Anderson-Brown back.

'I'm afraid that is out of the question. The university

80

was very unhappy about Dr. Anderson-Brown's deviations from the University's objectives, and as such, I couldn't possibly accept funding on such a basis.'

Professor Middleton tried to suppress his annoyance that someone had the audacity to try and tell him how to run his department.

'So, I'm afraid that if such conditions were placed on the funding, then the university would have to decline.'

Professor Middleton stood up to leave.

'Oh, I think not,' replied Nathan coldly, in a tone that sent a shiver down the spine of Professor Middleton. 'Sit down, please. I realise that Dr. Anderson-Brown is a little unorthodox, and that his career has been somewhat eventful, but then again your career is rather unique too, isn't it?'

'I'm not sure what you are implying,' said the Professor, hesitating, half fearing what Nathan was going to say next.

'Why don't we go back to Stanford University, then. Or was it really Stanford? I think not. I hardly think that you are in the position to criticise the ethics of Dr. Anderson-Brown. Adopting an education that wasn't yours must have looked wonderful on your C.V's and opened numerous doors throughout your career.'

Professor Middleton had gone white as a sheet. How on earth had he found out? If this got out, his career and life would be in ruins.

Nathan Grant continued. 'Still, I'm sure we could keep your little secret between ourselves. You can have your research grant, Dr. Anderson-Brown will be restored to his position with more freedom in his research than before, and no-one will be any the wiser about your little indiscretion.'

'I'm beginning to see the opportunities that your funding will bring,' replied the Professor carefully. He had no choice but to accept, since he had little doubt that Nathan Grant would carry out his veiled threat.

'Good, so you accept my terms then?' said Nathan, reaching out his hand across the table.

'Yes, of course,' replied the Professor, shaking Nathan Grant's hand whilst wishing that his own palm wasn't so hot and sweaty. 'I'll inform the university immediately.'

'Wonderful,' beamed Nathan,' I'll get my lawyers to draw up the necessary paperwork to put the funding in place immediately. Perhaps you could also have a word with Dr. Anderson-Brown about your change of heart. I would hate him to turn down this opportunity just because of a minor difference of opinion between yourselves – after all, he is an important part of this package.'

Professor Middleton nodded in agreement. The thought of him grovelling to Anderson-Brown and pleading with him to stay made him feel quite ill, but anything was better than having his secret revealed.

Nathan walked over and opened the door. Professor Middleton followed, the meeting not having gone how he had envisaged it at all.

'So, my men will be in contact with the university then,' said Nathan, shaking Professor Middleton's hand yet again.

Nathan closed the door and sat back behind his desk.

This afternoon had gone just as he had planned.

The following morning, Nathan received a phone call

The Legacy

from Dr. Anderson-Brown, accepting Nathan's offer.

The final part of the jigsaw had fallen into place.

The next couple of years were certainly going to be exciting.

Very exciting indeed.

4

The weeks that followed the Derby were for James Ryan the lowest point in his life.

He had tried phoning round all the big owners and trainers who prior to him signing up for Nathan Grant had been so keen for him to ride their horses.

Each one had declined his services.

In the past, he had ridden the odd winner for most of them when he wasn't needed by Grant and was still on amicable terms with most, but James thought he detected a coldness in their attitude, which previously wasn't there.

Perhaps he was being paranoid; after all, it had been a long time since he'd had to ring round for rides. Over the past couple of years as champion jockey, the owners had always phoned him, begging him to ride their horses.

Maybe they believed the newspaper propaganda that Nathan Grant's tabloids were spreading.

James had hoped that the bad press would die down after a couple of days, or that another newspaper group wouldn't follow the same story line, but no. They had got their hands on a good story that sold newspapers and, as so often seems to happen with a successful sportsman, were determined to bring him down.

The Legacy

It seemed that every narrow defeat in James's career was now being analysed and questions asked.

James found himself picking up rides from small trainers, who were delighted to find his services so readily available. The only problem was that the calibre of horses he was now riding was way below that he had become accustomed to. With James in the saddle, many of the owners thought their horse would be transformed and would exceed it's poor ability. James could only do his best and maybe improve their placing, but if the horse didn't have the potential or heart, then even James couldn't produce a miracle.

With each day, James's lead in the jockey's championship table dwindled, until he was overtaken by his arch rival. Within a couple of weeks he wasn't even in the top five.

His decline seemed to be spiralling out of control.

What made matters worse was that some owners and trainers were asking him to pull horses, to reduce their handicap for gambling coups in later races. 'After all' they said, 'he did such a good job of stopping Northern Lights in the Derby, no-one would have ever guessed.'

James had all but given up protesting his innocence. Any denial was greeted with a knowing nod and a wink. Only Northern Lights was his witness to the truth.

It wasn't long before James was becoming disillusioned with his career as a jockey. Somehow, the thought of starving himself to maintain his weight for riding in a seller at Ripon didn't have the same appeal as a ride in a Group One race in Deauville.

James soon realised that he had lost the heart and incentive to continue as a jockey.

He wished he could talk it over with his wife Jackie, but he knew that she was even more distraught at his downfall, for other reasons. It had meant an abrupt change in her lifestyle. No more holiday invitations to the Grant's Caribbean villa and no more invitations to all the important glamorous parties.

In a way, James felt he had let her down so badly in her expectations, but on the other hand, he wished she would be more supportive of him in this time of crisis. Instead they barely seemed on speaking terms apart from the odd everyday pleasantries. The problems in their lives were glossed over and ignored – pushed to one side in the hope that they would go away, but they were becoming worse.

One morning, James heard that the small flat racing yard where he had first started as an apprentice jockey had come on the market, the current owner having gone bankrupt.

In the back of James's mind, he had always wanted to go into training when his career as a jockey was over – he had no idea that it would be so soon.

James had certainly planned to continue riding for a few more years, to build up a good financial foundation to take over a larger, more prestigious yard, but his circumstances had changed and he now had to set his sights a lot lower.

The thought of a fresh start in racing filled James with an enthusiasm that had been sadly lacking over the past few weeks.

He loved horses, and racing was his whole life. He couldn't imagine being anything other than involved in racing in some way or other. Racing was all he knew and all he held dear.

He brought home the details of the yard and showed it to Jackie, who was appalled at the thought of them moving from their spacious, comfortable home to some cramped, damp trainer's house.

They had previously talked of a large yard, imposing house, prestigious owners and top racehorses. What James was showing her and was so enthusiastic about was quite the opposite. She could hardly imagine entertaining their wealthy owners in a dining room that was the size of their current bathroom.

James had already made an appointment to look round the following day, and as far as Jackie was concerned, he could go on his own. Hopefully, she thought, one look at the place and he would come to his senses.

The following day James arrived home from another unsuccessful day's racing to find Jackie out. He really had thought that she would change her mind and would at least come and look round the yard, after all, it was their future that was being decided. Instead he had to keep the appointment with the agent on his own.

As he drove through the narrow lanes on the outskirts of Newmarket, his spirits lifted as he began to recognise places and landmarks from his days as an apprentice jockey. He smiled to himself, remembering all the happy moments at the yard – the practical jokes the lads used to play on each other, Mick Flanagan, the head lad who struggled to keep the lads under control, often to no avail. Those were the days.

His excitement mounted as he pulled off the road and through the gates of Bishop's Place.

He was a little surprised to see the grass either side of the drive to be almost knee high. Mr. Reynolds, his old Governor, had always kept it as short as a bowling green.

The house ahead looked tired and unloved when once it had been the pride of Mrs. Reynolds.

The yard, where he had spent (or more often that not – misspent) his youth had certainly seen better days.

James felt rather sad to see the place so neglected, but considering the price he shouldn't have expected anything else. Still, he thought with growing enthusiasm, with a little hard work, the yard could soon be brought back to its former glory – just as he remembered it. The house too – but the yard would have to come first. He would have to get it up and running and start training as quickly as possible to start earning some money.

The agent was already standing beside the front door. James got out of his car and walked over. 'You must be Mr. Evans,' said James, shaking his hand. 'James Ryan.'

'Evening, Mr. Ryan. Did you have a successful day's racing?' the agent politely inquired.

'I've had better,' James replied, not wishing to go into details.

'Shall we start with the house?' enquired the agent, key already in the lock.

'No, I'd like to see the yard first.'

The agent looked surprised and put the key back in his pocket.

'Of course.'

They walked over towards the first row of boxes and James opened each door, wistfully remembering each horse that used to occupy the boxes during his time there. He had just reached the end of the first row, when a thin, stooped figure came round the corner.

'Well, well, if it isn't little Jimmy Ryan,' said the man in a soft, lilting Irish voice.

James looked closely at him and suddenly realised it was the old head lad.

'Mick Flanagan! What on earth are you still doing here?'

'Still minding the yard,' he replied with a grin, revealing numerous missing teeth.

James was quite shocked at his appearance. He had idolised Mick when he was at the yard and always wanted to be like him. Mick used to be wiry in build with a shock of curly ginger hair, green eyes and a pale complexion that was covered in freckles. Now he seemed to have aged 50 years. His hair was thin, grey and still wild, his face wrinkled and drawn and his body stooped. His cheeks seemed sunken, probably due to the lack of teeth.

'It's great to see you, Mick. How have you been keeping?'

'Times are hard, Jimmy. The luck of the Irish deserted me a while ago,' he said, shaking his head sadly.

'Still backing the wrong horses then,' James joked.

'Show some respect for your elders!' Mick exclaimed with his eyes twinkling.

It was good to see James again. He felt proud of what James had gone on to achieve and how he had played a role in his development. 'It's good to see you too, Jimmy. So, what brings you back to Bishop's Place? You're not thinking about buying the place are you?'

'Yes, I am, actually.'

'You must be mad. It'll take a lot to get this place

up and running again. Surely you could do better than this?'

'Times haven't exactly been kind to me lately either,' sighed James.

'So I've read. That bastard Grant stitched you up good and proper,' Mick said angrily.

'That's in the past. Now I'm looking to the future,' replied James, trying to sound optimistic. 'So, tell me – do you come with the yard?'

Mick grinned his toothless grin.

'I seem to have been here all my life, so I hope the new Governor would take me on, although I'm a bit long in the tooth, if you'll pardon the expression. The trouble is, I've got nowhere else to go. It was a relief when the agents said I could stay on and keep an eye on the place.'

Mick then proceeded to show James round the rest of the yard, leaving the agent trailing in their wake.

James remembered what a successful yard it had been all those years ago – small, but with an exceptional number of winners.

In the hostel, James looked in to the room he used to share with three other lads. On the old wooden door were still his initials and the date of his first win that he had carved in his euphoria all those years ago. It had cost him a £10 fine when the Governor found out, but it was worth it, and had started a tradition amongst the lads, so the door was now covered in initials and dates.

He fingered his carving gently, and cast his mind back to those days.

Life was strict at the yard but no-one ever complained. Their love of horses was a bond that brought them close together. Fines were commonplace for a variety of misdemeanours. If you got dropped by a horse – £5. If you let go of the bridle – £10.

James remembered fondly the time he was thrown, but managed to hang onto the bridle. Somehow, the horse managed to free his head and return riderless and without a bridle to the yard. James had followed ten minutes latter, clutching the bridle, to be greeted by cheers from the other lads. Despite protesting that he had held onto the bridle James was still fined £10. The other lads thought it so funny; they all chipped in and paid the fine for him.

These fines all went into a kitty towards the Christmas party and for any emergency a lad might find himself in. Needless to say, the Christmas party at Bishop's Place was renown for being the best in the area.

James fondly remembered the football matches they used to have between yards, and boxing tournaments where more often than not old scores were settled, with opponents leaving the ring the best of friends.

Mick could see the far away look in James's eyes.

'Those were the days, weren't they.'

'Yes. It's so sad to see the place like this now.'

Having viewed all the yard complex, James asked the agent to show him the house next.

Some parts of it he had seen as an apprentice lad all those years ago, but he had no idea what the rest looked like.

As he stood in the kitchen, Mrs. Reynolds' pride and joy, he was sad to see it in such a state of disrepair. She would turn in her grave if she could see all the cobwebs and dirt. The old aga still stood in the corner. James wondered if it still worked. The agent didn't know.

The lounge and dining area were adequately sized,

with big open fireplaces and windows overlooking the overgrown back garden where Mrs. Reynolds used to potter around tending the flower beds.

James followed the agent round the rest of the ground floor, wondering if the glowing running commentary he gave about each room really related to the same house that James was in. They then went upstairs – somewhere James had never seen before. He felt vaguely embarrassed to be standing in what would have been the Governor's bedroom. Two windows, the frames of which were in such a bad state you could put your finger through the rotten wood, overlooked the back garden. Two panes were also cracked. Easily replaced, he thought.

One wall was covered with a built-in wardrobe. A quick glance told him that there might be just enough room for Jackie's clothes – he would have to put his elsewhere.

There were three further bedrooms – one of which would make an ideal nursery for Joshua – and two bathrooms – both in need of new fittings.

The agent followed James back down again, and after a quick tour of the cellar they both went outside.

They then went round the paddocks which came with the property. The gates were hanging off their hinges and the post and rail fences were in a poor state of repair. The grass was thigh high, beneath which James knew was some of the best grazing in Newmarket.

Back at the yard James looked round the outside of the house again. Basically the structure seemed sound. Sure, there was a lot of work to be done, but a quick calculation told him that if he could knock £30,000 off the asking price, then by his estimates he could afford the property and all the repairs.

Mick reappeared.

'It's in a sorry state, to be sure,' he said, much to the annoyance of the agent, who had been doing his best to extol the virtues of this 'highly desirable property'.

James looked round again before turning to the agent. 'It'll certainly take a fair bit of money to cover all those repairs, so that asking price is a little unrealistic in my opinion.'

The agent looked crestfallen. James was the first person he had actually got inside the house. The few other prospective buyers had all turned round at the yard gate on glimpsing the sad view ahead.

'I'm sure there is some room for negotiation.'

'I should think so,' replied James, playing on what he sensed to be the agent's desperation to offload the property. 'Give me a few moments to think and have another wander round.'

The agent retreated to his Range Rover whilst Mick and James retraced their steps round the yard.

'Could it be brought back to its former glory, Mick?' asked James.

'I don't see why not. It only needs a few minor repairs, the right Governor with a love of racing, not to mention the right staff, and you're half way there.'

'The right horses help too,' sighed James.

'It all starts with the right Governor,' Mick repeated.

'Would I make a good Governor, Mick?' asked James.

'Me thinks you'd be a winner at whatever you did, Jimmy. I knew you would be champion jockey one day, and told the Governor that a month after you started.'

'But you always said I was useless,' protested James, thinking of all the times Mick had told him off for even the slightest error.

'Well, I couldn't have you getting too big for your boots too early on, could I? Besides, it would have upset the other lads if I had shown you any favouritism, and then they would have made your life hell.'

'That's true,' James said, smiling. 'So, do you think we could do it?'

'What – you mean you would keep me on!' exclaimed Mick with a degree of disbelief.

'Well, I would need someone to stop me getting too big for my boots, wouldn't I! Besides – you always got the best out of both man and horse.'

'I don't know what to say,' sniffed Mick, trying to suppress a tear of relief that the new owner wasn't going to make him homeless. 'But I do know that you would make a great Governor, and that it would be an honour and a privilege to work for you, sir.'

James smiled at the now deferential way Mick was treating him. In racing, the Governor was always treated with the utmost respect, and for Mick to call James 'sir' after all those insults that he had hurled at him when James was an apprentice, there was a wonderful irony to it.

'Let's do it then,' James replied firmly, his mind made up.

'You've done what!' exclaimed Jackie in total disbelief when James told her. 'How could you possibly put in an offer without me seeing the place or even discussing it with me?'

'You had the chance to come and see it today, but you wouldn't. Besides, we're not going to get anything better at that price, and with a bit of restoration it will be ideal,' James replied defensively.

He had been in such high spirits on the way home and had already been planning the running of the yard. He knew that Jackie might not be so keen, but the venom with which she reacted had left him reeling.

'Why don't you come out and have a look tomorrow? The agent said we could pick up the key any time.'

'I bet he did. I can't see him having people falling over themselves to look at it,' Jackie replied sarcastically. 'I suppose I should at least come and look at it.'

'Good, I'll make the arrangements for tomorrow morning. Perhaps your mother could look after Joshua.'

With that agreed, the remainder of the evening was spent in uneasy silence, each avoiding the other for fear of igniting the row again. The night was spent with equal coldness, James coming to bed to find Jackie curled up with her back to him, seemingly already asleep.

Breakfast the following day was eaten in silence, and on the drive to the yard, not a word was spoken.

When James pulled into the drive, Jackie's expression didn't alter. It bore the same stubborn scowl as it had for the last eighteen hours.

Jackie got out of the car and looked at the house and shuddered, pulling her jacket around her even though it was quite warm.

'Come on, I'll show you round,' said James, trying to temper his enthusiasm.

'If you must,' came the cold response.

They went from room to room with barely a word being

spoken. On reaching the main bedroom, Jackie opened the wardrobe doors to reveal a large damp patch on the wall, going black with mould.

'I suppose you expect me to put my clothes in here,' Jackie said, shutting the door quickly again, moving on to the next room before James could reply.

Things weren't going at all well, thought James. He hadn't even thought of looking in all the wardrobes yesterday, and all Jackie had done so far was pick fault with everything.

In the bathrooms, the suites were revolting.

The windows all needed replacing.

There was damp and probably woodworm, and it all needed rewiring and new plumbing, new heating, new everything!

To cap it all, she had found mouse droppings in all the kitchen cupboards.

'Well?' asked James, fearful of the reply.

'The place is disgusting and uninhabitable. The best thing for it would be to burn it to the ground and start again.'

'Oh, come on, Jackie, it's not that bad,' replied James defensively. 'Sure it needs a lot of work, but where's your sense of adventure? Can't you see the potential and how wonderful it will be once it's all done? I know it's not quite what we had planned, but under the circumstances, it's the best we'll get.'

'And whose fault it that, then?'

James wondered when she'd get round to that again. Lately, everything had been his fault. Jackie had seemingly begun to believe the rumours that James had thrown races, and his downfall was all his own doing. It hurt him more than he could bear – just when he needed her support the most.

Jackie continued. 'And if you think that I'm going to live here whilst it's all being done up, you've got another thing coming. Can you imagine trying to bring up Joshua in the mess that there will be? I really think that if you go ahead, I'll move back to mother's for the time being.'

James could see that in a way she was right as far as Joshua was concerned, but the thought of them living apart, even for a short time, upset him.

At that point, Mick appeared from behind one of the stable blocks.

'Oh, God, there's even a tramp here!' exclaimed Jackie with disdain.

'That's not a tramp, that's Mick, he used to be Mr. Reynolds' head lad in my days here. He's keeping an eye on the place, and if my offer is accepted, he'll stay on.'

'Well, I wish the two of you the best of luck then,' came Jackie's reply, as she strode back to the car.

'But you haven't even seen the yard,' said James, startled at the thought of her not having seen everything.

'I can't see it being any better,' came the reply.

James waved to Mick and shrugged his shoulders. Mick immediately understood. He was good at reading mannerisms, both human and equine. James certainly had his hands full with that one. Obviously highly strung, undisciplined and too used to getting her own way. Fillies like that were a challenge, and for once it appeared that James had taken on more than he bargained for.

James's offer was accepted immediately.

The contracts went through with lightning speed, the

main creditor obviously wanting to get rid of the property before it deteriorated any further and James being keen to start his new career.

Jackie moved back to her mother's, showing no interest whatsoever in the renovation plans for the house.

James wasn't too concerned – he was so keen to get the yard up and running so that he could start training. Renovating the house would come second.

James cleaned out part of the house and made it reasonably habitable. It had been a long time since he had to 'rough it', but he was so engrossed in renovating the stable boxes, putting in new water supplies to each box, re-fencing the paddocks and organising the band of workers that Mick had miraculously produced, that he barely noticed his living conditions.

James and his staff worked from dawn to dusk, and then a few hours more. After three weeks, the yard was at a point where they could start looking for prospective owners. Mick had put the word out amongst his contacts, and James put an advertisement in the *Racing Post*.

It wasn't long before half a dozen horses were installed in the newly refurbished stable block.

Each morning, James could see enormous progress in the renovation of the yard, and the first morning that he went out and saw horses' heads appear over the stable doors was one of the happiest moments of his life. His new career had begun.

James had been so busy; he had seen little of Jackie. He had taken her out for the odd meal, but she never enquired as to the progress. He had also gone round to see Joshua as often as he could, although it was not as often as he would have liked.

Jackie always greeted him with a coldness he thought she was incapable of.

He felt guilty for not starting on the house first, and vowed to himself that he would start the following week.

From the odd newspaper report he had seen, it was apparent that Jackie was far from pining for him. Having her mother on hand as permanent baby-sitter had allowed Jackie to party almost nightly with her old friends – a fact that Nathan Grant's tabloids reported with glee.

James tried to ignore the gossip, but he couldn't help noticing how happy she looked in all the photos.

He calmed himself with thoughts that the yard would soon start winning, better horses would follow, and he would be able to restore Jackie's lifestyle to something like it's former splendour.

As the number of horses gradually increased, so did the administrative work involved in the upkeep of the yard.

One of James's favourite times was spent in the kitchen with Mick, sitting at the old pine table he had recently bought, discussing the placing of their horses in forthcoming races.

The aga that James had serviced and restored to working order threw out a comforting warmth in the late autumn evenings.

James and Mick would spend hours studying forthcoming races and trying to work out the appropriate races for the horses in their charge.

There were so many factors to consider, some of which James had never realised as a jockey.

As a jockey, apart from riding out on the training gallops to get to know the quirks of the animals, his job was to turn up and get the most out of his ride.

As a trainer, there was so much more involved.

Some owners preferred their horses to run at a local track, since their business commitments meant they couldn't afford the time to travel further afield. Others didn't mind where their horse ran.

Did the horse like sharp tracks with tight bends or galloping tracks with sweeping bends?

Certain horses ran better on clockwise track; others anticlockwise.

Then there was the distance to consider, what going the horse ran best on, not to mention the prize money which would influence the standard of opposition.

Some horses thrived on running every week. Others needed time between races.

All these points had to be weighed up to get the best out of a horse, whilst keeping both the owner and horse happy.

Mick and James used to talk long into the night, planning their campaign for each horse. Mick's knowledge and experience was invaluable and James considered himself fortunate to have such a good head lad and friend who was willing to guide him through his transition from jockey to trainer.

Mick, in turn, felt rejuvenated in his 'new' job. He had learnt such a lot from the old Governor, Mr. Reynolds, but until now never had the opportunity to put it into practice.

He had guided James though his career from apprentice jockey to the peak of his profession, and felt sure that he could reach the top as a trainer (with a little help from him!)

Mick, in true Irish racing tradition, always had an eye on the betting potential of a race, and whilst he would never dream of attempting to influence a race in any way or form, was never backward in making the most of a gambling opportunity.

James, on the other hand, was not a gambling man and never had been. Certain aspects of the gambling world he found rather dubious, and as such he had no intention of getting involved, especially after the lies about race fixing that had been dogging him ever since Northern Lights' defeat. Besides, James had always considered gambling a mug's game. One look at Mick's circumstances confirmed his belief.

Whilst Mick did have the odd coup, more often than not he lost money, and the circumstances he was now in were ample testament that gambling didn't pay.

Mick had built up a good team of lads in the yard, many of whom were thrilled to work for James Ryan – ex-champion jockey – in the yard of the legendary late Mr. Reynolds. They all knew that James was blameless for Northern Lights' defeat and that he had in effect been hounded out of continuing as a jockey, and were all determined to do their best for James to make amends for the shabby treatment he had received from some of the racing world.

James was also delighted that Mick had found a couple of apprentice jockeys who were showing excellent raw talent, and, in James's mind, with hard work and good fortune were destined for the top.

*　　*　　*

The day finally dawned when the yard had its first runner – a four year old colt of moderate ability called Eldon Lad.

The morning of the race, James was so nervous that he couldn't face breakfast.

Mick brought the horse box round and coaxed Eldon Lad in.

James felt rather embarrassed at the state of the horse box. It was old and had seen better days, but had been cheap and Mick had assured him that it was a 'good little runner.' It had been meant to be used for moving horses from other yards and collecting straw etc., but with so much going on, James hadn't had the time to look for a more respectable one for public occasions.

Mick had grinned when he screwed a plate on the back saying 'Racehorses in transit.' Anyone driving behind would have thought it was a joke.

James vowed to make getting a decent horse box a priority; after all, the state of the horse box usually said something about the state of the yard and this vehicle was definitely giving the wrong impression.

It was a tough decision to pick between the two promising apprentices as to which was going to get the ride. After much deliberation, he decided on Alan, who rode Eldon Lad most mornings and so knew him better.

James decided to accompany Mick and Alan in the horse box, and they set off for Nottingham with the hopes and expectations of the yard resting on them.

Eldon Lad, however, was no world beater. He was a gutsy horse with a heart that far exceeded his ability. His finishing speed was also a bit suspect, but James thought he had found the ideal race for him. Time would tell.

Once at the racecourse, James went to find the owner
– Mrs. Evans. He spotted her easily in the crowd. Mrs.
Evans cut a matronly figure in her tweed skirt and
jacket, brown hat (which hid grey hair with a bad perm,)
and very sensible shoes. She was in her late fifties
and recently widowed. Eldon Lad had belonged to her
husband, and until then, her only experience of racing
had been accompanying him when his horse ran. Now,
as an owner with a responsibility for the horse, she had
become very enthusiastic.

Her decision to place the horse with James was taken
purely for sentimental reasons. James had always been
the housewife's favourite jockey when it came to the
annual flutter on the Derby, and she was astute enough
to disbelieve the rumours about him, so when she heard
that James was going into training, Eldon Lad became the
first horse in the yard – a fact that she would repeatedly
tell all her friends with pride.

James went over to her.

'Good morning, Mrs. Evans, wonderful day, isn't it?'

'It certainly is,' beamed Mrs. Evans, still hardly able
to believe that she was talking to the young, handsome,
famous James Ryan. He seemed so nice, ordinary and
easy to talk to, not at all affected by his fame. 'How's
Eldon Lad?'

'He's fine and in good form. The going's perfect for
him today. I've got high hopes for him.'

'Come now, Mr. Ryan, don't flatter me. My husband,
God rest his soul, never was the best judge of a horse. He
only bought Eldon Lad so he had an excuse to take the
day off when he ran. Sure, he always dreamt that one day
he would win, but you have to be realistic, don't you.'

'There are an awful lot of people like that in racing, Mrs. Evans, but Eldon Lad is a real trier, so let's see what happens, shall we? Now you must excuse me, I must get him saddled up. I'll see you in the parade ring.'

James went back, completed the formalities in the weighing room, saddled up Eldon Lad, and in no time at all was back with Mrs. Evans in the parade ring.

He felt very self conscious. It was the first time in the parade ring as a trainer, and he felt decidedly overdressed in his smart trousers, sheepskin jacket and trilby.

They surveyed the opposition. James was pleased to see that there was nothing that caught the eye, but then again, if Eldon Lad hadn't been from his yard, he wouldn't have given him a second glance either.

Mick was leading him round, savouring the atmosphere that he had missed for so long, with James wishing that he would stop grinning and showing his missing teeth.

The jockeys finally started to arrive. With them was Alan wearing the purple and orange stripes of Mrs. Evans.

'It's nice that you kept Mr. Evans' colours,' commented James.

'More out of sentimentality than anything else. My husband didn't exactly have much fashion sense, did he?'

James smiled but was too polite to agree.

He wished he wasn't feeling so nervous. So many people had come up to wish him well – all his old friends amongst the jockeys, staff from the other stables, staff from the racecourse, not to mention the odd owner who commented that they were keeping an eye on his yard to see how it progressed. The more people that wished him well, the more nervous he felt. It seemed as though everyone expected the former champion jockey to automatically be as successful in training. It made him feel very self conscious and alone.

The bell sounded and the jockeys mounted up.

'Remember, keep him in touch but not in front until the two furlong mark, then we'll see how much heart Eldon Lad really has,' James told Alan before Mick led them out onto the track.

Mick then returned to watch the race with James and Mrs. Evans as Eldon Lad made his way down to the start. He had stopped on the way to have a few pounds each way on Eldon Lad, although the odds were not as good as he had hoped, probably due to a few sentimental bets being placed because of the James Ryan connection.

Mrs. Evans was wringing the strap of her handbag with nerves, and with barely a word spoken between them apart from Mick offering up a quick prayer, the race was off.

Mrs. Evans was immediately jumping up and down, shouting like a fishwife. Mick was muttering words of encouragement which grew from a whisper at the start to shouting by the two furlong mark.

Alan had Eldon Lad in just the right place when he kicked for home. Nothing happened.

He gave him a couple of slaps with the whip. Nothing happened.

The shouting from Mick and Mrs. Evans increased as the horses approached the furlong post.

Suddenly, the horse appeared to change gear, and overtook the three who had been battling it out for the lead. By the time Eldon Lad passed the winning post ahead by a neck, Mick, Mrs. Evans and James were all jumping up and down, roaring encouragement.

Simultaneously they all fell into each other's arms, hugging each other with delight.

'You jammy bastard!' exclaimed Mick, forgetting that there was a lady present and that he was talking to the Governor. 'You have the luck of the Irish.' He then rushed off to lead the horse into the winner's enclosure whilst quietly calculating his winnings.

Mrs. Evans was beside herself with joy, and planted a big kiss on James's cheek.

'I feel wonderful, so wonderful!' said Mrs. Evans, wiping a tear from her eye. 'If only my Arthur could have been here to see it.'

'I'm sure he's here in spirit,' replied James, hardly able to speak, so stunned at the turn of foot that Eldon Lad had suddenly produced. 'Come on, let's get down to the winners' enclosure.'

As James, accompanied by a jubilant Mrs. Evans entered the winners enclosure, a big cheer went up from the crowd. It was the most popular win of the day. The housewife's favourite was back.

Alan was equally thrilled to have ridden his first winner, and he too received a big kiss from Mrs. Evans, who even planted one on Eldon Lad.

The rest of the day was a blur. The prize money was not a great deal, but would be enough to keep Eldon Lad in training for a few months, but to Mrs. Evans, the prize money didn't matter. It was her moment of glory.

Later that evening when they arrived back in triumph at the yard, a few bottles of champagne were opened, and Alan duly carved his initials and date on the door of his room. At last, the stable was on the racing map.

Following on from that success, over the next couple

of weeks, the yard had another winner and a few places, which filled James with enthusiasm and relief, and delighted the owners.

One morning, James received a phone call from an owner intending to place half a dozen horses with James, who wished to meet to discuss it.

On discussing it with Mick, James was rather perturbed to find out that the owner, a William Old, was a legendary gambler and a bit of a rogue. However, with the prospect of six more horses to add to the yard, James felt obliged to at least meet him, and an appointment was duly made at the local pub for the next day.

James walked in and was immediately recognised by a portly gentleman who got up and greeted him with a slap on the back.

'Well, well, James Ryan himself. Nice to meet you,' boomed William Old. 'What'll you have to drink?'

'Just a mineral water, thank you,' replied James, his back still smarting from the whack it had just received.

Old got the drinks from the bar and joined James, who had by now sat down at the table, which already had two empty pint glasses on it.

'So, how's the training business going?' Old enquired, taking a mouthful of lager, which seemed to drain at least a quarter of a pint out of the glass.

'Very well considering the short time we've been going.'

'Good, good,' came the reply. 'Still got a few empty boxes though, from what I hear.'

'Yes, but they are slowly filling up,' James answered,

sipping his mineral water, happy to follow the conversation.

'So, would you be interested in a few of mine then?'

'Of course, I'm always interested,' said James, quickly running through his mind the extra income another six horses would bring.

'Good. You see, I'm not too happy with one of my current trainers. Let's just say his ideas and mine don't seem to be quite the same.'

'And what ideas are those, Mr. Old?'

'Oh, come on James,' laughed Old, 'both you and I know that at this level of racing there's no way an owner can break even. The money's to be made gambling, and as a trainer, you're in a great position to influence the outcome.'

James put his mineral water down. He did not like where this conversation was leading.

'So, basically you want me to cheat – not only the horse but the general public too by stopping a horse running to its potential one race and then having a gamble on it when it's been dropped in the handicap the next. Well, I'm afraid that if that's what you mean, then I'm not your trainer. Any horse in my yard goes out and runs to the best of its ability, and I will not be a party to fixing results so that owners can line their pockets at the expense of the honest public,' James said, his anger mounting.

Mr. Old gave James a knowing look.

'Come off it, lad, from what I've heard, you're an expert at pulling horses.'

James stood up and looked Old straight in the eyes.

'Then your sources are very much mistaken.'

Before Old could reply, James walked out, shaking with rage.

How dare he ask him to cheat.

How dare he accuse him to his face of being a cheat.

James thought he would rather close his yard than be associated with the likes of Mr. Old.

Back at the yard, James found Mick in one of the stables.

'You were right, Mick, he was a villain through and through.'

'There's a lot of them about in racing,' Mick replied, shaking his head sadly.

The yard continued to attract more honest owners, much to James's relief.

In the house, the plumbers had installed a very expensive bathroom suite, which James had picked – not because he liked it, but because he thought that Jackie would.

Mick, when he saw it being unloaded from the lorry, commented that it was so posh, that if it were his he would have to have a bath before he could even go into the bathroom.

The electricians had also rewired the house, making even more of a mess than before. Next to come were the plasterers.

Despite James's attempts to get Jackie to have a look at how work was progressing, and trying to get her involved in some of the decisions, she steadfastly refused to set foot in the house, and rebuffed all attempts to get her interested.

James would retreat to the house and immerse himself

in work to block out the heartache he felt at Jackie's attitude and the fact that Joshua seemed to grow so much between every visit.

James, however, was not entirely alone in the house. Mick had taken it upon himself to get a dog.

'Every yard should have a dog – keeps the rats down,' Mick said with good Irish logic. The only fault with that was that the dog that Mick had come back with was an old black Labrador called Guinness, who spent most of his time asleep in a box in front of the aga, and at his age would have been incapable of catching anything.

'Well, good company for you then,' he said when James protested.

James also had the suspicion that with a name like Guinness, and the familiarity between Mick and the dog, the two of them were well acquainted and he had been set up.

After a couple of days, James had to admit that he had grown rather fond of Guinness, who never complained or argued, and was always pleased to see him when he came in.

Another stranger arrived in the yard – a small black cat which Mick found one day in the room where the oat and nut sacks were kept.

Mick promptly called him Oats.

When James protested about the cat, Mick's reply was –

'Well, you couldn't call him Nuts, could you. Besides, black cats are lucky. Out of all the yards in Newmarket he picked us. Lucky omen is that. Besides, he'll keep the mice down.'

James relented, and Oats was soon earning his keep, leaving an endless supply of headless mice on the back door step, which James often trod on with a big squish in the dark mornings when he wasn't quite awake when he went out.

When he wasn't mousing, Oats was to be found curled up with Guinness. In the early hours of the morning, after a successful evening's mousing, Oats would also creep upstairs and seek warmth on James's bed.

When James was in bed, he thought over what progress had been made in the yard and what the future held. He had a loyal group of owners and fiercely loyal, hard working staff. The horses he had, however, weren't ever going to be Group standard.

The flat season was beginning to wind down, although it still continued throughout the winter at a few tracks and on the all weather.

By next season, he hoped to have a few better horses so he could start aiming at the Group races where the real money was.

He smiled to himself as he turned out the light and pulled the duvet over him. As Mick would say – 'In racing, there's always hope.'

5

For the first two months after his meeting with Nathan Grant, Julian Anderson-Brown could barely believe his luck. His debts had been paid, his salary increased beyond that of his arch enemy, not to mention the fact that he seemed to be able to do what he liked with his research without getting summoned to the Dean's office for a dressing down.

He recalled the afternoon following the meeting at Grant Global Communications when he was called into the Dean's office.

Anderson-Brown had been about to leave when he received a message that William Middleton wanted to see him immediately.

His first thoughts were that it had been too good to be true – the research grant from Grant Global Communications, the salary and the bonus, and now the Dean was going to put a stop to it all.

When he walked into the Dean's office his heart sank. The office always depressed him at the best of times. It was dark, foreboding and smelt of damp, which seemed to epitomise the stuffy attitude that Anderson-Brown had come to despise.

William Middleton was sitting at his desk looking very

serious, his fingers strumming the worn leather desk top with agitation.

'Come in, Anderson-Brown,' the Dean said, motioning him to sit down. 'It would appear that the university owes you an apology and I have been asked to offer you your position back with the added latitude for research you appear to have wanted.'

Julian Anderson-Brown was astonished and fought to contain his delight.

'What, you mean I have a free hand with my research now?'

'It would appear so,' replied the Dean, trying to control his temper and the overwhelming desire to throw Anderson-Brown off the campus.

Julian Anderson-Brown was sitting there in front of him so smug and conceited; the Dean found it almost unbearable.

'So, I can continue with the experiments you previously objected to?'

'Yes,' hissed William Middleton through his teeth. 'The company funding the new grant wants me to give you a free rein. I trust you'll refrain from embarrassing the university with anything too outrageous.'

'I'll try not to,' came the reply.

Julian Anderson-Brown wondered what on earth had been said between William Middleton and Nathan Grant to prompt such a dramatic climb down. Either the university was getting an awful lot of money, or there was something underhand going on. Either way, Anderson-Brown didn't care. He could now do what he wanted in his laboratories without fear of interference from anyone.

In the following few days he had tested the Dean by

giving some very controversial lectures. When there was no resulting summons, he realised that at last he really was free to do what he wanted.

His research with the hamsters had gone really well now he had the time to devote to them. All the while, in the back of his mind, he was wondering how to apply it to racehorses; after all, he had a deadline to keep – or more importantly – a sizeable bonus to earn.

Nathan Grant had been in contact on numerous occasions, enquiring how their 'private deal' was progressing. Each time Anderson-Brown assured him that work was progressing well.

In reality, although he was convinced that his method in manipulating the appropriate gene was sound, trying it out on a hundred hamsters was one thing but he could hardly try it with the same number of racehorses.

Nathan Grant had arranged for him to fly over to his stud in Ireland to meet the vet and to get appropriate samples from the stallion and mare that Grant had chosen.

Anderson-Brown was thrilled initially at the thought of being flown there on Grant's private jet, but as the time drew nearer he began to wonder what exactly he had got himself into. It all seemed to be getting too serious for his liking.

A chauffeur-driven Mercedes met him at the small airport where he landed and took him to Nathan Grant's stud.

As they approached the stud, the scenery reminded Anderson-Brown of what heaven must be like. The paddock grass was greener than he had ever seen before, the post and rail fences round each paddock were in immaculate condition, and in each field were horses of equine physical perfection grazing lazily in the long shadows of the late afternoon sun.

The car pulled up at the administrative block of the stud and the chauffeur unloaded Anderson-Brown's bags and showed him into the reception area.

The secretary made a quick call to inform the chief vet of his arrival, and asked Anderson-Brown to take a seat as Dr. Popham would be out shortly.

Anderson-Brown gazed round the reception area. There were prints on the walls of all the stallions at stud there, together with photographs of Nathan Grant receiving trophies from various dignitaries after successful important races.

He then gazed out at part of the stable complex. He was astonished at how clean it was – immaculate in fact, with not a piece of loose straw to be seen.

Hanging baskets – still in full bloom – hung at regular intervals round the block, giving vivid splashes of colour to the mellow atone walls.

His thoughts were interrupted by a small, balding, studious looking man entering the reception from a door marked 'Strictly Private – Authorised Personnel Only.'

'Dr. Anderson-Brown? I'm Dr. Popham. I'm sorry to have kept you waiting. I trust you had a good trip?'

'Yes, very good, thank you,' replied Anderson-Brown, 'I was just admiring the complex.'

'Impressive, isn't it. I'm sure you will be even more impressed with the veterinary centre and laboratories. We have some of the most up to date equipment in the racing world here. Mr. Grant makes sure of that. It certainly pays when you can spot a potential problem with a horse and iron it out before it has a permanent effect on a horse's performance, and with what Mr. Grant spends on his horses, they are certainly investments worth taking care of.'

'What does he spend when buying a horse?' asked Anderson-Brown.

'Millions,' came the reply.

'I presume that's in total,' said Anderson-Brown, trying not to sound too ignorant.

'No, each.'

Anderson-Brown gulped visibly. He was used to experimenting on hamsters, which were bred in the university laboratories at very little expense. The thought of having committed himself to experiment on a multi million pound racehorse with no chance of a practice run was a very sobering thought indeed.

Suddenly, life seemed very complicated and he was beginning to have his doubts over what he had committed himself to.

Dr. Popham led him into the first of the laboratories.

Anderson-Brown was astonished to see the range of sophisticated equipment. Not just one or two pieces, but row after row, and all brand new. It was far better equipped than the university – for all its research grants and funding.

Dr. Popham showed Anderson-Brown round all the departments, answering his questions as he went.

He then showed him the two high-tech operating theatres before taking him back to his office.

Dr. Popham closed the door and motioned Anderson-Brown to sit down.

'I have to say that I am very uncomfortable with Mr. Grant's new venture,' he began, sitting down in one of the more comfortable chairs in the office. 'Firstly it contravenes Jockey Club regulations and secondly, from what I gather, it involves operating techniques that I am not familiar with in practice. However, as an employee of Mr. Grant, I must put my reservations to one side. It's not my position to query his decisions, just to carry them out.'

'My thoughts exactly,' replied Anderson-Brown.

'I trust you have performed this operation numerous times before?'

Anderson-Brown hesitated for a moment before truthfully answering.

'Hundreds of times.'

'Not on horses, surely?'

'No, never on a horse.'

An uneasy silence hung over the room as both men contemplated he predicament that Nathan Grant had put them in.

'On what then?' Dr. Popham asked.

'Considerably smaller animals,' Anderson-Brown answered evasively, looking at the floor with embarrassment.

'I see.'

Dr. Popham would have liked to pursue this line of questioning, but somehow he had the idea that he wouldn't like the answers he might get. He decided on a more positive approach.

'Perhaps you would let me have the details of your research and the techniques involved so I can start relating the procedure to equine physiology.

'Good idea,' replied Anderson-Brown, 'I've brought the full details for you.'

'Thank you. The staff here have been told who you are, but obviously not why you are here. As far as they are concerned, you are preparing a study for Mr. Grant on how to improve our breeding results by combining the genetic lines of the horses by – shall we say – conventional breeding. Needless to say, no one is aware of what your real job is here and it's imperative it stays that way. Even in a place like this where Mr. Grant demands the utmost loyalty and confidentiality, tongues wag and the world of racing is very small when it comes to rumours.

'A good cover story,' Anderson-Brown commented, feeling a bit like a double agent on a secret mission.

Dr. Popham sighed as he leant back in the chair and clasped his hands together.

'I have to be perfectly frank. As well as the illegality of it and the unfamiliarity of the operation, I do have personal misgivings about the whole project.'

'In what way?' asked Anderson-Brown, trying to suppress his exasperation at having come up against another sceptic to his work.

'Well, it's my job to keep Mr. Grant's horses fit and healthy, not to perform an operation on a perfectly healthy horse in an effort to produce a foal that could only be described as a freak.'

'That's a little strong, isn't it?' interrupted Anderson-Brown, affronted at Dr. Popham labelling the results of his work as 'freaks.'

Before he could get another word in, Dr. Popham continued.

'The whole thing about breeding racehorses is the element of chance. That's what racing is all about. You pit your wits against nature, selecting the best pairing of mare and stallion and hope that the combination of genes produces the desired result. It's a bit like cooking – if you pardon the analogy. With some ingredients you produce a sponge cake. With a little variation in the ingredients you produce a fruit cake. So it is with breeding racehorses – some combinations produce good sprinters, other combinations, horses more suited to distance races. Even then, there is the element of doubt. With the same ingredients you can end up with six totally different sponge cakes. Perhaps one will be excellent – one awful and the other four – average quality. So you see that even with the best combinations of mare and stallion, there is always an element of luck as to whether you can actually produce a foal that will go into the record books. That's the whole essence of racing – chance and luck.'

At last Dr. Popham drew breath and Anderson-Brown was now able to speak.

'I can see your point, but as a scientist don't you strive for perfection, which surely must be the most satisfying outcome for any experiment? Doesn't the thought of being able to produce the perfect racehorse have some appeal for you?'

'As a scientist, I have to admit – yes, but as a vet, I'm afraid it goes against my beliefs to operate on a mare to produce a foal that might possibly be produced naturally anyway. Finally, from a man who loves the sport of racing, to put it bluntly, it's cheating.'

Anderson-Brown thought carefully over his comments before replying.

'Well, whatever your or my misgivings we have a job to do, so we had better put aside our differences of opinion if we are going to achieve a positive outcome.'

'Yes,' replied Dr. Popham, 'he's the sort of man you don't want to disappoint.'

With their conflicting opinions temporarily forgotten, Dr. Popham offered to show Anderson-Brown round the rest of the stud.

The first stop was the stallion boxes.

'This is Coral Reef, the stallion Mr. Grant wants as sire. He's the best stallion here, narrowly missed out on the Derby four years ago. Just lacked that turn of foot.'

Dr. Popham got the groom to lead him out. Anderson-Brown was amazed at the power and strength Coral Reef seemed to have. His coat shone like polished mahogany, through which his muscles bulged – like those of a heavyweight boxer.

His neck was as thick and powerful as an Olympic weightlifter and a white blaze ran down his face. Overall Anderson-Brown was impressed – very impressed.

He had never been this close to a horse of such calibre before, and for an instant thought that it was the most perfect specimen he had ever seen, and wondered how on earth he could improve on that.

He calmed himself with the thought that it was not only what was on the outside that made a champion, but also what was on the inside. A little genetic modification to give more stamina, and Anderson-Brown could produce the ultimate racing machine – perfect.

Coral Reef was not too impressed at having his supper interrupted and snapped angrily at the groom whilst lashing out with his hind leg at Dr. Popham.

'Stallions are notoriously fractious,' commented Dr. Popham, giving Coral Reef a wide berth. He then turned to the groom. 'You had better put him back before he takes a chunk out of you.'

The groom led Coral Reef back into his stable, closing the door quickly behind him. Coral Reef lashed out again with a hind leg, hitting the door with a loud bang, making Anderson-Brown jump. It was Coral Reef's way of saying that he didn't want to be disturbed again.

They continued their tour of the stud, round the foaling boxes and ending up at the administrative centre.

'I'll show you the grounds tomorrow. It's a bit late and dark now,' Dr. Popham said eying his watch and noting that he was already late home for his dinner.

In his line of work, that was nothing new. His long suffering wife knew that and prepared meals which could easily be re-heated in the microwave whenever he came home late.

'I'll just show you to the guest room where you will be staying for the next couple of days,' he said, leading Anderson-Brown into the building that was the accommodation block housing the lads' hostel, grooms' quarters, a suite that was kept free for him in case he had to be called and stay overnight, and lastly a couple of guest suites.

Anderson-Brown was shown his accommodation, which was on a par with a luxury hotel – if not better. There was a lounge area equipped with TV, large sofa, antique desk and chair, coffee table, discreet lighting, and to Anderson-Brown's delight – a fully stocked mini bar. In the corner was a small kitchen area with fridge, microwave, cooker and all the necessary equipment for rustling up a quick snack.

The bedroom was enormous, with two queen size beds,

large oak fitted wardrobe, huge chest of drawers and another TV. The en suite bathroom was as magnificent as he had ever seen, with marble floor and walls, shower cubicle as big as his bathroom at home, sunken bath, two washbasins, bidet and toilet, not to mention the array of toiletries. The bathrobe and towels were thick and soft – not like the threadbare ones he was used to at home.

'Very nice,' said Anderson-Brown, trying not to sound overly impressed, whilst secretly thinking that he could get seriously used to this lifestyle. It was certainly going to be very pleasurable staying here and he made a mental note to arrange as many trips as he possibly could.

'If you hurry, you will catch dinner being served. They finish at 8p.m. Just head for reception, and the night porter will direct you. Breakfast is from 5–8am. I'll be in the lab from 8.30 onwards. In the meantime, I'll read over the paperwork you've given me and we can get cracking on the samples tomorrow.'

That night, having consumed the vast majority of the mini bar, Anderson-Brown slept like a log, and took a considerable time to wake when the alarm went off the following morning.

He showered and shaved, dressed, putting on the same clothes as he had on the previous day and then only just made it down for breakfast before they finished serving.

Anderson-Brown was full of excitement. The task ahead was, for him, the ultimate challenge.

With each week that followed, Julian Anderson-Brown was getting more and more anxious about his progress – or lack of it.

It was one thing to experiment using easily obtainable

animals, when at least he could repeat the experiment and perfect the technique, ironing out any problems that would inevitably occur.

What Nathan Grant had asked him to do was totally different. When he agreed, he hadn't even given a thought to the value of the mare he would be using, and now that he knew, the thought frightened him.

Not only that, but he had one chance – only the one chance – to get it right first time, and he was now beginning to have second thoughts about the whole deal.

Nathan Grant was becoming increasingly impatient with him, ringing him weekly for progress reports.

Anderson-Brown made one excuse after another, until Nathan Grant's patience ran out and he demanded a meeting. Anderson-Brown tried to get out of it by saying that he was at a critical time in his experiments and that he couldn't possibly be absent from them at this time, but Nathan Grant insisted in terms that he could not refuse.

The following day, he was sitting anxiously outside Nathan Grant's office at Grant Global Communications, not looking forward to the impending meeting.

It wasn't long before Janice showed him into Grant's office.

Nathan Grant was standing with his back to the door, staring out of the window at the buildings below.

'Good afternoon, Mr. Grant,' said Anderson-Brown, hoping a little politeness might defuse the tension he could sense in the room.

'Sit down,' said Nathan without even turning round. 'You're telling me that your work isn't progressing as well as you had hoped.'

'Yes, a few problems have arisen that I hadn't foreseen, and I don't think I'll be able to meet the deadline.'

'Let me make it quite clear,' said Nathan, turning round to reveal his thunderous expression, which made Anderson-Brown shrink into his chair. 'We have an agreement and no-one goes back on their agreements with me – do I make myself quite clear?'

'But . . .' started Anderson-Brown.

'No buts. You have another six weeks. If you have no positive news within the next four then I'll find someone who can. I don't take kindly to failures or people who let me down. I can destroy their career – no problem at all, and believe me – they are the lucky ones. I also don't like being lied to, so are you now trying to tell me you lied to me when you agreed the deadline?'

Nathan's face was red with rage as he leaned over the desk so that his face was within a foot of Anderson-Brown's.

'No,' stammered Anderson-Brown. 'It just proved to be a little more difficult than I had first anticipated.'

Nathan Grant turned and stared out of the window again in silence.

Beads of perspiration were beginning to run down the brow of Anderson-Brown, as his mind was trying to comprehend the veiled threat that Nathan Grant had just made. He had no doubt that Nathan Grant was capable of many things; Dr. Popham had often commented that Nathan Grant was not a man to be crossed and had recounted tales of destroyed careers and even disappearances – most of which Anderson Brown had taken with a pinch of salt – until now.

For the first time in his life, Anderson-Brown felt very much out of his depth.

'I'm confident that on my next trip to Ireland we can complete your project,' he stammered, realising that whatever happened, this was going to be his one and only chance.

'I sincerely hope that your confidence is not misplaced – for your sake,' came Nathan Grant's reply. 'I'll expect Dr. Popham to confirm the good news after your visit then, anything less will be unacceptable. Do I make myself clear?'

'Yes, sir,' stammered Anderson-Brown, wiping the sweat from his brow with the back of his trembling hand.

'Good. Then I had better not keep you any longer – you have a lot of work to do.'

Anderson-Brown stood up and held onto the desk for a moment, steadying himself and trying to regain his composure. It took all of his willpower to walk out of the office, since his legs felt as though they had turned to jelly.

In the elevator he felt quite sick and very much afraid. It wasn't the thought of his career being ruined – it had been in ruins a few times before and he had always managed to resurrect it – it was the veiled threat that had so worried him. What if those rumours Dr. Popham had told him about were true?

When he reached the outside of the building, he drew in a long breath to try and clear his head. It wasn't as though he still had a lot of work to do on the project – in fact he was ready to go ahead with it immediately. What was holding him back was the thought of only one chance to get it right.

He knew Dr. Popham was very concerned about performing the operation to implant the embryo, as it was a procedure that he had never tried before, but he had the good sense to keep his concerns to himself.

In a sudden blinding flash of inspiration, Anderson-Brown came up with the answer. Why not try it on another mare first – a sort of trial run. That way, he could see if it worked, Dr. Popham would be more confident to go ahead, and they wouldn't be trying it out for the first time on a £2 million racehorse.

'What a brilliant idea. Why didn't I think of it sooner?' he muttered to himself.

He would contact Dr. Popham as soon as he got back to the lab.

On the way back, Anderson-Brown stopped off at a bar for a quick brandy to steady his nerves and also to celebrate his flash of inspiration.

Numerous brandies later, he was in no state to return to work and was only just capable of taking a taxi home.

The call to Dr. Popham would have to wait until the morning.

'You must be insane,' came the reaction from Dr. Popham when Anderson-Brown told him of his idea. 'Mr. Grant would go mad if he found out we had impregnated two mares.'

Anderson-Brown hadn't thought of that and reacted quickly.

'He won't know what we don't tell him. Anyway, we needn't use a modified embryo with the first mare, just a normal one to try out the operating technique. I'm sure that we would both be happier operating on a mare of little value first, rather than messing around with one of Nathan Grant's pride and joy.'

'True,' said Dr. Popham thoughtfully, 'but how will we find a mare for the first op?'

Anderson-Brown's head was still thumping from the hangover, and he wished – as he always wished – that he hadn't drunk quite so much the night before. It dulled his mind and slowed his thoughts.

'What if I bought one and supplied it?' said Anderson-Brown, pleased with the solution he had come up with. 'It would have to be a cheap mare, but it would do the job serving as a guinea pig.'

Anderson-Brown had no idea how much a cheap mare would cost, but if it were only a couple of thousand pound it would be well worth the expenditure if the second op. went well, after all, it wouldn't make much of a dent in his bonus.

'Look, I would rather not discuss this over the phone,' said Anderson-Brown, realising that he still had some thinking to do over this new proposal. 'I'll come over to the stud and we can discuss it then. I'll make an excuse to Mr. Grant that I need to see you urgently and hopefully I'll be over in the next couple of days. In the meantime, you wouldn't happen to know where I can lay my hands on a very inexpensive mare?'

Dr. Popham laughed. 'Ireland's full of them. Leave it to me, I'll make a few discreet enquiries.'

'Thanks, I'll let you know when I'll be over.'

Anderson-Brown put the phone down and heaved a sigh of relief; little knowing that Dr. Popham was doing exactly the same in Ireland.

A quick call to Grant Global Communications revealed

that Nathan Grant was out of the country for a few days, much to the relief of Anderson-Brown who wasn't looking forward to talking to him anyway.

He briefly explained that he had to go to Ireland to collect some data urgently, and as Nathan Grant was expecting his report within the next couple of weeks he wouldn't want to have to delay it.

Janice duly made the arrangements, organising the flight and informing the stud.

She had been told the same as the stud staff – that Anderson-Brown was preparing a report for Nathan on breeding, which went some way to explain Nathan's involvement with Anderson-Brown, but why Nathan had agreed to his demands to be flown to Ireland so many times was beyond her. All the stud records were held on computer and could be accessed from England. On thinking about it, however, Nathan regarded the stud records as strictly confidential and would not want them accessed by anyone other than stud staff or himself, so maybe his access was supervised. Even so, it seemed all very strange.

Anderson-Brown arrived at the stud full of excitement and anticipation, with a wad of money in his bag and a frozen embryo in a canister of liquid nitrogen. When he phoned Dr. Popham to tell him when he would be arriving, Dr. Popham informed him that he had found a mare for 2000 Irish guineas. They agreed to operate the day following Anderson-Brown's arrival.

What Anderson-Brown had omitted to tell Dr. Popham was that the embryo to be used was from the same batch as he had prepared for Nathan Grant's mare.

Still, what Dr. Popham didn't know he wouldn't worry about.

The money was handed over and a horse box sent to collect the mare called Andaman Sea – a horse of moderate racing ability but with a leg problem that had ended a very uninspiring racing career.

The owner was delighted to have found someone willing to pay 2000 Irish guineas, since the horse was capable of only light work or a trip to the knacker's yard.

The stud staff were a little surprised to see a mare of such moderate ability in their stud, since the stud fees charged started at 5000 Irish guineas for the cheapest stallion, rising to six figures for Coral Reef. Still, as long as the stud fees were paid, who were they to question the owner's sanity.

That evening, when most of the staff were off duty and there was no chance of interruption, Dr. Popham and Anderson-Brown operated on Andaman Sea and implanted the embryo. It was a quick and uneventful operation – far easier than either of them had thought. Andaman Sea made a speedy recovery from the anaesthetic and was back on her feet in no time, wondering what on earth had happened.

Anderson-Brown invited Dr. Popham back to his suite to discuss the events of the day and between them they drained the contents of the mini bar in celebration.

Dr. Popham, unused to drinking in the same quantities as Anderson-Brown, was incapable of driving home and spent the night in the spare bed in the suite.

His wife wasn't surprised when he didn't come home that night. There was probably an emergency and he hadn't had the time or opportunity to call.

The following morning, with great trepidation, they opened up the door of Andaman Sea's box to find her munching away happily at her hay net. They congratulated themselves on their apparent success and fixed the operation for Nathan's top mare for the following Friday.

Anderson-Brown returned to the stud the following Wednesday as agreed with Dr. Popham. With him were the remaining embryos.

Nathan Grant was informed that the operation was going ahead on the Friday and on receiving the news demanded a report the moment the operation was finished.

Janice was informed that if either Anderson-Brown or Dr. Popham phoned, the call was to be put trough immediately – no matter what.

Janice just assumed that from the urgency of the instruction an emergency had arisen at the stud and that Nathan Grant was awaiting an outcome.

In that respect she was right, although even if the operation were a success, it would still take a little time to see if the embryo implant had been accepted by the mare.

Andaman Sea, meanwhile, had recovered well and as yet there were no signs of rejection.

Dr. Popham was visibly relieved that Andaman Sea's operation had been successful, and was now almost looking forward to operating on Nathan Grant's prize mare, Supernova.

Julian Anderson-Brown was also relieved that the operation had gone well. His reputation and more had been staked on it, and the bonus that he had been promised was now within reach.

The Legacy

The irony then struck him. He was in possession of a mare that was carrying the identical embryo that was about to be implanted in Nathan Grant's mare. The stallion had been the template for the embryos, and once the extra gene had been added, then the mare was merely a vessel in which the embryo would develop. The pedigree of the mare didn't matter.

Anderson-Brown would find himself the prospective owner of a foal every bit as good as Nathan Grant's – and only he knew it.

As far as Dr. Popham knew, Andaman Sea had been impregnated with a standard embryo, and stud records would show that Andaman Sea had been mated with Coral Reef. Nathan Grant knew nothing about the operation and Dr. Popham was hardly going to admit to having had a trial run.

All this left Anderson-Brown with quite a dilemma. What on earth was he going to do with the resulting foal?

He had seen the obscene amount of money that racing at the highest level could bring and he was within touching distance of it, but without compromising his position with Nathan Grant, how could he capitalise on it? Perhaps he could enter it in races that Nathan Grant wouldn't put his into and earn some prize money that way. Or there was always the gambling aspect.

If he played his cards right he might just get away with it, but he would have to be careful – very careful – not to arouse Nathan Grant's suspicions, or goodness knows what the consequences would be.

That Friday afternoon, Nathan Grant received the phone

call he had been expecting. All had gone according to plan. He walked over to his cigar cabinet and fetched out the biggest cigar he had.

He sat back in his chair having swivelled round to gaze out of the window.

Moistening one end of his cigar with his lips he then lit the other, smiling to himself as the thin coil of smoke wafted lazily towards the ceiling.

Anderson-Brown and Dr. Popham had done it!

Although his 'plan' was still in its early stages, the 'scientific technicalities' had been overcome and time would tell whether Anderson-Brown had lived up to his side of the deal.

There would still be some time before the foal would be born and some time after that until its potential could be assessed but at least the plan was now well underway.

Nathan Grant was usually an impatient man, but in this case, he would have to sit back and let nature take its course, having now come to the point where he couldn't meddle with the prospective outcome any further.

Following the successful operation on Supernova, Anderson-Brown spent that Friday night celebrating in one of the local pubs closest to the stud.

He had found that a lot of the stud staff went there, and he had taken to joining them and was soon regarded as an honorary local.

The stud staff didn't quite know what to make of the scientist who had been working so secretively with Dr. Popham. They made such an odd couple. Dr. Popham was the epitome of an upstanding professional person whose idea of a celebration might be a couple of glasses of wine at Christmas – that's if he even came to the staff party. He was aloof and rarely mixed socially.

Anderson-Brown, on the other hand, could drink as much as any Irishman in the bar and more often than not still be left standing at the end of the night. He certainly didn't dress like a professional person – no shirt and tie for him – it was usually cord trousers and a chequered shirt open at the frayed collar and with a couple of buttons missing.

Dr. Popham had a devoted wife and two children to go home to, whereas Anderson-Brown had no-one, so the pub regulars became his 'family.'

They also liked him because he was generous with his rounds and could tell a good yarn – and how the Irish loved a good tale.

Most of his tales were wild stories about his experiments, producing super animals the likes of which God never intended. They all took his stories with a pinch of salt – as all good Irish stories should be – since part of it they couldn't understand and the other part seemed impossible.

Despite this they all liked him, excusing the embellishments of his tales as an attempt to gain friendship by entertaining the locals – not to mention too much Guinness.

Occasionally the lads had to almost carry him back, whilst listening to his drunken babbling about genes, hamsters, super horses and Dr. Popham.

They laughed and humoured him and at the same time felt sorry for him as he seemed slightly insane.

Back at the university, Anderson-Brown continued his

drinking binges. He had worked long, hard hours to achieve Nathan Grant's goal, and now that the pressure was off he seemed unable to stop himself.

At Dr. Popham's insistence, Andaman Sea was removed from the stud at the earliest opportunity and put into livery close by where Dr. Popham could keep an eye on her.

Anderson-Brown was relieved that Dr. Popham had made all the arrangements since it had belatedly dawned on him that he now had the responsibilities that went with owning Andaman Sea, and if there was one thing that Anderson-Brown wasn't good at – it was in being responsible.

Dr. Popham kept him informed of Andaman Sea's progress and that of Supernova, and once the pregnancies were confirmed arranged for Andaman Sea to be taken to England and put into livery there to await foaling. He certainly felt a lot more comfortable with Andaman Sea out of Ireland.

Anderson-Brown now regarded his work as done. It was Dr. Popham's job to ensure that Nathan Grant's mare came to term successfully, and the lady at the livery where Andaman Sea was being kept was being paid enough to ensure the horse was being well looked after.

The thought that he had in effect double crossed Nathan Grant weighed heavily on his mind. He would have to be careful – so very careful – not to reveal the truth. God only knows what the consequences would be if Nathan Grant were to find out.

Anderson-Brown shuddered at the thought.

Perhaps he should get rid of the mare, but the thought of the value of the foal outweighed his fears, and greed got the better of him.

He worried daily about his secret and barely slept at night.

In an effort to forget about it, he carried on drinking long into the night. The only peace he got was in a state of drunken unconsciousness.

The more he thought about his predicament, the more he drank and the worse he felt.

Work, which he so used to enjoy, no longer interested him. How could he exceed what he had already done. Worse still, there was no-one he could tell, no-one to confide in, no lectures to give on it and no papers to write about it.

All seemed to be going according to plan when early one morning Nathan Grant received a rather disturbing phone call from William Middleton.

Middleton had insisted to Janice that he speak to Nathan Grant in person – immediately, and on mentioning that it was in reference to Dr. Anderson-Brown was put through straight away.

'Mr. Grant, William Middleton here. I'm sorry to trouble you, but I thought I should inform you that Dr. Anderson-Brown is becoming increasingly erratic in his work, and as he is working at the university at your insistence I thought it best to let you know.'

'What do you mean by erratic?' asked Nathan, irritated that William Middleton should be bothering him with this matter. After all, now that he had completed their 'deal', what he got up to now was of little concern to him even if Grant Global Communications were still funding the grant.

There was a slight hesitation on the other end of the

phone as William Middleton summoned up the courage to tell Nathan Grant – after all, he didn't want Grant to think that he was trying to get rid of Anderson-Brown, but just lately his behaviour had become intolerable.

'He's always late for lectures, that's if he bothers to turn up at all. His research seems to have ground to a halt through lack of interest, and on the odd occasion he has turned up at the university still drunk from the night before. It really has become intolerable.'

Nathan Grant thought carefully for a moment. He couldn't afford to upset Anderson-Brown in case he revealed their agreement, so he couldn't afford to invoke any serious disciplinary action.

'I'm afraid that Anderson-Brown is your problem. Discipline him how you like, but he remains at the university. Now, bother me again on this matter and you will have some serious personal problems of your own to deal with.'

William Middleton was about to protest when the phone was put down the other end.

It was all very well Nathan Grant insisting that he stayed on in his position, but the problems he was causing and the resentment from the other academic staff were becoming unbearable. However, with the threat of his past being revealed he would have to settle for having a quiet word with Anderson-Brown to see if he could at least moderate his behaviour.

Following the phone call, Nathan Grant had become quite concerned about Anderson-Brown's behaviour.

He recalled the first time they had met and how – after a few drinks – he had become quite indiscreet.

The last thing that Nathan Grant wanted was for Anderson-Brown to let slip their arrangement whilst on one of his drinking sessions.

There was only one way to find out. He picked up the phone.

'Janice, get hold of Brad Walters and ask if he can come and see me any time today. The sooner the better.'

Brad Walters used to be head of security at Grant Global Communications, but his unorthodox methods could have become a liability to the company had they become public knowledge. Nathan, not wishing to lose such a reliable and flexible employee, set him up in his own business as a private investigator.

Nathan knew he could rely on Brad to carry out any task that he didn't want his own security staff to get involved in. Usually it was checking the background of a prospective girlfriend, investigating his own staff he suspected of being disloyal or silencing the odd enemy.

There was nothing that Brad would not do or arrange to have done – for a price, and Nathan knew that it would be carried out with the utmost discretion.

Brad Walters arrived to see Nathan later that afternoon. He liked working for Nathan. It was more stimulating than the run of the mill missing person investigations or following the wife or husband of a jealous spouse. The case he had been working on he handed over to one of his staff, leaving himself free to devote his time to whatever Nathan wanted him for.

Nathan also paid him well, allowing him a lifestyle he wouldn't ordinarily have on the profits from his usual cases.

Janice showed him into Nathan's office immediately.

'Hello, Brad, how's business?' Nathan asked, walking over and shaking Brad's hand.

'Fine, Nathan, can't complain.'

Whenever Nathan looked at Brad, he couldn't get over how ordinary and insignificant Brad looked. He wasn't very tall at 5'8", was thin and wiry with a mop of fair hair, pale complexion and was almost feeble looking. Nathan knew, however, that Brad had muscles of steel, was a martial art expert, a crack marksman and could outrun all but the very best athlete at any distance. He also had powers of concentration beyond most men, and could out-think and out-plan anyone Nathan knew.

Brad's strength was that he was so ordinary looking and could therefore blend into the background when following a suspect or seemingly pose no threat if on a more complex mission.

'So, Nathan, what have you got for me?' Brad asked, hoping it would be more challenging than his more recent cases.

Nathan tossed him a file on Anderson-Brown which Brad glanced quickly through.

'Dr. Anderson-Brown has been working for me on a little private project whilst engaging in research work funded by Grant Global. It would appear that since the first part of the project involving his expertise has been completed, he has been celebrating the success of it to the extreme. As he is a man who drinks excessively, I am concerned that he might become – shall we say – a little indiscreet, and any indiscretion would have rather unfortunate consequences for myself. What I would like you to do is to get close to him and find out if he is revealing more than he should, and if so, to get back to me immediately.'

'So how will I know when he has crossed the line?' asked Brad.

'I'll decide that. Wire yourself up and give me the transcripts of your conversations. Just try to get him to talk about racehorses.'

'Sure, no problem.'

Brad took no offence that Nathan did not want to reveal what their "arrangement" was, and wasn't the remotest bit interested. Without knowing, he could carry out his job with a cold, clinical, unbiassed detachment that was his trade mark.

'And if you decide that he has overstepped the mark?'

Nathan paused before carefully answering.

'Then the outcome must be very unfortunate for him before it becomes unfortunate for me.'

A smile flickered on Brad's face. This could become a very highly paid job indeed.

'I'll get onto it right away,' said Brad, eager to start reading the file on Anderson-Brown and planning his campaign.

'He was also at my stud in Ireland, so you may need to go there as well. Here's a cheque to cover any expenses, together with your usual fee for the first week. I trust that's in order.'

'Yes, fine, thank you,' replied Brad. That's another thing he liked about Nathan Grant. There was never any quibbling over expenses, fees or moneys for a job like this. The extras could be negotiated later – if and when the time came. 'I've cleared my desk so this has my undivided attention and as soon as I have anything, I'll send the transcripts straight away.'

'Good. That's what I want to hear. Time is of the

essence,' replied Nathan. Every minute that went by was another minute that Nathan felt control of the situation slipping from his fingers and it was a feeling that he didn't like.

After Brad had gone, Nathan stood staring out of his office window, watching the heavy clouds roll over London, depositing their contents in sheets of rain, lashing the traffic and scurrying pedestrians below.

With a sense of relief, he sat back at his desk. Now that Brad was on the case, he would start getting the answers to those nagging doubts that had been troubling him since William Middleton's call.

Within a couple of days, the first transcripts were on Nathan's desk. They made uncomfortable reading.

Julian Anderson-Brown had been rambling on about his work, making references to hamsters, super horses, the Irish stud and how the world would one day stand up and take note of his work. Most seemed the incoherent ramblings of a drunk, but Nathan knew that if some of the comments made were elaborated on, then it wouldn't be long before Julian Anderson-Brown would reveal all.

A few days later Brad Walters returned from a trip to the stud with transcripts of conversations with staff and locals at the bar where Anderson-Brown seemed to have spent his evenings.

There was nothing that had raised any suspicions amongst them. In fact they thought him quite eccentric with wild tales of his work and the freaks that he had seemingly produced. Most of them had taken his tales with a pinch of salt and had listened to him more because

Anderson-Brown was generous with his rounds than out of interest in what he was saying.

As soon as Nathan had read Brad's latest report, he summoned him to his office.

'So, what's the verdict then?' Brad asked, eager to know if there was still unfinished work to be done.

'I don't think that he has done any damage yet, although he's getting very close to the mark on occasions. I have a feeling that it won't be long before he oversteps it.'

'My thoughts exactly,' replied Brad. 'I don't know what your arrangement with him is, and I don't want to know either – that's strictly between you and him – but I get the feeling that he wants to say more but is fighting to hold it back. This is eating him up inside, so he's drinking more and more.'

'I was afraid of that,' sighed Nathan, stroking his chin, deep in thought.

'So, before the consequences become a problem for you, you would like me to put a stop to any further prospective leaks?'

Nathan admired the way Brad was able to use such benign business terms for what he was proposing. At least it saved Nathan from having to use more direct terms.

'Yes, put a permanent stop to it as soon as possible.' Nathan thought for a moment before continuing.

'Dr. Anderson-Brown was due a nice bonus of £50,000 shortly. As he will not be needing it, let's make it your fee.'

'Most generous of you, Nathan,' replied Brad with a smile. 'I'll get on to it right away.'

After Brad had gone, Nathan sat down smiling to

himself. With Brad getting Anderson-Brown's bonus, this wasn't costing him any extra at all. What a wonderful irony there was to it.

That would then leave only him and Dr. Popham with knowledge of the deal, and he knew that Dr. Popham wouldn't reveal anything; after all, as a devoted family man he had too much to lose. There would be no problem keeping him quiet if the need arose.

Julian Anderson-Brown awoke with yet another massive hangover. His head was spinning, his eyes had problems focussing, his throat was bone dry and there was a sickly taste in his mouth. He also had a splitting headache.

He got unsteadily to his feet, holding his head in one hand whilst pulling himself upright with the other. He was still fully clothed from the night before.

He glanced over at the clock and groaned. He was already late for his first lecture. If he rushed, he might just make the second.

A few stumbling steps later and he realised that he wasn't rushing anywhere.

Groaning quietly to himself he walked tentatively to the bathroom, where he cut himself twice shaving and had to brush his teeth three times to try and get rid of that awful taste.

He changed and decided to give breakfast a miss, opting instead for two aspirins and a strong black coffee.

As he crossed from the accommodation block to the research block at the university, the fresh air sobered him up slightly and the aspirins had started to dull the thumping headache.

He vowed, as he did every morning, not to drink so much again.

He had missed his new friend and drinking partner Brad. Brad had turned up at his local a week ago, and the two of them soon became hardened drinking companions. Brad would tell wild tales of his days as a mercenary – tales which Anderson-Brown found hard to believe as Brad looked such a wimp – but were highly entertaining none the less.

Anderson-Brown tried to make his life sound as interesting; if only he could tell him about his big secret – now that would impress Brad. He longed to confide in his friend, but for the time being he dropped a little hint here and there about a hush hush deal he had going.

Brad had gone away for a couple of days, and Anderson-Brown felt surprisingly depressed drinking alone. He worried that he might have said too much without realising it, but Brad was such a good mate and never seemed to take much interest anyway. Besides, Brad was often the more drunk of the two of them.

He reached his office and found a message on his desk that Dr. Popham had called and wanted him to ring him back urgently.

After a second strong black coffee, Anderson-Brown returned the call, fearing that it was bad news about Nathan Grant's mare.

'Popham, Anderson-Brown here. How's the mare – no bad news I hope?'

'No, she's fine, how's Andaman Sea?'

'No news is good news,' said Anderson-Brown, guilty that it had been such a long time since he had checked on the mare's progress.

'So, why the phone call?'

'Look, there was a chap here yesterday and one of the lads says he was asking questions about you – what you were doing here – things you've been saying – that kind of thing. You've not been telling anyone about the project have you?' From Dr. Popham's voice he sounded very concerned.

Anderson-Brown thought for a moment.

'No, not breathed a word,' he replied, wondering why anyone would be investigating him.

'He even went down to the pub, asking the locals about you. Are you sure you've not said anything?' Dr. Popham's anxious tone had increased.

'No, nothing.' Anderson Brown thought again, but no, he couldn't think of anything he might have said, although there was the odd occasion when he couldn't remember anything at all.

'Well, I thought I had better let you know. For heaven's sake be careful. Mr. Grant is not the sort of man to cross.' Then almost as a afterthought he added, 'Oh, by the way, this man was short and thin with sandy coloured hair and fairly pale skin.'

Dr. Popham rang off leaving Anderson-Brown in a cold sweat. Surely not – it couldn't be Brad. Not good old Brad.

It tied in with Brad having been away. The more he thought, the more of a bad feeling he had about this. It was Brad who had befriended him, not the other way round, Brad who always bought that one extra round, and Brad who would ask about his work.

Anderson-Brown sat down stunned. All those drinking sessions he had with Brad – what on earth had he said?

Had anything got back to Nathan Grant? What if Nathan Grant were behind it?

His mind cleared instantly from the hangover as fear and adrenalin took over.

If he had been indiscreet, then he was in trouble – big trouble. If Nathan Grant was suspicious about him, then he was still in big trouble, and he knew what Nathan Grant was capable of.

He got up, locked the office door and took the phone off the hook. He had a lot of thinking to do if he was going to get out of this.

Not a lot of time passed before Anderson-Brown reached the uncomfortable conclusion that he was expendable. It was a very unpleasant feeling.

He then turned his thoughts to how he could get his revenge on Nathan Grant and what would hurt him most if the unthinkable happened. It was then he hit upon a master plan.

He phoned Mr. Pierce, his solicitor, and arranged an appointment for the following day.

He avoided going to his local that evening, fearful of meeting Brad there – just in case it was Brad who had been investigating him. Perhaps he was just being paranoid, but a sixth sense told him that something was very badly wrong.

Late the following afternoon he concluded his business with Mr. Pierce. It took a lot of persuading, but eventually Mr. Pierce had agreed to his demands and by 6p.m., with a feeling of great relief, he drove back to the university – a huge weight lifted from his mind. At least if the worst happened, he would get his revenge on Nathan Grant.

As he got into his car, he noticed a black car parked at

the bottom of the road well away from the street lights. He thought he had seen it earlier outside his flat when he left for the solicitor's.

He got into his car and headed for home, the car following. A feeling of fear and panic welled up inside him. He cursed.

His solicitor's was out of town and the main road back ran through open countryside for a few miles before reaching a built-up area again.

He accelerated slightly. The black car did too.

A car passed in the opposite direction, and as it did, Anderson-Brown looked in his rear view mirror. The driver of the car was momentarily lit by the passing car's headlights. He was small and had sandy brown hair and looked ominously familiar.

Anderson-Brown felt sick. He turned off onto a country lane, taking a short cut home.

He never made it.

A driver later phoned the emergency services saying that he had come across an overturned car. He had gone to investigate but found the driver dead in about a foot of water in the ditch beside the road. He had tried his best to revive him but was unable.

The police took his details and thanked him for his efforts.

The sandy haired driver then got back into his black Ford car and drove off, waiting until he had turned the corner before smiling at the thought of what an easy job it had been and the bonus he was about to collect.

6

In the months after her uncle's death, Emily tried to come to terms with her unusual inheritance. It had been a very difficult period.

Although she had very little contact with her uncle, she felt his loss more than she thought possible – after all, he was her last and only next of kin. At least before the accident, there was a member of the family out there. Now there was no-one.

The only other person she had to rely on was Greg, and he was becoming more of a disappointment to her with each passing day.

Greg – her rock, her companion and her best friend – was proving to be petulant, bad tempered, selfish and spoilt, who, on not getting his own way, would take his wrath out on Emily.

The subject of his anger was Emily's inheritance, or more specifically the money that came with it. Never had he been so close to such a sum, but the conditions for its use proved to be a source of great frustration and anger.

He couldn't understand or accept how anyone could leave that amount of money to spend on a horse, and despite Emily's best attempts at explaining the will, he couldn't understand how she just accepted the conditions without claiming that her uncle was insane – anything to free up the money.

He tried the romantic approach, wined and dined her, told her he loved her and what a wonderful life they could have together if only . . .

When that didn't work, he tried a different approach and stopped contributing towards the household expenses. After all, he argued, as she had inherited all that money, she could afford the bills.

Throughout it all, Emily tried not to lose her temper despite the feeling of anger and resentment that had built up inside her.

She loved Greg and needed him now more than ever, but he was becoming increasingly distant and cold towards her.

The only other person she could confide in was Mr. Pierce, the solicitor. She enjoyed their meetings to discuss expenses and the transfer of ownership of Andaman Sea.

Mr. Pierce admired the way that Emily had taken responsibility for the predicament her uncle had left her in, and by doing that had certainly made his life a lot easier. He also felt some degree of responsibility in not having talked Anderson-Brown out of leaving such outrageous conditions in the will.

He looked forward to their meetings, hoping that he could help Emily in any way, guiding her or just proving a person she could talk to.

It was at one of these meetings that they both reached the same conclusion – that there was barely enough money to carry out the terms of the will. There would, after all, shortly be two horses to budget for and then the training fees, which would be considerably more than the current livery bills. This left them with quite a dilemma. The terms of the will stated that the resulting foal must be entered in the Derby or be destroyed, but there was barely enough funds to carry out the terms.

Emily, practical as ever, came up with a solution. Perhaps she could offer to help out at Mrs. Forsyth's in exchange for a reduction in the livery bill – after all, she spent enough time there, why not do some work.

Mr. Pierce agreed that this was a wonderful idea and Emily duly negotiated a substantial reduction in fees in return for helping out.

Emily was overjoyed. Recently she had felt happiest at the stables, chatting to Mrs. Forsyth and talking to Andaman Sea, telling the horse all her problems which she would listen to with one ear cocked backwards.

Emily dreaded telling Greg that she would be working there part time since she knew what his reaction would be. When she finally plucked up the courage to tell him, the reaction was predictable.

'So, not only do you have to spend all the money on that damn animal, but you are going to have to work to pay towards it as well! You are unbelievable!'

'I don't have to do it,' Emily lied, trying to defend herself, 'I want to do it. I enjoy being at the yard and it will be a nice break from work.'

'You used to enjoy going out with me,' shouted Greg, his anger bubbling to the surface, 'but now you prefer to spend all your time with a bloody horse!'

'We can still go out in the evenings,' Emily replied, trying her best to pacify him.

'If you think I'm taking you out smelling of horse shit then you've got another thing coming!'

Before Emily could say another word, Greg was out of the front door, slamming it behind him with a force that made Emily wince.

It had gone exactly as she had expected.

Greg was right about one thing, she did prefer Andaman Sea's company far more than his at this moment in time.

The following Saturday morning Emily was roused from a deep sleep by the phone ringing.

She reached out from under the covers and after a couple of attempts found the phone next to the bed.

'Hello,' she said, still half asleep.

'Hello, Emily, is that you?'

'Yes,' answered Emily, still not alert enough to recognise the voice.

'It's Mrs. Forsyth, from the stables here.'

Emily was instantly awake.

'There's nothing wrong, is there?' Emily said, overcome with concern at the early hour of the phone call.

'No, don't panic, it's wonderful news. Andaman Sea produced a colt foal during the night. They're both fine. No complications or anything. The mare handled it like a real pro.'

'Oh, gosh,' was all Emily could say, she was so overcome with relief and emotion.

'Why don't you come down as soon as you can and see them? He's a strapping little lad and Andaman Sea seems so proud of him.'

'I will, I'll come down right away if that's OK,' Emily replied, half out of bed already.

'Yes, of course. You can have breakfast with me.'

'See you shortly then.'

Emily put down the phone and was dressed in a flash.

She glanced at the clock – it was just gone 6a.m. The half of the bed next to her was empty, as was the spare bedroom where Greg seemed to spend the nights when he bothered to come home.

Emily was almost relieved by his absence; she didn't want any of his sarcastic comments to spoil this special day.

She dashed downstairs, kicking off her slippers and slipping on her shoes. She grabbed her thick jacket and handbag, picked up her car keys and with barely a backward glance was off.

There was so little traffic at that time of the morning that Emily reached the stables in record time.

She dashed over to the office, where the glow of a light cast a faint shadow over the yard.

She burst into the office to be greeted by Mrs. Forsyth.

'How are they?' Emily asked, barely able to contain the combination of anxiety and excitement.

'Come and see for yourself,' beamed Mrs. Forsyth as she picked up her well-worn jacket from the chair before stepping out into the icy cold morning.

They went over to Andaman Sea's box where Emily peered in anxiously.

The mare looked over towards Emily, slowly came to the door then nuzzled Emily's outstretched hand so softly that it almost felt like silk brushing against her hand.

Behind Andaman Sea, Emily could just see the tiny foal. He was still a little unsteady on his legs, which seemed to have locked themselves in a rigid, slightly splayed state in an effort to stop him from falling over. His coat seemed almost fluffy and his mane stood up like the bristles of a brush. His little tail thrashed anxiously back and forth.

The foal looked apprehensively at Emily, almost peering out from behind his mother who seemed to be protecting him. His eyes were as wide as a child's at Christmas, taking in the wondrous world to which he had just been born.

Down his muzzle was a white blaze that zigzagged like a bolt of lightning down to his nostrils. Emily could also see that he had one white sock on his right fore leg.

He was so sweet that Emily had to bite her lip to stop herself crying. It didn't, however, stop a couple of tears from rolling silently down her cheeks.

'He's so – so gorgeous,' she eventually said, unable to take her eyes off him.

All the while the foal stared warily at Emily.

'And his legs are so – well – long and spindly!'

'Don't worry, when they're born, all foals seem to be slightly out of proportion in comparison to a fully grown horse.'

'Oh,' said Emily feeling a little silly that she didn't already know that.

She reached into her pocket and got out a couple of polo mints which she fed to Andaman Sea. The foal retreated even further behind his mother, a little frightened of Emily's movements, feeling safer with the protection of his mother between him and the strangers.

Emily watched them for about ten minutes in silent wonderment and sense of relief that her actions in taking up the conditions of her uncle's will had been vindicated.

The Legacy

'Come on, let's have some breakfast,' said Mrs. Forsyth, realising that she would have a hard job to drag Emily away from Andaman Sea and the foal. 'They need a little peace and quiet.'

'Oh – OK,' Emily replied, reluctantly following Mrs. Forsyth back to the house.

She had been so engrossed that she had barely noticed the cold, and pulled her jacket tighter for warmth.

Once back in the house, Mrs. Forsyth quickly busied herself in the kitchen, frying a breakfast that would have done a labourer proud.

Emily stood in the kitchen, lost for words.

'Here, a nice cup of coffee will soon thaw you out.'

Mrs. Forsyth handed Emily the cup of steaming coffee.

'Thank you, Mrs. Forsyth.'

'Oh, please, call me Mary. Mrs. Forsyth makes me feel so old. Come on, come and sit down and tuck in.'

They sat down to the enormous fried breakfast. Emily suddenly realised how hungry she was and it was soon devoured.

'So, have you any ideas for a name for the little chap?'

'No, I hadn't really thought about it,' Emily replied, wiping the grease from her lips with a napkin.

'Quite often a foal is named by combining the names or parts of the names of the sire and dam. Alternatively it can be something totally different.'

'I suppose I didn't want to name it until I had seen the foal and knew what sex it was,' Emily replied before draining her coffee cup.

'I know, how about "The Legacy"? After all, that's what he is.'

Mrs. Forsyth thought for a moment. 'That's true, and very appropriate.'

'And we could call him "Leggy" for short, since he has such long spindly legs,' Emily continued.

Mrs. Forsyth laughed and poured some more coffee.

'So, "The Legacy" it is,' said Emily with a sense of determination.

'Here's to The Legacy,' Mrs. Forsyth said holding out her cup of coffee for a toast.

'The Legacy,' Emily replied, holding up her coffee cup too.

They both laughed and drank to the newly born foal.

Meanwhile, back in his box, The Legacy stood close to his mother, comforted by her warmth and protective presence, blissfully unaware of the destiny that had been mapped out for him and the unusual circumstances of his conception.

A week later, in the early hours of the Tuesday morning, Nathan Grant was awoken by a phone call from Dr. Popham.

'Good news, Mr. Grant, Supernova has produced a colt foal.'

'That's great news, how is he?' Nathan replied, his excitement mounting.

'In fine health – couldn't be better. There were no problems at all, and he's the spitting image of Coral Reef, right down to that distinctive blaze and one white sock.'

'Good, that's good news, well done. I'll fly over as soon as I can to see him. In the meantime, I want a twenty four hour watch on him, I would hate for anything to happen to him.'

'Yes, of course, Mr. Grant, I'll make the arrangements immediately.'

'See you shortly then.'

Nathan put the phone down and started pacing up and down the bedroom floor. He could barely contain his excitement.

There had been many foals born at his stud but none so eagerly awaited by Nathan as this one.

He cursed at the thought of the full day of meetings ahead of him which were all too important to cancel. It would be difficult for him to concentrate during them, but Nathan Grant was a supreme businessman, and when it came to important business matters he could close his mind to all but the matters in hand.

Later he managed to rearrange his schedule for the following day and flew out as soon as the last meeting was over.

Dr. Popham stayed on late to meet him.

'So, let's see him then,' said Nathan without so much as a hello.

'Yes, sir,' replied Dr. Popham, keen to show his boss the foal that he had played such an important part in producing.

Dr. Popham led Nathan to the box where Supernova and the foal were.

Nathan peered eagerly in and on seeing the foal, chuckled.

'I see what you mean, spitting image of Coral reef, just as you said.'

'He certainly is, sir,' replied Dr. Popham, admiring the foal.

'Let's just hope he has a quicker turn of foot than him.

Anderson-Brown was certainly paid enough to see that he has. Shame about Anderson-Brown, wasn't it?' Nathan said, changing the topic of conversation without a flicker of emotion.

'Yes, it came as quite a shock,' Dr. Popham replied, trying to disguise the anxiety and doubt in his mind.

He had read about the accident and had an awful feeling that it was not quite what it had seemed. He only hoped that Anderson-Brown hadn't let on about the first mare, Andaman Sea. If so, then he himself was in real trouble.

Since Anderson-Brown's death he had become slightly paranoid, imagining people following him or his phone being tapped and he had a general fear of being alone.

He had problems sleeping at night and had lost his appetite, resulting in the loss of a good few pounds of weight.

The stud staff had borne the brunt of his short temper and irritability. These mood swings they put down to the pressure of the time of year with numerous foals being born. Late, sleepless nights were normal; combined with the odd emergency and the huge expectation that Nathan Grant had of the foal to be born to Supernova, then perhaps his moods were understandable.

'Let's go back to your office, there's a few things I would like to discuss privately,' Nathan said, turning and walking back towards the administration block.

Dr. Popham's heart thumped as he followed Nathan like a condemned man, wondering what it could be that had to be said in private. Dr. Popham could only fear the worst.

They reached the office and Nathan closed the door ominously behind them.

'So, we have a lot to discuss,' Nathan said, sitting down and fixing his stare on Dr. Popham.

'We have?' Dr. Popham replied nervously, fearful of what was coming next.

'Oh, come on now, Dr. Popham, you've done a marvellous job so far, but this is just the beginning,' said Nathan, smiling broadly. 'Has the foal been showing any of the characteristics that we've worked so hard to achieve?'

Dr. Popham tried not to look visibly relieved.

'It's far too early to tell. All one can say at the moment is that he is a normal, healthy, fine looking foal.'

'Healthy and fine looking, yes, but let's hope that he is considerably better than normal,' replied Nathan. 'I want you to keep a special eye on this one. I want full blood tests, the works, and a monthly report from you. If he shows any sign of enhanced ability I want to know immediately. We both know that this foal is different, and I want him treated as such. If Anderson-Brown did his job properly then the foal will be a world beater and I don't want anything to go wrong with his development – do I make myself clear?'

'Quite clear, sir,' Dr. Popham answered, whilst pondering the added workload all these tests and reports would mean for him. Still, it would be fascinating to study the foal in great detail.

'Good. He's to get the best of everything – no expense spared.

I'll leave the details in your capable hands. Lastly, I'll rely on your continuing discretion.'

Dr. Popham looked away to avoid Nathan's piercing stare.

'You can rely on me, sir, and I'll start on the arrangements straight away.'

'I'll call in tomorrow morning before I leave and look forward to your first report then.'

'Yes, sir.'

After Nathan Grant's departure, Dr. Popham was left wondering why on earth he would want a report the following day and what he could put in it that he hadn't already told Mr. Grant.

He looked at his watch and sighed. It was gone 9p.m. He picked up the phone and called his wife.

'Hello, darling. Mr. Grant wants me to prepare a report for first thing tomorrow before he leaves, so I'll have to stay here tonight. Yes, I'm sorry darling, you know how it is. I'll ring you in the morning. Give my love to the kids.'

He put the phone down and began preparing the report, starting with the uneventful birth to detailing the regime of tests he planned to carry out, together with a time scale of vaccinations, routine treatments, and even down to the first three months feed stuffs.

If he was going to spend half the night on this report, then he was determined that his boss would have to spend most of the day reading it.

With any luck he would soon get bored of such long winded reports and request them at longer intervals.

He fetched himself a coffee and sighed as he turned on the computer. It was going to be a long night, but it had to be done.

Nathan Grant was in his office a few moments after Dr. Popham.

'Good morning, Dr. Popham, how's the foal?'

'Fine, sir, I've just been and checked on him. He's doing well.'

'Good. And my report?'

'Here it is, sir.'

Dr. Popham handed over a thick document, the volume of which took Nathan by surprise.

'This must have taken you half the night to prepare,' he commented.

'Yes, sir, it did. When you read it, you'll see that I've laid out the next three months regime for the foal – from veterinary to dietary. I'm sure you will find that I've covered everything.'

'I'm sure you have. Very thorough,' came the reply as Nathan put the file in his briefcase. He would read it on the flight back.

'So, let's go and see him before I have to catch my flight.'

The foal, still nervous of the attention he was getting, peered out anxiously from behind Supernova, who looked a little irritated at the two people who were causing her foal concern. She nuzzled the foal to reassure him and then looked back at Dr. Popham and Nathan Grant.

'He's getting used to people,' said Dr. Popham, 'but at the moment it's best to leave them in peace as much as possible.'

'Agreed. I want the best staff to look after him. I'll leave you to make arrangements with the manager. I'll have a quick word with him to let him know that as far as this foal is concerned, you're in charge.'

'That would certainly help. I wouldn't want to upset anyone by usurping their authority.'

Dr. Popham had already told the staff that Nathan Grant regarded the foal as special. The staff had already guessed this, since any foal of Coral Reef and Supernova was bound to be special. Only Dr. Popham and Nathan Grant knew just how special he was.

On the flight back, Nathan got out the report.

Before reading it, his mind turned to a name for the foal.

He had often pondered a name for it long before it was born, and had eventually come up with the name 'Darwin's Choice.'

This amused him greatly, as Charles Darwin was the father of the theory of evolution and natural selection, and the foal was anything but a result of natural selection.

He smiled at his private joke. Darwin's Choice it was.

It would make him smile every time he thought of the name, and he was sure that it would have the same effect in the forthcoming years when he would be reading of his triumphs in the papers.

When Emily told Greg about The Legacy's birth, it was greeted with complete disinterest.

'You've called it The Legacy, what sort of a stupid name is that? Millstone would be more appropriate,' came the sarcastic reply.

Emily seethed with rage, but was careful not to let her emotions show.

'I just thought I would let you know. Anyway, I'll be spending most of tomorrow at the yard. Mary wants me to help her with a delivery of straw.'

'So, we're on first name terms now, are we? Still, it's

not surprising, you're spending more time there than you are at home.'

'At least I'm doing something and not sitting in front of the television or out with my friends drinking beer,' Emily replied with frustration and anger.

'I much prefer doing that to being Mary's skivvy,' said Greg, opening the newspaper and proceeding to ignore Emily.

'You would,' exclaimed Emily as she strode out of the lounge and headed for the sanctuary of the kitchen.

The situation between her and Greg was becoming intolerable. She wondered why he stayed if he despised her that much. Still, it was costing him nothing to stay, so why move out.

It had crossed her mind to throw him out, but she didn't want to be the creator of the inevitable scene that would follow.

She made herself a cup of coffee and sat down miserably at the kitchen table, opening a book on foal development that Mary had lent her.

Mary had proven to be a good friend and had offered a sympathetic ear to Emily on the odd occasion when Emily felt she had to talk to someone about the situation with Greg.

Mary had understood. Horses could take over your life, thoughts and emotions completely, leaving little room for anyone who didn't share the same passion for them.

Emily had kept to herself the plans that her uncle had laid out for The Legacy in his will. She would tell Mary at some point, but at the moment she still felt too embarrassed about the situation to tell anyone, and Emily certainly wanted to see if the foal had any potential before revealing her plans.

When she was at the yard, her mood would change instantly. She really enjoyed the work, no matter what it was, and with Mary's guidance was a quick learner and soon became invaluable.

The Legacy seemed to grow so quickly; he was no longer a gangly ungainly foal.

With the amount of time she spent at the yard, she and The Legacy soon became firm friends, and one of Emily's favourite times was letting Andaman Sea and The Legacy out in a paddock and watch the foal buck, kick and gallop round, enjoying the freedom of the open air, whilst Andaman Sea looked on like a proud mother watching over a hyperactive child.

Emily could watch them for hours. She would stand leaning against the gate with her elbows on the top rail and chin in her hands. Andaman Sea would quietly graze as The Legacy would career round the field, skidding to a halt before turning and galloping in the opposite direction for no apparent reason whatsoever.

Life seemed so uncomplicated on these occasions.

Mary often commented on how full of energy The Legacy was, and how poor old Andaman Sea must be worn out just watching him.

When it was time to lead them back, Emily would lead Andaman Sea and The Legacy would eventually follow, sulking like a spoilt brat that playtime was over.

After a couple of months, Mary felt the time had come to broach the subject of separating mother and foal, although The Legacy could no longer be regarded as a foal – he was a colt now.

One coffee break, Mary looked up and noticed Emily staring at Andaman Sea's box.

'Emily, it won't be long now before we'll have to separate Andaman Sea and Leggy; he seems to be getting a little coltish now towards her.'

Emily knew what Mary meant. She had read that there came a time when a colt would start to show an unhealthy interest in his mother. 'Yes, I know, but it just seems so soon,' she sighed, 'and he still seems so young.'

'He'll be OK, he's getting to be a big boy now.'

'I suppose so,' said Emily, sipping her coffee thoughtfully.

She had been dreading this inevitable moment.

'Have you thought of any plans for either of them?' Mary asked, aware that Emily had never spoken of their future.

Emily hesitated for a moment.

'I had hoped to race The Legacy,' she replied, being rather economical with the truth, 'but I don't know about Andaman Sea.'

'Race Leggy,' Mary said thoughtfully. 'Well, his sire was definitely one of the best and Leggy is certainly a live wire, but Andaman Sea's breeding is pretty modest as far as racing is concerned, as was her ability, but then again, a trainer would be better able to advise you on his potential. You do realise that having a horse in training is a very expensive business – far, far more than livery fees.'

'Yes, I know, but I've a little put by and I'd like to give Leggy a chance.'

Emily found the thought of sending The Legacy off to another yard heartbreaking. Mary's yard had seemed like home to her, Andaman Sea and The Legacy, and the thought of having to send him away was like breaking up the family, but it would be inevitable.

'And Andaman Sea?' Mary asked.

'I must admit that I haven't given her future much thought, so at the moment I really have no idea.'

'Shall we go through the possibilities?' Mary asked gently, aware that she had broached a difficult subject.

'Yes, it would certainly help having a second and unbiased opinion,' replied Emily, well aware that her judgement would be clouded by her over emotional attachment to the mare.

'You could put her back into training, but then you'll have the added expense, plus with her past leg problems I doubt whether she would stand up to the rigors of training.'

'Yes, I agree, so that's out.'

'You could keep her in livery, but once again there will be the ongoing expense of keeping her, plus The Legacy's training fees. You could send her to stud, but again, that would be expensive and you'll end up with a third horse.'

'Oh, no, two's quite enough to cope with,' groaned Emily, head in hands.

'There's selling her, and you could put the money towards The Legacy's training fees, but you wouldn't get much for her with her past leg problems. She may be fine now, but that would certainly count against her.'

The thought of selling Andaman Sea appalled Emily. 'No, that would really have to be a last resort.'

'Lastly, you could loan her to someone. I know a few people who have horses on loan. They take over the upkeep and expenses of the horse so they can ride them out as hacks or hunt with them.'

Emily looked up. At last there seemed to be a reasonable solution.

'You mean I would still own her but someone takes over everything else?'

'Yes, that's right. Of course you would be able to have her back at any time.'

'What about her bad leg?' Emily asked, concerned that this could be a problem.

'I tend to think that her leg trouble would only recur if she were in heavy training where a lot of intensive work is involved.

Anyone taking her on as a hack wouldn't subject her to the same amount of exercise, so I doubt the leg would give way. Besides, the people I know would all respect that there could be a potential problem and would adjust the work load accordingly.'

'That sounds to be the lesser of the evils,' said Emily, still reluctant at the thought of someone else looking after her.

'These friends of yours, would they still let me see her?'

'Of course,' Mary replied, patting Emily's hand for reassurance.

'In fact they usually use my stables, so Andaman Sea probably won't even be moved.'

'Would you give me a couple of days to think about it before making any enquiries?'

'Of course, take your time. It's not a decision to be rushed.

It'll be a week or so before we separate them, but rest

assured that if you go with the loan option, I wouldn't recommend anyone that I wouldn't trust with my own horses, so Andaman Sea would be in very good, kind, capable hands.'

"But not mine", thought Emily ruefully.

Emily thought over the matter and discussed it with Mr. Pierce the next time she dropped off the livery bills, which had increased dramatically since the arrival of The Legacy.

Mr. Pierce thought the loan option for Andaman Sea a wonderful idea as he knew how attached Emily had got to the mare. Also there was no provision in the will for the upkeep of Andaman Sea after the birth of the foal, so this seemed the best and most practical solution all round.

The evening, Emily went to the yard to do a couple of hours work and afterwards sat down with Mary and told her of the decision she had made.

'I think you're right,' agreed Mary, relieved that Emily had come to this decision. 'Loaning out Andaman Sea is the only option.'

'Could you ask around your friends then and see if anyone is interested?'

'Yes, of course, I'll give a couple of them a ring tonight.'

'I know it sounds silly, but would it be possible for me to meet them? I wouldn't want to hand over Andaman Sea to a complete stranger.' Emily asked, hoping the request was not too ridiculous.

'They wouldn't expect anything else,' laughed Mary. 'Besides, they would want to get to know you too. As soon as I have any news I'll give you a call.'

Before she left, Emily went over to see Andaman Sea and Leggy. Without so much as a greeting, Andaman Sea was trying to get her nose in Emily's pocket for the polo mints she always had with her.

'That's not very ladylike, is it,' laughed Emily, hastily feeding her a couple. 'Whatever happened to your manners?'

Andaman Sea crunched noisily on the mints and in a couple of seconds they were gone.

The Legacy pushed his mother out of the way for his mints, which disappeared with equal speed.

Emily sighed. The Legacy seemed to have grown every time she saw him.

She patted the mare's neck and stroked her soft muzzle. Emily felt so guilty that she was contemplating lending her to someone, but Mary was right; to keep her in a stable out of sentimental attachment just wasn't fair. Although Emily had started riding lessons since working at the yard, she wasn't up to the standard of riding a former racehorse and couldn't afford to keep the two horses anyway.

Andaman Sea would certainly be far better off and happier with someone who would give her the exercise she needed, not to mention a more interesting life.

Emily tried to think that she was doing it for Andaman Sea's benefit, but no matter how she put it, she couldn't help feeling that she was letting the mare down.

Back at the stud, the life of Darwin's Choice was being run like a military campaign.

Every hour was logged and reported on, everything he ate was monitored and recorded. The slightest rise in temperature prompted a battery of blood tests, and even his urine and droppings were analysed daily for good measure.

He was regularly weighed, measured and examined.

Dr. Popham threw himself into the project with renewed enthusiasm, relieved that his fears of him suffering the same fate as Anderson-Brown were unfounded.

His monthly reports to Nathan Grant were meticulous and thorough, so much so that half the time Nathan Grant had no idea what they meant.

Suffice in to say that Darwin's Choice was progressing well, and in some departments better than normal, which was what Nathan Grant wanted to hear.

Darwin's Choice's ability to run the other colts ragged in the paddock proved a particular delight to Nathan.

As soon as Darwin's Choice was old enough, he was separated from his mother, who was immediately returned to brood mare duties.

Life at the stud ran like clockwork, and there was no room for sentimentality. The stud, after all, was an extension of Nathan's business empire and he was never sentimental about business.

With all the blood tests, weighing, measuring, examining, poking and prodding, Darwin's Choice was rapidly developing into a surly bad tempered colt. He was not treated with any compassion or kindness, and as a result was soon able to give as good as he got.

The lads who looked after him often sported bite marks, bruises and the odd broken bones when they hadn't been able to get out of his way quick enough.

One lad, fearful of yet another bruising encounter, took a riding crop in with him whilst mucking out and when Darwin's Choice tried to take a chunk out of his shoulder, the lad gave him a couple of slaps on the rump. All hell broke loose and the lad had to be rescued by two others. When he was discharged from hospital the lad was instantly dismissed and it took a few days before the colt calmed down, showing the whites of his eyes and snorting at anyone he thought a threat – almost daring the lads to take him on.

It wasn't long before Darwin's Choice had the reputation of being the biggest bully in the stud, and the lads selected to look after him, who had previously been treated with envy at being selected to look after the star colt in the stud, were now regarded with sympathy.

Dr. Popham would include a little in his reports about Darwin's aggressive behaviour, but Nathan regarded this as an essential quality of a top horse and wasn't unduly worried, after all, you had to have an aggressive attitude to win.

Andaman Sea and The Legacy were parted and placed in separate boxes.

Emily could barely sleep that night, she felt so guilty, even though she knew it was for the best.

For a couple of days, Andaman Sea fretted and The Legacy seemed confused at being alone, but gradually they got used to it.

Emily met Kathy, a friend of Mary who was looking for a horse to have on loan. Emily like her immediately and knew that Andaman Sea would be in good hands. Kathy lived locally and wanted Andaman Sea to stay at Mary's, which delighted Emily as she could still carry on seeing her as often as before.

Meanwhile the situation with Greg was becoming more

Angela Woodward

awkward. Emily felt that she was like two different people – the happy one when she was at work at the stable, and the other person who was withdrawn and introvert at home, fearing when the next confrontation would occur.

Emily reached breaking point in late autumn, when she arrived home from a particularly stressful day at work to find that Greg had left a rather intimate note from a girl called Tina on the kitchen table. Perhaps he had done it on purpose, but Emily seethed as she read the contents and realised that they had been seeing each other for some time.

When Emily thought about it, she wasn't really surprised or upset about it, just angry that he had been deceiving her. Affection had long since disappeared from their relationship, but if he was still living with her surely a little loyalty was in order.

She waited for him to come home to confront him.

The key turned in the front door and she heard the door shut and his footsteps in the hall as she waited in the kitchen.

As he entered the kitchen, he saw the note on the table and Emily standing there with a thunderous look on her face.

'So, who's Tina then?' Emily asked, shaking with rage.

'Oh, no-one special. We're just good friends,' Greg replied unconvincingly.

'Come off it, Greg, credit me with a little intelligence! So how long have you been seeing her?' Emily demanded.

Greg had never seen Emily this angry before, and he couldn't really blame her.

'Um, a couple of months I suppose,' he said, resigned to confessing, as there seemed no point in lying any more. 'You can't exactly say that we've been getting on lately, can you?'

'Then why bother staying!' Emily said, fighting to control the anger.

'I don't know. I guess I didn't want to hurt you.'

Greg tried to sound convincing but it just sounded hollow.

'Come off it, you're doing it because it what suits you best. Free board and lodging, no expenses, you've just been living here like a parasite for the last few months!'

Greg stood sulkily in the kitchen, smarting from the truth of Emily's outburst. There was no way he could get out of this as he could see that Emily was in no mood to compromise.

'It's obvious that you and I are finished, so you can pack your bags and be out by the morning, and if you really wanted to do the decent thing you'd be out tonight!'

Emily stormed out of the kitchen, grabbing her coat and handbag on the way, slamming the front door behind her. She had no idea where to go or what to do; all she knew was that she couldn't bear to be in the same house as Greg.

She didn't want to go round any of her friends, being in no mood to discuss the ending of her relationship with Greg, so she eventually decided to go to the stables. Mary wouldn't ask any questions.

The hour or so that she spent there, talking to The Legacy and feeding him mints, calmed her down.

Realising that it was getting very late she reluctantly decided to go home.

Much to her relief, Greg had packed and gone.

She wandered round from room to room just to convince herself that he had really left. The house was in quite a mess as he had packed and left in a hurry. She decided to leave tidying it up until the next day.

Emily went into the kitchen and made herself a coffee. She sat down at the table, clasping the coffee cup with both hands as tears rolled down her cheeks.

She had no idea why she was crying. Maybe it was on suddenly finding herself alone. It certainly wasn't for Greg, as any love between them had gradually faded from the day that her uncle had died.

Perhaps it was tears of relief, the ending of one chapter in her life and the start of another.

As Emily thought of the future, doubt and insecurity overwhelmed her. It was as if her life was out of control and she had no idea where it would lead.

She finished her coffee and went to bed, curling up under the duvet, pondering what lay ahead.

No doubt life would evolve, and she would have to follow it as best she could, whatever the future held.

Nathan Grant was reading the latest report from Dr. Popham. Darwin's Choice was over a year old now, and last month had been broken – a bruising experience for the lad chosen for the task. The lad had never encountered such a mean, high spirited animal with the stamina to keep kicking and bucking when others would have stopped long ago.

Eventually, after a battle of wills, Darwin's Choice was

at last capable of being ridden, but was by no means easy to handle.

He was certainly proving to be an exceptional colt. With the best of everything money could buy, he had developed into a strapping, handsome animal. His jagged blaze stood out from his dark bay coat, which gleamed in the spring sunshine.

He was always on his toes, like a coiled spring, waiting to explode.

More often than not he was looking for the opportunity to lash out at whoever was handling him, letting the handler know just who was in charge.

Much to the relief of the stud staff, the time came for Darwin's Choice to be transferred to Nathan Grant's top trainer in England – Stuart Lawson.

Unknown to Nathan, the stud staff held a party the night after Darwin's departure, they were so relieved to see him go.

The staff all agreed on one thing – that for all his vices, Darwin's Choice was an exceptional colt and in the right hands would be destined for great things.

Although Emily knew that it was time for The Legacy to be broken, it took a good deal of talking to by Mary to get her to do anything about it.

Somehow just the word – breaking – seemed to imply the breaking of the sprit of the horse, and to Emily, The Legacy had such a kind nature that it seemed almost cruel.

Deep down she knew it had to be done and reluctantly allowed Mary to make the arrangements.

Out of a feeling of guilt she didn't go to the yard that

week and fretted at home, worrying about The Legacy. The odd phone call from Mary eased her worry a little, but Emily was still concerned that The Legacy would come out of the experience a changed horse.

The following weekend she went to the yard with great trepidation and went straight to The Legacy's box. To her joy he seemed just the same, demanding mints and attention. Perhaps he seemed a little older and wiser.

Mary told her that it was all going very well, and that Alan, the man who was doing the breaking, was very impressed with The Legacy. 'One of the finest horses I have ever worked with' was his comment.

During the next week, Emily was at the yard as often as she could make it, watching Alan and Leggy working together.

When Alan mounted Leggy and spent some time trotting and cantering round the paddock, it was such a marvellous sight that Emily had to bite her lip to stop the tears from welling up.

Alan saw Emily at the gate and turned The Legacy and trotted towards her.

'You have a fine colt here, Miss Lloyd, very fine indeed,' he said, patting The Legacy's neck as he tried to snatch at a particular juicy piece of grass that had got his attention. 'What are your plans for him?'

'I want him to go into racing.'

'He'll certainly do well. He's a bit of a baby still, but in the hands of a good trainer he'll soon catch up with the others of his age.'

'I hope so, and thank you for all you've done, Alan.'

The talk of putting him into training unsettled Emily. Although she knew it was inevitable, her uncle's plans seemed so far fetched that she tried to concentrate on life one day at a time.

She considered that she had done well so far – with which Mr. Pierce was in full agreement. She had taken her responsibilities seriously and her efficient handling of the finances had certainly made his life easier.

Emily realised that now the hard work would really begin. Sending The Legacy to a trainer would increase costs dramatically and she would not be able to see so much of him – if anything. To send The Legacy to a trainer felt to her like sending a child to boarding school – except he wouldn't be coming home for the holidays.

She dreaded the thought of not being able to see him, and cursed herself for becoming so attached to him.

Tentatively she broached the subject of trainers with Mary, who seemed to know everything about horses.

'Mary, have you any idea which trainer I should send The Legacy to?'

'I've been wondering when you'd get round to that subject,' Mary replied, aware of the fact that Emily had committed the cardinal sin of regarding The Legacy as a pet and not a racehorse. 'I've prepared a list of local trainers together with their fees. I've kept it local because I thought you wouldn't want him too far away.'

Emily smiled, appreciating Mary's thoughtfulness.

'Yes, you're quite right, thank you.'

Emily glanced at the list and suddenly realised that The Legacy's destiny lay with someone on this piece of paper, but which one?

'They all seem so expensive,' she gasped, looking down the rates with dismay.

'Unfortunately racing is a very expensive business and

these rates are just the start. On top of that there's vet's fees, blacksmith's and numerous others. It'll also be a while before The Legacy races, and even then you aren't guaranteed a decent return even if he wins. Prize money in all but the top races is pretty low. You really have to have an exceptional horse to make any money out of racing.'

Mary saw the look of dismay on Emily's face.

'Are you sure that racing The Legacy is what you really want?'

'Quite sure,' she replied firmly. 'Is there anyone on the list that you would recommend?'

They're all good trainers, although the last one on the list – James Ryan – has only been going just over a year and to be honest hasn't got much quality in his yard to work with so he hasn't been as successful as the others. I've included him because he was champion jockey three years ago and is an exceptional judge of a horse. Not only that, but because he's not been too successful he is the cheapest on the list.'

'The name seems familiar,' Emily recalled. 'Wasn't he involved in some sort of scandal?'

'Not a scandal really. A very wealthy owner who took exception to the way he rode one of his horses destroyed his career as a jockey which has also had an effect on him starting up as a trainer. It made me so angry at the time as it clearly wasn't his fault,' Mary replied angrily. 'It was outrageous. I mean, he came second in the Derby. It's a fantastic achievement to be placed!'

Emily sensed that this was a very sensitive subject with Mary and tried to change the subject.

'Would you mind if I took the list home?'

'No, of course not. I prepared it for you anyway. There's plenty of other trainers, but these are the more local ones.'

'Thank you, I'll give it some thought.'

Emily folded up the piece of paper and put it in her pocket.

She mulled over the comments that Mary had made about James Ryan. If he had ridden in the Derby and been placed, and was a champion jockey, then he must have ridden some of the best horses in some of the best races. He would therefore be capable of telling if The Legacy had any ability. Not only that but he was by far the cheapest trainer on the list.

She would ring Mr. Pierce in the morning with her thoughts, but in the back of her mind, whatever Mr. Pierce had to say, the next phone call she would make would be to James Ryan.

7

With the approval of Mr. Pierce, Emily rang and made an appointment to see James Ryan to discuss the training of The Legacy.

She gave very little information over the phone apart from his age, preferring to explain the predicament she was in face to face should she decide to place The Legacy with him.

In the few days up to the meeting Emily pondered the best way to explain her Derby aspirations for the colt. Whichever way she put it, the meeting was going to be very difficult.

Emily had never revealed the clause in the will to anyone apart from Greg, and his reaction of total incredulity had hurt her deeply. She had never even mentioned it to Mary, despite Mary being such a good friend.

She realised, however, that the trainer of The Legacy would have to be aware of his future and the thought of the reaction it would bring had given her many a sleepless night.

The morning of the meeting soon dawned. Emily, for some reason, had the best night's sleep in a long time, possibly due to the fact that she was about to share The Legacy's big secret.

She got up, showered and dressed, putting on beige trousers, a pale cream blouse and a moss coloured jumper.

She surveyed herself in the mirror.

With her tan boots and quilted jacket she looked every inch one of the horsey set.

Following breakfast of a slice of toast and cup of black coffee, she checked that she had all of The Legacy's documents in her bag, and on confirming the time set out for Bishop's Place – James Ryan's yard.

On arriving there she was surprised how immaculately clean it was.

A couple of the lads were sweeping away the odd stray piece of straw remaining from the morning's mucking out.

The stable blocks looked old, considerably older than those in Mary's yard, but were well maintained.

The nearby house, however, was a sorry sight of neglect.

She got out of her car and walked towards the yard.

A thin man with wild grey hair and a weather-beaten face appeared from one of the boxes and came to meet her.

'Can I help you, Miss?' he asked in soft Irish tones, his smile revealing numerous missing teeth.

'Yes, I hope so. I have an appointment with Mr. Ryan.'

'You must be Miss Lloyd then. This way,' he replied, motioning for her to follow him.

He led her into a room at the end of the yard which served as a tack room. James was busy checking one of the bridles, explaining to the young stable lad with him

179

the merits of using this particular bridle as opposed to the selection of others that were hanging there. To Emily's untrained eye they all looked the same.

'Try him with this the next time, John, it'll be a lot softer on his mouth,' James explained to the lad, glancing up at Mick and Emily as they walked in.

'A Miss Lloyd to see you, Governor,' Mick said in his best voice.

'Thank you, Mick. Please come in, Miss Lloyd. I believe you have a colt you're about to put into training.'

'Yes, that's right. I've just started to consider which trainer to place him with,' Emily said, hoping to sound as though she had a lot of options open too her.

'Well, let me show you round the yard and then we can discuss business later. I presume you would like to look at the yard?' James asked whilst looking Emily up and down.

She certainly didn't look like an average owner, seeming far too young and shy.

He put her in her mid twenties. Her shoulder length auburn hair was neatly tied back and she was well dressed without being too smart.

Her hazel eyes seemed to have a softness about them that James was instantly drawn to. He looked quickly away.

Emily, realising that James had been assessing her, started to blush.

'Yes, a tour of the yard would be nice, thank you.'

She too had been looking at James. He seemed far too young to be a trainer. The only ones she had ever seen were on the television, and they all seemed considerably older and taller, not to mention heavier.

James Ryan was about her height, slightly built with fair hair and the bluest eyes she had ever seen.

James led her out of the tack room and spent an hour showing her round the yard.

Emily was struck by the different quality of horses here compared to those in Mary's yard. Here, they were all in training – well groomed, fit and in excellent condition. In Mary's livery there was everything from children's ponies to the odd racehorse having a break from training – all breeds, shapes, colours and sizes.

James introduced each horse by name, patting each fondly on the neck as he went over his plans for each of them in turn.

His compassion and love of horses made a big impression on Emily.

His lads seemed industrious and hard working, toiling away in various boxes, greeting James with respect as he passed.

'You have just the one racehorse?' James asked as they walked round.

'Well, just the one I want to put into training. I also have his dam which is out on loan,' Emily replied. The butterflies began to rise in her stomach as the moment approached when she would have to tell him.

'I see. Is this your first racehorse?'

'Does it show?' laughed Emily a little nervously, trying to lighten the conversation a little.

'Well, not many owners come and give the yard the once over so thoroughly before sending their horses here.'

'Oh, I'm sorry. I hope I haven't interrupted you in any way,' she said, feeling a little embarrassed.

181

'No, that's quite all right. I like to meet and get to know the owners. It helps me to assess the expectations an owner has of their horse.'

'Talking of expectation,' Emily started nervously, 'is there anywhere we could go to discuss mine a little more privately?'

James frowned slightly, wondering what Emily could mean.

'Come in the house, we can have a chat over a cup of coffee,' James said, realising that Emily was looking a little pensive for reasons which were beyond him.

'That would be nice,' Emily replied rather apprehensively. She followed him across the courtyard, through the back door and into the kitchen.

James tried not to groan out loud when he suddenly realised what a mess he had left the kitchen in.

Emily looked round in wide eyed amusement and stifled a giggle.

After the pristine conditions of the yard the kitchen was an absolute mess.

The bottom kitchen cupboards had been replaced with new dark oak ones whilst the wall units hung sadly on the wall, their lurid green doors hanging lopsidedly from hinges that were giving way with age.

The walls were a grubby shade of white, yellowed with age and flaking in patches where the damp had risen through.

The large oak kitchen table was covered in paperwork, envelopes, many of which were unopened, newspapers and a couple of weeks of copies of the *Racing Post*. In the middle of this were three dirty coffee mugs and a couple of plates from breakfast.

In the sink was a pile of washing up, which must have amounted to a week's worth of dishes.

'Er, you'll have to excuse the mess, I'm in the middle of renovating,' James said sheepishly, totally embarrassed by the mess that he had previously been so oblivious to.

'That's OK,' Emily replied, finding his embarrassment rather endearing.

Unable to find a couple of clean mugs, James hurriedly washed two from the sink whilst the kettle boiled.

To clear a space at the table he merely pushed the papers to one side in a big pile.

They sat down at the table and Emily got The Legacy's documents out of her bag and handed them to James who read them quickly.

'His sire is Coral Reef – I'm impressed, but I'm afraid I've never heard of Andaman Sea, or many of her line. How come she was taken to Coral Reef?'

'I've no idea,' said Emily, realising that the moment of truth had come for her to tell all.

'Andaman Sea belonged to my uncle who was killed in an accident. I inherited her in foal, so when he was born I called him The Legacy.'

'A very appropriate name. So you have no idea why he took Andaman Sea to Coral Reef?' James asked, curious to know why her uncle would take an average ability horse to one of the most expensive stallions in Europe.

'I've no idea. I didn't even know he had a horse until his solicitor told me.'

'That must have been quite a shock,' James said, feeling rather sorry for Emily.

'That's a bit of an understatement.'

'Had you ever owned a horse before that?'

'No, the closest I had ever got to one was a donkey on the beach as a child,' Emily said, laughing nervously.

'So, why do you want to put The Legacy into training? After all, training is an expensive business. Wouldn't you have been better off selling them?'

Emily looked at James. There was something about him that she liked. He seemed warm, caring and kind – hopefully the sort of person who would understand her situation.

She took a deep breath and told him the details of her uncle's will.

James sat silently for a moment, trying to make sense of what she had just told him. Now he realised why she had seemed so reserved and almost embarrassed earlier.

He picked his words very carefully for fear of making the situation worse for her.

'So, you have no choice but to carry out his wishes?'

'None whatsoever. I would never contemplate having The Legacy put down. That's totally out of the question,' Emily said fiercely.

'I quite understand,' James replied gently. 'But how on earth did your uncle come up with the Derby of all races? I know that every owner dreams of running his horse in the Derby, and with a colt with Coral Reef's credentials I wouldn't hesitate, but Andaman Sea isn't even close to the calibre of horse needed.'

'I've no idea why he picked the Derby,' Emily said miserably. 'I don't know anything about breeding, horses or racing. All I know is that I have no choice. I will not have him put down!'

'I appreciate your problem, but the Derby.'

James shook his head sadly. What an awful position she was in.

'Sure I wouldn't hesitate to enter your colt in lesser races, but to be perfectly frank, with that breeding he just isn't Derby material.'

Emily looked down and fiddled nervously with her bag. It was the reaction that she had feared but at least he had let her down gently. She had one last hope – one last resort.

'At least come and look at him. Don't rule him out from looking at a piece of paper. Mrs. Forsyth and the man who broke him both say that he's an exceptional colt.'

Emily looked at James with such a pleading look. He didn't like to say that in a normal livery, it didn't take much of a horse to prove outstanding in comparison to the rest there.

He looked at her. She looked so vulnerable and sad. Realising that he would like to see her again he decided to agree.

'OK, Miss Lloyd, I'll come out and have a look at him, but I wont promise anything.'

Emily looked up, her expression changing from utter dejection to joy in a split second.

'You will? That's wonderful. When?' The words spilled out in her excitement.

'How about the day after tomorrow? About 11a.m.'

'Great, I'll pick you up, and please, call me Emily,' Emily replied, determined that he should have no chance of backing out of their arrangement if she picked him up.

As James walked Emily back to her car, he couldn't resist asking the question that had been bothering him since she revealed her plans to him.

'Why come to me?' he asked. 'After all, surely you would want a trainer with a track record of producing classic winners and with Derby experience. I admit I've ridden in many classics and three Derbys, but if you've done your homework, which I'm sure you have, you will have seen that I've only had moderate success in pretty average races so far.'

'Do you want the truth?' Emily asked, her eyes twinkling mischievously.

'Well, we've both been pretty truthful until now, so yes.'

'Firstly, Mrs. Forsyth recommended you, and secondly you were the cheapest on the list.'

James tried not to look too wounded by her comments.

'Besides,' she added mischievously, 'now that I've met you, I really like you, and I'm sure that you, The Legacy and I will get on really well.'

'James laughed.

'Out of all those reasons, I think I prefer the last one best.'

James watched Emily drive off before walking thoughtfully back to the stables. He couldn't work out which he was looking forward to the most – seeing Emily again or seeing her colt.

He was embarrassed to admit to himself that it was seeing Emily. He didn't hold out much hope for the colt, not with breeding like that.

As he reached the yard Mick appeared.

'Fine looking girl that. Did you sweet talk her into sending her colt here?'

Mick had seen the instant attraction between Emily and James, and from the length of time they had spent in the kitchen he took it as a good omen.

It had been three months since Jackie had served divorce papers on James, and since then Mick had been doing his best to act as matchmaker – so far with no success.

'So, is she sending the colt here or not?' he repeated, fishing for information.

'It's a bit more complicated than that,' James replied, not wanting to reveal Emily's plans for The Legacy. If he took the horse on, then he would tell him.

'I'm going out to look at the colt the day after tomorrow. Miss Lloyd has rather specific plans for him and she would like my opinion before any decision is made.'

'What plans?' Mick asked.

'If she sends him here, then I'll tell you,' James replied, trying not to sound too evasive.

'Miss Lloyd going with you, is she?'

'Yes, she's picking me up.'

'Good. About time you started taking an interest in women again.'

'It's not a date, we're only going to look at her horse,' James said in exasperation.

'If you say so,' Mick said with a wink, before returning to his jobs.

It was certainly a long time since James had found himself attracted to someone. This past year had certainly been a nightmare as far as his personal life was concerned.

He and Jackie had drifted further and further apart and James had soon begun to hear rumours of other men in her life.

James only began to take the rumours seriously when one name kept cropping up – a wealthy landowner with a string of top racehorses.

Jackie denied it and the divorce papers soon followed.

James had accepted them as inevitable, but it was the settlement she wanted that worried him.

Eventually a compromise was reached, whereby he would have to mortgage the yard to pay her off. He had no idea how he would make ends meet since the yard had barely been profitable without a mortgage. Now he had that money to find too and future prospects looked bleak.

Emily intrigued him, as did her colt. It wasn't unheard of for the colt of unfashionable breeding to become a classic winner, but to win the Derby – well, the odds would be astronomical.

He had nothing to lose in going to see the colt, and at least he would see Emily again. He just hated the idea of letting her down if The Legacy were not classic material, which he concluded would be the only outcome.

James went back to the kitchen and looked around him.

What must she have thought? The place was an absolute tip.

He had been so engrossed in training and his personal problems that he hadn't even noticed the mess.

James walked to the sink and started to run the hot water, which splattered everywhere as it hit the large amount of dirty dishes that were piled in there.

He had two days to tidy up before she came again.

James looked around with embarrassment and sighed before turning his concentration to the washing up.

*   *   *

Darwin's Choice's reputation preceded him, and when he arrived at Stuart Lawson's training stable the stable staff soon realised that all the rumours about the colt were true.

He was certainly a colt of undoubted quality, but his vices soon became apparent as he was being unloaded from the horse box.

The travelling head lad was having an awful job just to hang on to him as Darwin's Choice flung his head about, showing the whites of his eyes and snorting with great indignation. Occasionally he would rear up, shortening the length of his lead rein and flicking at the lad with his front hooves.

A couple of the lads went to give assistance and eventually, with the help of a bucket of horse cubes, enticed the colt into his box.

Darwin's Choice devoured them noisily whilst keeping a wary eye on the stable staff who had lined up outside his door and were peering anxiously in.

Darwin's Choice thrashed his tail in irritation and shifted his weight from one side to the other, like a thug spoiling for a fight.

The head lad who had travelled over from Ireland wisely decided to allow the colt to settle before he went to check on him to see how he had travelled.

Stuart had received instructions from both Dr. Popham and Nathan Grant as to the continuing care of Darwin's Choice, and whilst Stuart had realised that Nathan was pinning a lot of hopes on the colt, the tests and reports that he had demanded seemed to be ridiculously excessive. Stuart, however, knew better than to question his boss, and resigned himself to continuing the monitoring of the colt's progress.

Stuart had also heard that Darwin's Choice was a bit of a handful, and thought long and hard as to which of the stable staff he could allocate to him. Although each of his staff was extremely capable, it was apparent that Darwin's Choice would need someone exceptional, and following the performance that the colt had put on at his arrival, he was sure that they would hardly be queuing up for the job.

He eventually decided on the unusual choice of Maureen O'Connor, or Mo as she was known as in the yard. She was a diminutive, softly spoken Irish girl who was very reserved by nature and seemed to get on better with horses than with people. She seemed to have endless patience and a 'way' with the more difficult horses in the yard.

He sent his head lad out to fetch Mo. He could almost sense the relief of the other lads as Mo walked into his office.

'Come in and sit down, Mo,' he said, leaning back in his chair, studying the young red haired, freckle faced, green eyed Irish girl. 'Did you see the latest addition to the yard – Darwin's Choice?'

'I did, sir. A fine looking animal that one,' she replied nervously. Rarely had she been summoned to the Governor's office and she was unsure why she had been asked for.

'You no doubt saw that he was a bit spirited.'

'He is, to be sure,' she replied, twiddling her thumbs nervously.

'I would like you to look after him, if you think you're up to it.'

'I would, sir, of course. It would be an honour.' Her

green eyes sparkled with delight at the honour of the responsibility which she had just been given.

'Good, then I think that you had better get acquainted as soon as possible.'

'I will, sir, right away, and thank you sir.'

Mo got up out of the chair and almost ran out of the office, she was so keen to get to know her new charge.

Stuart smiled. That's what he liked about Mo. She might be tiny, but she was totally fearless when it came to horses. If a horse sensed fear, it would react to it, rather like a bully, but when someone wouldn't respond in that way the horse seemed to lose the advantage of intimidation and respect the person who had stood up to it.

He fervently hoped that Mo could stand up to one of the biggest bullies he had ever seen – Darwin's Choice.

Mo, meanwhile, had lost no time in introducing herself to Darwin's Choice. She peered over the door and the colt immediately turned round and stared at her. Mo looked away instinctively, knowing that if their eyes met, the colt would see it as a challenge. All the while she spoke softly to him.

She opened the door and went in, closing the door securely behind her.

Darwin's Choice eyed her, feeling a little puzzled. At the stud he had only been handled by men and the older and more difficult he had become, bigger and stronger the lads took over his care.

Here he was with a girl, something unknown to him, and a tiny one at that, hardly worth bothering about.

The way she spoke, so softly and almost musically, mesmerised him, so different was the tone from the deep, raised shouting voices he had become accustomed to.

She walked over to him, still avoiding eye contact, and held out her hand to touch his neck.

Instinctively he moved back and snorted, breathing in the air to sense her fear, but there was none.

She touched his neck and his muscles instinctively twitched and tightened, but instead of the slap and hard handling he was used to, her touch was soft, soothing and strangely pleasing.

He relaxed his muscles, enjoying the feeling of her tiny hand running down his neck and across his back.

All the while she talked gently to him.

Mo spent half an hour in the box, stroking him, rubbing his nose, feeding him mints and talking softly to him.

For the first time in his life Darwin's Choice relaxed and nuzzled her almost affectionately.

At long last he had found a friend.

Mo ensured that he had enough water and a full hay net and eventually left him to settle down for his first night at his new yard.

Mo was thrilled to have been given what she regarded as the best job in the yard – looking after Nathan Grant's most valuable colt for which everyone had such great expectations.

Sure he was a bit spirited and bad tempered but she regarded him as just a bit grumpy.

One thing was certain, she had never seen such a fine animal, and whilst stroking him she had never before felt such powerful muscles.

As she lay in bed that night, Mo couldn't believe how lucky she was. What she didn't know was that the rest of the yard were also counting their good fortune in having escaped the responsibility that Mo had been given in looking after such a temperamental animal.

In the weeks that followed, Darwin's Choice gradually settled in.

Mo had her moments with the colt, but with a little gentle scolding would soon calm him down again.

Stuart was delighted that the two of them got on so well together and congratulated himself on his choice of 'lad' for the colt.

Occasionally Mo would ride Darwin's Choice out, but more often than not it was Joe McGrath, a young jockey who Stuart had high hopes of. He was certainly very talented and was building up a good record at race meetings.

Darwin's Choice had got the better of Joe on numerous occasions, throwing him when he least expected it – almost testing him, but Mo explained – never lose your temper, never shout, just get back on, be firm, and most of all, show him some respect and kindness.

Joe was grateful for her advice, and he and Darwin's Choice seemed to regard their daily workout as a game rather than there being any malice in it. More often than not it would be Darwin's Choice who had the last laugh.

Stuart was delighted with the progress that the colt was making, and all the expectations that Nathan Grant had of the horse were proving to be true. Certainly, in all the yard there was no stronger, faster or fitter colt.

Joe McGrath was also very impressed with Darwin's Choice. He had ridden some exceptional horses in his short career, but there was something very special about this colt. He hoped that the Governor would see him and Darwin's Choice as a good partnership when it came to looking for a jockey to partner him when he started his racing career.

He felt quietly confident since a few of the other apprentices in the yard had ridden work on the colt and were more often than not unceremoniously dumped on the grass.

With any luck, he and Darwin's Choice would go far together.

James waited anxiously for Emily to arrive, surprised at how he was looking forward to seeing her. The fact that he was going to see her colt was an afterthought.

As he saw her car pull up, he had to stop himself from rushing out of the house to greet her.

"Play it cool" he told himself, "don't appear too keen, you might scare her off."

As Emily approached the kitchen door, James opened it and sauntered nonchalantly out.

'Lovely day, isn't it?' he said, immediately cursing himself for such a terrible greeting.

'It certainly is, and it'll be perfect if you take on The Legacy,' Emily relied with a huge grim.

'We'll see. As I said, I can't promise anything.'

On the way to Mrs. Forsyth's Emily chatted away nervously, asking James about all the horses he had ridden, which were the best and why.

James was pleased that she was leading the conversation, since he was surprisingly tongue tied and embarrassed in her presence.

It had been a long time since he had been remotely

attracted to anyone, and he realised that he had forgotten all the chat up lines he used to be so good at. Any that came to mind now seemed to be so old fashioned and faintly ridiculous.

On arriving at the yard, Emily introduced James to Mary and then asked after The Legacy.

'He was put out in the left paddock about five minutes ago with the other colts,' came the reply.

Emily led James to the paddock and leant on the gate, watching the colts chase round the field enjoying the freedom and open space and the chance to let off steam after having been stabled all night.

'That's him,' Emily said pointing to her colt, 'the one with the white sock and big blaze.'

James watched transfixed. He had ridded the colt's sire, Coral Reef, and was astounded at how alike they were. Not having known or seen the dam he couldn't say what characteristics he had inherited from Andaman Sea.

The Legacy was certainly a very well built colt, beautifully proportioned and was easily outpacing the others in the field with no apparent effort whatsoever.

After about ten minutes the other colts began to tire, and one by one slowed down, their nostrils flaring with heavy breathing and their coats damp with sweat.

Soon all but The Legacy were grazing peacefully. Not The Legacy. He was still going hell for leather round the field, almost as though he was showing off to Emily.

Emily called him and he wheeled round and looked at her.

He shook his head, almost irritated that she should interrupt his playtime, and trotted over for the polo mints he knew Emily always had in her pocket.

Emily could barely get them unwrapped quickly enough as he playfully tried to snatch the packet off her.

Emily laughed and chastised him.

'You greedy boy, showing yourself up in front of James here.'

James was amused by the obvious affection between the two.

He looked up at The Legacy and suddenly stared in astonishment. The colt was breathing quite normally and hadn't even raised a sweat, yet he had spent the last fifteen minutes at least galloping round the field. It was as though he had just come out of his box.

'I've brought a very important person to see you Leggy – meet James Ryan.'

The Legacy looked at James and crunched noisily on his mints.

James patted his neck and immediately noticed the strong firm muscles beneath his coat.

'What do you think of him?' Emily asked tentatively, worried that James might not be too impressed with him.

James tried not to show his excitement, but there was something about The Legacy that had 'champion' stamped all over him. He couldn't put a finger on it – he just had that 'feeling'.

'He certainly is a fine looking colt, beautifully proportioned and a good mover with nice balance. Would you mind if I rode him out for a few minutes to get a better feel?'

'No, please do,' Emily replied, delighted that he hadn't dismissed her colt out of hand.

They fetched some tack and it wasn't long before James was in the saddle.

He spent twenty minutes putting The Legacy through his paces whilst Emily fretted about what conclusion James was going to reach.

When she saw James coming back she dashed over.

'Well, how did it go?'

'With his breeding, I don't know how, but you have a good colt here – very good, but only time will tell if he's Derby material.'

'So, you'll take him on?'

'Definitely.'

Emily threw her arms round the colt's neck and hugged him.

James dismounted and took the saddle off. He had ridden a lot of classic horses in his career as a jockey and the feeling that The Legacy gave him sent shivers of expectation up and down his spine. He was so excited about The Legacy he was almost shaking.

The colt was like a dream come true for him. At last he had some definite potential in his yard, and what a potential it was. This could certainly be the start of something big.

He tried not to get too carried away or let Emily see his excitement. Racing could be a cruel, fickle game and anything could happen, even to the greatest horse.

'So, when would you like him to start?' Emily said, she was so keen to get the first stage of his racing career started.

'As soon as possible,' James replied, eager to take charge of The Legacy – his first decent horse with any great potential in his short training career.

'Good, let's see Mary and make the arrangements.'

Once The Legacy was back in his box, Emily and

James went to Mary's office, where Emily told Mary the good news. Mary was delighted that Emily had chosen James as trainer and was sure that the two of them would get on well together.

Arrangements were made for the colt to be collected the following day.

'I'll be sorry to see him go, he's such a character,' Mary said, realising that she would not only miss the colt but Emily too. They had become good friends over the past year and Mary hoped that Emily would still keep in touch and come and see Andaman Sea now and again.

On the drive back to the yard Emily kept asking James if The Legacy was good enough for the Derby.

'It's far too early to tell but he certainly has a lot of potential. Once he's done some work we'll have a better idea; after all, he's really still a baby in horse terms at the moment.'

'Yes, I suppose he is,' Emily sighed. 'Would you mind if I came to see him every now and again?'

'You can come as often as you like,' James replied, delighted at the thought of Emily spending a lot of time at his yard.

Once back at Bishop's Place James invited Emily in.

'Would you like to come in for a coffee and we can get down to talking over training fees etc.'

'Yes, I'd love too,' Emily replied, surprised at how much she was enjoying James's company.

Emily followed James into the kitchen and was astonished at its transformation. The sink was empty of dirty crockery, the work surfaces had all been cleaned and an attempt had been made to straighten the old cupboard doors. The pile of paperwork that had previously covered the kitchen table was now split between a small neat pile on the table and a big box under it.

Emily tried not to smile too much as James busied himself with making the coffee.

She then noticed the old black Labrador lazily eyeing her from his basket in front of the aga.

'That's Guinness,' James said, noticing Emily looking at the dog.

'He really belongs to Mick, my head lad, but he seems to spend most of his time in here.'

Emily gave Guinness a stroke and the old black dog sighed in appreciation.

James put the coffees down on the table and sat down.

'I'm not sure what your uncle left you to cover expenses. Training fees you know already. On top of that there will be vet's fees, entry fees, jockey's fees, transport, and blacksmith just to name a few. The trainer usually gets ten per cent of any prize money and the jockey seven to ten per cent. I know it all sounds rather daunting and I can't put an fixed figure on what final costs will be, but it's best to know what you're letting yourself in for at the beginning.'

'Yes, I appreciate that,' Emily replied, staring into her coffee thoughtfully. 'I certainly hadn't realised that there would be so many extra costs.'

Emily felt quite despondent. She knew that she had barely enough to cover the training fees alone.

'Is any of this negotiable?' she asked, hoping that they could come to some sort of arrangement.

'What had you in mind?'

'Well, what if you could reduce your fees by ten per cent for a ten per cent increase in your share of any prize money?'

James thought for a moment. He desperately needed every penny he could get from fees and it would be a while before The Legacy would race; however, the races that he had in mind for the colt would carry considerable prize money so this seemed like a sound proposition in the long term.

Before he could agree, Emily, having taken his hesitation as a negative sign added, 'Perhaps I could also help out here. I used to help out at Mary's yard and I know that you have staff to help you with the stable work, but what about your paperwork? You must be terribly busy with the practical side of running the yard and by the looks of it, paperwork doesn't seem to be your forte, if you don't mind me saying.'

James caught Emily looking at the box under the table which he had filled by clearing it off the table without even going through it.

He looked sheepishly at her and smiled.

'I certainly could do with some help in that department, so it's agreed.'

'Oh, thank you. I'll start with two evenings a week if that's OK with you.'

Emily drank her coffee with a great sense of relief. Now she had not only reduced the fees, but she had a good excuse to visit The Legacy at least twice a week.

James was also secretly delighted. He hated the office side of his work and felt continuously guilty about how behind he was, with envelopes and bills not even opened going back weeks in the box.

He hadn't realised that training would involve so much time out of the yard and he was happiest when he was with his horses.

He would also have the chance to see Emily twice a week.

Things couldn't have worked out better if he had planned it.

After Emily had left, he diligently washed up he coffee cups and put them away, smiling to himself at his change of attitude. Previously he would have added them to the pile in the sink.

For the first time in a long time, the future was looking up. He had a horse with great potential which, with any luck, would finally put his yard on the map. And there was also Emily. Just thinking of her gave him a warm glow of affection and he was already looking forward to the first of many visits.

He also realised that he would have to let Mick into their plans for The Legacy. James was going to have a lot of explaining to do.

Later that evening, when James and Mick were sitting at the kitchen table having their usual evening meeting, the subject of Emily was inevitably brought up by Mick.

'So, how did you get on with the lovely Miss Lloyd?' Mick asked, trying to sound very casual about it.

'Fine, thank you, Mick. We pick up the colt tomorrow morning.'

'Good, but how did you – you know – get on with her?'

James looked at Mick, knowing full well what he had meant the first time. He realised that he was going to enjoy stringing Mick along a little more as far as that topic of conversation was concerned.

'We had a very business-like meeting,' James replied, 'and I don't mix business with pleasure.'

'Pity,' said Mick with more than a little disappointment. Sensing that this line of questioning was going nowhere he decided to change the subject.

'So what's the colt like?'

'He's a fine colt. In fact I don't think I've ever seen one better.'

Mick's immediate thoughts were that his judgement had obviously been clouded by his attraction to Emily.

'Fine colt, eh. That's a surprise considering the dam.'

'Yes, I know, but these things do happen. The only problem is that there are a few complications,' James said with a sigh, realising that he would now have to tell Mick the plans for the colt.

'What's them then?'

'Emily inherited the colt from an uncle, who stated in his will that the horse must be entered in the Derby.'

'Be Jesus!' exclaimed Mick in astonishment. 'The Derby! The man must have been Irish to come up with a crack like that! He must be mad. Surely she can run it in something else.'

'Yes, but it must also run in the Derby. The will stated that if it didn't run in the Derby then it would have to be destroyed.'

Mick stared at James in disbelief, unable to take in what he had just heard.

'I take it back, he's not Irish, he's a monster. No Irishman would ever destroy a perfectly healthy horse on a whim!'

'My thought exactly,' James replied, trying to calm Mick down.

'But the Derby . . .' repeated Mick, shaking his head. 'You have to have a bloody good horse to enter it in that race.'

'But that's the odd thing about it, Mick, I think the colt is going to be good. I saw him and rode him out and I don't know why but I really think he's got the potential.'

'Are you sure you're not blinded by your feelings for Miss Lloyd?'

'I don't have any "feelings" for Miss Lloyd, and credit me with a little intelligence, I know what I felt about the colt. Anyway, don't prejudge him. See what you think of him yourself tomorrow.'

'I can hardly wait to see this Nijinsky!' Mick said, still shaking his head. 'So she inherited it from a mad uncle who says she has to run it in the Derby or have it put down.'

'Now you're getting it, Mick,' exclaimed James in exasperation that it seemed to be taking so long to sink in with Mick.

He couldn't blame Mick; after all, it was quite an outrageous situation.

'So, let me get this straight,' said Mick, slowly and thoughtfully, 'it's the Derby or dog meat!'

'You could put it like that.'

'The poor girl,' said Mick, suddenly feeling very sorry for Emily and great anger towards her uncle. 'If that man weren't dead already, I'd shoot him myself.'

'Spoken like a true Irishman,' James laughed.

A smile passed over the face of Mick for the first time in a few minutes.

James could understand his reaction, having felt the same emotions himself and knowing that Mick couldn't abide any animal being mistreated, let alone put down for no apparent reason.

'Poor girl,' repeated Mick, 'fancy being left with a choice like that – and where's she going to find the money for training?'

'Apparently her uncle left her some money to cover it.'

'That's the least he could do,' Mick replied sarcastically.

'The only trouble is I don't think he left her enough.'

'Jesus, poor girl,' repeated Mick for the third time. 'So what's she going to do?'

'Well, I agreed to a reduction in training fees for an increased percentage of prize money.'

'You can't afford to do that. Are you sure you're not in love?'

Mick wasn't sure whether to scold him or praise him for helping Emily out, but under the same circumstances Mick thought he would have done the same thing.

'And she has also agreed to come in twice a week and sort out the accounts and paperwork'

'Now you're talking,' Mick exclaimed, delighted that James wasn't only going to get the urgently needed help in the paperwork department, but he might now find something to distract him from the single minded obsession with training since his divorce from Jackie.

'Anyway, Mick, regardless of what your opinions are at the moment, I really do think The Legacy has great potential. Whether he's good enough for the Derby, only time will tell.'

'The Legacy, that's his name is it?' Mick said thoughtfully.

'Appropriate, isn't it?' James replied.

'I can't wait to tell my mates in Dublin about this one,' Mick said with relish, thinking of the crowd he would attract whilst telling this unbelievable tale.

'Please don't say anything, Emily would be so embarrassed. She feels bad enough about her uncle, without having it broadcast around Ireland. I promised her it would go no further.'

'OK,' agreed Mick reluctantly, out of respect for James and the lady in an awkward situation.

'I'll fetch him tomorrow and you can give me your opinion,' James said, trying to get down to more serious business matters.

'I can't wait,' Mick replied.

He wouldn't have long to wait before finding out if James really was being blinded by love or if The Legacy was the horse that every trainer dreams of.

James had been on the receiving end of such bad luck over the past two years, Mick hoped that his luck was about to change.

Perhaps it would be in the form of Emily's colt, not to mention Emily herself.

The following morning, Mick was full of anticipation as he waited for James to return with The Legacy.

The lads in the yard knew that a new owner was sending their horse for training, but none of them knew what Mick knew, and as an Irishman who loved to tell a good story, it took all of his willpower and respect for James to stop himself from revealing all.

The lads, however, couldn't help but notice how excited Mick was.

At long last James returned with the battered horse box containing The Legacy. He had meant to replace the old horse box, but lack of funds following his divorce settlement meant that he had to make do, and had ceased to become embarrassed by it.

James stopped and got out. Mick immediately came over and helped to unload the colt.

The Legacy looked around him in wide eyed confusion. All the familiar sights and people had gone. He didn't quite know what to make of it. He did, however, recognise James and soon realised that he was amongst friends.

James led the colt round in circles a few times to stretch the horse's legs after the journey.

The lads all gathered to look at the newcomer, each of them assessing the potential of the new horse.

Mick came over and looked The Legacy up and down before feeling each leg and finally running a hand over his hind quarters.

'So, what do you think?' James asked, desperate for Mick to confirm his opinion of the colt.

'Me thinks you could be right,' Mick replied thoughtfully. 'He's a fine looking animal – a bit on the thin side, but we'll soon build these muscles up, won't we lad. He sure moves well. I can't wait to see him gallop.'

Mick gave the colt an affectionate slap on the rump.

The Legacy wasn't sure what to make of the slap, but he had known as soon as Mick touched him, that he was in good, caring hands.

'When do you see Miss Lloyd again, then?' Mick asked, straight to the second point of business.

'She's coming tonight to make sure The Legacy arrived safely,' James replied with slightly raised eyebrows.

'Oh, no. She's not someone who regards a racehorse as a pet, is she?' Mick groaned, knowing from experience that these owners were nothing but trouble.

'I'm afraid so,' sighed James. 'Still, when you've never had a horse before and are suddenly in the circumstances she's found herself in, what do you expect?'

'So, we've got two to train, then.'

'It would appear so,' James replied.

'In that case, I'll look after the colt and you can take care of the filly,' exclaimed Mick, enjoying the uncomfortable look on James's face.

James looked at Mick and tried to summon up his most stern expression even though he was quite amused.

'I'd like to remind you that I'm the governor round here, and I will not have you talking about our new owner like that.

'Sorry, sir. I'll try not to let it happen again,' Mick replied with a twinkle in his eyes.

Later that evening Emily arrived, anxious to see how The Legacy had settled in to his new home.

James took her to the colt's box, where she was delighted to see him tucking into his hay net.

As soon as the colt saw her he snickered and went over to the stable door for his customary mints which he crunched and devoured immediately.

Once Emily had reassured herself that The Legacy was settled and happy she followed James back to the house.

Mick was already in the kitchen making coffee.

'Emily, this is Mick, my head lad.'

'Hello, Mick, we've already met but not been introduced,' said Emily, holding out her hand which Mick shook.

He was flattered that Emily had remembered him. He thought it must have been his Irish charm that had made an impression, oblivious to the thought that his lack of teeth might have had more to do with it.

'What do you think of The Legacy?' Emily asked with more than a degree of apprehension.

'I think you have a champion there, Miss,' replied Mick, who having seen The Legacy do a short gallop in the afternoon realised that his first impressions about the colt had not been misplaced.

'Well, if Mick thinks you have a champion, then we're half way there,' James replied. 'He's a very astute judge of a horse.'

Mick beamed with pride, even though he wasn't sure what astute meant.

After a few minutes in Emily's company, Mick warmed to her. He was not only a good judge of horses, but a good judge of people as well.

He felt so sorry for Emily. She was an ordinary, likeable girl in an extraordinary situation. He admired her belief and tenacity and the fact that the impossible burden didn't seem to be affecting her.

The only saving feature in the whole bizarre situation was that The Legacy, in his opinion, had ability – real ability.

Mick hoped that the colt's ability would be enough to fulfil her uncle's wishes and Mick made himself a promise that he would do all he could to help.

8

Stuart Lawson could not have been more pleased with the progress of Darwin's Choice under the care of Mo and careful riding of Joe McGrath.

Mo doted on Darwin's Choice and the colt flourished under her attention.

His temper, although always simmering under the surface, had been brought under control by Mo's gentle, but no-nonsense approach.

If there was anything that Darwin's Choice responded well to that was adoration – which he got plenty of from Mo and Joe McGrath.

Joe would never force the colt to do anything he didn't want to.

The odd painful experience had soon taught him that Darwin's Choice was too strong willed to be bullied by anyone.

One lad who just showed him the whip on the gallops one morning was instantly thrown and faced a long embarrassing walk back to the yard.

Nathan enjoyed coming to the gallops early in the morning and watch his colt fly past the rest of the string, making the other millions of pounds worth of horses appear very ordinary indeed. He was also delighted in that the horse was never out of breath after a gallop and would barely raise a sweat.

It seemed as though Anderson-Brown had worked his magic after all. Stuart and Nathan planned the colt's two year old campaign with the same attention to detail as his development.

His first outing on a racetrack would be in a two-year-old maiden stakes at Newbury in May. It would be his introduction to the totally new atmosphere of a racetrack, and knowing the temperament of Darwin's Choice, no-one could be sure quite how the colt would react.

The night before the race, Stuart could barely sleep, knowing what Darwin's Choice could be capable of if he was in the wrong frame of mind and if the colt played up in the way that he could, then it would be so embarrassing for Stuart and the yard, especially as Nathan had decided he would be there to see Darwin's debut.

To Joe's delight, both Nathan and Stuart agreed that he should have the ride as he was the one person in the yard who could get the best out of the horse.

The trip to Newbury was uneventful, much to Stuart's relief, and Mo seemed to have the colt well settled after the journey.

Since Nathan rarely came to see any of his horses run first time out, his presence was soon noticed amongst the racing journalists who concluded that Darwin's Choice would definitely be worth watching.

The presence of Nathan Grant, coupled with the impeccable breeding of Darwin's Choice, resulted in the on-course bookmakers immediately shortening the price on the colt to odds-on favourite, despite him never having run before and being up against a few very useful opponents of proven ability.

Stuart met Nathan about an hour before the race.

'He travelled well, sir, and Mo, his stable lass, seems to have a way of handling him and is doing a great job of keeping him calm,' Stuart said, relieved that so far the colt was behaving himself.

'Some women seem to have that effect on the opposite sex!' laughed Nathan, slapping Stuart on the back with such force that he had to take a step forward to stop himself falling over.

'I know what you mean, sir,' Stuart agreed, pleased that his boss was in such a jovial mood. He only hoped that Darwin's Choice would do the business today to keep his boss that way, or there would be hell to pay later.

His boss seemed to have an unhealthy obsession with this colt, like no other colt he had ever owned – and he had certainly owned plenty.

Nathan had told him early on that the Derby was his aim and Stuart had geared the colt's training from the beginning with the great race in mind.

Stuart had, however, been down this path before, with high expectations of a horse only for it to falter when it came to the final test. There was something, and he couldn't put a finger on it, something very special about Darwin's Choice. The only thing that Stuart could ever see beating Darwin's Choice was Darwin's Choice himself.

Nathan joined Stuart when he went to saddle up Darwin's Choice. The colt was standing quietly in the box whilst Stuart made a thorough check of the tack. All the while Mo was talking softly to Darwin's Choice and occasionally stroking his neck to reassure him.

There was something in the way that the diminutive red haired stable girl spoke to the horse, in that soft Irish brogue, and the way that she would gently stroke him with her tiny hand, that stirred a feeling of lust within Nathan.

If she could handle such a powerful animal with ease, wouldn't it be fun to find out if she could handle a man in the same way.

Nathan instantly dismissed the thought. It had been a long time since he had a fling with a mere stable girl. These days he had his pick of some of the most beautiful, not to mention talented, girls in the world. He only wished that some of them would speak to him the way this girl spoke to his colt.

Stuart gave Mo a nod, and she whispered encouragingly to the colt before leading him out into the parade ring. Nathan and Stuart followed, both trying not to let their expectations mingled with anxiety get the better of them.

Darwin's Choice eyed the crowd as Mo led him round. Much to Stuart's relief the colt seemed to be enjoying himself, walking round the ring with a seemingly effortless bounce to his stride, impressing fellow owners and race goers with his relaxed, flowing style and muscular physique.

Nathan watched his colt with pride.

Under Stuart's care he had developed into a handsome animal and looked far more advanced than the other two-year-olds in the field. 'Should be a walkover, eh Stuart?' he commented as Darwin's Choice broke into a bouncy trot for a few strides before Mo calmed him down again.

'It certainly should be,' replied Stuart anxiously. 'Let's hope Joe gets him to settle on the way to the start.'

As if on cue, the small figure of Joe appeared with the other jockeys.

'Morning Governor, sir,' Joe said, addressing Stuart and Nathan with a touch of his riding helmet.

'Make sure he doesn't pull too hard on the way down, keep him balanced and settled. Once the race starts, let him run at his own pace but at the same time, don't let him run off with you. Control him, don't fight him.'

'Yes, sir,' replied Joe, well aware that the race would be run the way Darwin's Choice wanted to run it, no-one else's way.

The bell sounded, Stuart gave Joe a leg up, and with one circuit of the parade ring, Mo led Darwin's Choice out onto the track, whispering good luck and giving him a final reassuring pat on the neck before letting him go.

Darwin's Choice bounded forward as he always did when he saw an open expanse of track in front of him, and Joe kept gentle but firm control of him as they cantered down to the start.

Joe was surprised and delighted how Darwin's Choice seemed to be taking it all in his stride. Rather than be wary of the crowd, the colt seemed almost to be enjoying himself.

Nathan watched Darwin's Choice through his binoculars, studying every movement and mannerism to see if he really was the special colt he was bred to be.

The horses were soon loaded into the stalls with few problems. Joe had insisted that Darwin's Choice be handled as little as possible, and with a few gentle kicks the colt walked into his starting stall like a seasoned professional – much to the relief of his connections.

Nathan barely had time to draw breath before they were off.

Darwin's Choice bounded out of the stalls and within a couple of strides was two lengths clear.

Nathan could see Joe keeping him settled, yet the colt seemed to be running with a freedom Nathan had never seen in a horse before.

After a couple of furlongs, the rest of the field were starting to bunch and were fighting for the minor places, Darwin's Choice having made his move from the start and produced an already unbeatable lead.

Darwin's Choice passed the winning post eight lengths clear of the field, with Joe hardly having made a move on the colt.

'Bloody hell! That was easy!' exclaimed Stuart, who despite knowing that the colt had showed enormous promise on the gallops, couldn't believe how easily Darwin's Choice had taken the field apart and destroyed it.

'Told you he'd be a champion,' Nathan replied in rather a smug tone.

'I knew he would be a champion, sir, but a performance like that for his first time out was something special.'

Nathan and Stuart reached the winner's enclosure just as a delighted Mo was leading Darwin's Choice in, telling the colt how proud she was of him, patting his neck and tweaking his ear.

Joe jumped off and was congratulated by both Nathan and Stuart who were both anxious to heard about the race.

'He felt so easy!' exclaimed Joe breathlessly. 'Right from the start I just let him have his head. He seemed to be on cruise control and was still accelerating at the finish. I had such a job pulling him up at the end, he could have gone round again.'

Stuart was looking over Darwin's Choice to ensure that he had come home sound.

'He's hardly raised a sweat!' Stuart exclaimed in astonishment, looking at the colt who had hardly changed his breathing rate. The second and third horses, meanwhile, were flecked with white patches of sweat that had built up into a lather under their saddles, and were blowing heavily from their exertions.

'Thank you, Anderson-Brown,' muttered Nathan, looking at the skies.

'I'm sorry, sir, I didn't quite catch that.' Stuart had been so engrossed in adjusting the winner's sheet on Darwin's Choice that he hadn't caught Nathan's last comment.

'It was nothing important.'

Nathan smiled to himself.

Anderson-Brown had done it – he really had done it. Nathan had to admit to himself that there were more than a few moments when he had doubts in his mind, but the sight of Darwin's Choice, the winner there in front of him having barely raised a sweat from his exertions, was a sight that he had dreamt of over the last eighteen months.

'Well done, Stuart, great job. The next race we'll have to step up in distance and in better company too. Then we'll have a better chance to see what he's made of.'

'It'll certainly be more of a test, but to be honest, on today's performance, I can't see him being beaten,' Stuart replied, still reeling from the ease with which Darwin's Choice dealt with the race.

The racing journalists present were already writing the headlines for the following day's papers. Reports that Stuart Lawson had an exceptional colt in his yard had proved to be true. Darwin's Choice had given a startling performance of speed and power.

Time would tell when he stepped up in class and distance if he had the makings of a true champion.

The following day a photograph of Darwin's Choice appeared in the *Racing Post*. Mick was the first to spot it, since he always managed to get hold of the paper before James.

'Jesus, Governor, will you look at that. Ain't he the spittin' image of The Legacy!'

James looked at the photograph with amazement and then quickly read the article.

'He's also from Coral Reef and I know Coral Reef had exactly the same blaze, so I suppose this colt and The Legacy got theirs from him.'

Mick grabbed the paper back and looked at the picture more closely.

'And will you look at the muscles on that. It makes The Legacy look like a wimp!'

'Are you criticising my horses and training methods?' James asked, not sure whether to take Mick's comments as criticism or not.

'Oh, no sir. Of course not, but you have to admit, he's a big, muscular horse.'

'And The Legacy is lean and fit,' countered James, 'and you don't have to be muscularly overdeveloped to run a good race.'

'I know, Governor, but you have to admit – he's a fine looking colt.'

'True, but so is The Legacy.'

'And have you read this? By all accounts he annihilated the field. If this horse enters the Derby, we'll have a real battle on our hands,' Mick said, sucking the air through his teeth, deep in thought.

'When The Legacy runs in the Derby, he'll have a battle on his hands with all of the entries, not just this one.'

James sighed as Mick became quietly engrossed in the *Racing Post*. It was at times like this that he felt the training of The Legacy to be a burden. It was as though he had taken the weight of responsibility off Emily and transferred it to himself. Now he had the expectations of Emily, Mick and himself to contend with.

There were moments when he had his doubts and reservations about The Legacy's prospects, but he only had to watch the colt on the gallops to have his spirits and expectations raised again and his excitement would return with more enthusiasm than before.

James had gone over Emily's budget with Mick and it was clear that there wasn't enough money to enter The Legacy in the sort of races that James would have liked in order to compare The Legacy's ability with other top colts of his age.

Mick, always the opportunist, had also pointed out that if The Legacy was virtually unraced and unknown as a

Derby entrant, then with his breeding he would be a rank outsider and with those odds it wouldn't take much of a bet to make some serious money.

James, at first, was indignant at Mick's suggestion of a betting coup, but, the financial situation getting more desperate by the week, James had concluded that unless things improved dramatically over the next year then he wouldn't have the resources see out the following season in training.

Desperate circumstances sometimes demanded desperate measures, and James decided that if things hadn't improved by then, perhaps he would have to put his pride to one side and for the first time in his life have a gamble.

He tried to turn his mind from his depressing prospects to Emily. She was coming over straight from work to spend one of the three evenings a week on James' accounts as she had agreed.

In a matter of a few sessions she had proved invaluable in organising the administrative side of the stables. She had also eased the cash flow considerably as she would spend hours on the phone, cajoling owners whose fees were overdue into paying more promptly.

It was a job that James had always hated, but Emily seemed to have a knack of doing it without antagonising anyone, and had even managed to persuade a couple of the owners to send more of their horses to the yard.

James was left to concentrate on what he loved doing the most – training horses.

Emily arrived promptly at 5.30 and after saying hello to The Legacy, settled down to the paperwork that had come in since her last visit.

James arrived back at the yard at 6p.m., having gone to collect some feed.

'Hi, Emily, how are you?' he asked as he walked into the kitchen to be greeted by Guinness.

'I'm fine, how's your day been?'

'Couldn't be better. The Legacy did a good session this morning. He's coming on really well.'

'Yes, he's certainly very happy and he seems to be maturing a bit now.'

Emily loved going to see The Legacy, but had become aware that in a racing yard a racehorse wasn't a pet any more, so the hours that she used to spend watching and talking to him she tried to curtail to fifteen minutes. Any longer and she would begin to feel embarrassed.

Mick then walked into the kitchen.

'Evening, Miss. Evening, Governor,' Mick said as he washed his hands in the kitchen sink, creating a huge amount of lather with the washing up liquid he had used.

'Hello, Mick, James tells me that The Legacy worked well this morning.'

'Always does, Miss. He's a fine horse, no mistake, and he'll be a champion one day, you'll see.'

Mick grinned at Emily who couldn't help smiling back at his lack of inhibition with his missing teeth.

'Can I make you boys a coffee?' she asked.

'That would be wonderful,' replied Mick, relieved that James wouldn't be making it – he made such awful coffee. Emily's coffee was the best – must be a woman's touch, he thought.

Emily cleared part of the table for James and Mick to sit at.

She loved this time of the evening when she would listen to them discuss how each horse had worked, or how it had run if it had raced that day.

They would plan the entries for the forthcoming race meetings, and Emily was always amazed at how complicated it was placing the right horse in the right race.

As she busied herself in her work, she would smile at Mick's rather forthright comments about some of the horses in the yard and James would glare at him for using such language in the presence of Emily.

It was during one of these evenings that Emily received a distressing phone call.

The phone rang and James answered it.

He listened to what sounded to Emily like a woman's voice at the other end. His expression turned to one of instant despair. James said very little, mainly listening to the other person before hanging up.

Both Mick and Emily immediately noticed his concerned expression and had both stopped what they were doing, looking at James with great concern.

'Mick,' James began, his voice sounding very strained, 'could you go out and check on the horses, please.'

'But I checked them an hour ago,' he replied, not quite sure why James was asking him.

'Then double check them, please,' James said with a firm voice, looking straight at Mick and then at the door.

Mick suddenly realised that James wanted to get rid of him, and feeling more than a little hurt, left. No doubt his boss would tell him what was going on later.

It was at that point that Emily realised that there was something very wrong.

'What's happened?' she asked, the colour having drained from her face on seeing James's serious expression. 'It's not The Legacy is it? Let me see him!'

Emily was half way to the door when James stopped her and put his arm round her, leading her back and sitting her down.

'No, it's not The Legacy. That was Mary Forsyth. Andaman Sea shattered her hind leg about an hour ago and has had to be put down.'

Emily looked at him, unable to comprehend the awful news.

'Put down? I don't understand.'

'Apparently Tracy had taken Andaman Sea out for a ride and Andaman Sea put her leg down a rabbit hole. I'm so sorry, Emily.'

'But surely something could have been done. Why didn't they ask me first?'

Tears started flowing down Emily's cheeks, her face now as white as a sheet.

'They called the vet immediately but there was nothing they could do.'

'But they could have called me earlier,' Emily sobbed.

'Emily, when something like this happens, it's kinder to put the horse down straight away. Andaman Sea would not have been able to stand up and would have been in great pain. You wouldn't have wanted her to suffer, would you? You couldn't have done or changed anything,' James said softly, realising the anguish that Emily must be feeling.

Emily's shoulders shook as she sobbed quietly.

James fetched a box of tissues and put them next to her, poured her a brandy and one for himself.

The sobs gradually subsided as the pile of sodden tissues built up beside her.

She eventually looked up at James, her eyes red raw and swollen from crying.

'What's happened to Andaman Sea now?' she asked, stifling another sob at the mention of the mare's name.

'The vet and Mary have made all the arrangements, so there's nothing for you to do.'

'So that's it – there's nothing left then?'

'Of course there's something left Emily, you still have The Legacy. Accidents like this happen. I know that's of no comfort to you now, but life has to go on.'

'I know,' Emily relied, wiping yet another tear away that was dangerously close to becoming a torrent again. 'It just hurts so much.'

James held Emily's hand, and pulling her out of the chair he put his arms around her, holding her close to him, wishing he could take some of the pain away and protect her from her anguish.

Emily buried her head in his shoulder and started sobbing again. Somehow his kindness and compassion had the effect of starting her tears off all over again.

At that moment, Mick opened the kitchen door and with one look at James and Emily, quickly retreated.

He wondered what had upset Emily so much, but he knew that she was in the good, capable hands of someone who cared a great deal about her.

Emily must have stood for about ten minutes in James's arms, the silence occasionally being broken by another bout of sobbing from Emily. James stroked her hair, trying to soothe the pain.

Gradually the sobs became fewer and James could feel Emily relax in his arms. He kissed the top of her head – he couldn't help it.

Emily looked up at him through her swollen, tearstained eyes.

'I'm sorry, I shouldn't have done that,' James said, suddenly feeling very embarrassed at the innocent kiss he had just given her.

'No, that's all right, it was rather nice,' Emily said, trying her best to smile.

'If it'll make you smile, then it was worth it.'

James then gently kissed her forehead.

Emily closed her eyes and then suddenly stepped back.

'Oh, no!' she exclaimed in dismay, realising how much her eyes were stinging from the crying and how red her nose must be. 'I must look an awful mess!'

'You look beautiful,' James replied softly, giving her a reassuring smile.

Emily wiped her eyes again and blew her nose.

'Here, have a sip of brandy. It always helps on occasions like this.'

James passed her a glass.

'Have you ever had a horse break a leg?' Emily enquired, having regained her composure.

'Yes, a couple of times, once on the gallops and once when the horse slipped going round a corner during a race.'

'That must have been awful for you.'

'Yes, those days are the worst ones in racing. As a rider you cannot help but feel responsible. Maybe there was something you could have done to prevent it, and there's

223

nothing you can say to the owner which will make you feel any better.'

'Oh God! Here's me thinking about Andaman Sea – I forgot about Tracy. How is she?'

'Apparently she's badly bruised but apart from that uninjured. Mary says that she's devastated.'

'Oh, poor Tracy. I must give her a ring. Would you mind if I used your phone?'

'No, of course not. Use the one in the lounge.'

Emily drained the rest of her brandy in one big gulp and picked up the box of tissues before disappearing into the lounge for twenty minutes before reappearing again – her eyes redder and more swollen than ever.

James looked at Emily with concern.

'I'm OK,' she said. 'We've had a good cry together and I think we both feel better for it. I also gave Mary a ring. She was so upset too.'

James poured Emily another brandy which she sipped slowly this time.

In an effort to take Emily's mind off the tragic events of the day, James talked about his early days as an apprentice jockey. How Mick would rule the yard with a rod of iron, keeping all the boisterous stable lads under control.

'I like Mick,' said Emily thoughtfully. 'He really seems to care about every single horse here, despite the things he says about some of them.'

James laughed.

'I think sometimes he says them out of affection more than anything else.'

'I'm sure you're right,' Emily replied.

She suddenly looked at her watch and realised how late it was.

'I really must be going. Thank you for being so kind tonight,' she said, a look of sadness reappearing on her face. 'I'm not looking forward to going home and being on my own tonight.'

'Then why not stay here? I'll make up the spare bed,' James said hastily.

'No, I'm sorry, I didn't mean that,' Emily said, embarrassed by the way her last comment had been taken. 'I couldn't possibly put you to all that trouble.'

'It would be no trouble. Besides, I wouldn't want to be responsible for you being over the alcohol limit and then driving home.'

'I hadn't thought of that,' Emily said. 'Are you sure it's no trouble?'

'Of course not. In fact – I insist.'

Later that night as James was trying to get to sleep, he kept thinking of when he held Emily in his arms. The smell of her hair, the softness of her skin, and the innocent kiss he had given her. He thought of that wonderful feeling when Emily suddenly relaxed in his arms, almost melting into them.

He groaned and rolled over.

James had vowed after his divorce that it would be a long time before he would get involved with anyone again, and here he was, attracted – more than attracted to Emily.

He rolled over yet again. To make matters worse, she was the owner of The Legacy – the brightest star in his yard. If he handled their relationship wrongly he could lose both of them.

James turned and lay on his back, staring at the ceiling in the darkness. His head told him to keep his distance and

banish all romantic thoughts of her from his mind but his
heart wanted to relive every second when he held her –
every smell and every touch.

He didn't even know what Emily felt about him.

What a mess he had got himself into.

He need not have worried. In the spare bedroom, Emily
was having the same problem sleeping.

James had been so kind to her tonight. It was a
long time since anyone had been that sympathetic to
her.

She lay there thinking about him.

He had held her so gently and protectively, stroking
her hair so softly, almost lovingly – and then kissing her
like that. Was he just being kind or was there more to it
than that?

Emily felt confused.

The more she thought about it, the more confused she
became.

Since Greg, she had been wary of sharing her emotions
with anyone – not that there had been anyone to share
them with – until now, but the way that James had
comforted her – was there more to it than just comforting?

Eventually Emily could barely think straight anymore,
the evening had drained her of all her emotions.

With dismay she thought of the next morning and how
puffed up her eyes would be despite having bathed them
in cold water before going to bed.

She groaned and pulled the duvet up to her neck. What
a sight she would look in the morning.

Emily was awakened the following morning by the noise

of someone going downstairs. For a moment she wondered where she was. Then she realised that she was in James's spare bedroom.

She looked at the clock and groaned. It was 5.45a.m.

Noises were also coming from the yard. Voices, laughter, horses whinnying and the sound of stable doors being opened.

Emily realised that by now the entire stable staff would know that she had stayed the night and would undoubtedly have jumped to the wrong conclusion.

She dressed hurriedly and went into the bathroom where she looked in the mirror.

Her eyes were still a little red and swollen from the night before but not too bad – considering. She bathed her face in cold water and had to use James's deodorant and comb.

Satisfied that she looked reasonably presentable, Emily went downstairs to find Mick and James in the kitchen.

'Sorry to hear about the mare, Miss,' Mick said with concern, James having briefed him as to the events of the night before.

'Thank you, Mick,' Emily replied, her heart still heavy from the upset.

'Would you like a cup of tea? I've made a pot,' James asked tentatively, not sure what emotional state Emily would be in this morning.

'I'd love one. Thank you. You start very early in the morning,' Emily commented, realising that most of the staff would have been up for nearly an hour already.

'I hope we didn't wake you,' James said, his voice full of concern.

'No, I didn't sleep very well last night, anyway.'

'Are you sure you're OK?'

'Yes, I'll be fine, thank you.'

Emily was touched by James's concern. It had been a long time since anyone had worried about her and she found it very comforting.

James poured her tea.

'So, what's the usual routine in the mornings?' Emily asked, trying to think of anything but Andaman Sea.

'It's mucking out, then first string ride out for about an hour, back for a light breakfast and then the second string goes out,' James explained. 'The Legacy will be going out with the first string. Why don't you come and watch him?'

'I'd love to. I should just make it in to work for nine, although I really don't feel up to it,' Emily said, realising how emotionally drained and tired she felt.

'Why not ring in sick? You can watch The Legacy work, and then if you like you can come with us to Newmarket. We've got two runners there this afternoon. You'd be more than welcome. I can get you in on an owner's badge, there's one going spare.'

'I don't know,' said Emily, hesitating. 'I really should go in today.'

'Come now, Miss. You look so pale and the fresh air will do you good. Can't have you feeling miserable in an office all day – can we?' Mick joined in, seeing a marvellous opportunity for James and Emily to spend the day together.

'And I can explain all about what goes on at race meetings, so when The Legacy runs you won't feel quite such a novice owner,' he added.

'Well, as you put it that way, I'll stay here with you two. I'll ring in after nine if that's OK with you James?'

'Fine by me.'

James beamed with delight at the thought of spending the day with Emily.

'But on one condition,' Emily said rather sternly.

James and Mick both looked up at the same time.

'And what's that?' James asked.

'That before we go to Newmarket, I can go home, shower and change. I can't go looking like this and smelling of your deodorant, James.'

'It smells better on you than it does on the Governor,' Mick said with a toothless grin.

They all broke into laughter and it was agreed that Emily would go home after the second string had been out.

They finished their tea and James drove Emily down to the gallops where the horses were about to start their work.

The Legacy seemed so mature now, it was hard to believe it wasn't so long ago when he was a new born foal peering out from behind Andaman Sea.

The thought of Andaman Sea brought a lump to Emily's throat, and she looked down at the ground, trying to regain her composure.

James realised that she had gone rather quiet again and in his concern put his arm around her.

'Are you sure you're all right?'

'Yes, I'll be fine. Sometimes I just can't get Andaman Sea out of my mind.'

'I don't think you'll ever get Andaman Sea out of your

mind, she'll always be there in your memories, but you will get over her in time,' he said gently.

The kindness that James was showing, together with the thoughts of the soft and gentle mare, made tears well up in her eyes again. She looked away and hoped that James hadn't noticed.

James hurriedly changed the subject.

'Look, The Legacy is about to start work. He usually gives the rest of the string a head start. Just watch what happens.'

Emily looked up and watched the string of horses start off in pairs down the gallops, leaving The Legacy behind. The colt was anxious to join the others, but the lad held him back. The Legacy jigged up and down, his eyes never leaving the other horses as they galloped away from him.

The lad looked at James, waiting for the signal.

James nodded, and the lad kicked the colt forward. The Legacy was instantly at full gallop, closing on the others, the ground being covered at a phenomenal rate.

Emily watched breathlessly. She had never seen anything so beautiful in all her life.

The colt's hooves seemed barely to touch the ground as the distance between him and the other horses diminished with each stride until he passed them, just before the end of the gallops.

'That was incredible!' Emily exclaimed, surprised that she could find the words, she felt so speechless.

'He certainly is a class act,' James said with pride. 'Your uncle may well have been right about the Derby.'

'Do you really think he's up to it?' Emily asked with excitement.

230

'He's certainly fast enough and seems to be able to gallop for ever. Unfortunately the other horses aren't much opposition for him. It would be nice to enter him in a race just to see how he handles race conditions and better opposition.'

'Yes, I suppose we should.'

'Why don't we talk it over tonight, after Newmarket? We could go over the fixture list and see what we can come up with.'

'I'd like that,' Emily said, pleased that she was being considered as part of the team, even though it was her horse.

The rest of the day passed so quickly. Despite Andaman Sea having been in the back of Emily's mind all the time, Emily felt a little guilty at having enjoyed herself so much.

Although neither of the horses were placed at Newmarket, both James and Mick were pleased with the way they ran, and were already planning the next races for them.

The day was rounded off with supper in James's kitchen, where the conversation inevitably turned to which race to enter The Legacy.

They decided on a fairly minor race that was in six weeks time, and Emily was already a little apprehensive at the thought of The Legacy's debut.

Mick diplomatically departed just before James made the coffee, leaving Emily and James together.

Over coffee they talked about some of the classic races that James had ridden in and some of the horses that he had partnered.

Emily realised that it was getting late, and knowing

now what an early start James always had in the morning, decided she had outstayed her welcome.

They walked back to her car together, the yard in darkness, the silence being punctuated by the noise of the odd horse settling down for the night.

'Thank you for a wonderful day,' Emily said, wishing that she didn't have to go.

'I really enjoyed myself too,' James replied, looking into her eyes which were so clear and bright in comparison to the red and swollen ones only twenty four hours ago.

'I'll see you Friday then.'

Before Emily could open the car door, James put his hands to her face and gently pulled he towards him, kissing her lips with the softest of kisses.

Emily was a little taken aback at first, but then put her arms round his neck and returned the kiss with tenderness and longing.

They drew even closer as they kissed, their locked shadows being cast on the driveway by the moonlight.

Eventually they parted.

'I really must be going,' Emily said reluctantly, trying – but not succeeding – to convince herself.

'Yes, I know.'

James kissed her again, not wanting the moment to end.

'I'll see you Friday,' she said as they parted to draw breath.

'I'll look forward to it.'

Emily got into her car and watched James wave as she drove away.

It had certainly been a couple of days of extreme emotion.

*　　*　　*

Although the Derby that The Legacy would run in was still a year off, the current year's Derby was only a week away.

Emily had never taken any interest in it before her uncle's death, but now she was keen to learn as much as she could about it, and read every report of the build up to it in The *Racing Post* and any other paper she could find.

The more she read, the more apprehensive she became.

She wondered what they would be saying about The Legacy this time next year.

When the Saturday came Emily went round to Bishop's Place to watch the race on the TV with James. She couldn't bear to watch it on her own, and was relieved when James had said he had no runners that day and invited her round.

James knew that the Derby could be quite overwhelming for even the most experienced of owners, so he couldn't imagine what Emily would make of it.

Mick would have loved to watch the race with them as well, but he diplomatically decided to watch it with the other staff in the hostel, leaving James and Emily alone together.

As the afternoon progressed, James was doing all the talking and explaining, whilst Emily watched, overwhelmed by the whole event.

After the race, James looked at her and realised that she seemed rather pale and subdued.

'Are you feeling all right?' he asked, his voice full of concern.

'I don't know. It's all so overwhelming,' she said weakly. 'All the owners are either millionaires or royalty. All the horses cost millions of pounds and as for the prize money of half a million pounds to the winner . . .' Her voice tailed off as she fought to compose herself.

'How on earth can I go there and mix with these owners? I mean, look at me. I'm only a secretary. And Leggy, poor old Leggy. He doesn't even have any decent breeding and he's got to race against some of the best horses in the world. I can just imagine the papers and everyone else laughing at us. It'll be awful. Damn Uncle Julian and his will!'

Emily put her head in her hands and closed her eyes, the enormity of what she had committed herself to only just beginning to sink in.

James firmly held her hands and pulled them away from her face.

'Now, listen to me,' he said sternly, immediately getting Emily's attention since he had never spoken to her like that before.

'Stop feeling sorry for yourself. The Legacy is one of the best colts I have ever had the privilege to be associated with, so I'm sure he'll be able to look after himself and put in a good performance without being disgraced. As for the owners, just because they are rich or royalty doesn't made them any better people than you. Underneath they are all just other human beings, the same as you and me. In fact, a couple of those owners are right bastards for all their airs and graces, so don't hold them in awe! And lastly, it's every owner's dream to have a runner in this race, so you are one of the very lucky and privileged few.'

Emily looked at James and realised that he was telling the truth.

'I'll try not to get too overwhelmed,' she said, 'but you may have to remind me every now and again.'

'You can count on me.'

'Yes, I know I can. There is another problem, though,' Emily added thoughtfully.

'What's that?'

'It'll take me a year to save up for an appropriate outfit!'

James laughed with relief.

'Silly girl, you'll look wonderful whatever you'll be wearing.'

As the date of The Legacy's race drew nearer, Emily's anxiety grew.

A multitude of doubts would constantly flash through her mind – how would he react towards the crowds, would the going be right and how would he compare with the opposition.

Mick and James seemed confident enough, but they were used to the pressures of racing. This would be Emily's first race as an owner.

One afternoon at work, she received a phone call from James. She was instantly concerned since James never rang her at work.

'Is anything wrong?' she asked immediately, sensing a tone of anxiety in his voice.

'Well, it's not too serious, but we'll have to withdraw The Legacy from the race next week,' James started to explain.

'Why, what's happened?'

'He cut into himself on the gallops this morning. Don't worry, it's nothing serious, only a superficial cut. It hasn't damaged any muscles or tendons.'

'On, no. Are you sure it's not serious?' Emily asked, concerned that James might be hiding something from her.

'Quite sure. The vet's been out and had a look and stitched the cut. He say's it'll be fine in a couple of weeks, just to keep him quiet to allow it to heal up, so I'm afraid I'll have to withdraw him.'

'Yes, of course,' Emily said, still concerned that she was not being given the whole story.

'Can I come and see him after work? I know it's not one of my usual nights, but I'd like to put my mind at rest.'

'I hoped you would come. Remember to bring some extra mints. Leggy could do with cheering up. He's a bit miserable, what with his sore leg and all the fuss he's had from the vet examining him, not to mention Mick! He's hardly been out of Leggy's box since it happened.'

'I'll stop and pick up some extra mints on the way. See you soon.'

Emily put the phone down and asked if she could leave early, having explained the situation and promised to make up the time by coming in early the next morning.

James was surprised to see her drive up only half an hour after his phone call.

'I left work early,' Emily explained, 'I wouldn't have been much use anyway, I was so worried.'

'It really is nothing to worry about. These things happen. We're just grateful that it's only a superficial cut and no deeper. Anyway, come and see for yourself.'

James followed Emily to The Legacy's box, barely

able to keep up with her as she was so anxious to see her colt.

She reached his box and peered in with trepidation.

The Legacy, on hearing her voice, turned round and snickered as he walked to the door. Emily instantly noticed that he seemed to be walking normally, much to her relief.

She looked down and saw the bandaged leg.

'What have you done, you silly boy,' she said, offering him a couple of mints which disappeared with barely a crunch.

'Look at you! You've got two white socks now!'

The Legacy seemed to look down a little shame faced to where Emily was pointing. He snorted, as if in agreement.

'Poor boy, and you've had the vet out too. I hope it's not too sore.'

Emily stroked his neck and then tweaked his ear which flicked back when she let go of it.

The Legacy greedily eyed the rest of the packet of mints she had in her other hand.

'At least it hasn't affected your appetite,' she said, for the first time feeling reassured that it wasn't a serious injury. When the bandage came off and she could see what had been done, then she would be more confident.

Having fed The Legacy the last of the mints she turned to James.

'What exactly did the vet say, then?'

'To put Leggy on light duties this week, just a quiet walk out to stretch his legs and relieve the boredom, to give the wound a chance to mend.

'Oh, dear,' Emily said with concern. 'He's never

done anything quiet in his life. He'll hate going for a quiet walk!'

'Yes, I know. I'll get Mick to walk the other side, he won't dare misbehave then.'

Emily laughed, the tension of the last hour having finally been released.

'Poor old Leggy! He'll be bored out of his mind.'

'Better that than opening up the wound,' James said, realising that The Legacy was not a horse that would take kindly to light work. He was the sort of colt who had so much energy that he needed a good daily gallop just to release it.

'Maybe if I could put Mick in his box with him, then they could bore each other to death,' James joked, laughing at the thought of it.

'That's a little unkind, isn't it?' Emily laughed with him as she pictured Mick telling all his Irish tales to the horse.

'What – do you mean unkind on The Legacy or unkind on Mick?'

They both dissolved into fits of giggles made worse when Mick arrived to check on The Legacy.

'What are you two laughing at then?' he asked, eager to share the joke.

'Oh, nothing,' James replied, trying to keep a straight face, not daring to look at Emily in case she set him off laughing again.

'Private joke is it?' Mick asked again.

'Yes – it's rather personal,' James replied.

'In that case I'd better get on and check on The Legacy.'

Mick opened the stable door and went in, running

his hand down The Legacy's leg as far as the bandage would allow before giving the colt a reassuring pat on the neck.

'There's a good lad. You'll be fine in no time – you'll see,' he said, stroking The Legacy's back.

James and Emily walked back to the house, trying their best not to break down into fits of giggles at the thought of Mick and The Legacy together.

Once inside, James proceeded to make the coffee as Emily sat down at the kitchen table.

'Has Mick ever been married?' she asked as James brought the coffee over.

'No,' James replied, 'I think he's too preoccupied with horses to get involved in any personal relationships. I suppose you could almost say that he's been married to a few horses. Some, but not many he's fallen out with, others he's drifted apart from, some have let him down and a few have broken his heart.'

'Poor Mick,' Emily said, realising how horses left so little time for anything else.

'But he wouldn't have it any other way,' James added.

'It's such a shame. I really like Mick. He's kind, caring and so uncomplicated.' Emily sighed, although she had to admit that she could never see Mick settling down to happily married bliss.

'Yes, Mick's one of the best. I don't know what I would do without him,' James said, thinking back over all the years that he had known him.

'As an apprentice jockey he taught me all I know, and now he's back, teaching me all I need to know as a trainer.'

Emily looked up at James a little surprised. On the

outside, James gave an impression of knowledge and confidence, but inside he seemed full of self doubt.

'And what about you, James? Do you see yourself becoming a lonely old man with only his horses for company?'

James looked thoughtfully at the empty coffee cup.

'I hope not, but I can't see anyone wanting to put up with me at the moment. Training has become an obsession with me. It's all I have left.'

'You're too hard on yourself,' Emily replied, putting her hand on his. 'I don't blame you for burying your-self in your work, but you're still young, talented and handsome.'

James laughed.

'It's kind of you to say so to cheer me up.'

'I'm not just saying it to cheer you up,' Emily said, looking into his soft blue eyes. 'I really mean it.'

She leant across the kitchen table and was just about to kiss him when they heard the kitchen door open.

Emily quickly sat down again and they both tried not to look like two embarrassed teenagers having been caught sneaking a kiss.

'The Legacy's fine, Miss,' Mick said, unaware that he had interrupted anything. 'He's settled down for the night and he'll sleep like a baby, I'm sure. I'll check on him again before I turn in, just to be sure.'

'That's good of you, Mick. Thank you,' Emily said, grateful that The Legacy was in Mick's capable hands.

'You spoil that horse, Mick,' said James, knowing that Mick wouldn't be quite so diligent with any other horse.

'He deserves spoiling,' Mick relied defensively. 'A colt

like that deserves a little special attention. He'll be a champion, mark my words.'

'Well, we'll just have to wait a little longer to find out,' James sighed, turning his thoughts to how long to give The Legacy to recover before he could race again.

'We'll have to wait until the vet is happy with him before we can consider entering him in any races. In reality, by the time he's one hundred per cent fit, there aren't any decent races to put him in, it's so close to the end of the season.'

'Quite right,' said Mick, deep in thought. 'And the going can be either hard as a rock or soft as a bog in September and October.'

'So, where does that leave us then?' Emily asked, wishing she knew what they were both thinking.

'Well, I propose that we give the end of this season a miss and enter him in a race early next year. What do you think, Mick?'

James looked at Mick, hoping for agreement.

Mick seemed lost in thought for a long time before replying.

'Shame, though, it would have been nice to see him run this season, but you're right, I think it's for the best. It's not worth running him in what'll be left of the season. Mind you, the going in the spring can be pretty boggy too.'

'What do you think, Emily?' James asked, realising that as the owner of the horse she ought to have some say in the matter.

'You're the experts, so I'll have to go with your decision. It's just so disappointing him not running this year, but as Mick said, it's not worth the risk.'

Emily tried not to sound too despondent.

Despite her disappointment, Emily knew that it was in The Legacy's best interest. In her heart, she was relieved that both James and Mick had the welfare of the horse foremost in their minds.

From what she had picked up whilst helping James out, she knew that there were some trainers who would have no hesitation in pushing their horses beyond their ability or fitness, usually resulting in the horse breaking down and the possible end of it's racing career.

It was such a shame, though. The next flat season seemed such a long way off.

9

The two-year-old career of Darwin's Choice had been an outstanding success and over the winter he was installed as the odds on favourite for the first classic of the season – the 2000 guineas.

Throughout the racing world the colt was regarded as invincible with the racing press calling him 'the flying machine' for his ability to win from the front or to toy with the field, passing them with a devastating turn of foot in the final furlong.

Darwin's Choice was also quoted as favourite for the Derby, despite the race still being many months away.

No-one could see the colt being beaten.

Stuart Lawson felt the pressure mounting on him during the winter months as Darwin's Choice enjoyed the break from the flat season.

As if it wasn't enough to have the expectations of Nathan Grant weighing on his shoulders, he also now had the expectations of the entire racing world.

There was so much that could still go wrong, Stuart couldn't bear to think about it.

Despite Darwin's Choice finishing the season as the top rated two-year-old, it often happened that the top juvenile would fail to make the transition to a successful three-year-old.

For Nathan Grant, the winter was also an anxious time. Illness, injury or sheer bad luck could ruin the colt's career and he fervently hoped that Stuart Lawson could nurture him as far as the Derby.

After winning the Derby, he could then retire the colt to stud and look forward with relish to the prospects that his offspring would bring – not to mention the fortune in stud fees.

Nathan and Lydia spent Christmas where they always did – in Barbados – where the high flyers of the racing world would flock for their winter break.

Needless to say, invitations to Nathan Grant's parties were coveted by all those invited and Lydia would enjoy hosting the ever increasingly lavish parties that everyone had come to expect.

It was one of the few times of the year when Nathan seemed to relax and actually enjoy life away from his business empire – although business, together with racing, always seemed to be the topic of conversation during the rounds of golf at the Sandy Lane golf course.

Stuart Lawson and his wife would also spend Christmas in Barbados despite the horrendous expense. It was expected of him by Nathan Grant. It also had the advantage of keeping him in close contact with other affluent owners whose services he might need to call on should he fall out of favour with his current boss.

Despite being on holiday, at social gatherings in the evenings virtually all the conversation was of racing – the gossip, the rumours and of course Darwin's Choice – the hottest favourite for the 2000 guineas in years.

* * *

The Legacy finished the season unraced but fully recovered from his injury.

Emily decided to leave him at Bishop's Place for the winter, where she was confident that he would get nothing but the best attention from Mick and James.

The Legacy soon grew his winter coat and no longer looked the sleek, glossy horse he had been in the summer.

When he was turned out into the field during the day he would soon roll in the mud, and despite his jute rug his coat would end up caked in dried mud, which added warmth against the chill winter weather.

Mick would mutter about the state he was in as he would lead him back to the stables in the evening, giving him a good brushing to get the mud out of his coat, knowing that the next day The Legacy would go out and roll in the muddiest patch he could find.

Emily found the winter so frustrating. By the time she finished work it was dark and The Legacy would have already been brought in and bedded down for the night. It was only at weekends that she could see him in daylight.

James had to assure her that his dull, muddy winter coat would return to its sleek, glossy condition in the spring, although to look at him sometimes she did have her doubts.

There was no luxury Caribbean holiday for James. His staff would have their holidays during the quiet winter period which meant that James would have to do a lot of the work in the yard himself, so he couldn't afford the time and was in no financial position to afford a weekend away, let alone Christmas in a warmer climate.

James decided to hold a Christmas party for the staff that had stayed on, friends, and any owners who could attend, although he had to admit to himself that it was really for Emily.

They had grown quite close over the weeks leading up to Christmas, but with Mick there in the kitchen every evening it was difficult for anything further to develop despite Mick's tactful disappearance early on in the evening.

Both Emily and James seemed to have an unspoken understanding that if their relationship was going to develop, it would be at the rate that they wanted and not because Mick expected it. The fact that their previous relationships had ended badly also meant a reluctance by both of them to let down the emotional wall that they had built up to protect themselves from further hurt.

Needless to say, at the party Mick was the life and soul, consuming vast quantities of Guinness that only a true Irishman could.

Emily and James laughed at Mick trying to teach one of the more mature owner's wives the Irish jig, whilst Emily had her toes trodden on by a few of the more elderly men as they tried to emulate Mick with his exuberant dancing.

James watched Emily with a feeling of warmth and pride.

When they had first met she seemed so quiet and subdued, but since she had been helping James her confidence had grown and she had really blossomed. She now literally ran the administrative side of the yard whilst James took care of the training.

Emily had also taken charge of organising the party, and in effect became the hostess.

In the early hours of the morning the number of guests gradually dwindled as a combination of excess alcohol and exhaustion from dancing took its toll.

Mick was one of the last to leave, staggering out of the door clutching a couple of cans of Guinness which he claimed were for a night-cap.

Emily and James were finally on their own amongst all the debris from the party.

Emily started to clear up the glasses when James came up and put her arms around him.

'Thank you for all the hard work you've put in to make this evening a success,' he said, taking the glasses from her and putting them back down on the table.

'It did go well, didn't it?' Emily said, half as a statement and half as a question, almost as if she were seeking reassurance.

'It certainly was a party to remember.'

James brushed the strand of hair which had fallen over her eyes. She looked pale and tired.

'Leave all this, I'll clear it up in the morning,' he said, having decided that Emily had done more than enough already.

'Are you sure?' she asked, moving ever so slightly closer to him.

'Quite sure.'

James could almost feel the electricity between them as he kissed her soft, inviting lips.

Emily responded for a moment before drawing away.

'I really had better ring for a taxi. It'll be ages getting here at this time of night,' she said, hesitating before kissing him again.

'Why?' he asked, in between kisses.

'I can't possibly drive home with the amount that I've drunk, silly!'

'No. I mean why go home. Why not stay here?'

He kissed her again and she responded passionately, her body pressed against his and her arms holding him ever closer.

They eventually parted, if only to draw breath.

Emily looked into James's eyes and any doubts that she may have had melted away.

'If you're sure,' she said, softly.

'I've never been so sure of anything in my life.'

Abandoning the mess of the party they managed to make it upstairs in between passionate, exploring kisses, discarding items of clothing across the landing until they reached the bedroom where the remainder of the night was spent reaching heights of passion that neither of them thought possible.

The following morning Emily rolled over and kissed James on his shoulder. It was then that she felt a strange weight at the foot of the bed.

Rather startled, she sat up, waking James from his deep sleep in the process.

'What is it, darling?' he asked, wondering in his half asleep state what was wrong.

'There's something on the bed,' Emily replied as she turned on the light to reveal a black cat curled up at the foot end of the bed, eyeing her with indignation at having been woken up.

'Oh, it's only Oats,' James replied reassuringly, pulling the duvet up to his chin for warmth. 'I'm sorry, I should have told you that he often comes to sleep here when he's finished mousing.'

'And here was I, thinking all this time that you were spending your nights alone,' Emily said, laughing at the thought of her getting it wrong.

'I'd much rather have you for company,' James replied, gathering her into his arms and kissing the soft nape of her neck.

Within a very short space of time, Oats retreated to the kitchen, unused to the strange activity that was going on under the duvet.

An hour or so later Mick stumbled into the kitchen for a coffee. His head was thumping and he had trouble focussing his eyes. Despite his enormous hangover he had still got up at the usual time to tend the horses, and was now in desperate need of a coffee and a couple of aspirins.

It was unusual not to see James this early, but Mick assumed that the poor lad had no doubt got to bed even later with all the clearing up that had to be done after the party.

One look round the room told him otherwise. The room looked vaguely as he recalled leaving it – glasses everywhere, plates and ashtrays too.

Then he noticed an indignant Oats, mewing in front of his empty dish, and Guinness sitting in his box looking rather neglected.

'Hasn't he been up and fed you yet?' Mick said as Oats rubbed round his legs and Guinness woofed in disbelief that his breakfast was this late.

'All right, all right, I'll sort you out!'

Mick quickly fed them before he put the kettle on for his much needed coffee.

It was when he looked round for a second time that he noticed one of Emily's shoes half way up the stairs and the other one at the top.

He quickly turned off the kettle and went up to Oats, who by now had finished his breakfast.

'It's about time them two got together,' he said, stroking the cat quietly who purred in appreciation. 'I'd better sneak out quietly and leave them to it.'

As spring approached, Darwin's Choice was brought back into training, and any lingering doubts as to whether he would make the transition from the best two-year-old to a top three-year-old were soon dispelled when winning his warm up race for the 2000 guineas in the same style as he had finished the previous season – with considerable ease.

The culmination of his pre Derby build up was winning the 2000 guineas way ahead of the rest of the field and smashing the course record in the process.

Stuart was euphoric.

The winter had been a worrying time for him with the expectations of Nathan Grant and the whole of the racing world hanging on whether the colt would emerge as good a three-year-old as he had been a two-year-old.

Now Stuart had no doubts at all. Darwin's Choice really was the 'flying machine' that he had been nicknamed throughout the racing world.

Such was the confidence of the bookmakers that Darwin's Choice was installed as shortest priced favourite for the Derby since anyone could remember.

Despite the outstanding calibre of his opposition, who in their own right would have been in contention for the

Derby, none could live with the blistering pace and endless stamina that Darwin's Choice seemed to possess.

Joe McGrath was delighted to have been booked to ride Darwin's Choice in the Derby. They had become a formidable partnership and the colt's victories had made Joe McGrath a household name. Needless to say, Joe was very much in demand now as a jockey.

If he had no rides for Nathan Grant, he had no problems in filling the gaps by picking up rides for others who were keen for some of Joe's talents to rub off on their horses.

This would be Joe's first real chance in the Derby, having only had one ride in it previously when he partnered a third string horse for another stable and finished at the back of the field.

For a first ride, the thrill of riding in the Derby alone had been satisfaction enough for him, but this year his expectations were for first place – and first place only.

The Legacy, meanwhile, was also back in training and Emily's now almost depleted budget would only allow James to enter the colt in a relatively modest race at Nottingham in May.

At least it would give The Legacy some racecourse experience and would provide far superior opposition than the rest of James's string on their morning gallops.

As James had promised, when spring arrived, The Legacy lost his thick, dull winter coat and now seemed glossier and more handsome than ever. He was also beginning to fill out and not look so lean as he had as a two-year-old.

As the race day approached Emily's anxiety grew. Until now, The Legacy was still her 'baby' and as soon as he made his racecourse debut she would have to share him with the rest of the racing world.

Part of her was looking forward to it and the other part was full of doubt and apprehension.

What if he wasn't as good as James and Mick claimed?

What if his temperament wasn't up to the rigors of competitive racing?

There were so many 'what ifs' that would spin through Emily's mind in the sleepless hours of the night.

The Legacy had also been entered at the first entry stage for the Derby, along with five hundred or so other horses. As each forfeit stage passed, fewer and fewer horses remained until the final sixteen were confirmed – fifteen of which were the cream of the racing world and the sixteenth was The Legacy.

Whilst a few racing commentators were waiting to see how The Legacy performed at Nottingham, the remainder had written him off as having no chance with his breeding and the fact that he came from a small, unfashionable yard that had failed to produce a single horse anything close to classic standard. This, combined with a jockey of very little big race experience on board led the bookmakers and racing experts to install The Legacy as the 200–1 rank outsider.

An unseasonable week of torrential rain resulted in the meeting at Nottingham having to be abandoned due to the course being waterlogged.

James and Emily were desperately disappointed since it meant that The Legacy would have to run in the Derby as a complete novice.

Mick was also a little disheartened, although with The Legacy not having shown the racing world what potential he had, the bookmakers left him as the outsider of the field.

With ten days to go before the Derby, Emily received a phone call from Mr. Pierce, the solicitor, asking her to an urgent meeting.

Emily could only assume that it must be something to do with what – if anything – was left of the finances for the upkeep of The Legacy, or perhaps it was to discuss what to do after her uncle's wishes in running the colt in the Derby were complete, as there seemed to be no instructions about what she had to do after that.

Not for the first time she found herself in the solicitor's reception office, waiting to see Mr. Pierce whilst chatting to the elderly receptionist she now knew to be called Violet.

Violet Evans, a spinster with three cats at home for company, proved to be a kindly soul, and knowing about the predicament Emily was in with The Legacy would offer a sympathetic ear if Emily needed to talk. She would always ask after The Legacy and James, having been a secret admirer of the young James when he was champion jockey.

Today Violet seemed particularly excited.

'Mr. Pierce has arranged for everyone in the firm to go to the Derby. He's even booked a minibus. We're going to take a picnic and everyone has to bring something towards it and Mr. Pierce has even said that he'll bring a few bottles of sparkling wine. It'll be such a marvellous day out – I can't wait!' Violet gushed in her excitement.

Emily smiled at Violet's enthusiasm and mused on the effect The Legacy had seemed have on the lives of those people she knew.

'I've got my best dress out – the one I wear at family weddings, and have put some new trim on my bonnet. Mr. Pierce has even hired a top hat and tails. Won't he look dashing.'

Emily couldn't image Mr. Pierce looking dashing, whatever he wore, but kept the thought tactfully to herself.

'And I'm even going to have a little flutter on him,' Violet said with a knowing wink.

The more Violet talked, the more Emily began to realise that it wasn't just her expectations and those of James, Mick and the rest of the stable staff that rested on The Legacy, but the expectations of the entire firm of solicitors, all her friends at work and all the other people who perhaps had drawn her horse's name in the office sweep stake or maybe had stuck a pin in his name in the papers for a random lucky bet. The Derby was an institution, and The Legacy was going to be part of it.

The phone buzzed and Violet picked it up.

'Mr. Pierce will see you now,' Violet said, rather disappointed that she wouldn't be able to chat with the glamorous client any more.

'Thank you, Violet, and I'm sure you'll have a wonderful day out, whatever the result.'

'I'll have my fingers crossed for you.'

Emily smiled as she went down the corridor to Mr. Pierce's office, again wondering what could be so urgent.

Emily knocked and walked in to be greeted immediately by Mr. Pierce.

'I do hope Violet hasn't been boring you too much about our outing,' he said with some degree of pride at having organised it.

It was the first time in his long career there that the

firm had ever considered organising such a trip and he was overjoyed when all the staff and their partners signed up to come, showing an enthusiasm he wished they would equally show in their work.

'No, I'm rather embarrassed by it. I only hope we won't let you down.'

'Oh, come now, Emily, just having come this far is cause for celebration; anything after that is a bonus.'

'Yes, but Violet says she's going to have a bet on The Legacy,' Emily said in despair.

'Don't you worry about Violet. She may look all prim and proper, but I know for a fact that she always has a flutter on the Grand National, and it's not as though she's going to become addicted to gambling,' he said reassuringly.

The thought of Violet sneaking into a bookmakers brought a smile to Emily's face.

'Anyway, Emily, I'm afraid it's down to business.'

Mr. Pierce sat down and opened the big file on his desk which Emily recognised from her previous visits as her uncle's. Her thoughts immediately turned to more serious matters.

'I think your uncle would have been proud of you to have got this far. I know I certainly am. I realise that it hasn't been easy for you, but it's only a matter of days until the big race and it's a credit to you that The Legacy has come this far.'

'I didn't exactly have a choice, did I?' Emily replied, feeling a little uncomfortable with the praise that Mr. Pierce has heaping upon her.

'You did have a choice and you made the right one,' he reminded her. 'Anyway, back to matters in hand. Your uncle also left this envelope on file to be given to you a week before the Derby, assuming you had got this far with his wishes. As you have, then here it is.'

Mr. Pierce handed Emily the thick manilla envelope; which for three years he had wondered about its contents.

Every time Emily had been to see him, he would get the envelope out afterwards and stare at it, wondering what more surprises lay in store for her.

He was now going to find out.

Emily looked at the envelope. Her name was written on the front and she immediately recognised it as the untidy scrawl of her uncle.

With more than a degree of trepidation she opened it, pulling out a letter which was wrapped round something. She untied the string and opened out the letter, revealing much to her astonishment a bundle of £50 notes.

She looked at the wad of money in disbelief and then looked at Mr. Pierce who also was staring at the money in amazement.

'What does the letter say?' he asked once he had regained some degree of composure.

Her eyes widened as she read the letter, and lost for words she handed it to Mr. Pierce who began to read it in a quiet voice to himself.

'Dear Emily, if you are reading this letter now, I thank you with all my heart for carrying out my wishes. I realise it couldn't have been easy for you and that you can't think much of me for putting you in such an awkward position. I had my reasons, but they are a secret I must take with me to my grave. As compensation for all the trouble I have put you to, I leave you the sum of £2000 to have a bet on your horse when it runs in the Derby, but you must put it on to win – and trust me – it will win. I've never been one for spiritual thoughts, but I hope that on the day I'll be watching from somewhere. After the Derby you may do what you wish with the horse, your obligations to me are fulfilled. Best of luck, your uncle Julian.'

Mr. Pierce loosened his collar a little more and peered over his half glasses at Emily.

'How could he!' exclaimed Emily with a mixture of sheer rage and frustration. 'Why couldn't he have left it with the other money. It would have made such a difference. The Legacy could have been entered in some more races and at least had a decent build up to the Derby.'

Hot tears welled up in her eyes and spilled down her cheeks.

Emily looked down, picked up her handbag and started rummaging through it for a pack of tissues, embarrassed by the scene she was creating and hoping that Mr. Pierce hadn't noticed.

'I'm so sorry. I really didn't know anything about this,' he stammered, avoiding looking at Emily and not knowing what to say to make Emily feel any better.

'And now he wants me to blow it all on a bet! One bet! And to win! James reckons he has a remote chance of being placed but how on earth is he going to beat that Darwin's Choice – the wonder horse of the century!'

Emily wiped her tears and blew her nose as quietly as she could, suddenly regretting her outburst which had obviously caused Mr. Pierce some considerable discomfort.

'I'm sorry, Mr. Pierce. I realise you didn't know. It's just so frustrating and so typical of my uncle to do something so – well, so outrageous!'

'Look, Emily, you've come so far now, just ask yourself one thing.'

Emily looked up at him through her tear filled eyes.

'What's that?' she asked.

'Do you have any regrets over the last few years?'

Emily thought for a moment and then smiled.

'No, to be honest, I can't say I have. The last few years have been different – very different, but no, I've no regrets. I've met a wonderful man in James, found so many new good, honest friends and have thoroughly enjoyed being involved in racing. As for The Legacy, I love him to bits,' she said quite honestly.

'Well, there you are then,' Mr. Pierce said with a smile. 'Take my advice. The Derby is a once in a lifetime event. Enjoy it. Make the bet and if you lose it, so what. It was never yours to start with and what you've never had, you'll never miss.'

Emily realised that what he was saying was the truth.

'Yes, when you think of it like that it puts it all into perspective.'

Emily was beginning to feel a lot better, although the thought of parting with the bundle of notes that lay on Mr. Pierce's desk on a bet still troubled her.

She decided to regard it as Uncle Julian's money and the bet would be the last thing that she would do for him.

Somewhere, she sensed he was enjoying watching all this.

Emily gathered up the letter and the money and put them back in the envelope before trying to squeeze them into her handbag.

Mr. Pierce came round the desk and shook her warmly by the hand.

'Good luck next Saturday, and most of all, enjoy yourself,' he said, still clasping Emily's hand. 'With any luck I might see you there, although you'll be mixing with all those rich and famous owners!'

'I'll keep my eye out for you,' Emily promised, 'and once again, thank you for everything.'

Emily leant over and gave him a little peck on the cheek which brought a flush of colour to his cheeks and turned his bulbous nose a deeper shade of red that it already was.

Emily walked out of the office, clutching her handbag tightly to her side.

'Good luck,' Violet said as Emily made her way out.

'Thank you, Violet. I hope you'll have a really good day out too,' Emily replied.

'It'll be a wonderful day, you'll see.'

When Emily arrived back at Bishop's Place Mick and James were having lunch in the kitchen. They were surprised to see her as she had said she was going straight to work after her appointment at the solicitor's.

As soon as she walked into the kitchen James noticed that she looked troubled and upset.

'What's the matter, Emily?' he asked, getting up and giving her a kiss. 'What happened?'

Emily opened up her handbag and took out the envelope, emptying the contents out onto the kitchen table.

Mick and James stared open mouthed at the pile of notes that unfolded seemingly with a life of their own in front of them.

'It would appear that good old Uncle Julian left me

£2000 to have a bet on The Legacy in the Derby,' she said in exasperation.

'The man's a star!' exclaimed Mick, his love of gambling rising to the surface.

'Mick!' James said sharply, realising that Emily was more than a little upset by this.

'If only we could have had the money for his training, it would have made such a difference,' Emily sighed and she sat down. 'And the worst thing is that it has to be to win, not a place.'

'To win!' Mick sucked in the air through his teeth making a strange whistling noise. 'To win, be Jesus!'

'This is going to be the last thing I do for my uncle regardless of any other surprises he may have in store for me,' Emily declared in defiance. 'Can you imaging me going into a bookies with all that, saying "£2000 to win" – I'll die of embarrassment.'

James thought wistfully for a moment of what a difference the money would have made before resigning himself to the situation.

'Mick's the one to put on a bet like that,' James said, knowing that if there was anyone who could do it, then Mick was your man.

'Would you, Mick? Please. I wouldn't even know which form to fill in,' Emily declared with some relief that Mick could be delegated to the task.

'Sure I will, no problem. I'll get hold of my contacts right away. We'll spread the money in little bets with lots of bookies so as not to make any of them suspicious of a coup. With any luck the odds will stay the same then,' he said, relishing the thought of organising such a coup. Shame, though that it was to win. He couldn't see that Darwin's Choice being beaten by anything.

'Good, I'll leave it with you, then,' Emily said, wistfully pushing the money over the table to Mick who took it and stuffed it in his jacket pocket.

The thought of Emily's £2000 being bet to win on a horse that he had trained made James lose his appetite for what remained of his lunch.

He pushed the remnants of his salad around with his fork before resigning himself to this unwanted added burden.

Surely there could be no more surprises in store for him as far as The Legacy was concerned.

The following day the first string of horses, including The Legacy, were out on the gallops. It was a miserable morning, windy and raining heavily. Like the rest of the string, The Legacy was hooded to keep his ears dry. The hood had eye openings and came down to his muzzle, covering his distinctive blaze. James had also bandaged him. With this greasy surface he didn't want him slipping and cutting into himself again.

Throughout the session James noticed a couple of men in waterproofs on the nearby hill, watching the Legacy through their binoculars.

James smiled to himself. They were probably either racing journalists or from another yard, gathering information on the opposition.

James had assumed correctly. They had been sent by Stuart Lawson to assess the potential of the only Derby entrant they hadn't seen run.

They watched through their binoculars, a little peeved

that they had been sent out on such an awful day to watch the no-hoper of the Derby on a training gallop. Still, instructions were instructions, and the sooner they got the job done, the sooner they could get back to the shelter of their car.

'That's The Legacy there – at the back. I recognise the jockey, Alan Johnson,' one said to the other.

'I see him. Nice looking colt. Must have got it from his sire. From what I gather, the mare was a bit of a pony.'

They chuckled in the rain and waited for The Legacy to start work.

The shorter man started his stopwatch as The Legacy sprang forward, eager to stretch his legs on the gallops.

'Nice mover too,' the shorter man added.

After a couple of furlongs the horses with The Legacy began to tire and peeled off to be replaced by two fresher horses.

This happened a few times throughout the one and a half miles, since none of the other horses in the yard had the stamina of The Legacy.

'The rest of the horses are pretty poor,' one commented to the other.

'Yeah, make The Legacy look something really special, don't they?'

'Anything would look special against that bunch of cart horses!'

They laughed again as they kept their binoculars trained on The Legacy, whose stride seemed to eat up the ground with ease.

As The Legacy passed the one and a half mile post, the shorter man pressed his stopwatch and wiped the rain off the front of it in order to see the time.

The Legacy

'Oh, shit! The rain must have got in my stopwatch, there's condensation in it!'

He stared at the time in dismay.

'Damn. It's really buggared it up. According to this he's as fast as Darwin's Choice and let's face it, nothing's as fast as Darwin's Choice.'

'The taller man grabbed the watch and studied it closely.

'That'll teach you to buy a cheap stopwatch. Next time, lash out on something decent. Now what are we going to tell the Governor?'

The shorter man thought for a moment.

'We'll tell him just what we saw. He's the best in the yard, nice mover, but let's face it, anything would look a class act in comparison to the rest of Ryan's string.'

'Yea, true. Shame we didn't get the time though.'

The two men hurried back in the pouring rain to their car.

Later they reported just what everyone had thought. The Legacy had no hope. His entry in the Derby was just an owner's dream of having a horse run in the great race, regardless of its ability.

They did have to reluctantly admit that the colt was a nice mover – very nice indeed.

When the second string rode out later in the morning, it seemed to be raining even more.

Half way through the session a horse slipped and the momentary unexpected loss of balance caused the jockey to fall.

James rushed over full of concern when the jockey failed to get to his feet immediately.

'Are you OK, Alan?' James asked, looking at the muddy Alan Johnson who was struggling to sit up, clutching his shoulder.

'It's my shoulder, Governor. It hurts like hell,' he said, his face contorted with pain.

'Can you stand?'

'Yes. I think so.'

With the help of James, Alan struggled painfully to his feet, still clutching his shoulder.

'We'd better get you to the hospital, see if anything's broken or if it's just dislocated,' James said before turning to Mick, who by now had managed to catch the riderless horse.

'Mick, get someone to take the horse back to the yard and finish the session. I'll take Alan to the hospital. Let's hope it's nothing serious.'

'Right you are, Governor,' Mick replied, his voice full of concern. Having seen Alan doubled up in pain and white as a sheet he thought it looked more than heavy bruising. Of all the bad luck. Alan was due to ride The Legacy in the Derby – his first ride in a classic.

James helped Alan to his car and sped off with him to the casualty department at the local hospital some ten miles away.

A few hours later, after a frustrating wait followed by x-rays and examinations, James returned to Bishop's Place with a very subdued Alan – his left arm in a sling.

Mick opened the car door for Alan and on seeing the devastated expression on his face, he knew it wasn't good news.

'Broken collar bone, I'm afraid, and severe bruising,'

James said before Mick could ask the question. 'It'll mean Alan missing out on the ride in the Derby.'

Mick looked at the distraught Alan. It was to have been his first classic ride – something that he had dreamt of ever since he could remember, and now with one unfortunate slip and fall, it wasn't to be.

'Hard luck, lad,' Mick said, resting his hand on Alan's good shoulder.

Mick knew that there was nothing that he could do or say that would make Alan feel any better, and with a painful shrug, the inconsolable Alan trudged miserably back to the hostel where he just wanted to be left alone.

'Poor lad,' Mick sighed, 'of all the bad luck. Who's going to ride The Legacy now?'

'Good question,' James said. 'I've already started thinking about it, but I'm afraid that there's no-one else in the yard up to it.'

'Shame you put on a few pounds since retiring, you could have made a comeback and ridden him yourself, but you're carrying too much condition now!' Mick said jokingly, trying to lighten the mood of depression that James seemed to be in.

'Come on, Mick. This is serious!' James replied rather crossly.

'Sorry, Governor. 'Twas only joking.'

Mick looked suitably chastised and crestfallen, and James immediately regretted getting cross with him.

'No, I'm sorry Mick. I shouldn't have snapped at you like that. Come on, let's see who we know is booked on Saturday, then we can draw up a list of possibilities.'

A couple of hours later, Mick and James were still

poring over the list they had drawn up when Emily walked in.

'What's up with you two?' she asked on seeing their long faces.

'Alan broke his collar bone on the gallops this morning and can't ride on Saturday.'

James recounted the day's events including the long wait in the casualty department.

Emily sat down at the table with them and all three stared silently into space, hoping for inspiration.

'So who'll ride The Legacy now?' Emily asked, breaking the uncomfortable silence.

'There's no-one else in the yard up to it so we're having to look elsewhere,' James replied, pointing to the list they had already drawn up.

'Unfortunately anyone half decent has either been booked for the Derby or is riding at one of the other courses. We've already rung quite a few, but with no success.'

Silence descended on the kitchen again – each of them lost in thought. James and Mick were racking their brains as to a suitable jockey whilst Emily was wondering what else could go wrong.

'Let's have a think about it overnight,' James eventually said. 'It's been a long, hard day and things might seem a bit clearer in the morning.'

'I hope so,' replied Emily, admiring James's optimism. 'It certainly couldn't get any worse.'

Stuart Lawson was relaxing at home that evening when the phone rang. A little irritated at having his peaceful evening interrupted he picked it up.

He immediately recognised the voice as that of Nathan Grant.

'Stuart – Nathan Grant here. I've booked Peter Rhodes, that South African, to ride Darwin's Choice on Saturday.'

Stuart thought for a moment, not quite sure if he had heard correctly.

'But Joe McGrath is booked for the ride,' he protested.

'Then unbook him,' came the curt response from Nathan.

'But sir, you know what an awkward ride Darwin's Choice can be, and he and Joe get on so well together and are unbeaten so far, so why split up a winning partnership? Anyway, it's a bit late to ask Peter Rhodes to get used to some of Darwin's quirks.'

Stuart realised that he had probably said too much, judging by the stony silence on the other end of the line before Nathan Grant replied.

'Are you trying to tell me that Joe McGrath is a better jockey than Peter Rhodes, who has already won the Kentucky Derby, the Arlington Million, Dubai Cup and Japan Cup, just to mention a few? What's McGrath won in that league? Zero!'

'No, sir, I wasn't questioning his ability, but Darwin's Choice is rather temperamental and Joe gets on so well with him.'

'I doubt that Peter Rhodes would have become the best in the world without knowing how to handle a difficult horse.'

'Yes, sir, but . . .' Stuart started, still protesting.

'No buts. Peter Rhodes rides. He'll be at the yard the

day after tomorrow to ride work on Darwin's Choice and
if you don't like it you can look elsewhere for a job.'

The cold, uncompromising tone of Nathan's voice made
Stuart realise that there could be no reasoning with him.

'As you wish, sir. I'll inform Joe straight away.'

Stuart put the phone down and a deep depression came
over him.

He had one hundred per cent confidence in Darwin's
Choice and Joe's partnership, and had no doubts that,
together, the Derby was theirs for the taking.

Stuart couldn't deny that Peter Rhodes was an excellent
jockey – one of the best in the world and undoubtedly more
experienced than Joe, but Joe knew the colt so well and he
had nothing but admiration for the way he handled him.

Stuart decided that he couldn't tell Joe over the phone,
so he got up and fetched his car keys. This was something
he would have to do face to face.

Joe was surprised to see Stuart Lawson pull up in his car
at such a late hour. He went out to meet him and his heart
immediately sank at the sight of his worried face.

'What's up, Governor? Darwin's Choice is all right,
isn't he?'

'Yes, Darwin's Choice is fine. Can we go inside?'
Stuart didn't want to break the bad news to Joe on his
front doorstep.

'Yes, sure, go on in. So why the visit and why such a
long face?'

Joe tried to sound upbeat, but Stuart's demeanour told
him he was about to hear some bad news.

Once inside and sitting in Joe's lounge, Stuart broke
the news.

'I'm afraid you've been jocked off Darwin's Choice in the Derby,' Stuart said, fiddling with his wedding ring nervously, not daring to look Joe in the face.

'Jocked off? Why? Who by?' Joe's voice sounded hoarse with disbelief.

'I got a call from Nathan Grant an hour ago. He's booked Peter Rhodes. I had no say in the matter whatsoever. I'm so sorry Joe, I did argue your case the best I could.'

Joe sat in silence and total disbelief. His dream of partnering Darwin's Choice to victory in the Derby now lay in tatters. Someone else had stepped in and would take all the honours and all the glory.

Joe put his head in his hands and sat there in total despair whilst Stuart fidgeted in the uncomfortable silence.

'I'm sure it was Rhodes who contacted Mr. Grant,' Stuart said, trying to break the silent gloom. 'He has a reputation for going straight to the owners and talking his way into the ride, and with the credentials he's got, Mr. Grant fell for it hook, line and sinker.'

Joe looked up despairingly.

'Doesn't Mr. Grant realise how awkward Darwin's Choice can be? Look what happens if anyone else in the yard tries to ride him. I know him. I know his little quirks and I can sense his moods. There's no way the best jockey in the world could get to know him the way I do in the few days left till the Derby.'

'I know Joe. I know,' Stuart sighed. 'I tried to tell Mr. Grant that, but he was adamant. I'm sorry, Joe. There'll be other opportunities, you'll see.'

'None as good as this, though,' came the despondent reply.

Joe put his head in his hands, shaking his head, trying to hide the devastating despair that he was feeling.

'It's too late this year now. I'll never pick up another ride – all the rides have been taken.'

Stuart stood up to leave. There was nothing else he could say that would lift Joe's despair.

'Next year, lad. There's always next year.'

Joe got up and followed Stuart to his car.

'Thanks for coming and telling me in person, Governor. I really appreciate it,' Joe said, acknowledging the fact that Stuart had come and told him in person when it would have been far easier to pick up the phone, but Stuart was a good Governor who looked after his staff. It was a shame that some owners didn't show such loyalty.

After a sleepless night, Joe drove to Stuart's yard to ride work as usual.

Mo already had Darwin's Choice saddled up for him.

Joe always looked forward to riding out Darwin's Choice, since every ride on the exceptional colt was something special. Today, though, he felt as though he would just be going through the motions.

'Morning, Joe. Darwin's Choice is fit and raring to go this morning. Like the rest of us, I think he's getting excited about Saturday too,' Mo said, leading Darwin's Choice out of his stable and trying to get the exuberant colt to stand still.

'You haven't heard the news, then?' Joe said, the tone of his voice flat and unemotional.

'Heard what?' Mo asked, realising that Joe wasn't his usual cheerful self.

'I've been jocked off Darwin's Choice on Saturday.'

'No!' Exclaimed Mo in utter disbelief. 'Who by?'

'Peter Rhodes, that South African jockey's got the ride now.'

'Why?' Mo said, wide eyed in astonishment.

'Because Mr. Grant says so.'

'Oh.'

Mo had been at the yard long enough to know that when an order came from Mr. Grant, there was no negotiating or reasoning.

'I'm sorry, Joe,' she said, patting Darwin's Choice on the neck and trying to calm him down as he jigged up and down, raring to get to the gallops. She gave Joe a leg up into the saddle.

'There's no way I'll find a replacement ride either – it's too late for that now,' came the despondent reply from Joe who was trying to stay on board the excited Darwin's Choice.

'What about the outsider – The Legacy?'

'What about it?'

'The grapevine says his jockey fell yesterday and is out for a few weeks. That ride could still be going,' Mo said thoughtfully.

Joe thought for a moment. He didn't doubt for a second that Mo was right, even though he hadn't heard anything himself.

Mo was usually right when it came to rumours in racing – she seemed to know anything and everything that was going on.

'It's a bit like going from the sublime to the ridiculous,' Joe said, thinking of the difference between riding the unbeatable Darwin's Choice he should have been on and the untested outsider and no hoper of the race.

'A ride's a ride, Joe. You'll not get anywhere by watching the race.'

'You're right as usual, Mo. I'll give his trainer a ring as soon as I get back,' Joe said, brightening up at the thought of a ride – any ride – in the Derby.

'James Ryan's the trainer. I'll have his number ready for you when I get back.'

'Thanks, Mo. You're a star.'

Mo let go the colt's bridle and Joe kicked him forward to follow the other horses out of the yard to the gallops.

Mo shook her head as she watched them go. Peter Rhodes partnering Darwin's Choice. She wondered what the colt would make of him.

True to her word, Mo had James Ryan's phone number ready when Joe came back.

Joe knew James, but not very well. James was champion jockey and rode for Stuart Lawson when Joe had first started as an apprentice at the yard. James was his hero, and when he was sacked by Nathan Grant, Joe was devastated by the injustice of it. It was then that he realised that there was nothing fair in racing. Despite all the hard work and effort you put into it, your fate was in the hands of fickle owners who could make or break your career.

He knew that James had taken up training and was surprised when he entered a horse in the Derby, since his yard definitely didn't have the calibre of horses for the Derby even if this one was half-brother to Darwin's Choice.

Joe had never heard of the owner, the horse had never raced and Stuart's 'spies' didn't think much of him, having seen the colt on the gallops. Still, as Mo had said, anything was better than no ride at all.

As soon as he could, Joe made the call.

'Hello, Mr. Ryan, Joe McGrath here – Stuart Lawson's jockey. You probably won't remember me – I was an apprentice at the yard when you were still there.'

'Yes, I remember you,' James replied, 'you were showing a fair amount of promise then. What can I do for you?'

'I believe there could be a ride going on The Legacy in the Derby on Saturday. Have you found anyone yet?'

'News does travel fast,' came the reply. 'No, we're still looking.'

'Would you consider me?' Joe asked, coming straight to the point.

'How come? Surely you're on Darwin's Choice.'

'I've been jocked off. Mr. Grant has booked that South African – Peter Rhodes – for the ride, so I've suddenly become available, as it were.'

James sympathised with Joe's plight and could only imagine the disappointment he must be feeling.

'Could you come out and ride him out tomorrow 6 am?' James asked, sensing the wonderful opportunity that had suddenly become available to book one of the best jockeys to replace the injured Alan.

'Yes, sure. I'll look forward to it.'

'Good. See you tomorrow. Oh, and the ride's yours.'

'Great, thank you. I'll see you tomorrow then.'

Joe hung up feeling elated, although he wasn't sure why

he should feel so overjoyed at the prospect of riding the 200–1 outsider when only twelve hours earlier he was almost guaranteed victory on Darwin's Choice.

At least he was back riding in the Derby, and for this year that would have to be enough.

James put the phone down and turned to Mick. The sense of relief on his face was plain for Mick to see.

'We've got a jockey for The Legacy.'

'Who?' Mick asked in astonishment, since they had no success with all the phone calls they had made.

'Joe McGrath.'

'Joe McGrath! But he's riding Darwin's Choice! Has Darwin's Choice been withdrawn then?' Mick asked, his eyes as big as saucers.

'No. Joe's been jocked off.'

'Who by?'

'Peter Rhodes.'

'Oh, him,' Mick said scornfully. 'Sweet talked himself round another owner, did he?'

Mick knew that Peter Rhodes had a reputation for pinching rides.

'Apparently so.'

'Poor Joe McGrath.'

'But lucky for us, Mick. He's coming down to ride The Legacy tomorrow. I'm sure they'll get on well. Joe's an excellent jockey – one of the best, and you know Leggy, he's as laid back as any horse I've ever known and seems to get on with anyone. We sure are lucky to get Joe. I'll give Emily a ring with the good news.'

'That we are,' Mick replied thoughtfully.

'Funny how luck can change, isn't it?' James said,

relieved that the problem of being without a jockey had resolved itself in such a satisfactory way.

Mick looked at him and smiled.

'That's racing for you.'

Joe arrived promptly at Bishop's Place to ride out The Legacy. It seemed odd driving to a different training stables, but he was relieved that he wasn't going to Stuart Lawson's to watch Peter Rhodes ride out Darwin's Choice – his ride – for the first time.

He worried about what Darwin's Choice would make of it and then he realised that it wasn't his problem, so pushed the thought to the back of his mind.

The routine in most training yards was usually very similar, so Joe would find it no problem fitting in.

James introduced Joe to Mick, who led him over to The Legacy's box. Mick opened the stable door and led the colt out.

'Bloody hell, he's the spitting image of Darwin's Choice!' exclaimed Joe in total astonishment at what he was seeing.

Joe looked the colt up and down in amazement. 'I know they're half brothers, but this is ridiculous!'

Even though Mick had known that they were pretty similar from having seen Darwin's Choice race, Joe's reaction amused him.

'Let's hope he's just as fast, then,' Mick replied, grinning his toothless grin which Joe found quite disconcerting.

'And let's hope he's not got the same vices as Darwin's Choice,' Joe added.

'The Legacy? No, he's a real gentleman of a horse,'

Mick replied, indignant that someone might imply that his beloved colt might have a few bad habits. 'Why, is Darwin's Choice difficult?'

'Difficult!' Joe laughed. 'Sometimes even the word bastard doesn't do him justice.'

'One of them temperamental ones, is he?' Mick said, nodding his head wisely, having come across a few of those in his long career with horses.

'I could show you the scars and bruises but you wouldn't think much of me as a jockey then,' Joe laughed, warming to Mick's easy-going personality.

The Legacy, meanwhile, was pawing the ground, anxious to get out on the gallops.

Mick gave Joe a leg up into the saddle whilst telling him what was expected of them on the gallops.

An hour later Joe rode The Legacy back to the yard. A beaming smile on his face – the first in thirty six hours.

James met them and held The Legacy as Joe dismounted.

'What do you think of him, then?' James asked, eager to get an unbiased opinion and comparison between The Legacy and Darwin's Choice.

'I'd never have believed it, but you've got a good – no – great colt here. He seems to have the speed and stamina of Darwin's Choice, although it's hard to compare when there's not much competition for him on the gallops. And they're so different in temperament. The Legacy doesn't seem to have an unkind bone is his body and is so honest and straightforward. Darwin's Choice is a bit of a nutter, but the way he's been brought up with the Derby in mind, Mr. Grant has treated him more like a laboratory experiment than a racehorse. He gets more blood tests, prodding and poking than the rest of the yard put together, it's no wonder he's got such a short fuse.'

'Do you think he'll give a good account of himself in the Derby?' James asked, hoping for a positive reply.

'I don't see why not, but to be honest I can't see him beating Darwin's Choice, providing he's in the right frame of mind,' Joe replied.

What he wanted to say was that he couldn't see Darwin's Choice getting beaten if he had been riding him, but that would have sounded rather big headed. What Darwin's Choice made of Peter Rhodes and vice versa remained to be seen.

'I would be grateful if you could keep your thoughts about The Legacy to yourself. Being the outsider, it takes the pressure off the owner and myself,' James said; keen to keep any over enthusiastic reports about the Legacy's ability private.

'They won't hear anything from me,' grinned Joe, knowing what James probably meant was that they would be having a big bet on the colt. Besides, he certainly didn't owe Nathan Grant any loyalty after what had happened and it would be fun if The Legacy would give some of the others a run for their money.

'Thanks,' James said with relief. 'I hope you can come and ride him out again before Saturday although you two really seemed to get on well today.'

'I'll try and make it tomorrow.'

Later that morning as Joe drove off, he smiled to himself. Maybe Saturday wasn't going to be so bad after all.

* * *

Angela Woodward

Emily arrived back at Bishop's Place after work. She spent most nights there now, and had taken over organising the renovation of the house as well as the accounts, quickly turning the house into a fine home. She couldn't wait to find out how Joe McGrath had got on with The Legacy.

James was waiting for her in the kitchen with a cup of tea and the good news.

'Great news, Emily,' he said after giving her a welcoming kiss.

'What's that?' Emily asked, taking off her jacket and hanging it behind the door.

'Joe McGrath's really impressed with The Legacy. He rode him out this morning. He reckons he'll give a good account of himself on Saturday.'

'He wasn't saying that just to please you, was he?' Emily asked suspiciously.

'No, I don't think so. Joe seemed genuinely impressed. I also asked him to keep it quiet. If the racing reporters get word that The Legacy is in with a remote chance they'll be round here like a plague of locusts.'

'Oh, I hope not,' Emily said, feeling sick at the thought.

'So, it's all systems go for Saturday, then. The Legacy's in fine shape, we've got a great jockey, the weather forecast is for a sunny day and I'll be accompanying a beautiful owner.'

Emily blushed. It wasn't often James said anything remotely romantic or complimentary – he wasn't that sort of man – so when he did, it made it all the more special.

'All we need now is a lot of luck,' Emily sighed.

'Regardless of what happens on Saturday, Emily,

278

you've made me feel the happiest, luckiest person alive.'

James looked at Emily and took her in his arms to give her a long, lingering kiss.

Mick walked in to the kitchen at that moment, saw them and walked back out again.

"I don't know," he said to himself, "it took long enough to get them two together, now there is no keeping them apart."

10

The day before the Derby Dr. Popham was engrossed in some routine blood tests when the manager of the stud came in.

'Do you want to have a go in the Derby sweepstake?' he asked, holding up a coffee mug full of pieces of paper with the names of the runners.

Dr. Popham looked mildly irritated by the interruption.

'Oh, OK then. How much?' he asked, realising that it would be easier to say yes than decline.

'Pound a go,' came the reply as the mug was held up for him to take a pick.

Dr. Popham rummaged through his pockets and found a pound coin, which he handed over. He wasn't a gambling man and oddly enough, despite being the chief vet at the prestigious stud of Nathan Grant, had no interest in horse racing whatsoever. It was the well being of horses which was his one and only interest in life.

He picked out a piece of paper and handed it over to the manager who took one look at it and laughed.

'Boy, you've picked the real turkey of the bunch with that one!'

He noted the name drawn out on a sheet of paper next

to Dr. Popham's name and put the piece of paper down where Dr. Popham was working.

'Better luck next year!' the manager said as he walked out of the laboratory, chuckling to himself.

Dr. Popham cursed himself for having decided to take part in the draw and tossed the piece of paper onto his desk, angry that it was littering up his nice tidy workstation in amongst the tests he was doing.

It wasn't until he had finished the tests and had sat down at his desk and completed writing up the results that he noticed the screwed up ball of paper.

He picked it up and sighed. It was just his luck that he had drawn the worst horse in the field. Life seemed to always be like that – one disappointment after another.

Dr. Popham gradually unfolded the piece of paper, muttering to himself for having parted with a pound. At least he might as well know the name of the horse that he had drawn.

He tried to straighten out the piece of paper by holding it down on the desk and running his hand over it.

Once it had uncurled and was legible he picked it up and read it.

'The Legacy,' he muttered to himself, 'never heard of it.'

If it had been Darwin's Choice, then he would have felt quite excited about it since that was the one horse in the race that he knew, and he certainly knew more about him than anyone else but Nathan Grant.

Darwin's Choice was the only horse whose career that Dr. Popham had even taken the remotest interest in following, not surprisingly given that Dr. Popham had a unique interest in the colt.

After Darwin's Choice had left the stud, he had copies of all the reports, both medical and training, sent to him, and had continued to study his creation as he developed into the outstanding horse that he was bred to be.

No horse could beat him tomorrow, so he had thrown his money away, and he felt unreasonably annoyed about it.

'The Legacy,' he read again.

Something under The Legacy's name made him stop to take a second look, and a wave on nausea suddenly swept over him.

The Legacy was by Coral Reef out of Andaman Sea.

He sat down and reread the piece of paper.

Owner – Miss E. Lloyd. Trainer – James Ryan.

No clues there, but Anderson-Brown was dead and he had no idea what had happened to Andaman Sea or the foal she had been carrying.

He could hear his heart pounding as awful thoughts raced through his mind.

Dr. Anderson-Brown had said that a normal embryo had been used for Andaman Sea, so surely there was no problem.

Despite trying to reassure himself the feeling of nausea persisted.

All the paranoia that he had felt after Anderson-Brown's death returned with a vengeance.

He had been involved in the bloodstock industry long enough to know that the chances of a mare of Andaman Sea's ability to produce a foal of classic standard was so remote it didn't bear thinking about.

It must have happened in this case, he tried to tell

himself. He couldn't think of any examples, but he was sure he had heard of some – or had he?

Dr. Popham sat down, the piece of paper quivering in his shaking hand.

He propped the piece of paper and put his head in his hands, feeling – for the first time in his life – like crying.

He shook his head and banged his clenched fist on his desk in frustration, telling himself to pull himself together.

He thought of all the reassurances that Anderson-Brown had given him and tried to think if there was anything that would have pointed to Anderson-Brown using anything other than a normal embryo.

He could think of nothing.

All he had was the word of a man who was now dead.

Surely it was a coincidence, nothing more. It had to be.

With it being the day before the Derby, Darwin's Choice would not be doing a full training session, just a 'pipe opener,' nothing too strenuous, just to keep him supple and to stop him fretting from lack of exercise.

Mo was pleased that Joe was going to ride him out, as she hadn't taken to Peter Rhodes at all.

She found it hard to forgive him for getting Joe jocked off Darwin's Choice when Joe had done all the hard work in getting the colt in such fine shape for the race.

She also didn't like his condescending tone of voice when the South African jockey spoke to her.

When she first offered advice on some of Darwin's

Choice's quirks he dismissed her out of hand, saying that there wasn't a horse that he had come across that had given him any problems.

Mo also found the way he treated Darwin's Choice hard to take. He seemed to have no respect for the colt and wanted to control Darwin's Choice by dominating him, and Darwin's Choice seemed very unsettled by it.

Mo sensed the colt's slight change in attitude. He seemed to be almost irritated. Perhaps it was her dislike for Peter Rhodes that had clouded her judgement, and the change in Darwin's Choice might be more to do with him sensing the atmosphere of anticipation that had built up in the yard as the big day approached.

She also knew that he was very quick to pick up on the slightest change in routine.

Mo tried to reassure herself that this was affecting Darwin's Choice, although he had never been so wound up before any of his other outings.

When Joe arrived she was pleased to see that he was looking reasonably happy. It was the last thing that she had expected with him having been jocked off the Derby favourite, but then again, Joe was so easy going.

She blushed slightly as he approached, realising suddenly that she had rather a soft spot for him.

'So, how's Darwin's Choice been behaving?' he asked, his broad smile sending her slightly weak at the knees.

'He's missed you,' Mo replied, wanting to tell him how much she had missed him too, 'and I don't think he's taken too kindly to Peter Rhodes,' she added, not quite succeeding in hiding her disapproval of the new jockey.

'I'm sure that Peter Rhodes is quite capable of handling

himself,' Joe added rather stiffly, still smarting from the fact that the ride had been poached from him.

Mo led Darwin's Choice out of the stable.

No matter how often Joe had seen the colt, the sight of him still took his breath away.

'Have you missed me then, boy?' Joe asked, as Mo gave him a leg up into the saddle.

Darwin's Choice wheeled round and Mo had a job holding on to him.

Joe managed to get his feet in the irons as the colt jigged up and down, anxious to join the other three horses that were running at Epsom but in different races, and would be joining him for their morning exercise.

Mo stroked the colt's neck and patted him before he set off for the gallops.

She sensed that his muscles were tighter than usual and thought it must be pre-Derby nerves getting to him. She would have to give him a good relaxing talking to when he got back from his exercise.

It wasn't long before Joe and Darwin's Choice returned to the yard, the colt still dancing up and down on the spot, the leisurely session having done nothing to release his pent up energy.

Joe seemed out of breath with the effort it had taken to hold the colt back.

Mo caught up with them and held the bridle as Joe dismounted.

'He's certainly fired up today,' Joe said. 'He dropped his shoulder a couple of times when I was least expecting it and almost had me off. Luckily he's tried that a few times too many already, so you can never really relax on him. Has he tried to throw Peter Rhodes?'

'I don't know. He hardly speaks to me. Talking to a mere stable girl seems to be beneath him. He's just so – so arrogant!' Mo said, trying to keep her anger in check.

'Never mind, you've only got to put up with him tomorrow, then he'll be off to pinch someone else's dream,' Joe replied, shaking his head sadly.

'I'm so sorry, Joe. It's so unfair.'

'Since when has racing ever been fair?'

They both stood silently for a moment, thinking of what could have been when Mo changed the subject.

'What's The Legacy like then? A bit of a come down after Darwin's Choice, I'll bet.'

Joe thought of the promise that he had made to James not to let on about The Legacy's true potential.

'He's not as bad as everyone makes out. I think he'll run a reasonable race,' Joe said, being fairly economical with the truth.

Mo nodded wisely. Poor Joe was trying to put a brave face on his partnering the outside or the field. How typical of him to be so generous with his assessment.

Mo looked at Joe a little shyly.

''Twill be odd, seeing you at Epsom riding someone else's horse.'

Joe thought for a moment and then looked at Mo who seemed so downhearted, even though she would be leading out the favourite tomorrow.

'I hadn't thought about it, but you're right, it will be very strange indeed.'

Mo bit her lip. It was every stable girl's dream to lead out a horse in the Derby, and it would have been such a perfect day if Joe had got the ride on Darwin's Choice. It wouldn't be the same with him partnering one on the opposition.

Joe sensed that Mo seemed more upset by events than she cared to admit.

'Why don't we meet up afterwards and go out for a drink?' Joe said in an effort to cheer her up.

'I'd like that,' she replied, beaming with delight at the thought of a date with Joe. If Darwin's Choice did win, she doubted whether she would be in the mood for the party that was bound to follow.

At that moment they were interrupted by Stuart Lawson's voice booming across the yard.

'Will you two stop gassing and see to Darwin's Choice!'

They both jumped, as did Darwin's Choice, before Mo resumed her work.

'See you tomorrow, then,' Mo whispered, feeling the happiest she had been in days.

Mick was sitting in the kitchen having a coffee, having spent the last night – as he had done every night this week – sleeping in the stable with The Legacy.

James said it wasn't necessary, but Mick insisted, recounting examples from Irish racing folklore on the nobbling of horses before races.

Emily tried to talk him out of it as well, but Mick was adamant.

'The Legacy is my responsibility and I will let nothing untoward happen to him,' he announced in rather melodramatic fashion.

As he was sitting drinking his coffee, he was beginning

to regret his act of bravado. Every bone in his body ached and he still had one night to go.

Mick sighed as he stretched his back first to the left and then to the right. He was getting too old for kipping in stables now, but it was going to be worth it to lead out The Legacy in the Derby, and he could tell them all in the pubs back in Dublin how he was sure that he heard people in the yard at night, and if it hadn't been for him, who knows what might have happened to The Legacy.

He had certainly had enough sleepless hours to create a multitude of daring stories, and with one night to go he might even come up with a better one.

The yard was relatively quiet with James out on the gallops with the first string, and Emily upstairs, probably still fast asleep.

The poor lass looked as though she hadn't been getting much sleep either, as the race day approached.

He smiled to himself. Emily spent most nights at Bishop's Place now, and she and James had become virtually inseparable. James seemed much happier too, now that he had more than just racing to occupy his mind.

Emily was more out going too, not the shy, timid thing that had arrived at the yard all those months ago, looking for a trainer for The Legacy.

He took a couple of mouthfuls of his coffee and put the mug wearily down again.

It had certainly been an eventful time from when that wide-eyed yearling had arrived in the yard to develop into the handsome colt that he was today, and Mick had to admit that he had seen none more handsome than The Legacy.

He felt his throat tighten with emotion and immediately chastised himself for getting too soft in his old age.

It had been fun, too. None more so than organising the £2000 bet for Emily on The Legacy. Somehow it was far more fun organising it using someone else's money rather than his own.

He had taken particular satisfaction in the fact that his contacts had been able to put on that amount without so much as a flicker of the odds. It was nice to think that he had achieved one over the bookies as far as the odds were concerned. The only disappointment to him was that it had all been put on to win.

Mick had put a few quid on himself, but wasn't going to let on that the bet was each way. Somehow the favourite seemed too much of a good thing to bet against winning.

Mick heard the first string arrive back and eased his aching body out of the chair. He walked over to the kitchen door, straightening up as best he could before going out to see the string back.

Breakfast would follow, but somehow he just didn't feel hungry. The change in routine and tiredness had dulled his appetite.

He promised himself that after the Derby he would take a week off work, down a world record quantity of Guinness and would then sleep for a week – in his own bed.

At breakfast he nibbled at his toast but left the majority of it.

As he sat there, he looked at Guinness and envied the black Labrador so cosy and comfortable in his box in front of the aga.

He heard Emily's footsteps coming down the stairs and painfully straightened his shoulder to stop himself from slumping across the table.

Emily greeted Mick with a cheerful good morning.

Mick tried to sound cheerful with his reply, but somehow it came out dull and flat.

Emily looked at him, full of concern.

'Oh, Mick, if you don't mind me saying, you look dreadful,' Emily said, worried about the tired look he had. 'I wish you wouldn't sleep in The Legacy's stable with him. I know it's a kind, good thought, but I can't bear to think of you out there all night.'

'And I couldn't bear it if anything happened to The Legacy, Miss. Besides, 'tis only for one more night. Anyway, I wouldn't be able to sleep in my own bed for worry,' he replied in his defiant tone, Emily knew that there was no was she could talk him out of it.

Emily looked at him again.

'Are you sure you'll make it to tomorrow at this rate?'

Mick straightened his stiff, aching back and smiled.

'Tomorrow, Miss, 'twill be no problem. I'll be fuelled up by adrenalin – you'll see. The sheer excitement will keep me going.'

Emily could see that the mere thought of tomorrow had brought the sparkle of anticipation back into his eyes and she had no doubt that come the morning, Mick would be back to his usual self.

James walked in and looked at Mick with equal concern.

'You're getting too old to kip in the stables, Mick,' he said, knowing full well that as far as Mick was concerned, it was a matter of principle and tradition that he wasn't going to change.

'I consider it an honour, not a burden,' Mick replied in a very self-righteous tone.

James looked at Emily who raised her eyebrows in exasperation as she busied herself clearing up.

Emily was grateful to have been given the day off work, her boss reasoning that with all the excitement she must be feeling, she would be more of a liability in the office than a help.

She decided to spend the day immersed in the yard's accounts in an effort to stop her from thinking about the following day.

Despite an almost surreal atmosphere of excitement in the yard with having its first Derby runner, the routine of the yard still had to be maintained, post to be dealt with, bills to be paid and goods to be ordered.

Mick and James had gone to see out the second string, leaving her alone in the kitchen.

She glanced at the *Racing Post* to see a picture of the Derby favourite – Darwin's Choice – in full gallop, the headlines asking if anything could stop Nathan Grant's flying colt.

He looked so much like The Legacy, but stronger and more powerful. Emily couldn't bear to read the accompanying article and pushed it to one side.

The rest of the day she spent engrossed in work, with James popping in briefly at lunchtime before going out again.

Half way through the afternoon Emily began to tire. The sleepless nights were beginning to take their toll. She decided to walk into the village and post the few letters she had done. The fresh air she hoped would do her good and clear her aching head.

It took about fifteen minutes to walk to the post office and a good hour to get back.

Everyone she passed stopped her and wished her well. People with whom she was only on nodding terms came up to her, shaking her hand and asking about The Legacy. It was as though the whole village had adopted The Legacy as 'their' horse.

Emily found it quite overwhelming.

Even little old ladies were telling her how they had put a couple of pounds on in the bookies, even though they admitted that they only usually had a flutter on the Grand National.

Everyone seemed to have banded together in support of The Legacy, Emily and the yard, delighting in the fame and recognition that it had brought back to the village – recognition that had been lacking since Mr. Reynolds's death. No one seemed to mind that The Legacy was the outsider of the field; the fact that he was taking part was enough.

The older villagers recalled when Bishop's Place was producing great horses under Mr. Reynolds, but those days were long gone and the younger members of the village tired of hearing stories of the champions that Bishop's Place had produced. Now they all had something to talk about, and if the spirit and enthusiasm of the village were anything to go by, then The Legacy would win by a mile.

Emily arrived back at the yard considerably later than she had planned, with having to stop and talk to so many people wishing her gook luck.

James had begun to get concerned and was visibly relieved when she eventually appeared and explained what had happened.

James smiled and hugged her close. 'You seem to be regarded as an honorary villager now. You're lucky, you've achieved it in record time. Unless you've been born here or lived here for at least thirty years, you're still regarded as an outsider. You've brought something really special to the village. Everyone's talking about The Legacy; even people who wouldn't usually talk to each other are discussing The Legacy's prospects against the rest of the opposition.'

He stopped and stroked a strand of hair that had fallen across her eyes.

'I'm so proud of you for bringing everyone together in such a way.'

Emily looked up at him, slightly embarrassed by what he seemed to be claiming that she had achieved.

'I'm sure that they would have been talking about the Derby anyway, even if The Legacy hadn't been running,' she said modestly.

'Some, maybe, but could you honestly see old Mrs. Jefferson from the post office having a bet on the Derby if The Legacy weren't in the race?'

Emily thought for a moment and then burst out laughing.

'No, definitely not. I just hope that The Legacy puts in a good performance. Everyone seems to be expecting so much of him.'

'No-one is expecting him to win, but they're all living the dream and I'm proud of you for sharing your dream with them, whatever happens.'

Emily wrapped her arms around James and buried her head in the warmth of his shoulder and comfort of his embrace.

'Thank you,' Emily said, looking up into his eyes.

'For what?' he asked, kissing her softly on her lips.

'For making it happen.'

'You have your late uncle, Andaman Sea and The Legacy to thank for that,' James said, holding her closer than ever.

Emily thought for a moment.

'There have been many times since Uncle Julian died when I've cursed him and wondered why he made his will out the way that he did, but all things considered, I have such a lot to thank him for, and whatever happens tomorrow, I don't regret a moment of it.'

Lydia looked at herself in the full-length mirror in her bedroom.

Not bad, she thought to herself, smiling at the transformation over the last year.

She had lost over ten kilos in weight, changed her hairdresser, changed her fashion designer and totally changed herself.

No longer was she the frumpy, dowdy, timid wife of Nathan Grant. Now she was more outgoing, confident, and smart, and had got involved in charity work and other people in general.

It irritated her that Nathan hadn't noticed, or if he had, chose not to comment. Not that she cared what he thought any more, she had done it for Matt.

Matt, that gorgeous young, six foot, tanned, brown

eyed muscular hunk that she had met on the beach in Barbados when she was there on her own a year ago.

She had trodden on something sharp in the sand and was hobbling back to the villa when Matt, who was jogging along this stretch of beach as he did every morning, stopped to help.

He had put his arm around her as she limped through the sand. She could feel the taught muscles flexing with every movement that he made, his sweat glistening on his tanned skin that rubbed against her and almost seemed to weld with hers.

Once safely back at the villa he had sat her down and brushed the sand off her feet, examining the painful foot with his gentle touch.

He never left the villa until she had to return to England, the whole of the time being spent in passionate encounters the variety and intensity of which never ceased to amaze and thrill Lydia.

It had crossed her mind that Matt was making the most of a good opportunity to become involved with an extremely wealthy woman who showered him with expensive gifts, but the expense and presents that she lavished upon him were well worth it. Besides, what if he had, thought Lydia, she didn't care, she was having the time of her life.

She didn't even care if Nathan found out. He would be pretty furious at the thought of the ridicule his wife would bring him with her toy boy, but so what, he couldn't talk with his endless stream of bimbos that he paraded so blatantly in public.

Lydia had made frequent trips back to Barbados, where

she and Matt would renew their passionate affair with the added vigour that separation brought.

It was because of Matt that Lydia had begun to realise what a sorry state she was in and had begun to lose weight and smarten up her appearance.

Matt would meet her at the villa on her arrival and lavish praise and attention on her that made her feel good – so good.

With regret, she turned her thoughts back to this evening.

She was hosting a dinner for Nathan who had invited, amongst others, an Australian businessman and his wife to dinner. He had also invited them to the Derby the following day.

The Australian had a foothold in a Chinese media company via a Hong Kong business colleague, and Nathan was keen to get involved in some shape or form. The thought of the enormous potential in the Chinese market that advertising would have had Nathan reaching for his calculator with excitement.

What better way to impress a keen Australian racehorse owner than to spend Derby day as a guest of the winning owner, Nathan Grant – or so Nathan thought.

It had been three years since he had been so confident about his horse, and look what had happened to Northern Lights.

Last year, Nathan didn't seem too concerned what happened in the Derby, he was so engrossed in his big hope of the future – Darwin's Choice.

Lydia had to admit that Darwin's Choice was an outstanding horse, but she was fed up hearing about him from Nathan.

It was – Darwin's Choice had won this, Darwin's Choice had done that – Darwin's Choice would win the Derby.

Lydia had booked her usual escape route to Barbados for the following week, not so much in case Darwin's Choice lost and she had to get away from any prospective angry mood that Nathan might be in – she was going to see Matt.

The thought of his muscular, tanned body exploring hers made her breathless with excitement.

Lydia looked in the mirror and blushed at the erotic thoughts that kept popping into her mind.

She had to pull herself together – she had an important dinner to host and one glance at her watch told her that their guests would be arriving shortly.

Lydia brushed a loose hair off the black beaded cocktail dress that she would never have dreamt of wearing a year ago, and with a final quick appraisal of herself in the mirror, she went downstairs to await the arrival of their guests.

Nathan was already in the drawing room, looking at some of the paintings he had commissioned of some of the more successful racehorses that he had owned.

He glanced round as Lydia walked in.

'Evening, dear,' he said before turning his back to her and pointing to the painting that hung over the fireplace.

'I think I'll have a painting done of Darwin's Choice and will hang it here. Quite a fitting place for a Derby winner, don't you think?'

'If he wins the Derby,' Lydia replied with a feeling of exasperation that he was talking about that damn horse again.

'Oh, he will win, don't you worry,' Nathan said with a conviction that Lydia had never heard in his voice before.

One thing was for certain, if that horse didn't win, the sooner she could get to Barbados the better.

11

All the stable staff at Bishop's Place were up early on the morning of the Derby in anticipation of an exciting day.

It was a beautiful morning and the weather forecast was for a perfect summer's day.

James let one of the more senior lads take the training sessions, as he wanted to ensure that everything was in order before setting off for Epsom. Not that he should have worried for Mick had already checked, double checked and checked again the tack, rugs, racing silks, passes and anything else relevant or otherwise.

Mick was back to his usual self; the aches and pains and lack of sleep from spending the last few nights in The Legacy's box had melted away and were now forgotten, as he busied himself with grooming The Legacy until his coat shone like polished mahogany. All the while he was grooming, Mick would talk the colt over the race. Occasionally The Legacy would snort and move sideways in his box. He had heard this story every night for the last week as Mick would tell him of the magnificent race he would run before eventually going to sleep.

Before setting off, Mick joined James and Emily for breakfast. They were engrossed in the *Racing Post*, reading out the horse-by-horse guide where there was a paragraph about each horse and the expert's verdict as to what sort of race each horse would run.

'Darwin's Choice,' James said, reading the write up for the favourite out loud. 'Unbeaten so far and rightful odds on favourite. Can win from the front or come from the back. Change of jockey to Peter Rhodes raised a few eyebrows though. Most likely opposition could come from Mirage.'

'Can't see Mirage get the better of him,' Mick commented, sitting down to the slice of toast Emily had made for him. 'He left him for dead in the 2000 guineas and it'll take a hell of an improvement to beat him.'

'Mirage,' James continued, 'bridesmaid to Nathan Grant's Darwin's Choice on two previous occasions, though the soft going in the 2000 guineas was not to his liking. Better suited by today's good going. Should have more of a race with Darwin's Choice.'

Emily listened to James reading through each of the horses in turn with Mick adding his acerbic thoughts on each for good measure until they came to The Legacy.

'The Legacy. The dark horse of the field. Unraced due to injury. Half brother to Darwin's Choice but the dam's not classic material. James Ryan's yard not exactly firing on all cylinders yet, and although training reports have been encouraging, odds of 200–1 seem about right.'

'That's a bit strong!' Mick exclaimed in indignation that anyone could write off his beloved Leggy like that.

'Strong, but true as far as they are concerned,' James replied, 'and thanks to my lack of training success you can hardly blame them for coming to that conclusion.'

'But Governor, before you had The Legacy, you've not had the horses to work with. I think The Legacy is a classy animal – no mistake, and he'll surprise you today,' Mick said, full of confidence.

Emily and James gave each other a wry look. They had heard Mick talking to The Legacy in the stable in the evenings, telling him what a wonderful race he would run, so that Mick seemed to believe in his own fairytale now.

'I'm sure he'll run a good race and I hope he'll finish in the top half of the field,' James said, trying to temper the optimism of Mick.

'I just hope he gets back sound,' Emily countered, beginning to feel very nervous about the day ahead.

James glanced at the clock.

'If you don't leave soon, Mick, he wont be running at all. You know you can't rush anywhere in that old horsebox!'

'I'll be off in no time,' Mick said as he disappeared out of the kitchen to change and then load The Legacy into the horsebox.

Once Mick was ready to go, James and Emily went out to see him off.

The obvious change in routine had slightly unsettled The Legacy, who had been a little reluctant to go into the horsebox, but with a little persuasion from Mick was soon safely loaded.

Alan Johnson, his arm still in a sling was already sitting in the cab. He might not be riding in the Derby, but he wasn't going to miss out on the occasion altogether.

Mick had also decided to take Simon, one of the other stable lads, for additional help.

Mick climbed into the cab and wound down the window.

'Sure you've got everything, Mick?' James asked out of habit, despite knowing how diligent Mick was.

'Quite sure, Governor,' came the somewhat exasperated reply.

'Drive carefully. We'll see you there, then,' James said, patting the driver's door as a signal for Mick to leave.

Mick started up the horsebox, which spluttered for a moment as black plumes of smoke coughed out of the rattling exhaust pipe.

As the horsebox pulled away, James thought to himself that he really ought to invest in a newer one.

He turned and put his arm round Emily.

'Come on, Emily, we had better get changed. You have a date with destiny this afternoon.'

'Oh, don't put it like that, I feel nervous enough about it already,' Emily replied, realising that the whole of the last three years had been building up to this one day.

They walked back to the house where Emily hurriedly cleared away the breakfast plates.

'Aren't you nervous?' she asked, wondering how James seemed to manage to look so calm.

'Slightly, but I've still got too much to think about. I will be when he goes out on the track and there's nothing more I can do; then I think I'll get really nervous,' James said thoughtfully.

They went upstairs to change and it wasn't long before James was back in the kitchen, anxiously waiting for Emily, who seemed to be taking forever to appear.

James felt slightly odd in his top had and tails. It had been a while since he had worn them, and he had been delighted earlier in the week when he had tried them on and found they still fitted. The tie, however, felt tight round his neck, and he fingered it nervously.

He turned as he heard Emily coming down the stairs and he stared at her in amazement.

'You look stunning, Emily,' he said when he had regained his composure, 'absolutely stunning!'

Emily giggled in slight embarrassment, feeling her cheeks warm as a blush spread across her face.

James looked at her with warmth and pride.

She was wearing a simple apricot dress cut slightly above the knee with a slightly longer matching jacket. Her auburn hair had been pinned up in a semi classical style and tucked neatly under a stylish hat.

'And don't you look handsome too,' Emily said to James, who was still feeling rather uncomfortable in his morning suit.

James went up to Emily and put his arms around her, pulling her close and giving her as passionate a kiss as he could without disturbing her hair or hat.

'What was that for?' Emily asked breathlessly when they eventually parted.

'For good luck and for being you,' James replied.

He looked at his watch and picked up his top hat.

'We really must be going.'

'So, this is it, then,' Emily said apprehensively.

'Yes, this is it,' James replied, leading the almost hesitant Emily to his car.

The closer they drew to Epsom racecourse, the more traffic there was and the more subdued Emily became.

Angela Woodward

By the time they reached the racecourse, the sight of the sheer numbers of people gave Emily a bad case of butterflies in her stomach.

James tried to keep her mind occupied by talking about anything and everything other than racing, despite beginning to feel rather apprehensive as well.

He parked in the trainers' car park and they set off to look for Mick to find out how The Legacy had travelled and settled.

After a while they found him, and he reassured them that The Legacy had travelled well and was fine. He was, however, annoyed at one thing.

'That pompous, officious little man at the gate wouldn't let me in at first. He took one look at the horsebox and said there was no way I had a Derby runner in there. I gave him the papers and a piece of my mind and he eventually let us in, having read the papers from front to back. Pompous little twit,' Mick ranted, 'I've got a good mind to report him.'

'He was only doing his job,' James said in an effort to calm the irate Mick.

'Well, he never stopped any of the other posh horse-boxes for so long,' Mick carried on, his Irish blood having been well and truly fired up.

'We're in now, and The Legacy is fine, so let's concentrate on the race ahead. Don't let a row with some officious gatekeeper distract you from that,' James said firmly, hoping to draw a line under the event, whilst feeling embarrassed at the thought of his old horsebox in the car park, surrounded by the luxury transport that all the other runners had arrived in.

'If The Legacy wins, James, I'll buy you a new

horsebox,' Emily said brightly, trying to lighten Mick's angry mood.

'If the Legacy wins, I'll hold you to that,' James replied, grinning broadly.

'If The Legacy wins, there won't be enough Guinness in all of England for my celebrations,' Mick added, flashing his trademark toothless grin.

Lydia was waiting for Nathan and their guests to arrive in their private box at the racecourse.

Nathan had a meeting with the Australian businessman, Paul Dunlop, in the morning, and had sent Alex back to chauffeur Lydia to the racecourse by herself.

She was quite relieved to be on her own, since Nathan had been so unbearably smug and optimistic this morning.

The dinner the previous night had gone so well that Nathan and Paul had arranged to meet up this morning to continue their discussions on the China venture.

Lydia had found the dinner rather tedious. Nathan and Paul talked all night about Darwin's Choice and China.

Paul's wife, Nadine, was a statuesque blonde whose phenomenal looks and long legs had apparently been obtained at the expense of her intelligence, and whilst trying to be the perfect hostess, Lydia had found trying to engage Nadine in an interesting and stimulating conversation to be almost impossible.

She sighed as she contemplated what she was sure would be an equally tedious afternoon with Nathan going on about that damn horse, the loud mouthed Paul and his intellectually challenged wife, and all the other boring entourage that Nathan invited every year.

Lydia looked round, saw the canapés and was immediately tempted by them, but the thought of Matt diverted her to the salad garnish on the plate, so she nibbled on a piece of cucumber instead.

Stuart Lawson arrived first and looked round for Nathan.

'Good morning, Mrs. Grant, Mr. Grant not here yet?'

'No, held up by a business meeting, but don't worry, he'll soon be here, he wouldn't miss this afternoon for anything,' Lydia replied, pouring herself a mineral water whilst feeling very self-righteous. 'I'm sure he won't be long. Do help yourself to a drink, please.'

Stuart picked up a glass of orange juice and had barely put the glass to his lips when Nathan walked in, accompanied by Paul Dunlop and Nadine.

Lydia had to stop herself staring at Nadine in astonishment. She was wearing an outrageously short dress that barely covered her modesty and an enormous wide brimmed hat which Lydia decided had more fabric in it than the dress.

Nathan made sure that his guests were given a glass of champagne before going up to Lydia

'Nice spread they've laid on, as usual,' he said, looking at her in rather a strange way before adding, 'You look – different.'

'Coming from you I'll take that as a compliment,' Lydia said rather acidly as she went to greet more guests who had just arrived.

It was the first time that Nathan had commented on the change in her.

Nathan watched her walk over to greet the new arrivals. There was something different about Lydia and he couldn't put his finger on it. It had been a long time since he had actually looked at his wife in detail, but she somehow looked smarter and was certainly more confident, judging by the way she had just spoken to him.

Must be her hormones, he thought, before dismissing Lydia from his mind.

He saw Stuart Lawson and immediately went over to ask about Darwin's Choice.

'He's, fine, no problems,' Stuart replied, 'and the going's perfect for him.'

'Good,' answered a relieved Nathan.

He had been waiting for three years for this day. It had all seemed so easy. The race was going to be a formality; nothing could touch Darwin's Choice now.

He circulated among his guests, revelling in their envy of him having what had been called the 'horse of the century.'

Even Paul Dunlop was impressed with the day so far, which delighted Nathan, since Nathan had the feeling that it would take a lot to impress the laid back Australian entrepreneur.

Paul had even invited Nathan and Lydia to the Melbourne Cup later in the year, which Nathan took to be a promising sign as far at their business discussions were concerned.

Racing was soon under way and after a couple of exciting races, Stuart excused himself to help with the saddling up of Darwin's Choice.

Nathan and Lydia followed a short while later and made their way through the crowds to the parade ring.

Lydia strode confidently in front of Nathan, much to his surprise. She definitely had changed, he thought, remembering haw she used to waddle embarrassingly behind him, struggling to keep up.

Nathan greeted some of the other owners like long lost friends whilst Lydia looked round and spotted James Ryan – one of Nathan's old jockeys, accompanied by a charming looking lady.

Lydia excused herself from Nathan and walked over.

'Hello, James, how are you? I hear you have a runner in the race,' she said to a rather surprised James.

'Mrs. Grant, how nice to see you. You look wonderful,' James replied, somewhat stunned by the transformation in her.

Lydia blushed slightly at the compliment.

'And this is?' Lydia asked, looking at Emily.

'Oh, I'm sorry. Mrs. Grant, this is Emily Lloyd, owner of The Legacy. Mrs. Grant is the wife of Nathan Grant, owner of Darwin's Choice,' James explained, introducing the two of them.

'Nice to meet you, Mrs. Grant,' Emily said as they shook hands, trying not to feel in awe of this extremely wealthy woman. 'You are so lucky in having the favourite for the race.'

'Not so lucky if he doesn't win, eh, James?' Lydia said, giving James a knowing look.

'True,' came James's reply.

Lydia had never forgiven Nathan for sacking James Ryan – he was such a nice young lad. Still, he seemed to have done rather well for himself since, and judging by the way he and Emily kept looking at each other, he had obviously found a new partner after his well publicised divorce.

'So, how many horses do you have, Miss Lloyd?' Lydia

asked, having taken an immediate liking to James's new partner.

'Only the one,' Emily replied, painfully aware that every other owner of horses in this race would own considerably more, 'and that was by default,' Emily added, feeling a need to explain herself.

'How come?' Lydia asked, intrigued by the last comment.

'I inherited a mare in foal from my uncle who was killed in a car crash, and he expressed a wish that the foal should run in the Derby, so here we are.'

'How romantic!' Lydia exclaimed. 'Isn't that the most wonderful story you've ever heard, James?'

James nodded in agreement.

'Anyway, please excuse me, I must be getting back to Nathan,' Lydia said, having noticed Nathan looking round, rather irritated by Lydia's prolonged absence.

'Best of luck,' she added.

'You too,' Emily replied, feeling considerably better having talked to someone in the parade ring who seemed to be quite normal despite her wealth, and very nice too.

'Who was that you were talking to?' Nathan asked with some degree of irritation when Lydia returned, not having recognised the girl with James Ryan.

'That's Miss Emily Lloyd, owner of The Legacy. A charming young lady, and it's so romantic; she inherited a mare in foal from an uncle who died in a car crash, and on top of that, I'm sure that she and James are an item,' Lydia gushed excitedly.

Nathan looked at Lydia with annoyance.

Some things never changed, and one of those was Lydia's love of gossip.

Meanwhile, a reporter who had been standing close by had overheard their conversation and had quickly jotted down the details.

He made a mental note to get an interview with this Miss Lloyd as soon as he could. What a wonderful story it would make – 'Girl inherits Derby runner from uncle.' He could just see the headline with his name underneath.

Dr. Popham hadn't slept a wink on the night before the Derby. He kept having visions of Dr. Anderson-Brown lying dead in the car accident. On the odd occasions that he did manage to doze off, he would have nightmares, seeing himself lying dead in the accident, not Anderson-Brown, and he would awaken from his dream in a cold sweat.

His wife tried to get him to stay at home the following day, fearing that his sleeplessness and cold sweats were a sign of the flu. Dr. Popham gruffly insisted that there was nothing wrong with him and as he was on duty, he would be going in to work. Besides, he needed something to occupy his mind.

As the build up to the Derby started, the staff at the stud began gravitating towards the staff room, to watch the big race on the TV.

Dr. Popham, not usually one to watch the race, found himself seated in the staff room, his hands clasping the side of his chair so tightly that the whites of his knuckles were showing. He stared at the TV, with an awful feeling in the pit of his stomach.

He watched Nathan Grant in the parade ring, waiting for Darwin's Choice to appear.

With ever increasing fascination he watched, as one by

one the horses appeared, then the commentator announced the arrival of The Legacy in the ring.

No – he must have got it wrong. The commentator seemed slightly flustered. The cloth under the saddle said The Legacy, but surely it was Darwin's Choice. There must have been a mix up somewhere with the saddlecloths.

Then, two horses later, Darwin's Choice entered the parade ring.

The cameras panned from one horse to the other.

The commentator, momentarily lost for words, suddenly started talking so fast that Dr. Popham couldn't make out what he was saying.

The stud staff stared at the screen in stunned silence as the TV cameras panned back and forth between The Legacy and Darwin's Choice.

A stunned silence had also momentarily fallen over the owners, trainers and Derby crowd as everyone gawped at the two identical horses.

'Oh, shit!' exclaimed Dr. Popham, as the colour drained from his face.

The stud staff, startled by the profanity which they had just heard from their normally dour chief vet, looked round in time to see Dr. Popham bolt out of the staff room, leaving the door to slam behind him.

Their eyes reverted to the TV and they all started talking at once.

Nathan was half listening to Stuart Lawson and half keeping an eye out for Darwin's Choice.

Suddenly he saw his familiar white blaze as the horse entered the parade ring.

He was annoyed not to see the usual stable girl leading him out, but a rather old chap with wild grey hair and a toothless grin.

He was about to chastise Stuart for replacing Mo with a totally unsuitable person to lead out his pride and joy, when he stopped and stared at the colt.

The name on the cloth read 'The Legacy.'

At that instant, Stuart realised what Nathan was staring at, and his mouth dropped open too. He wondered for a moment what the hell was going on, when he noticed another colt, two horses back, with an identical white blaze and the same matching sock. The name on the saddlecloth read 'Darwin's Choice,' and a pale, worried looking Mo was leading him.

'Bloody hell!' exclaimed Nathan and Stuart, almost in unison.

By this time, the stunned silence had descended on the parade ring as everyone watched the two identical horses in open-mouthed astonishment.

At the other side of the parade ring, James and Emily looked at one colt and then the other.

'Oh my God!' was all Emily could utter.

'I knew they were similar, but they're virtually identical,' James gasped once he had got his voice back.

James looked over at Stuart Lawson and Nathan Grant, who seemed to be as shocked as everyone else.

Suddenly it was if everyone started talking at once, the sudden noise startling some of the horses parading round. Some of them broke out into a trot whilst others wheeled round, almost yanking the arms of their handlers from their shoulder sockets.

'I knew that The Legacy was the spitting image of

Coral Reef, but he's almost identical to his half brother,' James muttered to himself rather than to Emily, echoing the same thoughts that Stuart Lawson was having about Darwin's Choice.

Extra TV cameras were hurriedly rushed to the parade ring and reporters tried to fight their way through the crowds to be in place to get a word from either owner when they left the relative sanctuary of the parade ring.

James looked at both the colts as they walked round. He was relieved that The Legacy seemed to be taking it all in his stride, which for a complete novice to put up with the entire furore that was going on around him was quite amazing, but Mick was doing a wonderful job of keeping him calm.

Mick seemed to be enjoying all the attention that was being focussed his way, whilst using all his experience to keep The Legacy from sweating up with nerves.

James then looked at Darwin's Choice. He was bouncing up and down, his pale-faced lass doing a sterling job, keeping the strapping colt in check.

James was astonished. Every marking, every peculiar zigzag of their blazes was identical. Even their white socks were a perfect match. The only distinguishing feature was that Darwin's Choice was far more muscular – a powerhouse of a horse, whilst The Legacy was leaner and more athletic looking.

The jockeys filed into the parade ring, anxious to see for themselves what had caused such a fuss in the crowd.

Joe McGrath kept his head down and made his way to where James and Emily were standing. He had a shrewd idea what the fuss was about. He knew that the two colts were very much alike, but seeing the two of them together made him stop and stare.

Joe glanced at Stuart Lawson and Nathan Grant who were glaring at him. For a moment he thought he should have forewarned them, but what the hell, they had shown him no loyalty, so why should he? His only regret was that he wasn't in the parade ring to see their expressions when they first saw the two colts, and hoped that he would be able to see it on a replay later that evening.

'You said he was like Darwin's Choice, but I had no idea they were that similar,' James said to Joe as they compared the two colts.

'I didn't realise quite how alike they were either,' Joe said, by way of an apology.

'If The Legacy looks like Darwin's Choice, then let's hope he can run as well as him,' Emily said, finally having got over the shock, although still looking rather pale.

Joe watched Mo leading Darwin's Choice round and caught her eye and smiled. Mo looked back at him questioningly back and he knew that he would have some explaining to do afterwards.

The bell sounded and the horses were led to the spots where their connections were standing.

Mick led The Legacy up and grinned at James.

'Well, he's certainly made it a Derby to remember already,' he said, patting The Legacy reassuringly as the colt played nervously with his bit.

'I haven't had so much fun in years,' he added, realising the attention he would be getting for the rest of the day.

James gave Joe a leg up.

'You'll have to let him run his own race. I know he's

got the speed and the stamina, and he's as honest as they come, and whatever happens I'm sure that he'll run the race to the best of his ability, but how he'll react to the race is anyone's guess,' James said, stroking The Legacy's blaze, almost feeling guilty about putting him under so much pressure first time out.

'We'll do our best,' Joe said, as Mick started to lead them away.

'Good luck,' Emily added, feeling awful at the thought of sending her beloved Leggy to do battle with the other far more experienced horses.

James had turned to lead Emily out of the parade ring when he noticed a barrage of reporters waiting for them at the exit.

Realising that Emily would have problems coping with this sudden unwanted attention, he held back for a while, before sandwiching themselves between one of the Saudi royal family and his entourage, thinking that there wouldn't be quite such a scrum if the reporters would treat the other owner with the respect that his status deserved.

'Keep your head down, keep walking and let me do the talking,' James said to Emily under his breath as they exited the parade ring.

It seemed to have the desired effect, with the minders of the Saudi royal family keeping the reporters at bay.

The majority of them decided to wait for Nathan Grant, whilst a couple of reporters continued to follow James and Emily, firing questions at them and getting no response from either.

Stuart Lawson, meanwhile, was trying to give Peter Rhodes his final instructions, although the mind of the

South African jockey was rather distracted by the furore that had been going on.

'And finally, don't touch him with your whip, whatever you do,' Stuart said, exasperated by the lack of attention from Peter Rhodes.

'Yes, Governor,' Rhodes replied, half listening to what the trainer had been saying.

Mo led them off for the parade, leaving Stuart, Nathan and Lydia to fight their way through the crowds of reporters who had been waiting for their comments.

By the time they reached the sanctuary of their box, Nathan wasn't in a very good frame of mind. This day was not turning out the way he had expected.

Emily and James managed to reach a reasonable vantage point from which to watch the race. They hadn't managed to shake off a couple of reporters who kept doggedly asking questions about The Legacy and Darwin's Choice.

James dismissed them by saying that it wasn't unknown for half brothers to have some similar characteristics, which in this case had obviously come from the sire.

Emily kept quiet, almost petrified by the intrusive reporters.

They managed to see the end of the parade in front of the stands, and then watched as Joe cantered The Legacy down to the start.

Through her binoculars, Emily could see The Legacy eyeing the massive crowd in the stands as Joe tried to get him to concentrate on the track ahead. The Legacy seemed to calm down a little by the time he reached the starting stalls, away from the crowds and finding comfort and familiarity amongst the other horses.

James watched as Joe walked The Legacy round at the start. From a distance, the only way he could tell The Legacy and Darwin's Choice apart was by the colours the two jockeys were wearing. Joe was in Emily's colours of blue with a green cross, white sleeves and cap, whilst Darwin's Choice's jockey was wearing the well-known colours of gold with a red circle, red sleeves and cap that belonged to Nathan Grant.

There was obviously a lot of banter between the jockeys. James could see the pointing and gesticulation through his binoculars, and could only imagine that the sole topic of conversation would be the similarity between The Legacy and Darwin's Choice.

From the corner of his eye, James could see that Emily was shaking. Her binoculars had a slight movement to them, which could only come from the trembling hands that were holding them.

He put his arm around her to reassure her. Emily glanced across at him and gave him a weak smile before putting the binoculars up to her eyes and squinting through them in an attempt to see her colt.

James had to admit to himself that his stomach was knotted with nerves. He had never felt like this as a jockey before such a prestigious race. As a jockey he still had a job to do, and although he used to get slightly tense and nervous on these occasions, it was nothing in comparison to how he was feeling now.

As a trainer, his job was done, and there was nothing else he could possibly do to help The Legacy; and the feeling of helplessness and anticipation seemed to be overwhelming.

He cursed as he noticed that his binoculars had started

to shake slightly too, and put them down for a moment, taking a couple of deep breaths to compose himself again.

James wished he could put his arm around Emily again, as much to draw comfort for himself as her, but he needed both hands to steady his binoculars.

They had started to load the horses into the stalls.

The Epsom crowd buzzed with excitement in the hot June sunshine.

The Legacy seemed to be a bit reluctant to go in at first, but with some pushing and encouragement from the capable handlers was soon safely installed. They had practised this successfully at home on numerous occasions, and James was not too surprised that the unique atmosphere had slightly unsettled him. He could only hope that it wouldn't affect his concentration during the race.

There were only two left to go in – Silver Bullet – a grey well known for his temperamental behaviour, and Darwin's Choice.

Every time Silver Bullet was led up to the stalls, he planted himself, legs rigid in defiance and refused to go in. Eventually the handlers blindfolded him and let him round in circles to disorientate him slightly before leading him back to the stalls. Instinct told Silver Bullet that the stalls were ahead and he stopped again, but with that element of doubt in his mind and the persuasion of a number of handlers he was eventually loaded into his stall.

Darwin's Choice was on his toes, watching all this going on before it was his turn to be loaded last, and much to Peter Rhode's surprise, went in with no problems whatsoever.

The starter then climbed up the steps to his rostrum, and on seeing that they were all in and checking the time, raised his flag.

They were under starters orders.

The Epsom crowd hushed in anticipation.

The stalls opened, the horses sprang out, the crowd roared and the race was off.

The Legacy jumped out in front, and was running the only way he knew how – fast and free.

Joe McGrath sensed that despite the blistering pace that he was setting, The Legacy was relaxed and well within himself.

A length or so behind, Darwin's Choice headed the rest of the field. Peter Rhodes didn't want his colt to be involved in any jostling for position, and was tracking The Legacy, stride for stride.

Rhodes was smiling to himself. The race was unfolding far better than he had possibly imagined. The Legacy was acting as the perfect pacemaker, and this green novice who seemed carting Joe McGrath would soon tire and be swallowed up by the rest of the field, and then Darwin's Choice would be in the lead.

The rest of the Derby crowd was echoing Peter Rhodes's thoughts. TV commentators were already saying that at least the owner of The Legacy had had a few moments of glory with her colt leading the Derby field for a short time.

Much to everyone's amazement, The Legacy was still heading the field as they rounded Tattenham Corner, and was showing no signs of tiring, with Darwin's Choice still tracking him a few lengths behind. The rest of the field, headed by Mirage, were now falling back, with the bizarre spectacle of the two identical offspring of Coral Reef pulling clear.

With three furlongs to go, Peter Rhodes was beginning to get concerned. The Legacy wasn't slowing, and if anything was beginning to pick up his pace. He decided to get to work, pushing with hands and heels, and Darwin's Choice lengthened his stride, changed up a gear and was soon up to the quarters of The Legacy.

Joe McGrath saw Darwin's Choice out of the corner of his eye, shortened his reins and shook up The Legacy, who responded and drew a length clear.

Peter Rhodes was now worried; he had a real race on his hands, and the winning post wasn't far away. He cursed himself for underestimating The Legacy, and pushed Darwin's Choice again, and again the colt responded, clawing back the gap between them until he was within a neck of The Legacy.

The crowd watched enthralled as the two identical colts battled it out, drawing ever further from the rest of the field.

The novice, The Legacy, far from blowing up in setting the cracking pace from the start, was giving the unbeaten Darwin's Choice a real race.

Half the crowd were shouting for Darwin's Choice, while the other half of the crowd, not to mention the bookies, were shouting for the underdog.

Emily was finding it almost impossible to watch. She had never seen The Legacy so focussed or under so much pressure. She realised that she had been holding her breath almost from the start, and tried to breathe normally but she was so tense that she could only manage shallow breaths.

James was urging The Legacy on, his voice getting louder and louder with each stride The Legacy made. He was almost euphoric that The Legacy would at least be placed – if only he could hold out, but Darwin's Choice kept coming back at him again and again, and with his reputation and record, surely The Legacy couldn't hold on.

From the balcony of his private box, Nathan Grant and Stuart Lawson were watching the race unfold with increasing anxiety.

At first, when The Legacy had led the field at such a gallop, they were delighted, thinking as everyone else was, that Joe McGrath had been carted on his first time out on The Legacy, and that he would soon pay for his blistering start. Darwin's Choice was just where they wanted him – in touch with the leader and in front of the rest of the pack, out of trouble.

It was when The Legacy seemed to pick up his pace on the downhill run towards Tattenham Corner that some concerns were beginning to show, but Darwin's Choice was still in touch and they knew that he could still change up a couple of gears if required.

Each time he changed up a gear, so did The Legacy.

Each time he drew upsides, The Legacy drew away again.

The winning post was coming up at an alarming rate. Nathan Grant willed Peter Rhodes to give one last final push, shouting for all he was worth, as though the jockey could hear him.

Through his binoculars Nathan Grant could see Peter Rhodes push Darwin's Choice to his limit, as he pulled up almost level with The Legacy.

Just one more effort would do it – one more push.

Nathan Grant saw Peter Rhodes glance at The Legacy, and to his horror, in a effort to get that extra stride out of Darwin's Choice, with the winning post only a few yards away, Rhodes gave Darwin's Choice a couple of cracks of the whip.

Rather than lengthen his stride, the colt's head came up just at the wrong moment and his action chopped as he changed his legs.

The Legacy, maintaining his long, flowing stride, passed the winning post at full stretch, a head in front.

Pandemonium broke out in the crowd. Never had they seen such a thrilling, not to mention unusual Derby before, and for such a rank outsider to beat the hottest favourite in years had the racing pundits reaching for their record books to see if such a feat had ever been achieved before.

The bookmakers, too, were cheering with delight. Their hearts had been in their mouths at the thought of a Darwin's Choice victory two furlongs out, and with The Legacy having beaten him, the result couldn't have been better.

Emily felt the release of all the tension wash over her like a tidal wave, and didn't know whether to shout for joy, laugh, cry or faint with shock.

James grabbed Emily, almost shouting at her with delight and kissing her until he realised that they had been surrounded by cameramen and reporters, and it wouldn't be quite proper for a trainer to be seen kissing one of his owners with such unbridled joy and passion.

Emily seemed oblivious to everyone else around her,

and once she had overcome the shock, clung on to James, wishing that this moment would last forever.

'I can't believe it!' she gasped, her voice breaking with emotion. 'He won, didn't he? It was so close, but he did win? Tell me I'm not dreaming!'

'Yes, he did win,' James said, his voice hoarse from all the shouting.

He kissed Emily again, and to hell with the pictures that might appear in the papers the following morning.

Nathan Grant put his binoculars down slowly. He couldn't believe what he had just seen. Surely he couldn't have been defeated when victory had been so close.

'Did you see that? That bastard of a jockey Peter Rhodes gave him a couple of cracks with his whip! Just as he was about to pass The Legacy in the final stride. What the hell did he think he was doing?' Nathan shouted, oblivious to the embarrassment that his outburst was causing his guests. His eyes were still fixed on the winning post, which should have marked a glorious victory for his magnificent colt.

Stuart Lawson, too, was staring at the track, his face ashen, oblivious to the noise of the crowd and everyone else around him. He was half listening to Nathan rant on about Peter Rhodes whilst thinking that if Joe McGrath had been riding instead in Nathan's choice of rider, then Darwin's Choice would undoubtedly have won. He wished he had the courage to say to Nathan Grant that he told him so, but he valued his job too highly and instead muttered in agreement.

It was the one thing that they did agree on, Peter

Rhodes had cost Nathan Grant the greatest prize in racing.

Nathan was taking the defeat of his colt as a personal humiliation. He had put so much time, money and effort, not to mention ingenuity into his breeding, only for him to be beaten by his half brother.

At that moment, the slightly inebriated Australian drawl of Paul Dunlop could be heard from inside.

'Jesus, Nathan, we don't have this much excitement at the Melbourne Cup. What do you do at your stud, clone them or something?'

If Paul Dunlop weren't so vital to Nathan for his Far Eastern business contacts, then Nathan would have knocked him out there and then.

Suddenly it sank in what he had said. He then recalled earlier in the afternoon when Lydia was prattling on about The Legacy's owner – what was it – yes, he remembered now – she had inherited the colt from an uncle.

'Lydia!' he shouted across the room to attract her attention, making everyone jump in the process.

Lydia could see the anger in his eyes and hesitated for a moment before going over to him.

'Yes, dear,' she said sweetly, which annoyed Nathan even more.

'The owner of The Legacy, what did you say about her inheriting it?' he demanded.

'Just that she inherited a mare in foal from an uncle who died in a car crash, and he expressed a wish that the foal should run in the Derby. Why?' Lydia asked, wondering why Nathan was suddenly taking an interest in a piece of gossip at a time like this.

'Did she say who he was?' he asked, dreading the reply he might get.

'No, she didn't say. Why?' Lydia asked again, curious to know the reason for his questions.

'Damn,' Nathan muttered under his breath, 'no reason.'

Nathan turned to Stuart Lawson.

'Get me Dr. Popham in Ireland. It's urgent. I must speak to him immediately.'

'Why? There's nothing wrong with Darwin's Choice, surely,' Stuart asked, concerned that Nathan had heard or seen something about Darwin's Choice that he had missed.

'Just get him on the phone,' Nathan shouted, making everyone jump again, and beginning to get even more angry with people asking him 'why' whenever he wanted something. 'And while you're doing that, I'm going to give that bastard of a jockey a piece of my mind'.

Nathan stormed off to where the horses would be unsaddled, with Stuart Lawson fumbling with his mobile phone as he tried to keep up with him. At least he was reassured by the fact that the jockey really was to blame this time, and as Nathan Grant had insisted on the jockey change, then ultimately Nathan Grant could only blame himself.

They reached the place where the unsaddling of every horse but the winner would take place, and awaited the return of Darwin's Choice. Stuart was still on the phone, and he eventually said a few words before putting the phone back in his pocket.

'Well, where's Popham?' Nathan growled, annoyed that Stuart hadn't handed the phone over to him.

'He's on duty, but he must be out in the stud some-where. They're out looking for him now and will ring back as soon as they find him,' Stuart replied, wondering why on earth Nathan would want to speak to his chief vet. They hadn't even seen Darwin's Choice yet, and from the way that he had run there would appear to be no problem with the colt himself.

They then spotted Nathan's colours through the crowd and could eventually see Mo leading Darwin's Choice towards them.

Mo looked pale and visibly upset, and Darwin's Choice was proving to be a real handful, tossing his head and almost lifting Mo off the ground. The colt was soon clearing a path for himself through the crowd, wheeling round, scattering onlookers and owners alike. The colt's nostrils were flaring with anger and the size of the whites of his eyes showed the extent to which he was annoyed.

Mo eventually succeeded in leading him up to where Nathan and Stuart were standing, trying to calm the fractious colt with gentle words, but to no effect.

Darwin's Choice was grinding on his bit with annoy-ance and stamping on the ground like a petulant child, occasionally giving a slight buck in an attempt to remove the rider whom he now hated with a vengeance.

Peter Rhodes's face was a picture of annoyance and concentration as he endeavoured to stay on board. He wasn't going to be humiliated by this devil of an animal throwing him in front of so many people, and he was relieved to eventually dismount.

Darwin's Choice, sensing an opportunity, wheeled round and tried to take a chunk out of the jockey who was now unsaddling him. But he was stopped by Mo hanging on for dear life, and the jockey's nimble footwork in getting out of the way just in time.

Nathan, in his anger, was momentarily lost for words, and Stuart decided to keep a diplomatic silence and proceeded to help Mo to try and calm the colt down.

Having successfully got the saddle off, Peter Rhodes turned to Nathan.

'What a bastard that horse is! We had the race won and he cracked with a couple of strides to go to the post!'

Nathan glared at the insolence of this upstart insulting his prized colt.

'The only bastard round here is you. You were told not to touch him with the whip, but you couldn't resist, could you? What was it – worried that your great riding capabilities weren't going to be good enough, so you had to use force despite your instructions! He would have won but for that.' Nathan's words came out in a raging torrent at the sight of this jockey blaming Darwin's Choice.

'I only showed him the whip to get that extra effort out of him!' Peter Rhodes said defensively.

'So what's this then,' Stuart joined in, pointing to two weal marks on the hindquarters of the colt.

Peter Rhodes looked at them for a moment, and for once was lost for words.

In the heat of the final furlong, he hadn't actually realised that he had touched the colt. It had all been instinct to him. Before he could say anything in his defence, Nathan stooped down and with his face contorted with rage in front of the alarmed Peter Rhodes said through clenched teeth.

'Get out of my sight, you little runt, and if you know what's good for you, don't ever call me again!'

The jockey scuttled off to the safety of the weighing room, relieved to have got away unscathed, thinking that the owner of Darwin's Choice was obviously as unbalanced as the colt. Still, he looked on the bright side, second wasn't so bad after all and would still have earned him a nice pay cheque.

Stuart's phone rang in his pocket, and despite being set on quiet, made Darwin's Choice jump. He answered it quickly before putting it back into his pocket, fearful of the news that he was about to give Nathan.

Nathan looked at him with annoyance at not having been handed the phone yet again.

'Well, have they found Popham, then?' he barked in irritation.

Stuart took a deep breath.

'He's not answering his pager, and the stud manager has looked everywhere for him and couldn't find him. They noticed that his car had gone from the car park and sent someone round to his house, but there's no one there. Apparently a neighbour said that the family left about half an hour before with a couple of suitcases and drove off without so much as a word.'

'The double crossing bastard,' Nathan muttered to himself.

'Sorry sir?' Stuart replied, not having caught the last comment.

'Nothing,' came Nathan's reply in a tone of resignation that surprised Stuart.

Nathan was thinking to himself. He would have to find out if the Legacy and Anderson-Brown were in any way connected. That could easily be done by finding out if Emily Lloyd and Anderson-Brown were related. He would then get Brad Walters to track down Popham for the rest of the answers.

'I'll leave you with Darwin's Choice,' Nathan said to Stuart, before heading back to his box.

He had a couple of phone calls to make and some questions that needed answering.

James and Emily fought their way thought the crowds, gathering an increasing following of reporters and cameraman, all wanting a word or photograph of the surprise winning owner and trainer. Eventually, with the assistance of some racecourse stewards they managed to reach the relative sanctuary of the winner's enclosure.

Emily was still in a state of shock, the enormity of what had been achieved still not quite registering yet, and the jostling of the reporters had also frightened her.

They could hear the cheering getting ever closer and eventually Mick appeared, leading a very startled looking Legacy with a jubilant Joe McGrath on board, who was punching the air with sheer delight.

Mick was beaming from ear to ear. He had often imagined what it would be like to lead a Derby winner into this enclosure, but never in his life had he imagined that he would get this opportunity, and now that he had, it had exceeded all his expectations.

Some over-enthusiastic punters in the crowd tried to lean forward and pat Mick on the back and touch The Legacy, who despite being unused to crowds, let alone one as excited as this, seemed to be handling the situation as well as could be expected.

With Mick leading him, The Legacy almost danced into

the winner's enclosure with his bouncy trot, nervously eyeing the enthusiastic crowd.

Mick wiped a couple of tears from his eyes as he reached James, who hugged him before giving The Legacy a congratulatory slap on the neck.

James then congratulated Joe, who was in such an ecstatic state that he was reluctant to leave the saddle, relishing every moment of his unexpected victory.

Emily gave Mick a huge hug and kiss on the cheek, which brought even more colour to his cheeks that were already flushed with excitement. She then threw her arms around The Legacy's neck and closed her eyes. It was the most wonderful moment in her life.

Joe McGrath eventually dismounted, after having given one last victory punch of the air, and was immediately hugged by Emily.

Few words had been spoken, they were all so overcome by the victory, but the expressions of sheer delight on each of their faces said more than words ever could.

Photographs were taken of any and every combination of The Legacy, Joe McGrath and the connections.

James eventually had the opportunity to ask Joe how the Legacy had run, and how victory had been achieved.

'Like you said, I just let him run his own race from the start,' Joe recounted, still out of breath from the exertions and excitement. 'I could hear another horse behind and I knew it would be Darwin's Choice and kept expecting him to pass us at any time, but The Legacy never gave up. When Darwin's Choice was almost upsides in the final furlong, The Legacy lengthened his stride and I still didn't believe that we would win until Rhodes picked up his whip. As soon as he did that, I knew we would win, but it was so close!'

He then turned to Emily, who had been listening to his account.

'What an unbelievable colt you have here, Miss Lloyd. I never thought anything would ever beat Darwin's Choice, but your colt is really something special, and he's all heart.'

Mick led The Legacy round in circles to wind him down a little as James, Joe and Emily talked about the race, their eyes fixed on The Legacy, who looked resplendent with his Derby winner's sheet on, his bay coat darkened and glistening with sweat.

Joe then left to complete the weighing-in formalities.

An official came up to congratulate the party and whispered something about the presentation in James's ear.

James patted The Legacy on the neck again, and after a quick word with Mick, who was still grinning from ear to ear, led the bemused Emily to where the presentation would be held.

Mick was left with The Legacy, who was still tugging hard, still with plenty of energy to spare.

He thought he would burst with pride as he led The Legacy down Epsom hill, being congratulated by all he passed, The Legacy still on his toes and fired up.

Mick didn't mind missing the presentation. He would be able to watch it later on TV if he managed to stay sober that long. Besides, he was where he most wanted to be – washing down and looking after The Legacy, winner of the Derby.

The presentation seemed to pass in a dream to Emily,

it was such a surreal experience. Fortunately, with the presentation having taken place fairly quickly after the race, she had little time to get nervous about it.

She shook hands with people, having no idea who they were, received congratulations from others, and had numerous photographs taken with combinations of James and Joe, all with their respective trophies. All the while she tried not to look at the crowds in front of her.

Once the presentations were over, the media scrum started, with questions being fired from all directions and microphones being thrust at them from all angles.

Emily let James answer the questions.

'Did you think that The Legacy would beat Darwin's Choice?' asked one reporter.

'We knew The Legacy would give a good account of himself, but he exceeded our expectations.'

'How much did The Legacy cost you, Miss Lloyd?' a voice from the crowd shouted.

Emily looked at James, who answered the question.

'Miss Lloyd inherited him.'

'And what now, James? Irish Derby? The Arc?'

'We'll be discussing these options later this week.'

'What about the course record, and clipping four seconds off it?'

James tried not to look stunned, as he hadn't heard this news.

The questions continued and James gave vague but diplomatic answers. In truth, they hadn't a clue what the future would bring; running in the Derby had been their only goal to date.

*   *   *

The Legacy

James and Emily left the racecourse relatively early, having declined numerous invitations to join various parties in their private boxes.

Mick followed behind in the horsebox. He couldn't resist making some comment to the officious little man who had stopped him earlier and tried to prevent him from coming into the racecourse. It had been a very sweet moment for him.

Alan Johnson, who should have ridden The Legacy, was in a slightly pensive mood, not quite able to join in the euphoria of the rest of them. If only he hadn't broken his collarbone, he would have had the ride. He could have ridden The Legacy to victory and gone down in the record books. He had to grudgingly admit to himself that with him on board, The Legacy would probably not have won, but it was one of those things in life that he would never know. Mick's infectious elation gradually began to affect him too, as Mick recounted the race over and over again on the journey back.

In the car in front, all Emily seemed to be able to say was 'I can't believe it.'

'You might when you see the video of the race when we get back home,' James said, still barely able to believe it himself.

It had always been his dream to ride a winner in the Derby – a dream that had eluded him, but to train a winner was something he had never even considered.

They talked over the day's events, still with a sense of disbelief that they had been a part of such an amazing day.

'I hope that now that you've trained a Derby winner, you'll get a few more good horses,' Emily said, hoping that this would be a turning point in James's training career.

'I'm sure I will. A few owners I've been speaking to today said they would be giving me a call. Let's hope they will,' James replied enthusiastically, beginning to look to the future for the first time.

'I really hope so, you deserve it,' Emily said quietly, putting her hand on his arm while trying not to distract him from his driving.

As they approached the village next to Bishop's Place, they had to slow down, for it seemed as though the whole village had come out to greet them.

The sight of so many smiling, familiar faces brought a lump to Emily's throat.

James pulled over and stopped the car.

'Come on, let's walk from here,' he said, keen to let the villagers share in The Legacy's triumph.

James got out of the car and walked back to the horsebox, which had pulled up behind them and said something to Mick.

To the delight of the crowd, Mick went to the back and unloaded The Legacy, and on making sure that his Derby sheet was straight and secure, led the colt down the main street, with James and Emily walking beside them.

The Legacy eyed the crowd as he bounced into a trot, his ears pricked, enjoying the moment as much as everyone else.

To lead the Derby winner past all his friends gave him almost as much pleasure as leading The Legacy into the winner's enclosure, and he thought it a wonderful gesture of James to share the joy of victory with everyone.

The villagers, too, were delighted by the gesture. They

had only gathered to cheer them as they drove through the village, and had never expected this. It was so typical of James, they thought, he was such a nice man and it was something that they would remember for the rest of their lives.

As they neared the entrance to the drive of Bishop's Place, James smiled. He thought back to when he first came to look at the place and how it had changed. The long grass either side of the drive was now neatly cut, just as his old Governor, Mr. Reynolds, would have expected.

He looked up at the sky and hoped that somewhere, up there, Mr. Reynolds was watching him, smiling in satisfaction that his yard was back on the racing map.

James's thoughts were brought back to the present by his staff cheering and waiting to welcome them back. Everyone was hugging everyone else, regardless of their status in the yard. Even the old boy, Walter, who looked after the tack, was given a hug by Emily, who was now looking radiant with joy at being back home again and amongst friends.

Everyone wanted to touch The Legacy and have his or her photograph taken, holding the rein of the handsome colt with his Derby sheet on.

A couple of cases of champagne appeared from nowhere, which caused James to look a bit puzzled.

'I took the liberty of ordering them before we left the racecourse. I told them to bill it to you,' Mick said a little sheepishly.

James laughed out loud and slapped Mick on the back.

'Well done, Mick. Thanks. I hadn't even thought of it. I'm glad you still kept your sense of priority!'

The champagne corks started to fly across the yard, startling The Legacy, so Mick decided it was time to settle him down in his box.

Before too much champagne had been consumed, James tossed his car keys to one of the lads, and asked him to fetch his car from the village.

'Oh, and you had better get Mick to fetch the horsebox, too, while he still can!' James commented, sure that it wouldn't be long before Mick had consumed a few too many to be fit to drive.

'That reminds me,' Emily said, mischievously, a broad grin covering her face.

'What's that?' James asked, topping her glass up with more champagne.

'I owe you a new horse box!'

12

Despite the pervading hangover which covered Bishop's Place like a hazy smog the following morning, the staff were all up at their usual time, shrugging off their varying degrees of nausea and headaches from the celebrations the night before, and were working with an enthusiasm which Mick had rarely seen.

Mick's head too, was pounding, but it was soon forgotten as he relived the previous day's events over and over again in his mind.

James appeared, his eyes looking darkened through lack of sleep, but he was grinning from ear to ear. Nothing was going to spoil the elation he was still feeling with having trained his first Derby winner.

Apart from having gone to bed rather late after the celebration party, James eventually had to turn off his mobile phone and take the main phone off the hook in order to get some sleep, since it hadn't stopped ringing following his victorious return from Epsom.

The Legacy was in fine fettle, and no one would ever have guessed that he had run in such a hard, gutsy race the day before.

Despite the euphoria that everyone was feeling, the routine of the yard still had to be adhered to, and stable life was quickly back to normal with mucking out, riding out, grooming and feeding.

Any semblance of normal life would, however, have to wait for James and Emily.

Reporters had gathered early for the traditional photographs of the Derby winner at home with the trainer, head lad and this time, the owner too.

More questions were asked of James about the race, the colt and the future, all of which he answered very diplomatically, evading the question of what the future held by saying that they were still discussing the possibilities.

The phone, since having been put back on it's receiver, hadn't stopped ringing.

Racing correspondents wanted to come and do articles on James Ryan's successful transition from champion jockey to trainer of the winner of the Derby.

Women's magazines, including *Hello* and *OK* were offering Emily what seemed to be vast amounts of money for photographs and interviews about her fairytale inheritance which had catapulted an ordinary girl into competing and beating the wealthiest racehorse owners in the world, not to mention the added spice of her relationship with James. The amount of money became more and more obscene with each refusal Emily made. It was not as though Emily had any dark secrets in her past, which could be uncovered, but she had no wish for her life to be made public property – she valued her privacy and integrity too much.

There were also owners ringing up, eager to send their horses to the bright new training star of the racing world.

Whilst James was out on the gallops, Emily answered the phone as best she could.

'No, I'm not doing interviews with women's magazines. No, not even at that price!'

'Yes, of course Mr. Ryan would consider training your horses. I'll take your details and he will get back to you as soon as he can.'

'Sorry, Mr. Ryan is out at the moment. You will have to ring back later for his comments.'

In the end, to maintain her sanity, Emily switched on the answer phone and busied herself clearing up from the previous night's celebrations, whilst waiting for James to return from the gallops.

Nathan Grant was in his office early the morning after the Derby – unusual for two reasons – firstly because it was early, and secondly it was Sunday. If he had any work to do on a Sunday, he usually worked from his study at home.

Lydia, when she got up and went downstairs, was relieved to find him gone for the day, and spent a long and relaxing breakfast reading all the reports of the previous day's big race, taking some satisfaction in his wonder horse being beaten on the nod. At least with Nathan out of the house, she could get on with her holiday preparation in peace – confirming the flight and packing her new wardrobe, which she had bought with Matt in mind.

She was about to take a second slice of toast, but the thought of Matt and his lean tanned body made her put it back.

It had taken a lot of willpower to lose all those excess pounds, and she wasn't going to ruin her new slim figure that Matt loved to explore with such enthusiasm.

Following the race yesterday, Nathan had reluctantly stayed on until Paul and Nadine Dunlop had left, despite it being fairly obvious to Lydia that he wanted to get away as quickly as possible. Negotiations with the Australian were at a critical stage, and it wouldn't have done to leave his guest of honour, even though his mind had seemed to be elsewhere.

Lydia assumed that Nathan had gone into work on a Sunday to prepare for another important meeting with Paul, and also to immerse himself in work in an effort to take his mind off his horse being the bridesmaid yet again.

She was wrong.

Nathan's first meeting was with Brad Walters.

Janice, who had been summoned in to work by Nathan, showed Brad in as soon as he arrived.

Brad wasn't the least bit bothered about being called in on a Sunday. As a private investigator, he worked every day of the week and any hours. Experience had taught him that fraud and cheating spouses never took Sundays off either, so to him it was just another working day of the week.

'Good morning, Nathan,' Brad said as he strolled in.

'I wish it was,' came the gruff reply from Nathan, who was sitting in his large leather chair, his hands clasped under his chin and his elbows resting on the desk. It was obvious that he was far from happy.

'What can I do for you?' Brad asked, sensing that Nathan was in no mood for pleasantries, so they might as well get straight down to business.

'Two things,' Nathan began. 'Firstly, I want you to find out if that Dr. Anderson-Brown you dealt with so satisfactorily a few years ago is related to a Miss Emily Lloyd, owner of the horse that won the Derby yesterday.'

'The Legacy,' Brad said. Even though he wasn't interested in racing, no one could have missed the reports in the papers this morning about the defeat of Nathan Grant's Darwin's Choice by an almost identical looking horse, and the outsider too.

'Yes, The Legacy.' Nathan could hardly bring himself to speak the colt's name.

'And secondly?' Brad asked, a little disappointed at the trivial nature of the first request, which he regarded as a poor use of his talent.

'Secondly, find out where Dr. Popham is.'

'What, the Dr. Popham from your stud in Ireland?'

Brad remembered the name from when he had been investigating Anderson-Brown. He never forgot names or faces.

'The same. He seems to have disappeared, together with his family — last seen mid afternoon yesterday.'

'Do you know why he disappeared – any funds missing or anything like that?' Brad asked. Any information helped to build up a profile on his quarry.

'The reasons don't matter, just find him,' came the blunt reply from Nathan.

'And when I've found him?' Brad asked, wondering if Nathan would need any of his special expertise.

'Let me know where he is. I've some questions to ask him, so I want him – how shall I put it – intact.'

Brad nodded, hoping that after their quick 'chat,' there could be a few extras to be added to the bill.

Nathan tossed over a manilla envelope.

'Your usual expenses,' Nathan said by way of explaining the envelope.

'It shouldn't take me long,' Brad replied, picking up the envelope and putting it in his pocket. From what he remembered of Dr. Popham, he would hardly be a match for Brad Walters, especially as he had his wife and family with him.

Following Brad's departure, Nathan pondered his next action over a cup of coffee.

He picked up the phone and dialled Stuart Lawson.

'Stuart, Nathan Grant here. How's Darwin's Choice?'

It was the phone call that Stuart had been dreading, as he had no doubt what sort of mood Nathan would be in.

'Darwin's Choice is sound, but he really has been a handful since we got him home. Mo's had a terrible time trying to calm him down. He certainly didn't take too kindly to Rhodes' use of the whip.'

Stuart suddenly thought that he had probably said too much, and that by criticizing Rhodes, he was in effect criticizing Nathan Grant's judgement.

'He'll get over it,' Nathan replied in a flat, emotionless voice.

'So, what can I do for you then, Mr. Grant?' Stuart asked, convinced that Nathan wouldn't bother calling just to ask after the welfare of his defeated colt. He usually lost interest in anything that was less than one hundred per cent perfect.

'I want you to give James Ryan a ring. See how much the owner wants for The Legacy.'

'What, you want to buy The Legacy?' Stuart asked in disbelief.

'Why not, he and Darwin's Choice would certainly

342

make a nice matching pair,' came Nathan's sarcastic reply, annoyed that Stuart would question his judgement. 'The colt should be pretty cheap, considering he's only had the one race. I'm sure a couple of million dangled in front of the owner will be more than she could ever imagine.'

'I'll get on to it straight away and see if the colt's for sale,' Stuart replied, thinking what a cold-hearted bastard his boss could be some of the time, with so little respect for anyone else.

'I didn't say see if it's for sale, I said buy it!' Nathan snapped, his patience wearing thin.

'Yes, sir, I'll ring him straight away,' Stuart hastily replied, keen to end the phone call with his boss being in such an obnoxious mood.

'See that you do!' came the curt reply before Nathan ended the call without so much as a goodbye.

Nathan had realised that he had to get that colt. If Anderson-Brown had engineered a second horse as he suspected, he couldn't afford for anyone else to have him.

He would pay anything for The Legacy, but if he got in quickly enough, he could probably get him relatively cheaply, and if Dr. Popham had the answer that Nathan suspected, then this would bc thc only option available to him to salvage something out of the entire mess.

The last twenty four hours had been a nightmare for Dr. Popham.

As soon as he saw The Legacy in the parade ring before the Derby, instinct told him that his worst fears were true.

He couldn't get out of the stud fast enough, stopping

briefly to remove the cash that he knew was kept in the office safe while everyone else was in the staff room watching the race. With any luck the money wouldn't be missed until Monday, and by that time he would be long gone, and to disappear, he would need all the money he could get.

His wife was initially surprised to see him arrive home before his shift had finished, but her surprise soon turned to shock when he told her to pack a suitcase, grab anything valuable and round up the children as they had to leave immediately.

She protested at first, demanding to know why, but his whole mood was such that she realised that he must be in desperate and in serious trouble, but he wouldn't say why.

She could only assume that he must have made some dreadful mistake at work, resulting in the death of one of the stud's best horses, and couldn't bear to face the consequences.

Part of her wanted to know, whilst the other part preferred to be in ignorance of anything that her husband might have done wrong.

They were just about to leave the house when his mobile phone rang. She picked it up and saw it was the stud calling, and handed the phone to her husband with trepidation.

He looked at it and threw the phone across the hallway. That act, and the look of sheer desperation on his face, realising that his absence had been noticed, caused his children to burst into tears. Dr. Popham's wife ushered the children into their car, trying to reassure them that they would be going on a little holiday, whilst wondering what on earth he could have done to make him react like that.

Dr. Popham decided to head for Dublin, and began to drive like a maniac, reasoning that the more distance he put between himself and the stud the better. His wife, Mary, hung onto her seatbelt for dear life, and the children were gradually reduced to a terrified silence, broken by the odd sob. As he got closer to Dublin he began to relax slightly. He thought that they would be safer there, with more places to stay and more places to hide.

Here he could plan what to do next, as his first instinct was to flee, with very little thought as to the consequences. He eventually parked outside a little hotel. His wife's concerns grew when he paid for the room in advance from a thick bundle of notes that he took out of his jacket pocket.

She wished that she were strong enough to demand an explanation, but she had always been quite a timid person and had always thought that she had been married to a pillar of society. Now, her world seemed to be crumbling around her.

Just as his wife was unpacking a suitcase, the children turned on the TV. To his horror, it was a replay of the final furlong of the Derby. His first instinct was to turn it off, but with a morbid fascination he couldn't take his eyes off the screen, watching Darwin's Choice and The Legacy battle it out to the winning line, reasoning that if Darwin's Choice won, then some of his troubles would be over at least, but The Legacy just hung on, crossing the winning line a head up on Darwin's Choice.

Dr. Popham couldn't believe it.

How wrong he was to have thought that things couldn't get any worse.

To the horror of his family, he sat down on the bed,

putting his head in his hands, and for the first time in his life, wept.

His wife led the children into the adjoining room, and left the distraught Dr. Popham sobbing in despair.

After a couple of the darkest hours of his life, he finally came up with a plan, and when his family went out to get something to eat, he sat down and wrote two letters, one to his solicitor and one to Nathan Grant.

As he sealed the last envelope he felt considerably better and calmer. He made one phone call, and then left the room asking the girl on the reception desk for some stamps and directions to the nearest post box.

Within five minutes he had posted the letters and felt as though a weight had been lifted from his shoulders.

On returning to the hotel, he found a distraught wife and children. They had come back to the hotel after their meal and found the room empty. Knowing the terrible state of mind that her husband had been in, Dr. Popham's wife had feared the worst, and when he reappeared, she flung her arms around him with relief. He knew that with any luck his problems were over.

He told her that he had phoned an old friend who ran a veterinary practice specialising in horses, and as one of the partners would soon be retiring, he had been invited to join the partnership.

She seemed overjoyed that some semblance of normality would soon be back in their lives again.

Dr. Popham, meanwhile, was still worried about the reaction of Nathan Grant.

Although the realities of The Legacy's victory were still only just sinking in, Monday brought some semblance of normality back to the yard, with Emily returning to work and James having a runner at Nottingham.

James had received a phone call from Stuart Lawson early in the morning, requesting a meeting. Despite numerous questions from James as to why he wanted to meet, Stuart was quite vague, saying that he would rather discuss it face to face.

James felt a little irritated at this unwanted interruption of his busy day for no apparent reason, but agreed to meet Stuart at Bishop's Place late morning, giving James just enough time to get to Nottingham in time to see his horse run.

Despite the history of James's sacking between them, James didn't hold a grudge against Stuart, reasoning that he was only doing his job, although he still felt as though Stuart could have stood up for him a little more.

Mick, however, on hearing of the meeting, cursed furiously, and spent the rest of the morning preparing for the trip to Nottingham, muttering to himself and making considerably more noise than he usually did. He had no time for Stuart and his apparent lack of loyalty to his staff.

James was just crossing the yard when he heard Stuart's car pull up, and went over to meet him.

'Morning, Stuart,' James said, shaking the hand that Stuart had offered.

'Good morning, James. I didn't get the chance to congratulate you on Saturday. It was a hell of a day, wasn't it?' Stuart replied with genuine warmth in his voice. 'How's The Legacy?'

'Oh, he's fine. I think all the attention has gone to his head a bit, and Darwin's Choice?'

'In as bad a mood as Mr. Grant,' Stuart said slightly mischievously. 'This time it really was the jockey that cost us the race.'

'Yes, Joe said that as soon as he saw Rhodes with the whip out, he knew he had won.'

They walked back to the house, talking over Saturday's events.

'So, how come the jockey change?' James asked, wondering why Stuart had split up the winning combination of Joe McGrath had Darwin's Choice.

'Mr. Grant's idea. Sort of backfired on him, didn't it?'

James agreed, and invited Stuart into the kitchen and offered him a coffee. The offer of a coffee was accepted, and as James busied himself boiling the kettle, he turned to Stuart, who had sat down at the kitchen table.

'What can I do for you then, Stuart?'

Stuart shifted slightly in his chair.

'Mr. Grant would like to buy The Legacy.'

James almost spilt the coffee he was bringing over to the table.

'Buy The Legacy!' he exclaimed somewhat incredulously.

'Yes, that's right. He asked me to come over and see if we could do a deal.'

'And what makes him think that The Legacy is for sale?'

James asked, still getting over the shock of the reason for Stuart's meeting.

'Come now, James, everything's for sale at a price,' Stuart answered, trying to sound more businesslike and confident than he felt. 'Besides, I'm sure that with what

Mr. Grant is prepared to offer, Miss Lloyd would find it a very generous price.'

James laughed a little cynically.

'Mr. Grant has never been generous in his life, Stuart. Besides, Miss Lloyd might not wish to sell The Legacy.'

'Perhaps not, but think of the practical aspects of it, James. Where do you go with The Legacy from here? You could run him again at the risk of him getting beaten, and that would bring down his value, and your yard, if you don't mind me saying, has hardly enough security for a horse of his calibre to keep him here.'

'I hope you're not implying anything by that last remark!' James exclaimed, well aware that the security needed tightening up, and not sure whether the last comment of Stuart's was a veiled threat.

'Oh God, no!' Stuart hastily replied, appalled at the thought that James had taken his last comment the wrong way.

He stared into his coffee, embarrassed by the mess that he seemed to be making of their meeting.

'Mr. Grant has instructed me to offer £2 million,' Stuart added, hoping to get back to business again.

'You're joking!' James replied with a dismissive laugh. 'We both know that he's worth more than that!'

'I'm sure that Mr. Grant could be persuaded to raise the offer,' Stuart said, pleased that at least James was talking figures.

'He can raise it as much as he likes, The Legacy is not for sale.'

'Have you discussed the possibility with Miss Lloyd, then?'

Stuart asked, deciding on a different approach.

'No, but I know Miss Lloyd, and she would never part with him,' James said, beginning to get a little irritated by Stuart's persistence whilst slightly enjoying the uncomfortable position that Stuart was obviously in.

'Perhaps you should talk it over. I'll ring you tomorrow when you've had a chance to discuss it. I'm sure there's room for negotiation. In the meantime, I'll have words with Mr. Grant and see if he could be more flexible with his offer,' Stuart said, trying to make it sound as though he was doing James a favour.

'Ring me if you like, but I don't see the position changing,' James said, relieved that this uncomfortable meeting seemed to be drawing to a close.

'Would you mind if I had a look at The Legacy before I go?'

Stuart asked, curious about the colt that had caused such a sensation.

'Yes, sure. Follow me.'

Stuart followed James over to The Legacy's stable. On hearing footsteps, The Legacy put his head over the door and snickered.

'They could almost be twins,' Stuart said, rubbing The Legacy's nose, who seemed a little peeved by the lack of mints on offer.

Stuart looked at the colt in amazement. They really were like twins, except in their demeanour. The Legacy seemed to greet him with genuine warmth, whereas Darwin's Choice would glower from his box, suspicious of anyone who came near him.

Stuart thought of all the hard times that Darwin's

Choice had given him, with his temper and tantrums. A colt with The Legacy's nature would have been such a pleasure to train by comparison.

'A fine animal, James.' He patted The Legacy's neck and sighed. 'Talk it over with Miss Lloyd and I'll get back to you tomorrow.'

They walked over to Stuart's car, talking about forthcoming races – Stuart, with his top horses entered in a few forthcoming classics, Darwin's Choice possibly running in the Irish Derby, whilst James thought of his horses entered in relatively minor races. They seemed worlds apart as trainers.

As James watched Stuart drive off, he did realise one thing. He would have to talk over the future of The Legacy with Emily. Important, difficult decisions would have to be made and made quickly.

His concerns mounted when later in the afternoon at Nottingham, he received a call on his mobile phone from Nick Cullen, the racing manager of Oasis Bloodstock, requesting a meeting the following day.

James knew that Oasis Bloodstock was a consortium of exceedingly wealthy Middle Eastern gentlemen, and they produced a lot of horses which went on to win under the very well known racing colours of Middle Eastern royalty.

James didn't need to guess that it was about The Legacy. Things were certainly going to get rather interesting over the next few days.

Emily arrived home, and as usual went to see The Legacy first. She was still in awe of the colt's achievements, but The Legacy seemed to be his usual self, and had soon sniffed out the customary mints and devoured them with great gusto.

'Still the same old Leggy,' she said, patting him on the neck, relieved that the enormity of his achievement appeared to have had no effect on him.

She had decided, half way through the day, to take the rest of the week off, as it had become impossible to get any work done, with everyone congratulating her and talking about the race over and over again, not to mention the uncanny similarity between The Legacy and Darwin's Choice.

In deference to her boss, who by late morning was despairing over the lack of work being done, she booked the rest of the week off, much to his relief.

She busied herself preparing a salad for when James and Mick would get back from Nottingham, every now and again being distracted by the pictures in the papers that were lying around in the kitchen, of The Legacy, James and herself.

It was quite an odd feeling having her photograph emblazoned across the papers. It was almost as though she were two different people – she still couldn't believe that the girl in the photographs was really her.

She heard the horsebox pull up, its exhaust blowing from the slight hole in it, and she smiled. She would get so much pleasure out of settling her little bet with James and buying him a new one. She had no idea how much one would cost, but was sure that the cheque that she would shortly receive as winning owner would more than cover it.

Having seen to the horse, James and Mick strolled back into the kitchen, talking about the afternoon's racing.

'Hi, James, Mick. How did you get on this afternoon?' Emily asked, pouring them a well-earned cup of tea.

'First in the Derby on Saturday to second last at Nottingham is a bit of a leveller,' James replied, with Mick nodding in agreement. 'Still, he's got room for improvement.'

'You can say that again,' Mick said with a little chuckle as he handed Emily the carrier bag that he had been carrying.

Emily peered in and gasped in astonishment at the sight of bundles of £50 notes.

'What's this, then?' she asked, staring at the contents of the bag.

'The first instalment of your winnings. I collected some this afternoon. I managed to get round a few of my contacts today. There's a lot more than that to come,' Mick replied, enjoying the genuine look of astonishment on Emily's face.

'More?' Emily muttered weakly. 'How much more?'

With the euphoria over the weekend, it had never occurred to her to work out how much money she had won.

'Now let's see.' Mick looked at James and winked, enjoying keeping Emily in suspense, as she seemed to have no idea of how much she had won.

'£2000 at 200–1 comes to £400,000, less tax.'

Emily sat down, speechless.

'I think you had better get the girl a brandy,' Mick said, rather amused by her reaction. She had never dreamt that it would be anything like that. There seemed to be so many noughts on the figure, perhaps Mick had got it wrong, but James confirmed what Mick had said.

Emily ate her salad in relative silence, trying to come to terms with her second surprise in three days, whilst Mick and James discussed the following day's fixtures.

Earlier, on their way back from Nottingham, James had indicated to Mick that he wanted to have a word with Emily alone, and so after tea Mick made some excuse and left them alone.

Emily was clearing the table when she noticed that James had gone rather quiet.

'Is anything wrong, James? You seem a little quiet,' she asked, thinking that it might have been something to do with the emotional roller coaster they had all experienced over the weekend.

'Have you had any thoughts about The Legacy's future?' he asked tentatively, knowing full well that they hadn't thought any further than the Derby.

'No. Why?' Emily asked as she started to wash the dishes.

'Come and sit down. We really need to talk about it.'

The seriousness of his tone made Emily stop what she was doing, dry her hands and join him sitting at the table.

'I had a meeting with Stuart Lawson today, the trainer of Darwin's Choice. His owner, Nathan Grant, wants to buy The Legacy.'

'But The Legacy's not for sale!' Emily exclaimed in horror at the thought.

'That's what I told him.'

'You never told me you had a meeting with anyone to discuss selling my horse,' Emily said angrily, not believing that James could have done such a thing behind her back.

'I didn't know why he wanted to see me – honestly Emily. You know I would never go behind your back about anything. I was as shocked as you when he came out with that,' James said, defending his actions.

'And what did you say?' Emily demanded, still feeling hurt despite James's explanation.

'I told him he wasn't for sale, but he asked me to discuss it with you and he would ring me tomorrow.'

'Well, there's no discussing it. He's not for sale,' Emily said adamantly, still reeling from the audacity of Stuart Lawson, before curiosity got the better of her.

'Just out of interest, how much did he offer?'

'He started at £2 million, but said that Nathan Grant was flexible and would probably increase his offer.'

'Two million!' Emily exclaimed in disbelief.

She had never considered putting a value on The Legacy. To her, The Legacy was priceless.

'Yes, I know. The cheek of the man, thinking that he could get him so cheaply; he's worth at least twice that,' came James's reply, angry at the ridiculously low starting price, thinking that Emily agreed.

'At least twice that!' Emily echoed weakly.

James then realised that it had never occurred to Emily what The Legacy was worth, and they had certainly never discussed it.

'Hadn't you realised?' James asked gently, realising that the colt's value had come as quite a shock to Emily.

'No, never. I had realised that before the Derby he was virtually worthless, or so the papers kept saying, comparing him with all the others, and I suppose, now that you think about it, winning the Derby has added to his value, but £2 million plus – that's ridiculous!'

'Not really. The value is in his potential stud fees. People would pay a five figure sum to take their mare to a Derby winner, so it doesn't take long to get your investment back,' James tried to explain as simply as he could.

Emily sat deep in thought for a while, feeling that the harsh reality of life had just woken her up from her wonderful dream.

'Another problem that we have,' James continued, not wishing to add to the burden, but realising that as the trainer of her horse he had a responsibility to point out some potential problems. 'With a horse that valuable, we don't have adequate security in the yard.'

'Security?' Emily said, not quite sure what James was getting at.

James thought for a moment how it would be best to explain the problem and decided to be as blunt as possible.

'Do you remember a horse called Shergar, going back a few years?'

'Yes, I remember,' Emily replied, not making any connection between Shergar and what James was trying to explain.

'He was kidnapped from a yard and vanished – they never found him.'

'Oh, no! I remember now,' Emily exclaimed in horror, suddenly realising what James was trying to say.

'He was taken from a yard with considerably more security than we have here,' James said, wishing he hadn't used such a dramatic example, since it had obviously upset Emily considerably. 'Not that I'm suggesting that anything could happen to The Legacy, but there are a few unscrupulous people in the world, and I thought it best to make you aware of the problem. I didn't mean to upset you.'

'No, James, I'm the one who should be sorry. It had never crossed my mind and you're right to have brought it up.'

Emily bit her lip and a feeling of emptiness came over her. It was as though she had suddenly discovered that she had a priceless painting and couldn't afford to keep it – but this was worse. She had nurtured The Legacy since he was a foal, and he was like a friend – but more than that – he was like a member of the family, the only family that she had left.

'I'll pay for more security,' Emily said, suddenly thinking of the prize money she had won.

'No, it's all right, I've already sorted out some additional measures with my winning trainer's percentage,' James said, trying to reassure Emily, 'I'm sure that will solve the short term problem, but you really have to look to the future too.'

'The future,' Emily said quietly, thinking that things couldn't get any worse.

'We could keep him in racing for another year or so, go for the Irish Derby or the Arc. If he wins, then his value increases; if he loses, then it goes down.'

'I don't care about his value,' Emily said defiantly.

'Yes, I know, but after another year of racing you ought to think about sending him to stud anyway. You can't keep him in racing forever,' James said, trying to be as realistic as possible.

'So what you are saying is that I would have to let him go sooner or later.'

On seeing the distraught look on Emily's face, James reached across the table and picked up Emily's hands, put them to his face and kissed her fingers.

'I just couldn't bear to part with him,' Emily said as tears welled up in her eyes.

'I know, but you don't have to do anything you don't want to. I just had to explain the position as a trainer, not as your boyfriend, and I hope that you don't think any less of me for that.'

'No, of course not. Thank you for putting it so honestly. It would seem that I've got rather a lot of thinking to do.'

Emily stood up and went to the sink to finish washing up, her heart heavy with the harsh reality that James had revealed to her.

James got up and put his arms round her, pulling her close and stroking her hair.

Emily tried not to look up, for fear of letting a flood-gate of tears open up and just buried her head in his shoulder.

Despite the warmth and closeness of his embrace she felt terribly alone with the decision that she – and only she – could make.

Earlier that afternoon, Nathan grant received a phone call from Stuart Lawson.

'How did you get on?' Nathan asked, eager to find out if Stuart had clinched a deal to buy The Legacy.

'Ryan says the colt's not for sale,' came the reply that Nathan didn't want to hear.

'How much did you offer?'

'£2 million, just as you said, but I hinted that it was

negotiable. He said he would talk it over with the owner tonight and I'm ringing him tomorrow morning,' Stuart said, indicating there was room for negotiation.

'If you have to, go up to £4 million,' Nathan replied angrily, annoyed that Miss Lloyd had turned down what would have been a fortune to her.

'I'll keep you informed,' Stuart said before finishing the call, relieved to have kept their conversation brief.

Nathan walked over to the window and stared out over the city, trying to quell the frustration that he was feeling.

There seemed to be too many unanswered questions and too many loose ends for his liking. He hated waiting for people he relied on to produce results. Patience was not one of his strongest points.

He turned his mind to the meetings that he had been having with Paul Dunlop. At least those negotiations seemed to be going well, and the positive response from Paul's Far Eastern partner indicated that a deal wasn't far away.

Nathan returned to his desk and studied the agenda for their meeting later that day, pushing all thoughts of The Legacy from his mind as the prospect of finalising a lucrative deal took his full attention.

His concentration was soon broken by a phone call.

'What is it, Janice,' Nathan snapped angrily, annoyed at the interruption.

'Brad Walters on the phone, sir,' she said, nonplussed by the annoyed reaction of her boss whose moods she had long since come to expect and ignore.

Without so much as a thank you to Janice, Nathan took the call from Brad, his mind switching back immediately to The Legacy.

'What's the news then?'

Nathan's curt reaction told Brad to keep his report brief and to the point.

'Firstly, the uncle that Miss Lloyd inherited the colt from was a Dr. Anderson-Brown, an old acquaintance of ours. A copy of the will is being couriered round to you. You should get it before the end of the day.'

The double-crossing bastard, Nathan thought as Brad paused for breath before continuing.

'Secondly, Dr. Popham seems to have done a runner with his family. It would also seem that £20,000 is missing from the stud safe – disappeared while everyone was watching the Derby.

The staff say that everyone was in the staff room watching the horses come into the parade ring when Dr. Popham swore, went white as a sheet and bolted – hasn't been seen since.'

'Any luck tracing him?' Nathan said coldly, his venomous thoughts turning to his ex chief vet.

'His wife's credit card was used in Dublin last night, so I'm on my way there now – and when I find him?'

'Let me know immediately. I've a few questions that I want to put to him.'

The icy tone of Nathan's voice sent a shiver of pleasure down the spine of Brad Walters.

It sounded as though Nathan Grant was really annoyed with Dr. Popham, and once he had finished with him, then there could be a few lucrative 'extras' in this investigation after all.

When the alarm went off on Tuesday morning, it seemed to Emily as though she had hardly slept a wink.

The points that James had made to her the previous evening had gone round and round in her mind in never ending circles, with no prospect of resolving anything.

Every creak and noise in the night had startled her as she imagined hooded figures trying to steal The Legacy from her under cover of darkness.

James too, had slept very little, aware of the tormented thoughts that Emily must be having. He too, would listen for any unfamiliar noise, despite having arranged additional security and for a security firm to patrol round Bishop's Place during darkness.

He had lain in his bed, hoping that Emily would think he was asleep, not wishing to add his concern to hers.

The first thing that Emily did when she got up was to check on The Legacy, who seemed surprised at seeing Emily so early in his morning routine.

James had himself intended to check on the colt as soon as he got up, but as Emily had beaten him to it, he stayed in the kitchen and made them both a coffee.

Emily looked pale and tired when she came back, and was relieved to see a mug of coffee waiting for her.

'How's The Legacy this morning?' James asked, trying to lift the cloud of depression that seemed to hang over Emily.

'Fine,' came the tired reply as Emily rummaged through the cupboard, trying to find some aspirins that would alleviate the headache that followed the sleepless night.

'Are you all right?' James asked with concern, worried at how quiet and listless Emily seemed to be.

'I'll be fine, it's just a headache,' Emily replied. One great big awful headache, she thought, almost wishing that she could turn the clock back a week to when everything seemed to be so much simpler.

'First string's due out, so I'll see you later,' James said, giving Emily a peck on the cheek, which she hardly seemed to notice.

She watched James cross the yard and saw The Legacy being saddled up, ready for his morning's work.

The colt looked so fit, handsome and raring to go.

Tears sprang to her eyes as she watched him trot out of the yard at the back of the group.

It seemed to her that it had all been too good to be true.

An hour later, James was back for breakfast. He decided to tell Emily about his meeting with Nick Cullen later in the day.

'It seems as though the vultures are circling,' Emily replied in a rather dull, tired voice.

Mick, having been made aware of the situation by James while they were out on the gallops, looked up from his toast.

'Come now, miss. It's not that bad. It's not as though they are going to take him off you. If you feel that strongly about it, all you have to do is say no,' Mick said, trying to put things back into perspective.

'I know, Mick, but you make it sound so simple,' Emily replied with a big sigh, toying with her toast, not feeling the least like eating it.

'Sometimes you women make things too complicated,' Mick said, trying to sound as philosophical as he could. 'Go with what your heart says.'

'That's easy for you to say.'

Emily walked over to the kitchen window, hoping for divine intervention that wasn't going to come.

'My head says that maybe I should sell him – at least he would be safe in a more secure yard, but my heart can't bare to part with him – it would be like selling a member of the family!'

Mick nodded, as he knew what torment she was going through, even though it was a nod confirming to himself that she had become far too attached to the colt.

'You've made the right decision before, and you'll make the right one again,' he said, not quite convinced of the logic behind his last comment, but at least it sounded reassuring.

'It's a shame there's no way to compromise between your head and your heart,' Emily replied wistfully.

Emily's last comment made James sit up. Compromise – maybe that was the answer to the problem.

James was on his way to meet Nick Cullen when his mobile phone rang. It was Stuart Lawson.

After they exchanged pleasantries, Stuart got straight to business.

'Did you discuss Mr. Grant's proposition with Miss Lloyd?' he asked, hoping for a positive response.

'Yes I did, and the answer is still no,' came the reply from James.

Stuart cursed under his breath. Obviously the owner was playing hard to get and was holding out for more money.

'As I said yesterday, Mr. Grant is fairly flexible on the offer. Would she consider £2.5 million?'

'I'm sorry, Stuart, but Miss Lloyd doesn't want to sell The Legacy,' James said, wondering how many times and in how many different ways he would have to spell it out before Stuart got the message.

'£3 million?' Stuart said hopefully.

'She's not interested.'

Stuart thought hard about having to break the news of his failure to do a deal to buy The Legacy. The prospect didn't appeal to him at all.

'Is there any way she might change her mind – more money?'

Stuart, by this time, was clutching at straws.

'I haven't discussed it with her, but there is a possibility. Miss Lloyd is very fond of the horse, and having inherited it from her uncle makes it all the more special to her. She might be persuaded to sell a share in him.'

James could almost hear Stuart's mind working as he thought through the possibility.

'I'm not sure what Mr. Grant would say to that,' was Stuart's reply. The proposition had somewhat thrown him, but at least he was still negotiating.

'I'll give Mr. Grant a ring and will put it to him.'

'As I said, I'm not sure if Miss Lloyd would even consider it, but I could discuss it with her if Mr. Grant is interested.'

James wondered how annoyed Emily would be at him discussing the possibilities of selling even a share in The Legacy, but he felt that he had her interest at heart to explore all options that might be open to her.

'OK, James, I'll ring you as soon as I have any news.'

James put the phone back in his pocket and turned his thoughts to his meeting with Nick Cullen.

* * *

James was slightly late when he dashed into the lounge of the hotel where they had arranged to meet.

He quickly glanced round and noticed a slim, tanned, dark haired man sitting on a sofa, reading the *Racing Post*. It could only be Nick Cullen.

The man had noticed James come in, recognised James and put his paper away, giving him a quick wave.

As James walked over, Nick stood up and shook his hand.

James was surprised how young Nick seemed to be to hold a responsible position as manager of such a high-powered bloodstock agency. He was also tall and wore an extremely expensive suit, his tan probably coming from flying all round the world to more exotic climates in his role of overseeing the agency's empire.

Once introductions were over, Nick summoned a member of staff and ordered coffee.

'That was an impressive performance The Legacy put in on Saturday, beating Darwin's Choice and smashing the record as well. I must admit I couldn't see Darwin's Choice getting beaten beforehand,' Nick said. James warmed to the genuine enthusiasm that Nick seemed to be showing.

'Yes, I have to admit, we were also rather surprised. I half hoped for a place, but a win certainly exceeded our expectations.'

They were momentarily interrupted by the arrival of the coffee.

'The Legacy certainly showed a lot of courage to hold off the challenge of Darwin's Choice,' Nick said, stirring a spoonful of sugar into his coffee.

'Yes, he's all heart and one of the most genuine

horses I've ever known, and believe me, I've known a lot.'

A momentary silence fell between them as the exchange of pleasantries ended.

'You've probably guessed that I wanted to meet to discuss The Legacy,' Nick began, taking a sip of coffee.

'I didn't think that it would be to discuss any other horse in my yard,' James said, with a broad smile.

Nick grinned too, taking an instant liking to James and his honest, forthright attitude.

'The Oasis Bloodstock Agency have asked me to sound out the possibilities of buying The Legacy,' Nick said, coming straight to the point of the meeting.

'I thought as much, and I'm sorry that you've had a wasted journey. The Legacy is not for sale. Miss Lloyd and I had quite a discussion about it last night.'

'I see,' Nick replied, not the least bit put out by the outright refusal. 'Any particular reason?'

'Miss Lloyd is very attached to The Legacy, having inherited the dam while in foal, and I'm afraid she regards it as one of the family,' James said, trying to emphasise the great attachment she had for the colt.

Nick thought for a moment, going over the possibilities in his mind.

'I can understand that. Some horses you can't help but develop a great sentimental attachment to, and given those circumstances, it's not surprising.'

James looked up, surprised at the genuineness in Nick's voice; who really did seem to understand, rather than say it because it was what James wanted to hear.

'So you can see then that she doesn't want to part with him for any price.'

'What if the Oasis Bloodstock Agency bought a fifty per cent share in him? Of course I would have to discuss it with the consortium. What would Miss Lloyd think to that?'

James tried not to look too delighted that the suggestion that he had hoped for came from Nick.

'It's not something that Miss Lloyd and I have discussed, so I'm not sure what her thoughts on the matter would be,' James said, as he finished off his coffee.

'OK, give me a moment while I make a few calls and see if the group would be interested.'

Nick disappeared to make the calls whilst James waited anxiously for his return. He wondered what Emily's reaction would be, but he felt that he had a duty to explore all possibilities.

About five minutes later Nick reappeared with a beaming smile on his face.

'The group feel quite comfortable with a fifty per cent share, so let's run through some figures so that you can put the full package to Miss Lloyd,' he said, opening up his briefcase and getting out a notepad, pen and calculator.

They spent the next couple of hours hammering out a deal which James thought that Emily would find acceptable.

The more they talked, the more James grew to like Nick. He didn't seem to be out to get The Legacy on the cheap – unlike Nathan Grant.

Nick was treating the negotiations as a prospective partnership, which would involve mutual trust and respect.

They ended the meeting as good friends, with James

promising to call Nick the following morning, once he
had a chance to go over the deal with Emily.

Nathan Grant was in even more of a foul mood the
following morning.

Lydia had left for Barbados in such apparent happi-
ness that it annoyed Nathan even more. She seemed so
damned pleased with herself that Nathan found it a bit
disconcerting.

When he got to work, Janice brought in his post,
together with his usual coffee.

He sat at his desk and flicked through the mail.
Amongst the letters was a manilla envelope marked
strictly private. It bore an Irish stamp and postmark.

Putting the rest of the mail to one side he opened the
envelope and pulled out the contents. He unfolded the
letter and to his surprise found that it was from Dr.
Popham.

He read the letter with increasing anger.

Dr. Popham explained how Anderson-Brown had
talked him into carrying out a trial operation on
Andaman Sea, implanting what Dr. Popham was assured
was a normal embryo. He hadn't told anyone of this
operation for fear of his skills as a vet being brought into
question, and also for his own peace of mind to ensure
that the procedure was safe before repeating the operation on Supernova.

It wasn't until the Derby that Dr. Popham suspected
that anything other than a normal embryo had been used,
and even now he couldn't be one hundred per cent sure.
That secret had died with Anderson-Brown.

Dr. Popham apologised for taking the money from

the safe, and regarded it as his final payment and pension.

The letter went on to say that a copy had been sent to Dr. Popham's solicitor, together with the records of both operations, and that if anything untoward happened to either him or his family, then the documents were to be opened and made public.

He finished by saying that he was sure that Nathan Grant would wish him and his family a long and accident free life.

Nathan smashed his fist on the desk with rage, making the coffee cup jump and splatter its contents across his desk.

'The double crossing pair of bastards,' Nathan raged as he paced up and down his office, trying to work off some of the anger that was boiling to the surface.

He pressed the buzzer on his desk.

'Come and clear up this mess, Janice,' he barked.

Janice appeared immediately and mopped up the spilt coffee and cleared the cup and saucer away. She didn't dare ask if he wanted another one – she had never seen him so angry.

Nathan reached for the phone and called Brad Walters. His first instinct was to wreak revenge on the hapless Dr. Popham, but he stopped just in time, realising what the consequences would be.

He sat down in sudden despair, knowing that there was nothing he could do about it.

He called Brad anyway.

'Brad, Nathan Grant here. Have you found Dr. Popham yet?'

He listened for a moment as Brad started to tell Nathan

how he was closing in on the family before Nathan interrupted.

'Forget it Brad. I've got the information I was after. No, you don't need to find them, just pack up and come back – now! Yes of course you'll still get paid,' Nathan said with irritation before putting the phone down.

Throughout the morning he kept trying to call Stuart Lawson, but his calls were diverted to a message service. Eventually, just after lunch Stuart rang.

'Where the hell have you been? I've been trying to get hold of you all morning!' snapped Nathan, who had spent most of the morning prowling up and down his office, annoyed at his trainer not answering his phone.

'Training your horses,' came Stuart's rather irritated reply.

'Well, what did Ryan say?'

'The Legacy's not for sale, not even for £3 million. He did suggest that she might consider selling a fifty per cent share in the colt.'

'I don't want a fifty per cent share! I want the colt! Offer £5 million.'

Nathan slammed the phone down with such force that Janice could hear it from outside his office.

She grimaced slightly before getting on with her work.

Emily was waiting for James to return from his meeting. He seemed remarkably cheerful considering he had been discussing selling The Legacy.

'Well, what did he say?' Emily asked flatly, having been unable to pull herself out of her depression.

'Stuart Lawson has upped Nathan Grant's offer to £3 million.'

'Still not interested,' came Emily's toneless reply.

'Now come and sit down and I'll tell you about Nick Cullen's offer.'

'I can't see what they can offer to make me change my mind,' Emily said, not wanting to get involved in any discussions for fear of weakening her resolve.

'At least hear me out, Emily.'

Emily reluctantly sat down next to James as he went over the proposal. The more James explained, the more interested she became.

'They want to pay £2 million for a fifty per cent share in The Legacy.'

'A share?' Emily asked, not quite sure what he meant.

'They own half and you own the other half, so to speak,'

James explained before continuing.

'All decisions regarding The Legacy would be jointly discussed and would have to be accepted by both parties. The Legacy would not be entered in any more races, but would be sent to their stud in Newmarket.'

'He wouldn't be far then,' Emily said, thinking out loud.

'No, he wouldn't. You would get fifty per cent of the stud fees after deductions for expenses, which would amount to a considerable yearly income. Their security is like Fort Knox, and is reviewed annually with no expense spared. Oh, and they wouldn't mind if you wanted to go and see him.'

'They wouldn't?' Emily said beginning to take an interest in the proposed deal that James had come back with.

'No, not at all. Nick Cullen seemed to be a really nice bloke, someone you could trust, unlike Nathan Grant.'

'What do you think I should do?' Emily asked, hoping that James could help her to make up her mind.

'You know I can't help you with this decision, Emily, it has to be your decision and yours alone. As far as the deal is concerned, I don't think you will get a better one than Nick's.'

'I'll think about it overnight,' Emily said, realising that she would have to resolve the dilemma herself.

That evening she spent a lot of time talking to The Legacy, trying to explain the choice she had to make.

He listened with one ear and occasionally seemed to snort in the right place.

Most of that night, Emily tossed and turned in bed, jumping at every noise that came from the yard, worrying about The Legacy's safety and the future.

James would hold her when he sensed that she needed holding, and would let her go as she tossed and turned – her mind in turmoil.

Morning dawned, and James was surprised to see her in the kitchen looking remarkably bright.

'I've come to a decision,' Emily announced before James had time to speak. 'I'll accept Nick Cullen's offer providing I can spend the money how I like.'

'Of course you can, silly. It's yours, Emily, all yours,' James said, puzzled by her comment.

'Yes, I know, but the condition is that the money I receive I want to invest in Bishop's Place!'

It was James's turn to sit down in astonishment. He didn't have time to open his mouth before Emily continued with such determination that he dared not interrupt.

'With all the interest you've had since the Derby, you'll need to expand, and I've been doing your accounts for long enough now to know that you're in no position to, and I doubt that the banks would be interested in lending you the money either. I think that the calibre of horses that you've been offered could turn everything around, but you need more boxes and better facilities. So, what do you think?'

'You're mad!' was James's immediate reply.

'Accept my conditions or there's no deal with Nick!' Emily said defiantly.

'That's blackmail,' James replied weakly.

'No, it's a sound business proposition. I want to invest my money, and I can't think of anywhere better. So, what do you say, partner?'

James looked at Emily, her hazel eyes glistening with excitement at the prospect.

'I still think it's blackmail,' James said, trying to sound reluctant, but what he really wanted to do was pick her up and spin her around in his arms with the excitement of the prospect.

She held out her hand for him to shake, but just as he was about to, she stopped.

'Oh, there's one other thing,' she added mischievously.

'What's that?'

'I'll have to come and work here full time. Firstly there will be all the added work with the expansion and new owners, and secondly to safeguard my investment,' Emily said, giggling.

'Now that's a deal I can't refuse,' he replied, forgoing the shaking of hands and sealing it with a kiss instead.

'I'll ring Nick after breakfast,' James said, unable to let Emily go.

Mick walked into the kitchen at that point and gave the two of them a withering look.

'It's a bit early for that, isn't it?' he muttered as he put the kettle on, thinking that they had been too busy smooching to make the coffee.

'It's business, Mick. Strictly business,' came James's reply.

It was quite a day.

Stuart Lawson phoned, saying that Nathan Grant wasn't interested in a fifty per cent share, and had upped his offer to £5 million. James politely refused, saying that he was about to do a deal to sell half a share in the colt.

After he put the phone down he smiled at the thought of the flurry of phone calls that were about to be made between Stuart Lawson and Nathan Grant.

James then phoned Nick Cullen, and with a little more negotiating agreed on a deal. Nick said he would ring later in the week to arrange a meeting when all the paperwork had been drawn up, ready for signatures.

Mick appeared half way through the afternoon with two more carrier bags full of Emily's winnings, which she just managed to get to the bank before it closed. The teller raised his eyebrows as she deposited the bags on the counter, despite this having become a regular occurrence. Even the bank manager, who now regarded Emily as one of his most important clients, helped to count the money.

Emily asked Mick if he didn't mind if she and James ate alone that evening. Mick didn't mind at all. He could go down to the local pub and have a snack with numerous pints of Guinness and recount the huge gambling coup that Miss Lloyd had landed on her horse, even though the regulars thought that the figures that Mick claimed must be wildly exaggerated.

James arrived back to a delicious smell wafting through the kitchen.

Emily came in and greeted him with a kiss. He stopped and stared at her. She looked fabulous in a new, black dress with thin shoulder straps, which accentuated her curvaceous figure.

She led him through to the dining room.

'What's the occasion then?' he asked, stunned at the subdued lighting, candles, soft music and bottle of champagne in an ice bucket next to the table.

'Just cementing out business partnership,' Emily said lightly as she went into the kitchen and brought out the first course of smoked Scotch salmon.

They talked throughout the dinner about their plans for the yard, updating some of the facilities and building others.

After they had cleared up James sat on the sofa with Emily in his arms.

Emily suddenly went rather quiet.

He looked at her questioningly.

'It's OK,' she replied. 'It's the thought of The Legacy going away. It must be like when a child you've reared has suddenly grown up and leaves home. I suppose, in a way, The Legacy has grown up too, and it's time for him to leave.'

James hugged her close, realising how she felt but glad that she had managed to put it into perspective.

Angela Woodward

'I've got a surprise for you,' he said, kissing the top of her head as she snuggled into his arms.

'What's that?' she asked, looking up at him.

'I managed to add a bit to the deal when I spoke to Nick earlier,' James said, looking rather pleased with himself.

'Oh?'

Emily tried to sit up but James held her tightly in his arms.

'The first year that The Legacy is at the stud, you'll have free loan of one of the syndicate's best mares to be sent to The Legacy.'

Emily managed to break out of James's arms.

'You mean a foal of Leggy's?'

'Yes, that's right, in a couple of years you'll have son of The Legacy to contend with.'

'Or daughter!' Emily exclaimed, joy written all over her face. 'That's wonderful James. Thank you!'

'It just seemed the right thing to do with The Legacy going away,' he added, pleased at the delight that it had given Emily.

'It does rather. A bit like fate,' she said thoughtfully.

'Or destiny,' James replied.

'Now there's a thought,' Emily said, looking as though she had just had a good idea before snuggling back down into James's arms, giggling to herself.

'What's that?' James asked, wondering what had amused her.

'Destiny – we can call the foal Destiny.'

DESTINY

To celebrate the opening of the new London Racecourse, an extravagant day's horse racing has been organised. The prize money and prestige of the races attracts the elite of international entries, the calibre of which has never been gathered for one meeting before.

For Peter Miller, it's his chance to make his name as a racing correspondent, having recently retired from the saddle.

Record crowds are present to enjoy this 'once in a lifetime' event.

After the second race, Peter receives an anonymous phone call. A deadly virus had been released in the stables. All the thoroughbreds could die within seventy two hours unless a cure is given, for which the blackmailer demands £20 million.

Peter notifies the authorities, racing is suspended and the stables quarintined.

A veterinary expert is called in and it soon becomes apparent this is not a hoax.

The expert turns out to be Eleanor Wright, an old flame of Peter's, and he tries to renew their relationship to gain inside information into the investigation, but soon finds himself falling for her again.

The squabbling of the owners, who include some of the richest and most influential in the world, is hampering investigations. Some want their own experts involved; others have brought in their own security staff to find the blackmailer.

Could the blackmailer be a disgruntled ex-employee, an opportunist or a terrorist organisation looking to swell their funds? Could it be another owner, who, with the elite horses dead would find his own promoted to the top?

Peter is also under suspicion, having been the person contacted by the blackmailer,

He decides to use his connections in racing to mount his own investigation and clear his name from the list of suspects.

Time is running out to find the blackmailer and the cure, as is the patience of the owners.

ISBN 1 903892 015
Available from www.cowanpublishing.com